A LIGHT IN THE HEART

Kathleen O'Brien

To Ronna,
I hope you enjoy my story! Thanks so much for coming to my author event! Kathleen O'Brien

Plicata Press
Plicata Press
P.O. Box 32
Gig Harbor, WA 98332
www.plicatapress.com

A Light in the Heart is a work of fiction inspired by one true event. All other characters, incidents, and dialogues are products of the author's imagination and fictitious, and are not to be construed as real.

Cover Design by Mary Smith, Harbor Design Services
Gig Harbor, WA

ISBN: 978-0-9828205-3-7
LCCN: 2011923238

O'Brien, Kathleen
A Light in the Heart/Kathleen O'Brien
1. MontanaFiction 2. Cape CodFiction 3. Burnfiction
4. LiteraryFiction 5. Women'sFiction
6. RelationshipFiction 7. RomanceFiction
8. InspirationalFiction

TO MY FAMILY

AND

IN LOVING MEMORY

OF MY SISTER

CHRISTINE MARY CONRAD

19 FEBRUARY 1951, Wisconsin Rapids, WI

19 OCTOBER 1971, Boston, MA

TO JOE: WHO MISSES HER AS MUCH AS I DO.

Beauty is not in the face;
beauty is a light in the heart
~Kahlil Gibran

LOSS

Cape Cod, January 20

THE ACCIDENT

It's hot; cramped. Legs trapped, arm pinned. Pain beats at my body.

Voices enter, leave.

Acrid smell burns nose, eyes.

Flames tease fingertips.

Try to scream; no sound.

Voices return, screech like pebbles tossed against glass. Tinkling, falling glass carving away beauty, ear to chin.

Flashes of light. Flashbulbs? Turn; smile.

Can't move.

More flashes. Ghosts with cameras dance by my cocoon, suck away the air. Where'd it go?

To Donna? Where is she?

Voices scream at me to hang on. Don't want to.

I reach for death.

Metal tears at my cocoon then life pores in through an opening.

Thick brown hands appear out of grey clouds.

Voices shriek, "Miller, get away. Fire."

Miller? A grunt then refusal from the man with bronzed hands. Through darkened firelight fingers become graceful, palms turn upward toward paradise —then urgency beckons.

Go away.

A voice reaches my conscious, unconscious mind, "Grab my hand—now."

Need to rest.

"C'mon let's get you out; this thing's ready to blow."

Rough hands grab shoulders, pulling limb from socket—it hurts. I resist. He pulls harder.

Consciousness and clarity rage against euphoria and eternity—each fighting the other.

Which will win? Life? Death?

Only fate and this man named Miller know for sure.

Boston, January 20

THE HOSPITAL

"Christine. Christine, can you hear me?"

A pinging reverberates then a whisper.

"You've been in an auto accident. You were airlifted from the Cape to Boston Metro Hospital."

I try to open my eyes. Too bright.

Another voice, brusque and authoritative demands, "Christine, I'm Dr. Talbot, look at me."

Fingers lift eyelids. Light assaults. I try to shove him away; my arms won't move.

"We're going to help you."

Head heavy; body floating. Cold, so cold.

"Come back, Christine."

Shouting. Rapid beeping screams a warning.

"Paddles. Now."

" Clear."

****

White blurry images fade in and out, turn into clouds, into frilly dresses and white cake then morph into flames that crawl up my legs, singe my stomach and hands.

Oh, god, the pain—make it stop.

Haloed silhouettes hover. Angels? Miller? One moves closer, slips a hand under my head.

Donna?

Pain stabs at my cheek.

Something lifted off my face; air grows thin.

Fingers pry at my mouth. I bite. "Christine, we're going to put a tube down your throat to make it easier for you to breathe."

Pressure. I fight. Gag.

"That's it, you're doing fine. Nearly done."

Air fills my lungs.

Where's Donna? I lift my head to see. It hurts.

"Keep her still. Up the morphine."

A cloud lifts me above random voices.

"Driver broken arm."

Donna's okay?

"Other driver drunk. Senator's son."

"Passenger gashed face, burns, critical."

Someone whispers, "Will she make it?"

Head pounds, a roar in my ears. Sobbing—not mine.

A voice warns, "No, no, sir, don't touch her. I know you want to comfort her, but we can't risk infection."

Nick?

Daddy?

****

Castanets echo an annoying tune. That band's not playing at our wedding.

Strobe lights flash. I open my eyes.

Florescent lights race above me.

A man dressed in blue leads my bed down a long hall; it clangs and rocks. "Good, you're awake. We're moving you to ICU."

My body quivers under soft fabric.

The man wheels me into a room. Nurses who don't speak hook me up to monitors and someone in the hall whispers, "Horrible. Did you see her face? And her burns ... third degree."

Terror and an overwhelming sadness collide.

The tears are now mine.

****

A distant voice wakes me. "Is she okay?"

I want to scream, no, I'm not fucking okay.

Voices in hushed conversation: "A drug induced coma? How long?"

I open my eyes.

Daddy stares at me. Mother cowers behind him.

Dr. Talbot moves into view. "We're not sure, Mr. McMurray, but this is the best treatment for Christine."

Daddy clears his throat. "Her face?"

My stomach turns, my heart empties.

He continues, "She's a model, you know."

Dr. Talbot turns his back on Daddy and looks at me, disgust darkens his face. "We'd like to make sure she lives, sir, before we worry about the modeling."

Daddy doesn't quit. "I don't like it. Her burns aren't noticeable, face is more important. I want that addressed first."

"Sir, Christine is what?" Dr. Talbot flips a page on the chart. "She's thirty-two. The decision is hers."

Boston, early March

POST COMA

They woke me a week ago. The plump nurse with the pixie cut that makes her face look bloated says I'm lucky I was asleep when they debrided and grafted. Not so lucky I tell her. While everyone's life went on, mine stalled, filled with nightmares of burning flesh and death. When I tell her I pray for a dreamless night she cocks her head, pats my bandaged hand and leaves ... as they are all doing now. Daddy, Mother, Dr. Talbot, nurses, techs—no one lingers; no one wants to talk to the scarred woman who used to be beautiful.

They won't give me a mirror. Nothing to see they say; bandages are still on.

"At least, dear, your face wasn't burned. The scar will heal nicely and you can go back to modeling," Mother says.

Yet the truth is in Daddy's face when he looks at me—my beauty is gone.

No face, no job. No job, no life. Death would be better than this.

Ten years working my way up ended in the time it takes to breathe in and out—taken away by some drunk.

My life. Stolen. Gone. Everything I've worked for—lost.

"How are we this morning?" The nurse bursts into the room.

I roll away from her.

"Honey, we're moving you to another floor where you can have regular visitors."

"Go away, let me sleep."

"None of that now. Your friends want to visit you." I'll bet they do. See the freak.

"Don't want to see them."

"They're worried. Your fiancé Nick, and Donna—that friend from the accident—call all the time. Miller, too, and some guy with a weird name. Anders, I think. You see, lots of people care about you."

Anders?

Before I can object, another nurse comes in the room. They disconnect cords, scoop me up, help me into a wheelchair and push me past the debriding room where other patients scream—the ones not lucky enough to be put in a coma.

An image slips through: nurses peeling layers of charred skin from my stomach. I cringe in pain from the memory that I'm not sure is mine.

Boston, end of March

VISITORS

The TV drones on while my friends look out the window, pace the room and mumble about needing to be somewhere else. Two months of my life has been taken from me, yet they're the ones who complain: can't stay, gotta go, back to the office, to my gig, to the shoot, to our lives, to the parties, to the next big thing. So they leave. Ten minutes is what Nick gives me, Donna even less. They leave together heads pressed close, chattering like school children. With backward glances they give me a quick wave and " ... see you soon. Take care now."

Daddy and Mother shift in their chairs, sigh and talk about nothing until I scream at them to go.

Detectives circle my bed like vultures asking questions about things I don't remember. The Senator visits too, but not the son. The Senator wants to pay me off so I don't sue, but I can't stand the sight of him. Can't stand any of them.

Except Anders and Miller. They stay, they see ***me,*** *not past me; they hold my hand even when I yell at them. They take my abuse and tell me I'm looking better. I believe them. I believe them because I have to. Anders and Miller are my strength.*

The nurses tell me Miller followed the ambulance to the hospital and stayed all day. Now he sits beside me giving me courage. The man who saved me is still saving me.

Anders just appeared one day and said he wasn't leaving the hospital until he knew I'd be okay. Nick's jealous; it's good for him. Nick is weak, but he has Donna to lean on. I have Anders.

Who knew that a meaningless affair in Montana five years ago would be the only thing I cling to now? Anders tells me I need to return to Montana; that the air, the mountains and the beauty of it will help me heal. I could stay at the ranch; paint, fish, and recover. He tells me Lotte wants me to stay there. He says she's convinced I will love it this time. But how can I? I'm marrying Nick this summer.

PART I

FALL BACK

"And forget not that the earth delights to feel your bare feet and the winds long to play with your hair."~Kahlil Gibran"

ONE

Montana—late September the following year

For the third time Christine tugged at the "For Sale by Owner" sign. It wouldn't budge. She dug her left heel into the earth, lifting the pressure off her bad leg, and with her hands clasped the metal frame and tried to loosen it from the clay soil by rocking it back and forth. Her hands still didn't work properly; the skin on her palms taut and unyielding. The exercises that were supposed to promote more flexibility weren't working fast enough. She clutched the sign tighter, leaned her body into it for more leverage and pulled. It inched up then stuck, the earth holding it hostage.

Frustrated, hot and sweaty, Christine straightened, blew upward at a loose strand of hair and wiped her forehead with the sleeve of her sweatshirt. Her leg ached; she wanted to sit, but the ground was unwelcoming and she knew her body would fail her when it was time to stand again.

Her body, the sign—what else would fail her? She felt inadequate and angry. Before the accident tasks such as this had been easy. Since the accident, nothing had been easy. Her journey back from the edge of death had been filled with pain, depression and an overwhelming sense of irrelevance. Feeling alive was limited to snippets of time, mostly since she'd come to Montana. Yet no matter how hard she tried the fact that she would never model again loomed larger than anything else. Or, so she thought, until Nick dumped her. If it hadn't been for Anders call in July, she'd still be in seclusion at her parents' house, wallowing in self-pity.

On the ridge above her the trees rustled; a breeze drifted down the hill, lifted off the creek and reached her, cooling her frustration. After a few moments her mind surrendered, then her muscles, and finally she allowed herself to welcome her surroundings. When she opened her eyes she let them linger over the land; she breathed in the sweetness of blooming purple clover and listened to the distant rumble of the creek. It was hers now—seventeen acres of undulating Montana land. The dry terrain, replete with brittle sagebrush and a sea of grass, spread out before her; for nearly three hundred feet it rolled out flat until it reached Rainbow Creek where shale stair-stepped to a butte fifty feet above. There the sun had settled into the trees and unfurled the shadows.

Christine shielded her eyes and watched as Anders lanky silhouette, framed against the late afternoon sun, walked along the precipice, stakes in one hand and a camera in the other. He wove around tall aspens toward the planned site of her house. Today they'd outline its footprint. An eagle soared above him, caught an updraft and rode the thermals until it disappeared.

Anders had told her about the thermals and updrafts. He'd filled her with insight about the creatures of Montana, about the people, about herself and how being here would change her life. She should have been excited. After all, the adversities of the last year and a half were behind her and the fears that followed quelled by the tranquil setting and reassured by Anders presence in her life. Yet, the lurching in her stomach had returned telling her something was amiss. Buyer's remorse? Or had something deeper seeped into her psyche and spread like the fiery fall colors through the Gallatin Valley? Insecurities about her disfigured face, scared body and damaged leg were always with her, but then she'd gone and done something foolish—she'd bought land. Anders had said come to Montana to heal, not to purchase land, build a house, or start a new life. What had she been thinking? But she knew. She'd been thinking get as far away from memories of the accident, from Boston and her past life as she could.

Christine cleared her throat, cupped her hands around her mouth and shouted, "Anders." When he didn't answer she tried again. "Anders. I'm coming up."

Anders stopped and yelled down the hill, "Hold on. I'll come down to help you."

She waved him off. "No. Stay there."

"Take it slow. Don't hurt yourself," he said.

She ignored him. Lumbering around sagebrush, thistle and negotiating boulders, she stopped only to pick sprigs of grass out of sandals. As she approached the creek, which meandered tight against the rise and followed the curvature of the steep knoll, the earth became damp; it squished underfoot and the soggy soil crept up the sides of the sandals. Another step and she sank deeper into the soft cold earth; it oozed between toes until her feet were overtaken by the muck. Soil pushed against unprotected skin and trapped her, reawakening a past emotion. Air sparse, her mouth went dry. The therapist said this would happen anytime she felt trapped—no matter the cause. He'd said not to worry, it would pass in time. Easy for him.

Christine yanked each foot free and slid them into the icy creek, swishing them until the dirt disappeared. She bent over, dipped a hand into the water and splashed her face, lingering too long on the reflection. It became distorted and revealed itself in a ghoulish image: mouth and nose monstrous, eyes tiny black sockets, the scar, which ran from the tip of her ear to the edge of her mouth, seemed to pulsate.

"You okay?" Anders' voice drifted down the hill.

She waved him off again, slipped the hood of the sweatshirt over her head and pulled it tight to hide the scar. Gingerly stepping on flat rocks, she traversed the creek where it narrowed and plodded up the hill along a trail carved out two days earlier by Lotte's crew. She grasped twigs and sprigs of grass when she could, touching the earth for balance whenever her leg grew tired. By the time she reached the top sweat dripped down her back.

The land flattened here with acres of tall grass, aspens and one massive willow. She walked toward it, sat, leaned against it and tilted her head upward to catch her breath. Heavy branches spread out above, limbs twisted and gnarled. Christine raised each arm, spread fingers so they overlapped the branches; hands healed, but no longer beautiful, no longer useful.

By next spring a house would sit on this level plot with the willow to its back, the front opening up to the valley below. The plan, fleshed out on a napkin the day after she'd signed the final papers, would come to fruition. Soon she'd be sitting in this very spot, surrounded by a flagstone patio that Jake would build. French doors from the kitchen would open onto it and she'd fill large pots with brilliant flowers, the willow serving as protector from the summer sun. The upstairs master bedroom window would face the dawn, a reminder of the creation of each new day and the beauty of life—a life she'd once taken for granted.

"Christine, where are you?"

She got up, walked toward Anders' voice and found him crouched amidst tall dry grass, patting the ground. She said, "I'm right here. What are you doing?"

"Taking pictures of the valley. Then I noticed this." He pointed, indicating an area where the grass had been matted down.

Christine knelt next to him, but pain shot through her leg and she fell back.

He extended a hand. "Can I help?"

She brushed the offer aside. "Nope, I'm good," she said and pointed to the flattened section of grass. "What does it mean?"

"Not sure. At first I thought it might have been from last night's storm, but when I looked closer … perhaps they were taking an afternoon nap."

"Who?"

He poked at the earth. "Elk, deer, maybe even moose." Anders stood, resting his hands on his hips—faded jeans slung low on his lean frame, blue shirt wrinkled and un-tucked, boots caked with dried mud. Blond hair blew across his forehead; brown eyes searched the woods behind them. His tanned face expressed control, but compassion and vulnerability simmered just below the surface—she knew, she'd seen it more than once.

He dropped his hands and frowned. "Can't make out anything. Maybe they're hiding." He sighed. "So." He looked down at her. "Ready to put those stakes in the ground?"

"Yes, let's do it," she said.

Before she could stop him, he picked her up and lifted her onto his shoulder.

"Put me down, I'm not a damned invalid." Her head bobbed as he carried her. Clumps of blond curls fell and covered her face. The scars on her stomach burned. She brushed hair out of her eyes, lifted her head, slid her arms to his shoulders and pushed up. "Anders Larsson, put me down."

****

They'd been walking the perimeter of the clearing, dropping stakes at random intervals trying to remember the layout. They'd both forgotten Spencer's plan back at the ranch, yet Christine blamed Anders. Frustrated, she pulled a rubber band from her jeans and gathered damp hair into a ponytail.

"Well, I don't know where they go." She glared at him, threw down the stakes and slowly sidestepped down the hill. The day had gone sour. She shivered; the weather had turned cold and threatening, and her stomach was twisted in knots again.

"Aren't we a bit testy?" He pretended to scowl, then slid in beside her, cupped an elbow with one hand and wrapped the other arm around her waist. "Hold on now; let me help you."

By the time they reached his truck, her anger had dissipated.

"Will you look at that?" Anders said and pointed to where the for sale sign had fallen over.

"Damn it. I couldn't get the stupid thing out and now ..."

"Shush. Not the sign. Look over there," he said. About twenty feet from his truck, a bull moose had risen from the high grass. "Get inside, Christine."

"He's not dangerous ... is he?"

"Usually not, but they can be unpredictable." Anders guided her to the passenger side of the truck, opened the door, helped her in and slammed the door. He got into the driver's seat, set the camera between them, put the key in the ignition and started the engine.

"Wait, stop. I want to see him." She lifted the sun visor and pressed her face close to glass. "My goodness, he's immense."

The moose stood motionless. Steam poured from his nostrils, the dark coat of hair glistened, as if he'd been swimming. His sides heaved. His antlers were light colored not covered with the dark velvet she'd heard so much about. Without turning she whispered, "I can't believe people really shoot them. Don't they know?"

"Don't they know what?"

"Don't they know all life is precious?" She shook off the solemnity. "Is he getting ready to shed his antlers? Is that why the velvet is gone?"

"No. Not until winter. We should go, babe. Lotte's waiting dinner for us."

This time she shushed him and felt his impatience. This was old stuff to him, but the first wild moose she'd seen this close. Anders shifted, the springs on the old bench seat creaked. The moose's ears laid back and the hair on his hump rose, yet he stayed, watching them.

"One more minute, please? He's beautiful, so perfect." Christine turned toward Anders touching her lips to the air, hoping he'd relent, viewing it as a promise for later in the evening. The lines around his mouth softened and he smiled.

He stroked her hair. "You're beautiful, too."

"I used to be." Sadness and regret collided, and she pushed his hand away.

'C'mon, I think you're perfect." His eyes lingered on her face. She pulled more hair from the rubber band and let it fall, hiding the scar. She ignored him. He grunted and said, "Let's go, it'll take us over an hour to get back."

As if sensing their impending departure, the moose turned and headed toward the creek. Christine craned her head, watching until he disappeared. Anders eased the truck into reverse. Backing over rocks and slipping into deep ruts, the old truck creaked and groaned. Anders pulled onto the highway, an uncomfortable silence occupying the space between them. Christine slid across the cracked red leather seat and rested her head on his shoulder.

"Thanks for trying to help me. Sorry I snapped at you."

He patted her knee and smiled. "Next time I won't be as forgiving."

The main highway took them north past smaller ranches and farms. The last lingering rays of the fading sunlight cast a pink glow on the roof tops, leaving houses in shadows. Christine squinted. The houses disappeared and the roofs seemed suspended, as if nothing anchored them to the earth. It was how she often felt: floating above life. She wanted to be a participant, wanted to be comfortable with her damaged body, yet those two things eluded her. Would everything change once she moved here and made it her home?

It was after 7:00 p.m. when they reached the ranch. Lotte Brugmann, caretaker of Larsson Ranch, met them at the door, apron askew, hair disheveled, whiskey on her breath. "It's about time. You two think we got all night?" She led them into the dining room where foreman Jake Manor and the other ranch hands sat waiting for dinner.

****

"When you gettin' your butt in gear and movin' here permanent?" Lotte leaned back, feet propped on the table.

Christine shifted, uncomfortable with the question. Remnants of the evening meal lay scattered on plates, mostly wiped clean by thick slices of fresh bread. Leftovers were meager: roast chicken, its carcass picked over like crows on road kill, rosemary sticking out of its ribs; a few browned potatoes mixed with baby carrots. Garlic, roasted crisp, dotted the tablecloth. Lotte's homemade lemon meringue pie rolled in Christine's stomach, but her queasiness was more a reaction to the impending move which at times made her feel as if she was being dragged by a runaway horse. It was Friday night and most of the staff had gone into town. That left Anders, Jake and Christine to face Lotte's inquisition.

"I'm waitin' for an answer. You've been here two damn months, what ya waitin' for?" A toothpick hung from Lotte's upper lip, she caught it with her tongue and swept it inside her mouth. Before Christine could answer, Lotte spit it out. "Now damn it girl, you've got to get on with it. Don't you like that piece of land Anders found you? They're clearin' it in a few weeks, ya know. 'Fore you know it, it'll be done and you'll still be whinin' about ... hell ...who knows what."

Anders said, "Let her alone. She'll do it when she's ready."

"I can speak for myself." Christine turned to Lotte. "I've got a lot to do before I pack up."

"Excuses, excuses." Lotte cut her off, "You know what they say ... everyone's got one and they all blow smoke." A smirk twitched at the edges of Lotte's lips, a sure sign she knew she'd inter-mixed two slang expressions. Before Christine could protest, Lotte held up a hand between her face and Christine's. "Talk to the hand," she said, embracing another old and tired gem.

It would do no good to argue. Christine reached over, pulled Lotte's hand down until it rested on the table. "I need to find a new roommate for Donna. I owe her that much."

"No you don't," Lotte said.

"Wait, let me finish. I'm walking out on our lease."

Lotte jumped in, "You don't owe that woman nothin'. Where was she when you were in the hospital tryin' to get better? Out partyin' wasn't she? Didn't take any of the blame did she? So don't talk to me about what you owe her."

The rest of Lotte's diatribe was lost in the lengthy melody of chimes that indicated it was forty-five-minutes past the hour. Too much stress for one night. Christine's head pulsated; her forehead felt like canvas stretched tight across a wooden frame. She focused on the grandfather clock while they talked around her again.

No one had to remind her how hurt she'd been when Donna, who was partially responsible for the accident, seemed apathetic to her injuries. While Christine fought for her life, Donna was released from the hospital within a few days, suffering only a broken arm and mild concussion.

Filigree hands on the old grandfather clock in the dining room clicked away, Christine mumbled short responses to their questions, not really listening, no longer caring. New fears surfaced: finding someone to rent-share wasn't going to be easy, and that was only the beginning. She'd have to tell everyone, and then listen to reasons why she shouldn't move: too soon after the accident; too soon after her treatments; too soon for those who didn't want her to move on. Montana was too dangerous a place; too risky; too whatever popped into their heads. Tears sprang into her eyes and hung there ready to bubble over.

"Hey, are you listenin' to us?" Lotte pounded on the table. Seeing the terror in Christine's face, Lotte "gentled down" as Jake would put it. She put her hand over Christine's. "I'm sorry, girlie; I should know when to shut up. Jake says I talk way too much."

Christine willed the tears away, concentrating on Lotte's hands that were thick and chapped, the knuckles large. Dirt had embedded itself deep in her fingernails. The palms of Christine's hands, which she kept hidden as much as possible, were scarlet. She envied Lotte's masculine, working hands—symbolic of her gruff exterior, but which belied a tender heart.

Eyes dry, Christine held Lotte's gaze. "I'm fine. You don't need to worry about me."

"You're not foolin' anyone. I know you're still hurtin' deep inside from that accident and those folks out there aren't helpin'. I see you mopin' around, talkin' to them on the phone, and they're makin' you cry. Tell 'em to go jump and let's get started on that dream house of yours."

Christine pulled her hands away. "Are you going to help me build it?" But, she knew the answer. Lotte could hardly wait to swing a hammer. When a fire destroyed part of the ranch in the mid-1960's, Lotte, at the age of twenty-four, helped Anders' grandfather rebuild.

Lotte's round face lit up. "Help you? You bet I am. Just get me them plans Spencer drew up and I'll be out there buildin' walls myself." She shed her glasses, rubbed her eyes, and leaned across the table. "Just tell me when, and I'm with ya."

Lotte's eyes were narrow, almost almond shaped and green. Jake once said when she was mad, her eyes were like two fiery arrows, striking at a man's heart and letting it bleed slow-like—painfully slow, until she's ready to forgive. Christine had heard that she could inflict that pain for days, sometimes months, to those who didn't treat her or her adopted family right.

Lotte shoved a clump of stray hair back into the loose bun she wore low at the base of her neck. Her full upper lip curled and twitched, baring unexpectedly perfect white teeth. She rose, struck an Elvis-like pose—knee cocked inward, imaginary guitar strapped to her torso—and said, "I'm with ya, baby."

Jake, who had said very little all evening, whispered to Christine, "You know she does a perfect rendition of Hound Dog. Should get her to do it sometime."

"Hey, what's that whisperin' about?" Lotte snarled at Jake. "Don't you be talkin' about me when I'm doin' my Elvis impression. That boy was something. I can still remember seein' him for the first time on the Ed Sullivan show. We were livin' in Indiana at the time. It was rainin' cats and dogs; roads were flooded and water was comin' up the porch steps. Lightnin' was flashin' and the thunder was a rollin', but we were all huddled around the TV just waitin' to see Elvis. I remember ..."

Knowing Lotte would continue her tales long into the night, Christine quietly slipped away when she had the chance. She crept up the massive staircase that was the centerpiece of the entry hall, making sure she held close to the right, and quieter, side. When she got to the top of the stairs, she walked down the long hallway to her room. The door creaked when she opened it. A full moon illuminated her bedroom and laid a path of light from the open window to the doorway. Eyelet curtains flapped in the September wind, causing the cane rocker next to it to slap against the wall. Christine walked over to the window to close it and, gazing out past the corral toward a distant campfire, she remembered a portion of a Michael Gurnett poem: *"The campfire glows and the hobbles are on, I'm feelin' I've found the place I belong."*

Maybe she had, even though she hadn't liked it the first time—there hadn't been enough action, just old cowboys and oppressive heat. Five years ago, a clothing catalogue sent her and Donna to the ranch for a photo shoot; Anders was the photographer. Though the brochure for Larsson Ranch offered "...

wide open spaces, horseback riding and the best fly fishing in the whole state of Montana" as well as high-end amenities for the discriminating traveler." Their experience hadn't lived up to the hype, leaving them longing for Boston's nightlife. The aridness, the constant swirling dirt had been oppressive. Its beauty eluded her—the only beauty that mattered was her own. Anders had been a mild distraction during their brief ten day stay. After the shoot she went back to Boston and Nick. Anders returned to his work. They had little contact after that and she rarely thought about him until he called a few days before the accident to tell her he was coming to Boston for a job. He wanted to see her. By the time he arrived, she was in Intensive Care.

Christine undressed and buried herself underneath piles of blankets and a down comforter. She lay in bed staring at the ceiling, conflicted about the impending move, Anders growing affection and her hesitation. She'd led him to believe they would be together tonight, but she wasn't ready to let him see her ravaged body. Later when she heard the door to Anders' room close, it was sadness and fear that crawled in beside her.

TWO

"You're not serious. You can't walk out on our lease." Christine held the phone away from her ear while Donna ranted. She was mad, but what had Christine expected? Their friendship had always been about Donna.

Christine had tossed and turned all night—not just from indecision; her leg had continued to throb, keeping rhythm with her heart. Nothing helped—not a pillow under her knee or sleeping in the rocking chair. Finally, about three in the morning she took a pain pill and fell into a fog of burning cars and twisted metal. Once awake, she knew the only way to quiet some of the fears was to get it over with and call Donna.

In the background, Matt—Donna's boyfriend for the last three years—chattered; his voice grating like the annoying jabber of a Stellar Jay. "It's because of that cowboy, isn't it? Tell her those cowboys are never faithful. Tell her …" Christine resisted the urge to hang-up; luckily the rest of his words were drowned out by a plane on approach to Logan Airport.

"Tell Matt he doesn't know what he's talking about—Anders isn't a cowboy. And, I can't hear him anyway," Christine said.

Matt was wealthy by birth, lazy and pretentious. Donna used him to get what she wanted: an apartment in Boston's exclusive Beacon Hill and endless connections in the modeling and film industries. But, that was Donna: vain, sometimes ruthless, self-absorbed—and beautiful. "That's ridiculous," her father would say, "you're much prettier. Donna's too large on top to be a proper model." He was wrong, of course, and since Matt had an 'in' Donna had no trouble getting jobs.

"Shut up Matt, I can't hear her," Donna screeched. "God damn planes are driving me crazy. They're using those damn east west runways again. Fog's rolled in this morning—it's like a friggin' white-out without the snow. I'll never make my ten o'clock shoot—can we hurry this along, please?" Rumblings again, this time it wasn't a plane. Donna screamed, "I said shut-up, Matt."

Christine repeated, "I'm moving out here. I'll be in Boston in a month or so to pack up. I'll help you find someone to rent my room."

"Don't bother," Donna said.

"Look, don't try to talk me out of it. Your life wasn't torn apart. You're still modeling aren't you? You've got your gig, now I want mine. This is my chance." Silence from the other end—guilt provoking silence. The kind designed to make Christine change her mind, the kind she used to give in to. Not this time. "Are you there? Or did you hang up?" She fidgeted with the phone cord. "Look, I'm hanging up if you aren't going to talk to me."

"Your dad's gonna be pissed—how do you plan to deal with that?"

"That's my problem. I'm not a child. I've let him influence my life for the last thirty-three years; not anymore."

This time Donna sighed, then whimpered, "But what will I do without you? Who will I get to move in here? You're always thinking about yourself."

Again from somewhere in their apartment, a tunneled utterance from Matt, "I'll move in with you."

The whining stopped. Donna said, "Now see what you've done."

The line went dead.

Christine replaced the receiver and stared at it. Donna was right; her father was going to be furious. He was convinced Christine would return to Boston, have cosmetic surgery and resume a modeling career. He assumed that's what she wanted. It wasn't. Until the accident, and for as long as she could remember, she'd been daddy's beautiful little girl yet when Christine returned to her parent's house on the Cape to convalesce from the accident, her father wouldn't look at her, diverting his eyes whenever he saw her. She knew it was hard for him—he thought beauty was one of God's ultimate gifts. He would say "You're lucky God made you beautiful; now use that God-given talent to earn some money."

Most fathers wanted their daughters to be 'more than a pretty face' but not Boyd McMurray. He began grooming her for a modeling career when she turned five, entering her in contests and dragging her to auditions. Christine's stage mom was a middle-aged male who flirted with the mothers and fabricated stories about himself. Always in touch with the latest get rich scheme, he'd been out-of-touch with her real interests. It had saddened and angered her when she'd realized that his main obsession with her modeling career was its potential for big money and fame. But, she'd disappointed him—never quite making the grade, never becoming the Heidi Klum of the modeling world as he'd envisioned. Then fate intervened.

The downstairs clock chimed eight. Christine's stomach grumbled for food, but more than that she needed coffee. She hobbled down the stairs, massaging her hip where the pain localized. In the kitchen she downed two ibuprofen, then poured leftover coffee and sat at the table replaying her conversation with Donna until it began to weigh on her. She took a deep breath and shrugged it off—done being the victim.

Sun streamed through white café curtains over the kitchen sink and filled the room; a kiss of fall air blew through the open window. She shivered. September was cooler than she expected. During her first month at Larsson Ranch, the old kitchen, with its white metal cabinets, yellow flowered wallpaper, black and white checkered floor, became her refuge whenever she couldn't sleep. She'd raid the refrigerator at night, piling spoonfuls of homemade ice cream into the same orange Fiesta®Ware bowl, carefully washing and putting it back in the cupboard so no one would know. Each bite cooled the burning in her stomach and the ache in her heart. By the time the sun broke over the mountains she'd be back in bed.

Finally one day Lotte said, "You can't be mopin' around here and sleepin' 'til damn near noon every day. This is a workin' ranch and you may as well make yourself useful; get out there and help with the chores."

Lotte put her to work, doing odds jobs in the stables and housecleaning when she could. It helped her sleep through the night and shed some of the pounds she'd gained.

Gravel crunched; a car door slammed, heavy footsteps approached. "Gol darn woman, why can't she do it herself?" Jake flung the door open, slamming it back on its hinges, crossed the kitchen tracking mud across Lotte's spotless floor. "Any coffee left or you drink it all?"

"Aren't we a bit cranky this morning?" Christine learned to throw it back at the other men, but this was the first time she'd had to do it with Jake.

He rubbed a day-old beard with one hand and tugged at the back of his bleached out jeans with the other. Wiry brown hair speckled with grey curled out from under his John Deere hat. He looked distraught. Drops of perspiration slid down his cheeks, in and out of crevices scoring his leathered face. He paced, but managed a weak, "Yep."

"Well snap out of it." No change. She studied him. Kind of good looking for a guy in his seventies, though certainly nothing like the men she knew in Boston—most of them models, many of them gay. Feminine beauty oozed from several of her ex-boyfriends. Too bad there had been nothing girl-like about their personalities. Not like Jake, who underneath his gruff pretense and masculine exterior, had a heart ready for "easy pickins"—Lotte's words. Working the ranch had made his six-foot frame lean and muscular with biceps that still had definition. He had Paul Newman eyes that, right now, wouldn't meet hers.

"Alright Jake, if you're going to pout at least you can tell me what's wrong." When he didn't answer, she changed the subject. "Where's Anders? I thought he was staying in today."

Jake poured the last of the coffee into a worn cup with gothic print spelling out "Yellow tone" the's' rubbed out. He kicked a chair out from under the table, dropped in it and took a swig of coffee. "Don't know. He didn't go out with us. Must be still in bed."

"Oh, I didn't think about knocking on his door."

"Ain't you two bunkin' together?" The worm holed pine table creaked as he leaned toward her, this time his eyes locked onto hers.

It was a question they'd all been dying to ask. Her body stiffened and she changed the subject again. "Now what's eating you?"

He grinned. "Nice try honey, but if you want to do it right you got to say "waaz eatin' ya?" He laughed and rubbed his eyes. "It's that woman again."

Ah, Lotte problems. Christine smiled—Lotte drove the hands crazy with "… that damn stubbornness." But they were as loyal to her as they were to their own mothers and sisters. Christine had grown accustomed to Lotte's gruffness, but it wasn't always that way. During her first trip to the ranch, she and Donna nicknamed her "macho Lotto".

"What's she done now?" Christine said, always enjoying Lotte stories.

Jake tossed his hat on the table, rubbed his knuckles across the top of his head. "She's got us takin' the last of the vacation folks into town to catch the bus to the airport. I don't get those people—don't they ever do anything for themselves? Word is they forgot to make arrangements—ha, they're just lazy and all high and mighty."

"I was one of those 'high and mighty folks' when I came the first time."

"I remember. You and that Donna were a real pain in the ass. Always complain' about gettin' dirty and whinin' about that hair of yours." He laughed, leaned back in his chair and continued, "You had poor ol' Anders runnin' around doing your errands. Had that boy tied up in little knots. Sure were a little brat, ya know."

The muscle across Christine's forehead tightened, her head ached; the desire to strike back was too much.

"Okay, you can just shut up now. You're not so great yourself. You're a grumpy old man. All Lotte has to do is snap her fingers and you follow her around like a wounded puppy. People say you . . . "

And there it was; she'd done it, returned to the Christine she hoped she'd left in Boston. Jake slammed his fist on the table, leaned across it so hard that its legs swayed. "What those damn folks say? You tell me now right now what they say about me and Lotte?"

She flushed, ready to fight back but as swiftly as her anger erupted, it left. She slumped back in her chair. "I'm sorry. I didn't mean anything."

The fire went out of Jake's eyes. "Hell, I'm sorry, too. Havin' a bad day."

The door slammed. "Who's sorry for what?" Anders looked at Christine. "Damn it Jake what'd you do?" They hadn't heard the door open, hadn't heard Anders' truck, hadn't heard him walk into the room, but he was there—Christine's knight, body rigid, poised to attack an old man.

"Oh, for goodness sake Anders, relax. I'm fine." Why was the protectiveness Anders had shown in the hospital, a protectiveness she'd coveted, slowly becoming an annoyance? "Jake and I were just doing a bit of reminiscing. Weren't we, Jake?"

"Doesn't look like that to me," Anders said, glaring at Jake. "Lotte's looking for you. She said the van's loaded up and you better get it to town before the bus leaves for the airport. She's says if you don't hurry and if anyone misses their plane it'll be coming out of your hide."

Jake picked up his hat, groaned and grabbed at his back when he stood. He headed toward the door, stopped, turned and pointed at Christine. "You're good for this place. You forget what I said."

****

"She really hung up on you?" They'd moved past Jake. Christine was telling Anders about her argument with Donna.

"Yeah, she was mad. I knew she would be." Christine scurried around the kitchen armed with sponge and a bottle of cleaner, attacking mud left from Jake's boots. Lightheaded from the chemicals, but not finished, she moved to the worn red laminate counter tops, scouring spots until some of the color faded. It was only 10:00 a.m. and she'd already fought with two people, three if she counted Matt.

Anders' slipped in behind her, resting his chin on her shoulder. "I don't want to get you mad, but Lotte was right last night—Donna is selfish and you know that. She never did apologize to you."

"But, it wasn't her fault." The knot in her stomach was growing, filling up with suppressed resentment toward Donna. "The guy that hit us was drunk, remember?"

Their traffic light had just turned yellow. Even now it blinked in her dreams: car approaching, take diversionary action. Donna hadn't seen the light; hadn't realized the car coming from the east wasn't going to stop even though its light was still red. Donna was applying lipstick when it hit them. Christine remembered the sound more than anything else. The screech of brakes, the crushing metal, and breaking glass. Glass falling, cutting, slicing through her skin, the searing pain in her leg. Then the heat. She shuddered and tried to pull away from Anders. "Can we talk about something else?"

He turned her to him, studied her face and gently pushed her hair to one side. "You okay"

"Yes, fine."

But, she wasn't.

He stared at her. "You know what? You need a break. I don't have anything going on today. How about we pack a lunch and head down to the river, or maybe take a drive into town and see how Spencer is coming with the revised plans?"

Agitation and sorrow disappeared, and she let him in. The tension left, she rested her forehead against his chest. She felt safe.

"You shower and get ready. I'll fix lunch," he said.

She paused in the doorway, watching Anders pull turkey and cheese from the refrigerator.

"Go," he said and pointed at her.

This was all new: the selflessness, the protectiveness, his self-assurance, the cooking. She'd never been around men who cooked or men who were good to women. More than once she'd been seduced by men like her father. More than once she'd been taken in by dark eyes and a ready smile.

THREE

Anders carried the wicker picnic basket to the truck. Christine followed with a blanket and sketch pad. They piled everything inside including Anders fishing equipment, camera and tripod then headed out. The day was cool; a breeze drifted through the aspens, coaxing burnished yellow leaves to flutter against the sapphire sky. Jake's last message to her still resonated, clear and forceful, "You're good for this place." This place was good for her, too—forget Donna, forget her father.

Christine rolled down the window, let the wind touch her face and clear her mind. A whisper of white topped the distant mountains in the west; she settled in, unencumbered.

"What are you smiling at?" Anders stared at her, his grin spread from one ear to the other like a cliché. Though he was not as breathtakingly handsome as some of her previous men, he was breathtakingly kind. And cute—there was that.

She kept her answer light. "Feels good to be alive. What a glorious day, what a glorious place. You're very lucky to have grown up in Montana. Don't know how you could have left." She paused. "Why did you?"

As he always did when she asked that question, he changed the subject. "Since you are in love with this place, where do you want to go?"

"Spencer's. I thought we were looking at house plans first."

"I talked to Linda, he's busy. Let's drive to Emigrant, set up by the river then stop by Grandma Jo's for pie on the way home. Okay?"

"Not so fast, darlin'," letting her tongue languish on the roof of her mouth, mimicking Lotte, "I want an answer to my question."

"First mine. We're nearing the highway."

"Geez, okay, go to Emigrant; I like the idea of riding for an hour. Now tell me. And," she turned and pointed at him, "you're not getting out of it this time."

They turned off the gravel driveway and into what Jake referred to as "that dang city traffic." They'd eventually head south on Highway 89 which ran along the Yellowstone River, a meandering, scenic highway past open meadows, through narrow canyons and skirting dense forest.

She turned to Anders, "Well?"

"What?"

"You know all about me, it's time for you to do the talking."

"No, I don't know all about you, babe. You haven't told me much about your childhood. If I'm talking, so are you. We've got all day, let's get to it." He gave her a gentle nudge. "You up for it? I tell, you tell?"

Could she? She turned to him. "You first."

"There's nothing to tell. I had a fight with my dad when I was eighteen, packed up my bags and hit the road."

"What about?"

"The same thing every teenager fights about—control. He wanted it; I didn't want him to have it."

"C'mon, you gotta give me more than that." The noise from passing cars drowned out Anders' response. "I can't hear you," she said.

They rolled up the windows, he turned toward her and smiled, "Better?"

She nodded, "Go on."

"He kept pushing me to be more involved in Grandpa's ranch. I wanted to go to college in California and he thought it was a waste of time." He grunted. "To be fair, I guess he wanted to keep me close, but the more he pulled, the more I resisted. He never got over my mother's leaving and when my older brother up and left, it nearly killed him." He glanced at her. "I know; I hate talking about it. Mom was a bit of a free spirit. Her Crow heritage was what attracted my dad in the first place and ultimately it's what drove them apart."

"You're part Indian?" It shocked her; he didn't look at all Indian—he was blond. Maybe his brown eyes; maybe the high cheekbones? His jaw was a bit wide—and tight; right now it was set and tight.

"People here say Native American. What do you easterners say?"

She knew he wasn't really looking for an answer, just making a point. Her family had always been a bit wary of other cultures. Until Miller, she'd never been friends with a person of color. "But Anders is Swedish, right?

"My real name's not Anders." He cleared his throat. "You'll laugh."

"No, I won't."

"Don't worry; everyone does. My parents couldn't agree on a name. My dad wanted to name me Arle—that's his name, but Mom hated it, so a few weeks after I was born she named me Arapoosh."

"Arapoosh?"

"Apparently, I was very colicky and Arapoosh means 'sour stomach' in Crow."

She swallowed, stifling a giggle. "No, really?"

"Yeah, she was a bit of a nut case."

"How did they get Anders out of Arapoosh?"

"My dad insisted my middle name be Swedish. Anders is my great-uncle's name."

"Well, it's sure a lot better than Arapoosh. My god, what was she thinking?" Christine chuckled, but he wasn't laughing. "Look, I was kidding. You surprised me. I don't care if you're part Indian or Chinese, really." It came out wrong. "What I'm trying to say, is that, well, I don't know. It doesn't matter."

"It mattered when I was a kid. I was the brunt of a lot of jokes; the perfect target. Anders, Arapoosh—both names were different; it didn't matter what I called myself. Didn't have a lot of friends and as soon as they met my mom they backed off. She wore her hair in braids that reached down to her waist and sometimes she'd dance around with these long scarves. I hated it. I mean, I loved her, but hell, I was a kid; all I wanted was to be liked. Then she left when I was twelve and it was almost a relief."

He was driving faster now, flying over ruts in the road. Christine braced herself against the dash and pushed both feet into the floorboard. Their conversation seemed less important as fear grew. "Could you slow down a bit?"

He shot her a blank stare. "What? Oh, sorry."

"It's okay I just got scared for a minute."

Anders slowed the truck and eased off the road into a narrow turnout. "Really, sorry 'bout that."

Her ears were ringing and her legs cramping. She kicked off her shoes, wiggled her toes to get the circulation going, and rolled down the window for air. They'd stopped in front of a small grey ranch style home. A petite grey haired woman walked the yard with a cane, bending over occasionally to pull a weed from pristine flower beds that rimmed the perimeter of the yard. When the woman heard them, she stood up, shifted the cane inch by inch until she faced them. Her lips pursed, she squinted and stared, then hobbled toward them. Christine turned to Anders, "Do you know her?"

Anders shook his head. "But it looks like she knows us."

The woman approached. Christine noticed the cane was more like a garden tool she'd seen on info channels. Four arms extended from its staff, each covered in rubber, making it easier for the woman to maneuver. It was unlike the hand-carved wooden one Anders had given her. She'd thanked him, but buried it deep in her closet where it sat, unused. The woman approached the truck and stopped; realizing they were strangers, she turned and shuffled back toward the house. Christine fought the sadness aching deep in her chest.

She glanced at Anders; he was staring at her. He opened his mouth, but she cut him off, "Now what were we talking about before you pulled over." She gave him a wink and wondered if he could see through her smile. "And, why did you pull over?"

"You were nervous about my driving; I thought we could talk about that for a minute."

"Naw," she lied, "I'd rather talk about that Native American heritage of yours."

"Let's not; let's save it for another day. How about a cup of coffee?"

About a half-mile down the road, he pulled into the parking lot of Rocky's Café and jumped out of the truck, ran to her side and helped her down. "C'mon."

"Wait, I don't want any coffee. Hey, wait up."

He kept walking. She hesitated; she hated Rocky's. The coffee was lousy, nothing like what she was used to in Boston, and the food wasn't very good: greasy breakfasts and greasier lunches. Plus it was the local hangout for long haul truckers and nearby ranchers—nobody she had anything in common with. There was a rumor that their backroom satisfied hunger of another kind. She scurried after Anders, trying to keep up, but her leg throbbed. Anders disappeared through a heavy, intricately carved wood door that didn't fit the place. A lackluster red and yellow sign, evidence of the café's longevity, hung lopsided over the door, announcing Bayern Beer Here. It was flanked by two smaller signs one proudly proclaiming World's Best Buffalo Burgers, the other Help Wanted. She pushed her way inside.

A chalky haze hung in the air of the testosterone filled room. A long, grayish counter ran the entire length, dividing the kitchen from the dining area. Men in denim dungarees and overalls occupied most tables; the only sign of femininity were a couple of waitresses in tight fitting black skirts, white blouses, ratty, trussed hair and red lips. Smoke stung the membranes in Christine's nose and her eyes watered; she squinted and scanned the room. Anders had stretched out in a corner booth. The owner's daughter, Janice, a seductive redhead with emerald eyes, stood next to him. Christine bit her lips for color and ran a hand through her hair until it fell over the scar. Head down and eyes averted, she maneuvered through the maze of tables. Most of the men were deep in conversation yet she felt their eyes on her. The smell of bacon grease and burnt toast made her nauseous. She reached Anders just in time to see Janice brush his hand.

"There you are. C'mon and sit down." Anders patted the bench. "Christine, you remember Janice?"

A flash of red lips, a quick, "Heard you were back, nice to see you again," and Janice turned and walked toward the kitchen, swinging an ample derriere.

Christine slid into the booth. "Why didn't you wait?"

"I don't like to rehash my past." Anders kissed her cheek. "No bickering."

"Here's your coffee, hon." Janice loomed over Christine holding a cup. "Can you lean back so I can get this to Anders without spilling it on you?" She reached over Christine, set the coffee in front of Anders, breasts spilling out of her blouse. "You want anything, Chrissy?" Janice drew out the 's' until it sounded like a hiss.

"Sure, I'll have some and, Janice, it's Christine, not Chrissy."

When Janice left, Christine turned back to Anders. He was smiling at her.

"Why do you let her get under your skin?" he said.

"For god's sake, she, Donna and I hung out together, remember? Now, she acts like she doesn't know me. It's all a show, you know; all for your benefit." The day was getting worse by the moment, a picnic no longer sounded like a good idea. "She's not the least bit attractive; I really don't know what you saw in her in the first place."

"It was high school, I was a kid." His voice became light and playful. "You're jealous, aren't you?"

His smugness annoyed her. "Not in the least. In fact I think the two of you are perfect for each other."

The smile gone, his voice low, he said, "C'mon, why'd you do that?"

"Do what?" She glared at him.

"You know what I mean. Why do you attack like that? I was teasing you." He frowned. "Sometimes you make it difficult to care about you, but then maybe that's what you want."

"Don't be ridiculous." Sometimes she wished he'd just blow up. His calmness, his confidence, his kindness were all traits she couldn't live up to; they'd never been part of her make-up. There were times when he seemed much older than thirty-nine. She often felt like the child and Anders the parent, like the six years between them was a river she'd never be able to navigate.

Another cup appeared, steam inching its way toward her skin. A flash of heat poured through her body, panic set in and for a moment she felt her skin blister and pucker in anticipation of spilt hot liquid. "Can you take this before it burns my hand? We're out of saucers and these damn cups get really hot," Janice said.

With a trembling hand, Christine reached for it then changed her mind. "Would you please just set it down?" Her voice raspy, the words tinged with irritation. Feeling bad she said, "Can you sit with us?" Stupid, stupid. What had she done?

"Sure the rush is over—the girls have things under control. Let me grab my own cup."

"Now why'd you do that?" Anders said as Janice disappeared to grab her cup off the counter. "If she makes you uncomfortable …" Before he could finish Janice plopped down across from Christine and scrutinized her face.

Janice drew a finger along her own cheekbone. "Ya can hardly see it now."

"Thanks. Been using a lot of vitamin E."

"How's the modeling going for you?" Janice took a sip, peering at Christine.

Christine resisted the urge to avoid the question. "I don't model anymore. I'm more interested in art and this spectacular Montana landscape. In fact, I've bought some land and plan to build a house." That'll shut her up.

If Christine's revelation unnerved Janice, it didn't show.

"Well, honey that's great. Everyone deserves a dream. You know what I always wanted to do?"

Christine stared at the dark liquid in front of her and delayed answering by diligently stirring the coffee. She lifted the cup to her mouth, blowing to cool it and hoping one of them would fill the silence. When neither did, she felt compelled to ask, "No, Janice, what was it you always wanted to do?"

Something changed in Janice's demeanor. She leaned into the table, her breasts crushed against the metal edging that encased the grey Formica table top, her eyes wide. "Law. I wanted to be one of those attorneys that works with the ranchers around here."

Christine looked from Janice, to her coffee, to Anders. Amusement played with the fine lines rimming his eyes and twitched at the corner of his mouth. He was waiting for her to say something. Sarcasm pushed from her mind to her lips, but something in Janice's behavior stopped her. "Wow, Janice that's great. Why didn't you?" She glanced at Anders, this time his eyes held a tenderness that made her uncomfortable.

Janice hesitated, fiddled with her cup. "Anders knows the story. I got knocked up when I was eighteen—the father was a guy from Oregon, out here for spring break who wanted nothing to do with me or the kid. I'd already been accepted to Montana State when I found out. Everything changed then. I had a little boy, the cutest little thing. I couldn't give him away, though everyone said I should. He's grown now. Studying to be an environmental something or other in Idaho. He'll graduate this June." Her pride obvious, her smile wistful.

Christine reached across the table and patted Janice's hand. "You could still do it you know. It's really never too late."

Janice pulled away. "Oh you know, honey, that's a real sweet thing to say, but you go on and follow your dream and leave mine to me."

"Where the hell are you? I need you out here." The voice surged toward them like a freight train; the voice hit its crescendo with, "Janice, now." A large bald man behind the counter pointed at Janice and yelled again. What must have been an everyday occurrence didn't stop the din of conversation, pots clamoring or dishes clanging.

Janice shrugged. "Boss's calling. You two have yourself a nice day now. See ya." In a rush of bravado laced with a smattering of seduction, Janice rose, gave them a quick wave and said to her father, "Geez, just hold onto those britches of yours. I get a break once in a while. I'm your daughter damn it."

"I wish I could hear that conversation. Janice can be pretty feisty," Anders said with a tinge of admiration.

Christine's face felt hot and her hands tingled. She wanted to lash out at Anders, at Janice, but she wasn't sure why. "I suppose you could always follow her into the kitchen," she said, trying to keep her tone light.

Anders tipped his head to the side, stroked his chin and said, "You are jealous, aren't you?"

FOUR

Like a scene from a movie, the hawk gained altitude then disappeared above the gold of the aspens and dark green of the fir trees that embraced the Yellowstone River on both sides. Random autumn breezes sent ripples over the river's surface and sabotaged Anders's efforts at catching trout using a blue winged olive. Before she met him, Christine would have thought a blue winged olive was something that grew on a tree in Greece and was especially tasty drenched in vodka with a splash of dry vermouth in a martini bar in Boston's Back Bay. Now she knew better. Best way to catch a trout in September, he'd told her.

They'd left Janice and the arguing behind, spending the remainder of the morning relaxing: Christine sketching, Anders snapping pictures and later, fishing. Neither had brought a watch, but stomach rumblings coincided with the sun high overhead. Christine hobbled along the shoreline with the heavy picnic basket; her progress, though cautious, was methodical and determined. The river was low and clear, as it usually was at the beginning of fall. In one of her favorite photography books about Montana, she'd read that its clarity often depended on their summer: It became turbid with sediment if it had been unusually wet or if there had been a heavy snow pack the previous winter. Today it bubbled clear. It surged over large boulders, ambling northward through crevices left by years of erosion etching a path until it would eventually join the Missouri on the border of northeastern Montana and North Dakota—a place that Anders had promised to take her next summer.

The occasional call of an eagle and the slap of a trout breaking the surface, settled on her like a protective glove and without immediately realizing it, her limp abated. She found a flat boulder at the bend in the river just out of Anders' sight, spread the green, red and yellow flowered tablecloth over the enormous makeshift table and opened the picnic basket. Anders had packed enough food for six: sliced turkey on soft dimpled bread that Anders called focaccia with a cranberry spread and some mild white cheese. He'd 'thrown together' a pasta salad with leftover pesto he'd made with the basil from Lotte's garden, brought fresh fruit, and chocolate turtles from Sammie's Sweet Shoppe in town.

She rose, walked to a spot where he could see her, waved her arms and called, "Time for lunch."

****

"Where'd you learn to do all this?" She snatched the last turtle and spread her arm in a half arch indicating what remained of their meal.

"Say, I wanted that," he said.

"I left you the fruit."

"Oh, sure, the healthy stuff." He reached for a small green apple, inspected it, wrapped his mouth around half and bit. "Wow, that's sour."

She'd been trying to coax him into talking more about his past, but he was evasive so she tried playing to his ego. "I'm impressed. None of the men in my life cook. Are you just a natural, or did someone teach you?" She scooted, moving to a comfortable spot on the rock, rolled to her side, rested her head on her hand and stared at him.

He mirrored her movements and answered, "I did a lot of cooking when I lived in California."

She waited. "And?"

"And what?" He nudged her elbow and shot her a grin. "You want me to continue with my dysfunctional history?"

"Of course."

The rock seemed to soften underneath her and the stress of the morning conversation was carried away by the song of the whippoorwill settled somewhere in the trees behind them.

"Okay, you win. I left home right out of high school and stayed with the Nicholson family in California. They were regular guests at the ranch when I was a kid. They told me if I ever wanted to visit California I could stay with them. Dad would never let me, but when I was eighteen and they called for help with their horse ranch, I left. I lived with them for six years, 'til I finished college."

"How long did you stay in California?"

"Lived in Santa Barbara until three years ago."

"Really? I thought you came back a long time ago."

"Nope, came back to help out three years ago when Grandpa died and Dad went to Alaska to live with my brother. I think he left so I'd have to come back and help Lotte. Rather selfish of him, I'd say."

"Then when we met five years ago, you were what? Visiting?"

"You mean when we hooked up, and you never called like you promised."

She blushed and pointed at him. "You didn't either."

"Kidding; I was a different guy. Much more interested in my work than getting involved. But, yes, I was kind of visiting. My agent got me the gig."

"How'd you get interested in photography?"

"Jenna Nicholson was a photojournalist. She taught me. I worked my way through college at UCSB as a photographer and got my degree. Been freelancing ever since. Was lucky—Jenna helped me at first. Eventually I made my own way. Got a few assignments for Montana Magazine so I was able to come home fairly often. Then the one for the fashion magazine that you did, followed by the one in Boston when you were in the hospital, and you know the rest."

"Do you miss California?"

"Can't go back. Lotte and Jake need help."

"Would you want to?"

Anders stretched, stifled a yawn and rolled to his back, resting his head on the roots of a massive tree stump that protruded from the bank above him. "Aw, babe, I'd miss the people here." He leaned over and kissed her. His lips familiar, stirred memories from their past.

She pulled away, slid forward to the edge of the boulder, maneuvered her body until she lay on her stomach resting her chin on the smooth surface of the rock, and dangled a hand into the water. Deliciously cool, she let it lap at the tips of her fingers. She felt Anders rise and move away. A chill carried by a puff of autumn air drifted through the light cotton blouse coaxing goose bumps to rise on back and arms; she shivered and wished she'd brought a sweater. She closed her eyes and felt herself drifting into an afternoon siesta.

****

Something wet on her face. Cold. Where was she? More water, droplets on her hand, water trickling from her scalp onto her face. Her arm ached. The surface underneath was hard; something covered her body. Terror flashed through her body. Accident. Hospital. Then she remembered; they were at the river. Christine rolled to her back. A slap and water splashed onto her hair; the fish were jumping. "Anders? Did you fall asleep too? The trout are feeding." She sat up, pushed the tablecloth off and rubbed her legs. The sun had moved beyond the trees, creating shadows around her. She squinted. Where was he? Her eyes resisted focus, still wanting to close.

"Anders, you here?" She looked around. The picnic basket sat at the top of the bank. She strained to listen, concentrating beyond the deep hum of the river to see if she could hear him. Nothing. Perhaps he'd returned to his fishing spot. Christine stood, stored the tablecloth in the basket and headed out to look for him. She found him in the middle of the river, water up to his waist.

"Hi there, sleepy head."

The line from his fly rod rose from the water, Anders arched his arm over his head, flipping the rod and fishing line behind him, then whipped it upstream, touching the surface of the river several times before coaxing the fly at the end of the line toward its final resting spot. Methodically he drew the line in, his face intent, waiting for a strike.

Christine sat on a tree stump where the bank met the woodland. She loved watching him fish; the graceful arc of the line, rapid movements touching ripples in the river's surface, the outstretched arm directing the precision-like placement of the fly. The beauty of it was much akin to watching a great conductor coaxing an orchestra to a crescendo. She saw it happen once at the Boston Symphony, the first and only time she'd attended—she was eight, her sister Meredith, ten. Her great-grandmother had sent Audrey, Christine's mother, three tickets with a note saying to take the girls—explaining " … if one introduces children to culture at an early age, one might be able to save another generation from society's attempt at making philistines of us all." Christine's great-grandparents were cultured and pretentious. They raised Audrey after she was orphaned at the age of thirteen when her parents were killed in a plane crash. They could be overbearing and disliked Christine's father.

When the tickets for the symphony arrived, there was none for him. If he was angry he didn't show it, instead focusing his attention on Christine, insisting she have her hair and nails done. It was the first time Christine realized the power of beauty. The attention had been addictive: the smell of the expensive lavender shampoo, the beautician's fingers working up a lather, the gentle tug of the brush as she pulled it through Christine's hair, telling her she was pretty and lucky to have such beautiful blond hair. As the cosmetologist buffed her nails, Christine closed her eyes and imagined herself on a stage wearing expensive clothes, all eyes focused on her. At the store, the saleswoman fussed over her, commenting how adorable she was and what a cute little figure she had. They'd all laugh now if they saw her in faded jeans, Lotte's hiking boots, broken fingernails and hair pulled into a ponytail.

The night of the concert she'd felt like a princess. Once the conductor raised his baton, Christine sat mesmerized, watching the movements—fluid, yet precise; jabbing toward the bass section, moving cleanly and effortlessly to percussion until the instruments came together in such a harmonious union that had resonated throughout her entire body. It had been a moment she'd never forgotten. Watching Anders' movements now, she felt the same thrill. This moment was close to perfection. Anders, the river, the serenity and the accord with nature united with the intensity of that night and she felt a sudden urgency to get to Boston, pack and return to Montana.

She pushed up from the ground, ignoring the pain, and called to Anders, "Shouldn't we get going? It must be close to five."

With the rush of rapids swirling around him, Anders trudged upstream toward her, fishing line trailing behind him. He rose from the river, cheeks ruddy, hair tousled, water dripping off his army green waders; at that moment, ruggedly handsome. He held his pole over his shoulder like a javelin then laid it gently on the shore. "What's wrong?"

The words stuck in her throat, she swallowed and tried again. She looked around. "It's perfect. It's what I need. It's clear to me that this is where I should be. I need to book my plane ticket back to Boston. Gotta get packin' as Lotte would say." Christine laughed. "She's right you know; I've put it off long enough."

"Okay, then. Let's get started on your new life."

They decided to forgo a visit to Grandma Jo's and apple pie. Instead Christine wanted to see her land again. She needed a touchstone here in Montana. One that she would remember if leaving her life in Boston became difficult.

This time they stayed in the truck. They sat by the road, windows down, so she could breathe in the air: the earthy smell of grass, the dampness from the billowing deep grey clouds gathering overhead, and the unmistakable scent of the silky locoweed.

"Do you think I can do it?" she said.

"Of course you can. You've worked too hard on yourself not to succeed."

They were both quiet; her thoughts rummaging around her future, playing with each scenario like a puppy with a new toy. His thoughts? She could only guess. Hard to say when she'd return. The holidays loomed; maybe she'd spend them on the Cape with her parents. No matter. She needn't make that decision now.

Christine reached over and stroked Anders hand. "I'll miss you."

Without saying anything, he started the engine.

****

The plane fare to Boston had tripled since the last time she checked—not that it mattered. Money wasn't an issue. It was her consolation prize for being a passenger in a car hit by the son of an influential Senator with a multi-million dollar liability umbrella who didn't want to be sued. The settlement would keep her comfortable until it didn't matter anymore.

The Sunday morning internet connection slogged along. Last night it had been impossible to use the only computer at the ranch because Lotte was paying bills. Right now it choreographed its way through millions of other sites, gathering data, until the archaic computer screen burst with new information. Roundtrip Bozeman to Boston, seven hundred dollars, if she left on a Wednesday it dropped by forty. Not enough incentive to worry about. She started to book a ticket for the following week, but remembered something was happening next month. Then she remembered—Lotte's seventieth birthday celebration. Anders and Jake had been planning it for a long time. Close to one hundred people were expected. The cabins were completely booked. That meant Christine wouldn't leave until mid-October.

Lotte had bristled when they finally told her about their birthday plan. "Now why would I want to go and celebrate getting old?"

One night last month they were gathered around the fire pit at the edge of the backyard, most of the guests had gone back to their cabins. Only staff remained. Sparks danced from one to the other, while each of them stared at the fire, no one wanted to be the one to take Lotte on until Jake leapt up. He stood over her, pointing a finger close to her nose. "Because we said so. We're gonna celebrate until we ain't got no celebration left in our bones, ya hear me?" And that was that.

"You've got mail." A cheery automated computer voice declared—the minimized icon flashing. Should she peek? The computer belonged to the ranch, but everyone used it. Lotte only signed on to keep track of the ranch finances and play Solitaire.

Jake e-mailed his sister in Maine and Anders used it when he misplaced his Blackberry or IPad.

Who had signed in to check e-mail and not signed out? Curiosity had done Christine in more than once. Nosey is what her sister Meredith called it. Should she? No one was around. Most of the staff, including Anders, had gone to the local Farmer's Market—Anders taking photos, everyone else shopping. They wouldn't be back until mid-afternoon. No one would know, unless Lotte walked in. The clock ticked. Rain slapped at the window. Her palms grew sweaty, her heart pumped; she tiptoed to the door and listened. A whirring sound—the vacuum. Lotte was upstairs. It was safe. Dare she? Just a quick look. She settled into the chair, fingers tentative, clicked, minimized one window, opened the other. *Good morning, photoguy.* The mouse took on a life of its own, moving quickly to the mailbox icon. Click. She saw enough of the return e-mail address to spur her on. Dated today, sent by *fairmaiden*, subject header, *you have a sister.* The vacuum stopped. Her heart beat faster. Do it now, or … Footsteps coming down the stairs, "Christine, you down here?"

Arapoosh, I'm your half-sister, Peta. That's all she read before Lotte burst into the room.

"What's the matter with ya? Can't you answer me when I holler? Damn men, can't take off their boots, dirt everywhere."

Heavy moccasin-like slippers covered Lotte's own feet, thin strands of grey hair fell onto her cheeks and hid her eyes, she blew air upward, each tress returned, dropping lightly like a feather from a molting bird.

"Damn hair," she said and pushed it back behind her ears, plopped into the arm chair in front of the desk, grabbed an old wool blanket from the floor and pulled it to her chin. "It's chilly in here. Sixty yesterday and it feels like it could darn near snow today." She wrapped the blanket tighter. "What ya doin'?"

Christine's forefinger slid to the left button of the mouse, pressing down she checked the box marked *Keep as New*, closed the window; the *Checking Flights* window reappeared. Anders had a sister. Should she tell? Couldn't—she'd been nosey. This time Meredith was right.

"What'd you find?" Lotte turned the screen toward her, peering at flight information. "Looks pretty expensive to me, but, hell, you got lots of money now. Get on with it, girl."

Lotte pulled her glasses down onto the tip of her nose making it appear even larger. She peered at Christine who, feeling guilty, averted her eyes, concentrating on Lotte's nose which started out straight, then slanted toward the left, widened and turned toward her right cheek at the bottom.

It was hard to believe Lotte was once a beauty, but pictures from thirty years ago showed a different Lotte. Blonde hair, small nose, smaller lips; age had dulled and widened her. Yet the beauty was there, one only had to look.

Lotte tapped on the screen so Christine could no longer ignore her. "Do it now."

"I will. I'll go after your birthday."

"Humpf, no need to wait for that. Not sure I'll go myself."

"Of course you'll go."

The game continued. "Why should I?"

"Because everyone loves you. Not one person has declined." Lotte gave her a dubious look, but Christine continued, "C'mon, you know you want to. You can't disappoint all those people, now can you?" All those people—anxiety tingled through her body, unabated. Too many people. So many staring at her scars.

A deep rumbling sound followed by a wheeze, rose from the chair. Lotte had fallen asleep. Christine refocused on her trip. She'd fly into Providence instead to visit her parents on the Cape before going to Boston. Leaving the return date open, Christine booked the outbound flight for the twentieth, the day after the celebration. Good time to go. Everyone would be busy with guests—no fanfare, no long good-byes, and no expectations. She pushed her chair back, closed out of the travel site, decided against looking at Anders' e-mail. If and when he wanted her to know, he'd tell her. She tiptoed out of the room into the hall. A quick look at the clock told her it was 3:15 p.m. at the Cape. Her parents would be back from church, they'd have had their Sunday dinner and Meredith, Carl and the kids would be gone. Her mother would be in the kitchen scrubbing pots, probably still sipping the one glass of wine she allowed herself. Her father would be lounging in the recliner, the Sunday paper scattered on the floor. Might as well call them to let them know her plans.

The old stairs creaked as she climbed them, but no limp. In the last few weeks it had diminished. The doctors said that would happen, but they'd also said the scar on her cheek would fade—it wasn't fading fast enough. Christine reached the last step. She hadn't tripped, hadn't stumbled and the ache that usually shot up her leg and into her hip was dull, not sharp as usual. She walked down the hall and sat on the tiny wicker chair, pushed her head deep into the phone alcove so she could talk without being heard. She lifted the receiver. The dark, heavy mass of molded plastic rolled awkwardly in her hand—palm to fingertips and back. How much should she tell them? She inserted her finger into the rotary phone's first hole, hesitated, then dialed. The addition of each number carried her across the country until the last number pulled her right into the heart of her parents' living room.

"Hello, this is the McMurray residence." The voice was familiar and soft, with a slight lilt, and a touch of affectation that remained from years of living a privileged life as a child—though her mother might disagree with her daughter's assessment.

"Hi, Mother, it's me."

"Oh, Christine, it's good to hear your voice. Wait, dear, let me get your father to pick up the extension."

"Mom. Mom. Wait, I don't have much time."

Her first lie.

"Mom?"

"Yes, dear?"

"I'm coming back next month, on the twentieth."

"Wonderful dear. Are you all right? Will we get to see you?"

"Yes, and yes. Just take this down. I'm flying into Providence, so I can see you guys before heading to Boston. I get in at ten at night. I'll rent a car; you guys don't have to pick me up."

Her father's voice crackled over the bedroom extension, "Kitten is that you? Did I hear your mother say you were coming home? Should we … "

"Boyd, she's …"

"Shut-up Audrey I want to hear everything from Christine. Why don't you go on back to the kitchen and finish those dishes."

For the second time in two days Christine felt empathy, this time for her mother; this time she suppressed the feeling.

A subdued voice returned, the cheery inflection gone. "Good-bye dear, I'll see you in a few weeks." The line cleared, then clicked on again. "Oh dear, I forgot, Miller called again. He said you had called him before you left, but he's been out of the country. Should I give you his number?"

Her father interrupted. "Forget it, Audrey, she doesn't need to talk to that guy. Now hang-up." Then to Christine, "Have you given up that crazy idea of living out in cowboy country?" He would be standing, stretching his five foot ten inch frame to appear taller. His chest extended, face bloated with smugness, a smirk on his lips.

"I haven't made any decisions yet."

Her second lie.

"Good. I talked to your old agent and he's sure he can get you some jobs. He even said the accident might make some magazines more interested in you. You know, local model's comeback. He said you could make a lot of money promoting your story. And, that reporter still wants to talk to you."

"Dad, stop. I'm not modeling anymore. I was already too old before the accident, now I'm not marketable at all." She heard the intake, then the growl from deep, like a dog ready to attack. She braced herself, but this time she wouldn't let him berate her. "Oh, Dad, someone's here. Got to go, see you in a few. Mom's got my schedule. Love you."

Her third lie.

She dropped the phone before he had a chance to say anything, before she had a chance to change her mind and not go back at all.

The downstairs screen door whapped against wood then slammed shut. They were back. “Dang it woman, you sleep the whole day away. Anders, get in here you gotta see this one,” Jake said.

Anders response was drowned out by Lotte’s booming voice. “What the hell you yellin’ about? Near gave me a heart attack. I wasn’t sleepin’ anyway, just giving my eyelids a rest. What’s it to ya?”

Jake boomed back. “Well you don’t have to get all huffy. Was just givin’ ya the what for. In case you was wondering, we had a good day. Got the green stuff you wanted, Anders even bought ya some flowers.” He lowered his voice, but Christine could clearly hear him. “He got some pretty flowers for Christine, too, didn’t ya boy?”

She started down the stairs then remembered the e-mail—Anders had a sister named Peta

FIVE

September slipped into October. Unnoticed it disappeared into the blustery days of the first full month of autumn. Christine noted personalities at the ranch also became inclement. Though Anders hadn't mentioned his e-mail or the discovery of a half-sister, he appeared edgy and ill-tempered. Preparations for the party overwhelmed all of them. Christine's curiosity about Peta subsided but her apprehension increased. She kept busy helping the men and, like today, made several trips in town to meet with Spencer about last minute changes to the house—a mountain style cottage really, with lots of windows. Spencer disapproved. He told her winters would be harsh and 'encouraged' her to reduce the number. He was convinced she would regret deciding on light rather than warmth. Pine floors and a river rock fireplace were also on her list of 'must haves'; his displeasure with these decisions was obvious.

He stared at her. "Impractical," he said with a shake of his balding head. "Now this is your money of course, but since I'm your architect and responsible for the end result, I need to advise you that the decisions you are making are not very sensible. Pine is inherently soft and the smallest movement, like the scrape of a chair, can leave a mark that cannot be fixed. And river rock is overused. Why don't you think about something like a flagstone or slate surround? " Before she could answer, he continued. "You're quite young, you know, to be taking this on yourself, and since you are a woman ..."

That's when she stopped him, rising from the chair abruptly and shoving the plans back to him. "Now you listen, Spencer. I may be young in your eyes and, yes, you are amazingly observant, I certainly am a woman ..." She waited to see how her sarcasm settled on him and when she realized it hadn't she continued, " ... but since I'm paying you, we can either work together or I'll call someone else." She was bluffing of course. There were very few architects in the area, none with Spencer's reputation.

Anders had warned her Spencer was a man who was used to working with wealthy ranchers and business owners, all male, building palatial houses and sprawling business complexes. Spencer pursed his lips and bristled, "Well it's your money and if you want to waste it, I guess I'll do whatever you want. Though I think it's a big mistake." He clucked like a woman, shook his head and pointed to the chair, "Now sit, dear, and let's get this done."

His mannerisms were exaggerated and dramatic, so much that she'd often wondered if he was gay. "Aw, he was just henpecked by his ma—still is," Lotte had said when Christine mentioned her suspicions. "Both them Madigan boys are that way; they never grew up. Hell, his brother Mason is married and has two kids and still acts like he's six."

Right now Spencer was acting like a two-year-old, ready to throw himself on the floor kicking and screaming. Instead he pointed to the chair again. "Sit, I said."

Damn, you'd think he was talking to a dog. She hesitated trying to decide between need and principle—she decided on the former.

After an hour of discussion, and the more she explained the vision for the house and property, the more vested he became. "I still think you are making some irresponsible decisions here, but it sure is going to be a beauty. Who's going to build it for you?"

"Stan Merkel's outfit. They're going to do most of it, but Lotte and the boys at the ranch have offered to do some of it, and Anders has a bit of construction experience. I'll oversee it until I leave for Boston, then Anders will take over."

His eyes narrowed. "You're taking on a big project, here. If you want it done by spring you'll need a professional to stay on top of it. I could recommend …"

He was at it again. She stood up, extended her hand. "Thanks, Spencer. Would you make those final changes in the next two weeks? I'd need them before I leave on the twentieth."

He held out his hand and shook hers. "You're a strange one, Christine McMurray, but I've got to hand it to you—you've got spunk. I'll have it for you by the end of this week. Take care, now." He laid his other hand on the small of her back and eased her out the door.

****

Two days later Christine received the revised plans along with a curt message: "I hope these changes are satisfactory. I'm afraid any other additions will have to be handled by my associate, Ken Jacobson, as I've taken on another project that will keep me occupied for the next year. Good luck to you." His name sprawled across the bottom of the page like Montana bindweed in the heat of summer with the only discernable letter a phallic-like "S" that rose above the rest of the signature. Though she no longer had need of his services, the note irritated her and she showed it to Anders along with the plans.

Anders rested his hand on her shoulder. "Don't take this personally. I told you he was a busy man."

"He's an arrogant S.O.B.," she said.

Anders then passed the finished plans around the ranch amidst declarations of "oh's and ahs". It seemed there was a unified consensus of admiration especially when she told them the original design and floor plan had been sketched out on a restaurant napkin. In the past they'd looked upon her artistic attempts, which consisted primarily of caricatures of each of them, with coy smiles and elbow prodding intermixed with a few "that don't look nothing like me" comments. Rudimentary sketches of the Montana landscape were hidden in her room away from curious eyes and criticism. She'd experienced enough of that from her father. "A waste of time," he said. "You'll never make any money with that scribble. Your face is where the money is; you'll see you'll be making millions before you know it."

Of course she hadn't and now she never would.

SIX

It was October 15th. Christine, Anders and half a dozen men from the ranch gathered in the middle of her land with the plans, stakes, twine, backhoe and excavator ready to plot and clear the spot where the house would stand. The weather wasn't cooperating and hadn't for the last three weeks, which was why they were behind schedule. This was their first opportunity to clear the land and she felt time slipping away. A front from the Rockies funneled a brisk wind through the canyon and heavy rain pelted them amidst intermittent sun breaks and periods of hail.

"C'mon Christine, we've been here for over an hour waiting for this thing to blow over. It's not going to. I've got to get back and get these guys working on cleaning out the barn." Anders stood hunched over, his back braced against the wind, the hood of his jacket pulled tight, covering his head and face. Her own hat soaked; hair so wet that rain drops streamed down the collar of her coat and saturated her back. The jeans, tucked into boots, clung to her thighs and rain seeped through to wool socks. Some of the men began to retreat to the truck for cover. She knew she should give in, but couldn't. She needed to have an imprint of the house, one that would remain in her mind's eye while in Boston.

"I'll stay, you go," she said.

Anders shifted. "Don't be ridiculous, Christine. We'll come back tomorrow and do it."

She moved in front of him. "You can't, nor the next day, nor the next and you know it. This is the only day before I leave." She pulled her hand from deep in her coat sleeve, her fingertips numb, his hand warm when she touched it. "Let me stay, I need to do this. Besides, look, there's blue sky." She pointed east where a window of blue had opened amongst a layer of grey. As if to mock her it disappeared, covered by a rush of darkness. "I'll be fine."

He turned from her and scanned the men who stood leaning against the truck. "Mitch, you stay with her." Then to her, "I'll drive the backhoe down the hill. I'll leave my truck here; Mitch will drive you back." She attempted to protest, but he was having none of it. "That's the way it is. You don't agree I'll throw you over my shoulder and take you back now." He paused. "You let Mitch help you set the stakes, then come home. We can clear it while you're gone."

So he thought he could talk to her like she was a child. Who did he think he was, her father? Anger raged through her like a brush fire out of control. "Don't you tell me what to do. If I want to stay here all night by myself, I'll do it. If I want to lie down and wallow in the mud and drown in the rain, I'll do it." She shook a finger at him, her insides trembling. "Don't you ever … " She was irrational, but she couldn't stop and poked her finger into his heavy denim coat.

Anders grabbed it; she yanked it back. "I never intend to control you," he said and lowered his head, glanced at the men, then back at her. This time his eyes were cold. "It's good you'll be leaving soon. I think we need the break."

She wanted to protest, to tell him it wasn't him, it was her. That she was terrified of returning home, that fear had taken over, running rampant destroying rational thinking, playing havoc with her emotions. Instead she said, "Perfect. I couldn't agree more."

It took him only twenty minutes to get the equipment down the hill and onto the trailer. Anders worked fast yelling at the crew to get the lead out, then hopped in the Mitch's truck and spun out onto the road.

She tried to make small talk with Mitch while the rain continued destroying her day. The cold penetrated her hands so that gripping the measuring tape was difficult; Mitch pulled the end and Christine yelled, "Stop." At the appropriate spot she pushed the stakes into the saturated earth, wrapped the twine around each one, measured again, and moved to the next, trying to keep the line taut. The twine slipped from the sodden and splintered stakes with each attempt. Mitch, his hands constantly in pockets and head down, showed no signs of going beyond what was required of him and when Christine asked him for solutions, he just shrugged.

Resentment of his apathy and frustration with the inclement weather welled; she covered her face with her hands, her body trembled and she sobbed. "Can't you please ... " The words wouldn't form; she heard him shift and walk. He was going to try to comfort her, she couldn't let that happen. She moved away from him and rubbed her eyes with a coat sleeve and looked up. He wasn't walking toward her he was walking away, toward the truck. The last of the stakes were thrown on the ground, the twine and tape beside them. Fine. Didn't need him, didn't need anyone. She laid the end of the tape on the ground securing it with a rock, pulled it until it reached the desired length, set the stake, wrapped the twine around three times and moved to the last and final one. Done. She skirted the outside perimeter of the layout, walking through the mud, letting the rain soak her, but not her spirit. She imagined herself inside watching the rain, a fire roaring, a woolen blanket on her lap, face clear, body slender and flawless, pain gone. An imaginary door opened and she stepped inside. The sun broke through the clouds; its rays beat down and spread until they encompassed the entire house.

"Hey, Ma'am, let's get going, it's pouring. You're gonna get sick."

Silly man, couldn't he see the sun shining on her, on the house, on her life. How could he say it was pouring? She raised her face to the sun—liquid rays washed away anger.

When they returned to the ranch, Anders avoided her, ignoring attempts at explanation and apology. He dismissed her with a wave. "It's who you are, Christine. No need to explain." Yet she needed to explain. But, she decided, he wouldn't understand so why bother.

The chill in the house, evident to everyone, affected their mood. Tension built, tempers grew increasingly short; Christine sensed she had ruined Lotte's celebration and that saddened her.

Two voices played the 'blame game' in her head. The stronger one, and the one she eventually came to accept, assuaged her guilt with indignation; the other voice, which oozed culpability, was overruled by her own offbeat sense of logic. It was just as well. She'd be leaving soon and Anders hadn't even told her about Peta. How could she trust a man who wouldn't share his secrets?

SEVEN

Preparations for the party kept everyone busy. Jake, his son Vic, Mitch and a handful of men from neighboring ranches cleaned out the old barn for the celebration. The men worked feverishly to give it new life with fresh hay over loam, white paint sprayed with abandon in random strokes that when finished resembled a creation by Andy Warhol and covered the perpetrators with specks of white, dotting cowboy hats and eyebrows. The rest of the crew cleared a grassy area adjacent to the barn where tents would be erected and heat lamps would keep the chill out. October weather could be unpredictable—either bone chilling cold or cloaked in warm temperatures, fooling everyone into thinking spring was just around the corner.

The barn—primarily used for the storage after the new one was built last year—when viewed from a distance, appeared to lean precariously toward the east one day and to the west the next. A trick played by the eyes, Anders told her. Weeds sprouted thick around the barn's splintered siding. Sunlight streamed through the knotholes in the decaying structure in a divine artistry making Christine want to shout out "hallelujah." The gaping holes and missing boards had increased with each storm, but Jake had assured her the barn was sturdy and dependable; by her own assessment it not only looked like it was ready to fall down, it looked lonely and forlorn.

Christine, wrapped in a blanket, relaxed on the back porch in one of Lotte's rocking chairs to get away from curt responses and ill tempers. She'd just leaned her head back, closed her eyes and tried to clear her mind when Jake emerged from the barn and called to her.

"We got it all covered." He chuckled when he realized he too was 'covered' in a cloud of white, looking as if he had been dusted with flour. She nodded at him as a gust of wind carried men's voices through the empty barn to the porch where their words dropped as fast as the earlier rain. It sounded like Vic who said, "Where'd Anders get off to anyway? Funny how he's never around when there's work to be done." Mitch threw her to the wolves and in this case a pack she'd been trying to befriend, when he said, "Are you kidding? He couldn't wait to get away from Christine. She was being a real bitch and … "

"Quit your complaining and get back to work," Jake yelled over his shoulder, then poked at his ear. "Sorry 'bout that. Don't pay no attention to them. They're just pissed 'cause they've got to work extra between now and Saturday."

She'd had enough of Mitch. Forgetting what he said was easy. "Where'd Anders go?"

Jake said, "Don't know for sure. Said he had to meet someone in Livingston and asked if we needed anything picked up in town. Told him to get the tent, tables and foldin' chairs from the Rent Me place. They close 'bout five, then I guess he'll be back by supper."

Jake watched her, waiting for a response, obviously curious about Mitch's remarks, but she wasn't in the mood to explain. Instead she said, "Think Lotte would mind if I picked the last of the fall flowers for some of the cabins?"

"Naw, go ahead," he said.

Christine pushed the blanket from her lap, stood and slipped her arms into the jacket that hung on a hook near the back door. She grabbed the pruning shears hanging next to it and picked up the basket designated for flower and vegetable gathering. Two flower beds lined the stone path that led from the house to the old barn, one of the few feminine touches at the ranch added by Anders' grandmother in the early forties. Heritage roses, asters, geraniums and the last of the dahlias would make nice bouquets for the cabins. She clipped flowers while Jake followed her, taking a cigarette break. The silence grew increasingly uneasy; it was Jake that broke it.

"That barn hasn't been used for nothin' for a spell, critters all over the place, but we got the cats out there and they're havin' a field day with them field mice." He chuckled at his attempt at humor. "All we got left to do is take apart a few more stalls and spread more hay around. We'll put the band in there with a bunch of plywood on the floor for dancin'."

She tapped the wet flowers against her leg soaking her jeans. "Pretty, aren't they?" Not really expecting an answer, she continued, "There's a band? I didn't know that."

"Couldn't have a party without music. Lotte loves to dance, ya know. I talked the band into playin' her favorite Elvis songs." He moved closer and lowered his voice. "Tom Jenkins' son is an Elvis impersonator in Reno, Nevada. Now don't you go spillin' the beans, but he's drivin' up, stayin' with Tom and Sara and comin' to the party." He tugged on the bill of his hat, pulling it down and tight over his eyes. "Yep, we're sure goin' surprise that gal." He poked at the dirt with the toe of his boot. "Yep, she's goin' be speechless when I get through with her."

Bellows from the barn, followed by hoots, then gun shots stopped their conversation. Jake dropped the cigarette butt on the ground, crushed it with his heel and stormed back into the barn. "What the hell's going on in here?" Voices crossed over each other, the only words she clearly heard were "rat" and "over there". Time to go inside.

Steam from the kitchen rolled out when Christine opened the door. The kitchen smelled like boiled dirt. Lotte stood over the sink scraping skin off cooked potatoes, brows pushed together, mouth stern. Christine walked to the white-pine cabinet that housed most of the vases as well as extra glassware for the cabins. The antique hutch with its worm worn insides and stubborn specks of orange paint that still remained after its restoration was one of her favorite pieces. The entire farmhouse was a sanctuary for discarded and unwanted furniture. Lotte picked up collectables every week, Jake lovingly restored them and they were added to the cabins or brought in the house. The ranch house was nothing like the home where Christine grew up. Her father insisted on new—no stray furniture, dogs or cats. He permitted nothing through their front door that was recycled. Except for her great-grandparents' grandfather clock and bedroom furniture, her father sold all of the furnishings and jewelry from their estate while her mother sat meekly in a corner of the Manchester craftsman style house weeping. Christine and her sister had tried to persuade her father to keep some of it, by reminding him many pieces were the only things their mother had left of her own parents. Her father was far more interested in the money it would bring in. "Best to forget the past," he'd reminded them.

Christine took out several vases, set them on the table and began arranging. She turned to face Lotte who still hadn't acknowledged her. "I picked the last of the flowers for the cabins—hope you don't mind." Nothing. "Is something wrong?" Christine moved next to Lotte and lightly touched Lotte's shoulder.

"Oh my, you scared the livin' tar outta me. Where'd you come from?"

"Are you okay? You look upset."

"Just madder than hell at that boyfriend of yours."

"He's not my boyfriend."

"He took off outta here and left us with all this stuff to do without so much as an explanation."

Lotte muttered something unintelligible and grabbed at potato peels clinging to the sides of the old porcelain sink and threw them into the waste bin. She turned toward the antique yellow refrigerator, yanking hard on the long, chrome handle.

"Didn't need no birthday celebration in the first place, now I gotta do half the work for my own damn party. Wish people'd just leave things be and mind … "

The last of her complaint shared with the refrigerator; its only response, a slow gurgle. That seemed to satisfy Lotte because when she turned, her arms were loaded with celery, bacon and brown mustard—tonight's menu included Lotte's German potato salad with a warm vinegar dressing and crisp bacon. She looked up at Christine and said, "I guess you was wantin' to talk to me about something. Shoot."

Should she probe about Anders or pretend there had been another reason? Easy choice really, when dealing with an angry

Lotte. "Nothing specific, really. I picked flowers for the cabins. That okay?"

Lotte's frown returned. "Sure, but why we need to go to all that trouble for folks that ain't paying? I mean I think if they gonna be here they should pay for the cabins, but Arles called and said no one should pay. Shocked the heck outta me, I'll tell you. Arles is one of the tightest men I know and not one of my favorites neither."

Arles. Christine hadn't heard his name mentioned in a while. Gruff and stern, he'd grunted a greeting when Anders reintroduced her to his father in July soon after she'd arrived. He'd been back for a short visit to check up on things. He'd kept his hands stuffed in his pockets and when she said it was nice to see him again, he turned his back to her, body stooped, thinning grey hair with an exaggerated comb-over sweeping from ear to ear.

"Arles will be back for the party?" Christine asked.

"Don't know, don't care. Don't really care if he ever comes back as long as he keeps payin' us. He and Anders fight all the time. I tried to tell Anders to stay in California, but he wouldn't listen. Said we needed help and he'd been gone from his home long enough and it was time to get back to his roots. Whatever that means. The roots he should be lookin' for are gone, flew the coup when he was just a young-un."

Pieces of celery flew off the cutting board onto the floor from Lotte's rapid knife movements. When she was finished, she reached into the upper cabinets and pulled down an enormous butter colored bowl, scooped up the chopped celery and dropped it in the bowl. Next she attacked the onion in a similar fashion, wiping her eyes with the towel she'd stuffed in her apron. "Damn onions, you'd think if they could put a man on the moon they sure as hell could find a way to grow 'em so they wouldn't make you cry."

How to approach it? So many questions: curiosity about Anders' mother's disappearing act; his father's anger, his brother's departure and now this new sister. Finesse seemed like a good tactic. "What can I do to help?"

"You can go track that boy down and drag him back here." Lotte looked up with tears streaming down her face. "Well, what ya waiting for?"

"Uh, I don't think that's a good idea."

"Got ya." Lotte swiped at her eyes with the back of her hand and winked. "I just messin' with ya. Let him be. I imagine he's got enough on his mind with you leavin and all."

And Peta, she thought. "No one knows where he went?" Christine plucked a paring knife from the silverware drawer, pulled a couple of potatoes from the sink and sliced them into the celery filled bowl. Lotte just grunted.

"Didn't he say anything?" Christine kept her eyes lowered, concentrating on keeping each cut uniform, drawing the knife through until the pressure of the blade pushed on her thumb. When she looked up, Lotte was staring at her. Not saying anything she stared back then noticed Lotte was wearing new jeans. Not her usual overall-type-jeans; these were trendy. They rested just above ample hips where soft flesh visibly protruded through a dungaree shirt. They flared out slightly at the ankle.

"You got new jeans." Lotte flushed, turned toward the stove, yanked a cast iron skillet from the cabinet next to it, opened a package of bacon and began frying."They look nice, really. I was just surprised. You're usually in overalls or sweats. I'm sorry if I embarrassed you."

Lotte bristled, "Got 'em off the computer. Easiest purchase I ever made, just move that little pointer around, click, fill in a few questions and next thing ya know they're deliverin' stuff to your door. Perfect Fit Jeans they call 'em. 'Perfect for the women with curves', is what they said. Sure something, that internet."

"Sure is. I love e-mail, especially. My dad's kind of weird about it, but Mom and I communicate pretty well with it. How about you?"

"Can't figure the darn thing out. One minute I've got my own, if I make one wrong move, I'm kicked out or reading some obnoxious advertisement for Bag Balm® or some company wantin' me to enter their million dollar contest. Tried that once.

Took me all over the place, askin' questions 'til I'd had enough. When I tried to get out, it just kept flashin' a little window with dollar signs. I had to shut the whole damn thing down and when it turned on again, I was in Jake's letter box."

Adrenaline surged through Christine; the opportunity was too good to pass up. "That happened to me once. I was online and didn't realize it was signed onto Anders' home page. I figured it out when a window popped up saying new mail had arrived."

Christine was about to confess her indiscretion when she looked out the window and saw Anders' truck pull up next to the barn. He opened the door and jumped out. Dark jeans hugged a fit backside, a sweater and black cashmere jacket covered an un-tucked light blue shirt. Her breath shortened, her stomach fluttered, a sense of familiarity flushed through her, an involuntary reaction; one she wished she wasn't having at this moment. He reached back into the cab and pulled out a manila envelope and a stack of papers. He turned toward the house, grinned and touched his forehead with his index finger, acknowledging he'd seen her watching him. Guess he wasn't mad anymore. He hollered something to the barn; men emerged and pulled tables from the truck bed, then Anders headed toward the kitchen door.

****

"What's she like?" While everyone else in the room sat in stunned silence, Vic had uttered the one question everyone wanted to ask. They'd finished dinner and had gathered in the living room: Lotte, Jake, Vic, Mitch and one other guy whose name Christine could never remember. Anders had summoned them to tell them about Peta.

Lotte lounged on a velvet covered settee, arms crossed, legs stretched and resting on a tiny needlepoint stool with curved legs, so delicate it teetered whenever she moved. Jake leaned against the archway that divided the room from the hall, periodically clearing his throat, arms crossed, fingers digging into a heavy flannel shirt. Christine looked around the room; everyone's arms were crossed. Why was everyone so tense?

Anders shifted and said, "She's a typical fifteen-year-old whose mother is too loony to stay in one place long enough to take care of her." He rose from the oversized leather chair, kicked the ottoman and paced. "Look everyone, I know you think this is a bad idea, but. "

Jake cleared his throat again. "How d'ya know she's really your sister? Maybe she's just playin' ya."

"Why would she do that, Jake?" The question, sharp with challenge, hung in the air. Jake lowered his eyes and didn't answer.

"She has pictures of my mother." Anders paused, stared out the window. "And, she has a photo of us. Peta said the photo was the one thing her mother left behind when she disappeared last year abandoning her to the care of an eighty-year-old grandmother and sickly aunt." He challenged them with his eyes. "She left a note telling Peta about Isak and me and how to find us in case anything happened, which it did. Grandma died and the aunt's in the hospital."

"Where's her father, Anders? Hell, maybe we should be asking, who's her father?" Mitch said.

Before Anders could answer, Lotte leaned forward, motioned for him to help her out of the chair and said, "Think I've heard enough for now. I need a drink. Anyone else?"

An affirming chorus rose above the tension with a list of spirit laden drinks. While Lotte was out of the room, Christine pulled Anders aside.

"That's where you went today?"

"Sorry I didn't tell you about her. I didn't want to say anything until I'd met her." He cupped Christine's elbow, maneuvering her into the hall and out the front door. They stepped onto the porch where the cloudless night, thick with autumn, drew attention to the harvest moon which threw a dusting of light across the lush green yard. The star-filled sky illuminated the hills across the highway; the mountains beyond cloaked in darkness.

Christine reached for Anders' hand. "It's beautiful here."

She didn't want to talk about Peta now; she was leaving in a few days.

"Yeah, it's nice." Anders dropped his hand and scratched his head. "I have a sister, go figure. Wonder how many other siblings I have? How many of them are without parents?"

"Having parents around isn't always the best thing either."

"Not now, okay?" His body slumped and he leaned against the railing next to her. "I know yours weren't ideal, but let's not talk about them." He rubbed his eyes. "This thing with Peta brought back a lot of past emotions about my mother. I was only a couple years younger than Peta when she left me."

His sadness weighed on her. She sighed and didn't know what to say to comfort him, so neither said anything. The air became thick with silence. It was only broken when a breeze from the south caused two rocking chairs on the porch to sway making a clicking sound. Christine stared at the blackness of the night.

"What's wrong? You're not mad because I didn't tell you?" Anders face, half hidden by the darkness, had softened. He pulled her close, brushed his lips against her hair. "You're sad because you're leaving, aren't you?"

It was strange how well he knew her; it thrilled and terrified her. She turned her face into his chest, rubbed her nose into his wool sweater and breathed deeply. It smelled like the earth, like home, like Montana.

"Oh, I'm fine." She pulled away and sat. "Come sit." She patted the rocker next to her. "Tell me more about Peta."

Someone closed the front door, muting the voices inside, conversation interrupted only by occasional clinking of glasses and sporadic laughter.

"She's only a kid. Exuberant and thinks her life is just a bowl of cherries." He laughed. "Really, that's what she said. What teenager is that cheerful and uses such a silly cliché?" He shook his head.

They settled into their own thoughts, the quiet night insulating them in a shroud of intimacy.

He broke the silence. "It's spooky—she looks like my mom did at her age. At least from pictures I've seen."

Anders rocked, the sound of grit being ground into the wooden porch—screeching with each forward motion.

"I knew about her, you know." Christine placed a hand on the arm of Anders' chair to restrain the grating sound from continuing.

He stopped, leaned into her, ran a thumb down the edge of her cheek. "I knew you knew." He smiled, touching his lips to her mouth, warm and soft.

Instinctively she pulled back; he mirrored her movement, his lips now securely set in a smug smirk. "Thought you were pretty smart, didn't you. Snooping around my e-mails."

She tried to explain. Again he leaned toward her, put his finger over her lips and kissed her. "I'm going to miss you, you know." Something in her memory stirred again; something in her body responded.

The window behind them flew up. Lotte poked her head out. "What the hell you doing out here? Get yourself back here—we're ready for more." The window slammed, but not before they heard her grumble, "Damn inconsiderate. Leave us sittin' in here wonderin' where the hell ..."

Christine moved first, but she rose too quickly and her dress caught on a piece of splintered wood. She fumbled with the delicate silk organza trying to remove it from the seat of the chair without tearing. It was vintage; her grandmother's—the only item Christine had taken when her great-grandparents died. She wasn't sure why she wanted it; it was unlike anything she owned and certainly not at all like the trendy clothes she modeled. Donna had laughed at her when she brought it home. Now it was going to be ruined.

Anders slowly eased the fabric from the cracked wood. Long strands of white and grey fibers hung from the hem creating undesired ruching.

"Here, wait, don't pull on it, you'll tear it," Christine said.

"Hold on now." He brushed his hand over the surface of the delicate fabric easing it back into shape until the threads disappeared. A tiny hole appeared at the center of the snag, the dress now permanently scarred.

"Damn it. I can't keep anything nice." It surged upward, closing her throat, reaching its peak and spilling from her eyes: the anger, the resentment, and somewhere, the sorrow. "Damn it, Anders, why don't things stay perfect?"

He put his arms around her waist, pulled her close and whispered, "It's just a dress, Christine, just a dress."

"It's not *just* the dress." How could she explain to him that it wasn't about the dress, it was representative of every imperfection in her life? It was about losing her temper; it was about leaving in three days; it was about him finding a sister; it was about her scars, both inside and out.

"I know, I really do." He stroked her hair. "Perfection isn't reality. Nothing is perfect. What happened to you was tragic. Horrible beyond any explanation, but nothing changed, really. Sure you have some scars, but they're not a symbol of who you are." He stepped back, tilted her chin until she had no choice but to look at him.

The porch light came on, then off. The light momentarily rested on her face. Panic came in waves; she moved away from him, frantically searching for a tissue. "I must be a mess."

He grabbed her this time, pulled her back, then whispered, "Look at me, please. Christine, look at me."

When she did, she glimpsed what she'd been trying to avoid. He wanted her, desired her, maybe loved her; at the very least he was falling in love with her. Confusion replaced the panic—her true feelings always intertwined with her gratitude to him.

She fumbled in the pocket of her dress, avoiding his eyes, "I really need a handkerchief; do you have one?" It appeared, crumpled and yellowed and smelled like sage. She quickly wiped her eyes and blew her nose, gathered herself and said, "Let's get in there before she sends out the troops."

Anders lightly touched her elbow. "Wait, please. You need to hear this. I mean really hear this. You are beautiful, Christine. Don't you know that?"

It wasn't a question she could answer, but it was at that moment she knew they'd moved to a different stage in their relationship. The light came on again; moths flew recklessly into the beam.

****

They'd come inside to a barrage of questions about Peta's legitimacy as Anders' sister. Unnerved, he'd left the room then returned with two photos and tossed them at Jake who took one look, locked eyes with Anders and said, "Yep, she's your sister all right."

Christine couldn't help feeling jealous of all the attention Peta was receiving and wondered how it was affecting Lotte whose party was just two days away. The brightly lit room and animated conversation became too much. Christine retreated to the kitchen for solitude and a cup of tea. The men left an hour later and she heard Lotte say, "Well, this old gal's had enough excitement for one night. Tell Christine she can come out of the kitchen now, we're headed to bed."

What must Lotte think of her? Crazy woman come all this way from Boston just to build a house and get Anders to fall in love with her. Crazy woman not sure of her own feelings come all this way from Boston just to hurt her boy. That's the way Lotte thought of Anders. Her boy. Yes, Lotte must think she was about as unstable as the motherless wild filly Jake found up in the mountains last year. No matter how hard he tried, he couldn't tame her and finally had to sell her at auction in Livingston. Was that the way it was to be for her? Untamable and unattainable.

Christine wrapped her hands around the warm mug of Earl Grey tea, took a sip, and then pressed it to her cheek. The heat felt soothing; she moved it to the other side of her face where there was little sensation. Glass from the accident had cut her so deeply that nerve endings had been permanently severed, leaving the lower left side of her face with little feeling. She moved the cup from one side of her face to the other; for some reason the incongruity pleased her.

When she was finished, she set the tea cup in the sink and walked out of the kitchen. The hall was dark with the exception of a lit marble lamp that teetered precariously on a narrow, spindly-legged parsons table. The base of the lamp was a sculpture of a robust naked woman, her arms reaching upward toward the rose-colored lighted globe. Anders' photos of Peta were stacked on the chair sat next to the table. Murmurs from the porch—Anders and Jake were outside. Christine picked up the photos and sat on the chair. The photo of Peta appeared recent. Braces covered a brilliant smile, brown eyes rimmed in thick dark lashes and brunette hair cascaded in ringlets around frail shoulders. The resemblance to Anders held lightly around the shape of her eyes and strength of her jaw. The other photo was of a family. A younger Anders awkwardly cradled his infant brother, unease showed in his eyes. The father, stoic, stood behind the boy. Arle's upper body bent slightly forward, his hand supporting the baby's head. It was the only part of his body that touched any member of his family. The father's unease captured in his tightlipped expression. The mother, barely discernible in the dark background, appeared detached and though her brown eyes stared into the camera, the blankness in her gaze palpable. Christine held the two photos next to each other; it was difficult to tell if mother and daughter shared a likeness. Christine turned one over—the names, Juanita, Arle, Anders and Isak, were printed in rudimentary scrawl on the back. Interesting. Anders' mother's name was Juanita.

"What do you think?"

She jumped; the photos slipped from her fingers and onto the floor. Anders, ankles crossed, head resting on the doorframe, stood in the open doorway.

"My god, you scared me. I didn't hear you come in." The flush that began somewhere between stomach and heart reached her face. Didn't matter how hard she tried to hide it, emotion always colored her cheeks better than blush ever did. Of course, the deeper the emotion, the rosier the complexion. She bent down, picked up the photos and ran a finger over the glossy surface of Peta's face and said, "She does look a lot like you. The resemblance is remarkable." When she looked up he was next to her.

"I'm tired. I really don't want to talk about Peta anymore tonight. Okay?" He ran his hands over her shoulders and down her arms. "I'm going upstairs now. Will you come with me?"

It was a question he'd asked many times and she repeated the answer she always gave him, "I'm not ready."

He dropped his arms and sighed. "Will you ever be ready? We do have a history, you know. It's not like it's the first time."

"I can't. Not yet."

"I suspected that, but I'm not going to wait forever. You know that, don't you?" He kissed her lightly on the cheek and left.

****

The cream oozed, filling the cracks between her fingers. Quickly she slathered it on her legs, then arms and chest. She stood naked in front of the full length mirror trying to see what Anders might; trying to remember her body before the accident. It was certainly trimmer then. There was no rhyme or reason to the burn scars. One breast, flawless; the other an ugly red, purple under the fold where coagulated fat met ribs. Her stomach and upper thighs dimpled and scarred where they'd been grafted. Her arms untouched, her hands brutalized by the fire. Her face. She allowed her eyes to rise upward, pausing briefly to examine her neck. It was fine. Dare she look further? The best part of her face: her lips, full and pink, opened slightly and an inaudible intake of air escaped when her own eyes ascended to meet those of a stranger. This person who she didn't know stared back at her. This person with sad eyes, set too far apart, not quite blue, not quite green now softened and filled with moisture, tears escaping and racing down her cheek, growing smaller and smaller until they dissipated at the edge of her chin. Who was this person and what had she done with Christine? The model, the beloved daughter, the pretty sister; prom queen, desired friend and lover. Her scarred, puckered skin was the external branding for what she now knew to be a damaged inside. One that unknowingly had been damaged for years, before the accident, even before she thought that being beautiful was important.

She turned away from the mirror, covered herself with the thin flowered cotton robe and climbed into bed, settling under the thick layer of blankets to get warm. Would she ever be desirable to anyone again? Would she ever let a man see her naked? Not Anders, not yet. They'd kissed and touched since she'd been back in Montana, but nothing that would require removing any garments. Part of her missed the intimacy she'd known before the accident: the feeling of being desired and sexy; the rising passion, succumbing to one's needs; then, the afterglow. The moments when she and a partner remained in each other arms, marveling at the beauty of their respective bodies and boasting of each other's sexual prowess. They'd lie about their feelings for one another, she as much as her partner. The sex act had been about the sleekness of her body, and her ability to seduce. She'd really never given the whole love thing too much thought; hadn't loved Nick the way a prospective bride should. Maybe because she'd seen what love had done to her mother and her sister. It had aged them, depleted them and made them too needy. Yet she too needed men to find her desirable and she needed Anders to want her. She touched her face as he had. He was a good man. Why did she always feel something was missing? But the answer always came to her as another question: was it something missing in him or was it in her?

EIGHT

October 19th

No one had expected the wind to be as bad as it was. No one had expected it to blow through the barn like a runaway locomotive. The morning forecast had predicted rain and breezy conditions, intermixed with a few flurries, but nothing like what happened. At noon the forecast was more troublesome: heat from the south was expected to collide with a cold front from Canada. When it did hit around 3:00 p.m., two hours into the festivities, it brought sleet and snow; then torrential rain and turbulent winds.

The forty-foot tent they'd set up as a bar next to the barn was its first casualty. Chairs had been arranged in a circle around the perimeter of the canvas enclosure, a layout that concerned Christine and was not at all pleasing to Lotte. When she and Lotte complained to Jake, he told them, they had no say. "It's the one time you gonna have to just trust me." And, that's the way it was when the first gust came up. Many guests had moved there to escape the music and have a smoke. The wind came up so fast some were still seated when the anchors that secured it to the ground gave way, leaving everyone exposed to the elements. The top flew into the corral, spooked the horses and left two sides of the tent flapping on bent steel poles. Those who had been sitting under it rushed into the barn.

The band and the Elvis impersonator had just finished singing *I Can't Stop Loving You* to Lotte and had begun a rendition of *Jailhouse Rock.* The music blared so loud that no one noticed when a crowd of guests rushed into the barn from outside. Christine had been dancing with one of the summer visitors and Jake pulled Lotte off her chair yelling for everyone to "cut a rug." Folks spilled onto the dance floor, oblivious to the storm raging outside. It wasn't until the first rotted piece of the barn's roof broke away and fell into the barn, landing on the food table that Jake grabbed the microphone and urged everyone to get out. The crowd flooded toward the barn's entrance as the wind surged sending pieces of the roof and siding crashing onto the dance floor.

Without thinking Christine ran toward the closest table, lifted the tablecloth up and ducked under it. She squatted on the hay strewn dirt floor, the white linen cloth encasing her and slapping at her face. She sat, pulled knees toward her chin and buried her face. Above her, rain pounded on the decaying roof and leaked into the barn. It seeped into crevices and furrows created by insects and the barn's furry inhabitants. Dampness saturated the hay, soaked through her black cotton skirt and reached her panties.

A flash, then darkness. People shrieked obscenities and bumped her table as they ran toward safety. Screams and the thumping of feet became too much; Christine cupped hands over her ears, closed her eyes and concentrated on breathing as much to squelch the panic as the voices that began to swirl in her head. Voices she'd hoped had gone away. Her closeted surroundings became a prison, then a haven, so much so that when Anders reached his hand under the swirling fabric and shined a light in her face, she recoiled. The flashlight, the hand too reminiscent of the accident, paralyzed her.

"Christine, is that you? Come on, get out of there, the whole place is coming down."

She pulled back from him, swatted at his out-stretched hand. "Go away, just go away."

"Damn it, Christine, look at me." When she didn't respond he grabbed her arms trying to pull her to safety and shouted "Get up, now. For god's sake, what's wrong with you?"

Something heavy and loud crashed onto the floor nearby. A scream, then Lotte's voice surged over the pandemonium, "Jake's been hit; he's bleedin'. Somebody help."

Anders yanked on Christine's arm. She fell forward onto her knees, pain shot through her damaged leg, settling into her calf with a dull ache. Mud stuck to her knees and hands as she crawled out into darkness and chaos. Someone opened the massive, wooden doors and light burst into the front of the barn casting pools of brightness onto the dirt floor; the distant sky ominous, bruised with indigo clouds. Guests fled toward the exit struggling to keep the heavy doors open as they banged back against the fragile siding.

Lotte yelled again, "Anders, where the hell are you?"

Anders turned the flashlight toward the back of the barn, then back at Christine. "You okay?" She nodded; he pulled her up. "I've got to go help Lotte."

"Yes, but wait." She tried to grab his shirt. "Anders, wait, I'll come with you." He disappeared into the crowd, in the direction of Lotte's voice.

Christine's became disoriented in the ensuing bedlam and she stumbled. Someone grabbed her elbow and said, "Christine, you alright?" The ache in the leg persisted, ears pounding, she barely heard the voice repeat, "Christine, are you alright?"

Christine tried to brush the dirt from her hands by wiping it on her skirt; a hand from the unknown savior took her chin, pulled it upward. Janice, red lipped, mascara running down her face, hair a mess, kind, beautiful, Janice. Christine's head cleared; she threw her arms around Janice and hugged tightly. "Yes, yes I'm okay. What about Jake?"

"Don't know. Let's get the hell out of here before the whole damn place falls apart."

Janice wrapped her arm around Christine's waist and helped her toward the barn's opening. Rain spat through holes in the roof and wind swirled through the barn upturning tables, tossing food and tableware. The Elvis impersonator rushed by Christine singing *Shake, Rattle, and Roll*, his white beaded cape flapping behind him, making him look more like the Flying Nun than the King of Rock. His white boots sloshed through puddles splashing mud on pristine bell bottoms. As he neared the entrance to the barn he turned to Christine, grinned and said, "Quite a party. What else do you guys do for fun?" He jumped into a waiting white half-cab pickup with *The King* and a caricature of Elvis on the side panel.

The truck's tires threw mud in all directions, covering exiting party goers who screamed and gestured to the departing entertainer.

By the time Christine and Janice reached the outside the wind had decreased to a robust breeze and the rain had diminished. She and Janice sat on the steps of the back porch; drenched, muddy, and weary. In the distance, the siren from an approaching ambulance cut through the turmoil, the sound growing louder until it pulled into the driveway.

"Jake's hurt. I have to go back," Christine said.

She stood just as Jake, supported by Anders and Mitch, hobbled out. Lotte, cursing like a trucker, followed, holding Jake's hat. "Gol darn, party. Wouldn't listen to me. No, had to go full on like a bull looking for a heifer in heat. Shoulda made him stop."

"Wasn't your fault. Shoulda had the boys check out the old barn years ago." Jake's voice turned to a whisper. He sucked in air, cleared his throat and tried again. "I'm okay now. Lotte, you just go on and help all these guests get on home."

"Anders, Mitch, set him here, he's drippin' blood on his shirt," Lotte said. Christine and Janice stood while they eased Jake onto the porch step. A three-inch gash over Jake's right eye, gaped, oozing thick, ruby liquid. "He's gonna need some stitches," Lotte said and turned toward the ambulance where a short, redheaded, freckled paramedic was pulling on rubber gloves, while the other paramedic, a tall woman, grabbed a metal box.

"Ma'am, I'm going to have to ask you to move aside here, and let me help him." The male paramedic knelt in front of Jake and gently probed at his cut. "Sir, I'm going to have to take a look. Tell me where it hurts."

"It hurts damn near everywhere. When you get to be my age, son, it's hard to tell where you don't hurt." Jake grinned, but when the paramedic didn't, Jake rubbed his hand across his chest and said, "Hurts a bit here when I breathe."

"Okay. I'll need to take your vitals."

"You're gonna do what with my vitals? Now I might have somethin' to say about that. Don't think I want you exposin' me to the ladies here." He winked and chuckled, then fumbled with the buttons on his white shirt. His hand trembled when he tried to loosen the thin black tie around his neck.

"Now wait, sir, we are going to help you do that." The paramedic reached over and gently pulled Jake's hand down, unbuttoned his shirt and helped him slip it off his shoulders.

"If you don't quit calling me sir, I'm gonna have to get up and smack you. Name's Jake. And you?" Jake held out his hand to the now red-faced younger man.

"I'm Mathew, sir. Now let's get your blood pressure." The woman, who Mathew called Carey, handed him a stethoscope and blood pressure cuff.

Guests mingled around them, talking in whispers, until one of them asked Lotte how they were going to get their vehicles out. Most were parked in the pasture next to the corral and the ambulance blocked the driveway.

"Look, I can't be worrying about you folks getting' outta here. I got ma man hurt here. Can't you see that?" Her eyes rimmed in red, her face twenty years older.

Janice moved in between Lotte and the guest, led him past the ambulance and down the driveway. Ten minutes later, Janice was directing cars through the pasture and out to the road.

The paramedics had taken Jake's vitals and were slowly probing his extremities. Mathew's hands, pale and freckled, tapped on Jake's back, then he placed the stethoscope over the area of Jake's heart and listened intently. "You doing okay?" When Jake nodded, he rose and said, "Think we'll transport him, just to be safe. We'll need to stitch him up at the hospital anyway, so we may as well give him a ride. How 'bout it, Jake, that work for you?"

Jake nodded again, rubbed his arm. "My arm's kind of achin' right now. Must've bruised it when I was pushin' the roof off me." He snickered at his own attempt at a joke, and wheezed. "Look's like my asthma's actin' up again."

The storm had moved through. The sun broke for a moment then slipped behind the mountains and dusk crept around them.

Amidst Jake's moaning and Lotte's curt direction, the paramedics lifted Jake onto the gurney and slid it into the ambulance.

Lotte walked over to Christine. "We're followin' Jake to the hospital."

The hospital—she couldn't go with them, hadn't been in one since last year. She did all her post hospital exams in the out-patient clinic. "Uh, Lotte, I can't."

Lotte interrupted her, "You stay here. Can't have anything else happen. I'm takin' Anders with me. You don't need him now. I do."

Christine was taken aback. "Sure. We'll be fine. You go on." She turned to give Lotte a hug, but she was already walking to Anders' truck.

Janice and some of the guests stayed at the ranch, picking up trash from the party and debris from the barn. It looked like half of the roof had blown off. What was left sagged dangerously in the center. An occasional gust caused the barn's skeleton to sway.

When they were finished, Christine and Janice threw the last garbage bags in the trash can and went into the kitchen to wait for someone to let them know how Jake was. Hours passed; no one called. Christine tried Anders cell phone, but got voice mail. She stammered through one explanation after another before being cut off. Frustrated she sent him a text and still there was no response from Anders or Lotte.

"It's odd we haven't heard from them," she said, nervously picking at dried egg that dotted the kitchen table.

"Don't do that, it's gross." Janice reached over and pushed Christine's hand away. "Your hands … "

Christine drew back and tucked her hands under her thighs, fingertips up, that way the scars on the back of her hands were pressed into the soft cushion of the chair. She dug her fingers into the black fabric of her skirt.

"Yes, my hands are scarred, too. I don't want to talk about that right now."

"Oh, for Pete's sake Christine, I was just going to say how good they look." Janice pushed her chair back, rose, put the tea kettle back on the stove and turned to Christine. "More tea for you?"

"No, thanks. Sorry 'bout my outburst. I'm still a bit sensitive"

"A bit. Ya think?" Janice flashed a smile, flipped her hair back.

They both heard a motor before the motion detector on the side of the house came on. They rushed outside as Anders' truck pulled up to the barn. He jumped out ran to the passenger side and helped Lotte out. She leaned on him, head down, shaking, muttering to herself. Her tentative steps, hunched over demeanor and Anders' tense expression pulled the air from Christine's lungs. As they neared the porch, Anders let his arm drop from Lotte's waist and cupped her elbow to go up the stairs; Christine rushed over and supported Lotte's other arm. To Christine's surprise Lotte allowed both of them to help. Frantic, she tried to catch Anders eye and when she did, he said, "He had a heart attack on the way to the hospital."

"Oh, no."

"No, no he's fine. Well, he's not fine, but he's alive."

When they reached the top of the stairs, Lotte pulled her coat tight and stood upright. "He's gonna be just fine. I know it. Them docs are gonna fix him up good as new." Her voice weak, her conviction unconvincing. Anders opened the screen door, led Lotte to the kitchen table, and eased her into a chair.

Janice, who hadn't said a word since the truck pulled in, stroked Lotte's hair and leaned down to whisper, "Course he's going to be alright, he's Jake, isn't he? That man would never let anything like an old heart attack keep him down."

Lotte encircled Janice's waist with her arm. "Thank you sweetie, you always know what I'm wantin' to hear. Not sure if it's the truth now, mind you, but I like hearin' it."

The affection in Lotte's voice, much like Christine's own mother's when she spoke to her grandchildren, was difficult to hear. Strange how grandparents became effusive, hugging, babbling wimps. Babies' rosy cheeks became kissable, chubby thighs became precious and cooing was accepted as the normal way to communicate. All the things she had to look forward to tomorrow. Oh, no, it was tomorrow. How could she go now with Jake in the hospital? Christine pulled a chair next to Lotte and sat. Anders had gone to make some calls; it was only the three women. Christine reached for Lotte's hand and gently squeezed. "He's a fighter, Lotte. He'll do just fine. Can you tell us what happened and what the doctors said?"

Lotte withdrew her hand and slid out of her coat. "They say he might need some kind of operation. They're doin' a bunch of tests and told us to go home. That's all I know." She rose from her chair and paced. "Now where's that boy? Anders, where'd you get to?"

Anders voice echoed through the kitchen from somewhere above them. "I'll be down in a minute."

"Never mind, I'm comin' up."

"Hold on, Lotte, I'll help you."

It did him no good to try to try to stop her. Lotte was already down the hall and walking toward the stairs.

"What should I do? I can't leave tomorrow; they'll need me," Christine said.

Janice stood, "You go; that's what you do. What good would you do here anyway? Lotte will take care of Jake and Anders will take care of Lotte."

Sure and you'll take care of Anders, Christine thought.

As if Janice had read her thoughts, she said, "And, don't worry about Anders, he's big boy. He can take care of himself until you get back. When are you coming back? And, who's going to watch out for your house while you're gone?"

"I'll probably be back in January sometime. Spencer's partner is working with the builder to make sure the house gets going before the bad weather really hits—the foundation poured, I guess, and the framing done. They hope to get the outside walls up and roof started before any major snow storm, but that's yet to be seen. Anders said he'd go out every couple days to make sure everyone's doing their job, but heck now that Jake is sick and Peta's a part of his life, I don't know what's going to happen."

Anxiety settled in her neck, tightening the muscles across her head and onto her temples; then she felt the nausea creep in. A migraine; she hadn't had one of those since leaving Boston. The flashes began in her right eye then progressed to her left, until she couldn't stand it any longer. She pushed on her temples, rotated her neck and closed her eyes.

"You okay?" She felt Janice's hand on her back.

"Migraine. I better go upstairs."

She dug out her migraine medication from her carry-on, popped two in her mouth, lay on the bed and wrapped the bedspread around her like a cocoon.

****

She found Anders' note on the refrigerator early the next morning. The scrap of paper from *Bozeman Towing, From Our Truck to Your Car*, read: "Christine: Didn't want to wake you. Janice said you weren't feeling well. The hospital called; they're doing surgery on Jake now. We'll call."

Damn it. It didn't say when "now" was; didn't say who "we" were. No signature. Why the hell didn't they wake her? Now what should she do? Damn it. Her flight left at 3:45 p.m. She needed to talk to Anders.

"Christine, you do what you need to do. I can't tell you." His voice brusque, using the same tone as the other night when she wouldn't follow him to his room. Then it softened. "Look honey, I'm up to my ears in this mess. I can't leave Lotte here alone; you'll have to decide. But for what it's worth, I think you need to go, deal with home and get back as soon as you can."

"But shouldn't I stay for Lotte?" She was whining now and knew it. It always worked on her father, but usually annoyed Anders. She heard him murmur to someone.

"Lotte says go. She thanks you for thinking of her but knows you need to settle things in Boston. Oh, wait, the doc is here. I'll call you back." The phone went dead.

When the return call came, it wasn't Anders but Janice who told her Jake had come through the surgery just fine, but would be in the hospital for a while, then convalescing at home for weeks, maybe months. It was Janice that relayed Anders' message that he would be home in time to take her to the airport. It looked like it was Janice they were leaning on. It looked like maybe they didn't need her at all.

PART II

IN THE DEAD OF WINTER

"Every mile is two in winter"~George Herbert

NINE

Christine leaned forward and peered past the sleeping passenger in the window seat, past the darkness to lights flickering in the distance hoping to catch a glimpse of something that would ground her. She found nothing. Rain slashed against the plane's window and a whisper of cold air wafted from the air duct above the open middle seat. She reached up, twisted it off and wrapped the blanket tighter.

They'd bumped around the stormy sky since leaving Bozeman, settled a bit out of Minneapolis, but the turbulence began again thirty-minutes later. Her thoughts had bumped along at the same pace. Early in the flight questions without answers beat a constant and unwanted rhythm against her temples. Resting her eyes didn't help; each time she dozed, loud snorts from the man in seat A woke her. The two aspirin she'd discovered in her jean's pocket, partially decomposed and covered in fuzz, had only given minor relief. Concentrating on the positive things in her future hadn't helped: Anders, the land, the house. Nothing seemed to melt away the pressure that moved unabated from temples to neck. Finally somewhere over Ohio, she'd tucked a pillow behind her head and given in to the rhythm of the flight. Sleep briefly replaced anxiety. Then panic set in as they began their descent, and reality replaced reverie. Montana left behind, now she had to deal with her parents.

In keeping with their turbulent flight, the plane slammed onto the runway at Providence International eliciting gasps from some of the passengers. The seatbelt dug into her flesh and she was thrown back in her seat. The plane slowed, made a sharp left turn and seemed to skid into the gate. The apology came from a male crew member. "Sorry 'bout that folks. Just trying to avert a collision with a mouse on the runway. Welcome to Providence International where the local time is 10:12 p.m. Eastern Standard

Time. Weather here is a balmy forty degrees with overcast skies and a light rain. We'll be taxiing..."

Christine tuned him out and glanced out the window; lightning flashed and rain dotted the porthole size window. A perfect metaphor for her mood. The lights came on and the 'all clear' chimed as hundreds of passengers rose in unison and moments later crushed toward the open door. Before she had a chance to catch her breath the man in the window seat, who smelled of stale cigars, stood and hovered over her making it clear he was ready to deplane. He sidestepped into her, pretending to look forward and nudged her toward the aisle. She felt the pressure of his foot against the heel of her shoe and when his body pressed against her, she turned and glared at him.

"What's a matter, missy, not in a hurry to get off this bucket," he puffed at her. Tobacco and garlic lingered, filling her nostrils; nausea pushed up into her throat. She swallowed and reached into the overhead bin. She struggled with her bag and let it slide slowly onto the top of the seat. Cigar man continued to snicker and nudge. She took her time putting on her coat. Let him wait. Then she tied a black cashmere scarf tightly under her chin, pulled it over her cheeks to cover her scar and wrapped the ends around her neck.

"You gonna take all day?" Ignoring him, she moved into the aisle, opened her purse to pull out gloves. "Man you got some nasty scars on those hands. What happened to you anyway?" This time she didn't look at him and hurried down the aisle and out of the plane.

Once on the jet-way the cold hit her like Anders parting remark, "I hope you sort things out and come back soon, but I'll understand if you don't." What the hell was that supposed to mean? He'd understand not sorting things out or not coming back? Before she could ask he'd brushed his lips against her cheek, reassured her that he would oversee the construction of her home and walked away. He'd understand if she doesn't come back? Of course she'd be back. He was the one who seemed distracted, practically shoving her in the car to make sure she got to the airport so he could get back to the hospital.

In crowded gate area, a whoosh of warm air greeted her. Outbound travelers milled around the door like runners at the start of a race, barely moving as she tried to pass. One woman struggled with a small baby, while the husband grabbed the other child as she ran toward the open door.

"Jack, can't you keep an eye on her? I can't do everything." The angry mother glared at her husband as the child wailed and pulled away.

In the ensuing mayhem, someone bumped Christine, causing her to drop the rolling carry-on. When she tried to bend over to pick it up, her leg gave out and she fell, causing her scarf to fall off. The small child fell against Christine, smiled shyly and reached out to touch her cheek and said, "Yucky."

The father rushed over to grab the child and said, "Sorry, Miss, are you okay?"

She nodded as another hand reached down to help. Yellowed fingers, nails clipped close, the face of her seatmate smirked at her. She pulled away and stood. "I got it, thanks." She struggled to right the bag while walking down the corridor and grappling with the scarf until she found the nearest restroom and hid in one of the stalls. The momentary commotion of flushing toilets, running faucets and children crying echoed through the tile-covered restroom drowned out her weeping. She leaned her head on the grey enclosure and closed her eyes, willing her tears to stop. Muted music sounded somewhere close. Her phone. She grabbed toilet paper and blew her nose, frantically searching for the phone at the bottom of her purse.

"Hello." Her voice cracked, but whoever it was had hung up. She fumbled with the phone trying to read the caller ID. Number Unavailable.

In baggage claim she picked up a second bag and moved on to the rental car area. Long lines had formed at each of the major car rental companies and she heard one very angry man demanding to know why he had to wait. When she approached Luxury Car Rentals there was a sign that instructed her to proceed to the rental car location on the bottom floor.

Perspiration dripped down her neck. When she reached the bottom of the second escalator, she stopped, pulled off her coat, and scanned the garage for the rental car location. The deserted, dimly lit area unnerved her and the eerie sounds of screeching tires didn't help. In the distance she could see car after car skidding down the exit ramp. She pulled off her gloves, stuffed them in her purse and plodded toward an unknown destination. As she rounded one of the concrete pillars she caught sight of a small yellow sign, Rent Luxury here. A scruffy rental car attendant leaned against the corner of a bright yellow structure, staring at her. As she approached, the attendant dropped his cigarette, crushed it with his heel and moved inside. She shivered.

"What can I do for you?" The attendant leaned over the counter; his eyes ran the length of her body then stopped at her face.

She waited, but saw no reaction. He was young, probably barely twenty-one, round with a uniform that hung on him making him look more like Humpty Dumpty than Jack the Ripper. Her anxiety slipped away.

"McMurray, Christine. I have a reservation for a BMW. The small one." It was one of the ways she indulged herself after the settlement: nice cars, new houses.

"None of those fancy cars here, lady. You'd have to go to Logan to get a car like that." The attendant looked down and began texting on his cell.

"But, I specifically reserved that car. Luxury cars are supposed to be your specialty and your eight hundred number assured me you had one."

"Well, lady, we don't and there's not too much left. All I got …" he paused, set his phone down and riffled through some paperwork then peered through the window and pointed, " … is that white Lincoln there in slot B55. That good enough for you?"

Oh, no, not a tank for a car. "Nothing smaller?"

He picked up his walkie-talkie. "Hey Pete, got a customer out here wants something smaller than that Lincoln, got anything almost ready?"

Pete's response came back crackled. "Nope."

"Well, lady, looks like you're out of luck. It's the Lincoln or nothing. Hertz might have something. Should I call 'em." The attendant, who was now visibly irritated, cocked his head at her.

She shook her head. "Never mind; I'll take it."

The attendant grunted, filled out the paperwork, asked for a credit card and she drove away feeling like she was driving a bus.

Traffic on I-95 was light; Christine accelerated and set the cruise control. It was a nice enough car; soft leather seats, iPod adapter, GPS, and a hands-free phone that she didn't know how to operate. She reached for her cell and pushed the number programmed for the ranch.

"Hi, you got there okay?" Anders said.

"How'd you know it was me?

"Caller ID. We've got all the latest technology out here you know?"

"Of course. Forgot. Well, I'm here and on my way to my parents. How's Jake?"

"It's Christine," his voice echoed, then returned clear, and clipped. "He was doing better when we left, but he's got a long road ahead of him. Probably will be in the hospital for a week or more, then months of rehab. I tried to call earlier, but you didn't answer. How was your flight? How's the weather there?"

"Flight was bumpy, otherwise uneventful, though I had some moron next to me. Weather's awful, it's raining like crazy." Nice. They'd resorted to platitudes. Silence followed until she couldn't take it any longer. "I'll call you in a few days after I get settled. Give Lotte a hug for me." She waited.

"Will do. You take care now."

"Okay, you …," The line went dead. You take care now? What the hell kind of response was that? Take care of what? Me? My parents? The damned car?

Bright lights in the rear view mirror came up fast, swerved around her, horn blaring. What the heck? She glanced at the speedometer. The car had decelerated. The cruise had disengaged; another car swerved around. The phone jumped in her hand.

"Gol darn Anders hung up before I could say hi. Hi, then. How you doin' out there?" Hearing Lotte's voice was like coming home.

"Good. I'm glad Jake's doing well. How are you?"

"Better now that ma man has pulled through. Doc says he's goin' to have to watch all that fat he takes in and do some walkin', but if he minds the doc, he'll do just fine." Lotte continued, "I don't want you worryin' too much and there's no need to call us every day. You know, we're doin' just fine here. You need to take your time, get things settled and packed up. If we need ya, we'll call."

Thoughts fused into uncertainty, then irritation. "Well, I hadn't really planned on calling every day."

"Oh, now there, we knew that, just don't want you wastin' your time when everything's fine. Plus you'd be gettin' a lot of answers from the answerin' machine. We're gonna be really busy at the hospital and tryin' to figure out how we're gonna keep the ranch goin' without Jake. Anders already got a call into Janice's brother to come help. And, well, I guess we didn't have a chance to tell ya; Peta's comin' to stay for a spell."

Great. That's the way it was—Janice and Peta. Christine's out and they're in. "Say, Lotte, got to go. Traffic's all around me and the weather's bad. I'll call when I can."

She hung up. Feelings of rejection and insecurity drained her heart, leaving it empty. Nearly missing the exit which would take her from I-95 onto I-195 toward the Cape, she slid across two lanes of traffic to the off ramp and accelerated, entering the interstate. Her heart pounded, her mind again flooded with anxiety filled with the voices of Lotte, Anders and her parents. Christine flipped on the radio and tried to focus on the road. It would be an hour before she crossed over the Sagamore Bridge onto the Cape, then nearly another hour on Highway 6 before she reached her parents' house in Gale Harbor. The steady hum of the road and muted strains of Beethoven or maybe it was Bach, she never could keep them straight, made her wish she could keep on going. Drive to P'town, as it's known to the locals, where the highway ended, take a room at The Inn at Cape's End and shut everything out, sleep the next few weeks. No one to disappoint her, no one for her to disappoint.

In high school she and her friends would go there to escape their boring lives and feed their curiosity about the offbeat people who lived there. Though she'd heard stories of P'town in the 1970's when it was a community of hippies and artists, free spirits of another segment of society, the gay community, later moved there. Those changes unnerved some of the Cape's residents, including her father. He called it "HomoTown, a haven for degenerates and perverts." He'd forbidden her from going there, but to his dismay, his condemnation of alternative lifestyles had only proven to be a catalyst for her curiosity. P'town's charm captivated her artistic side. The narrow streets lined with old pastel colored buildings and a resident population just as colorful, were subjects for her sketches and watercolors whenever she could sneak in a visit without her father knowing.

When she was a freshman and Nick a junior, six of them piled into his 1966 restored convertible Camaro. Though temperatures hovered around thirty degrees they'd bundled up in down jackets, heavy gloves and scarves and, with the heater blasting, sipped from thermoses of hot cocoa for the entire forty-five minute drive to P'town. She'd told her father they were going to the National Seashore to take photos for her photography class. Instead, they'd parked and walked up and down the deserted town, stopping now and then in the local alternative stores, laughing and examining the different sex toys and erotic clothing until they were asked to leave. When a winter thunderstorm moved in, they took cover in the doorway of the local book store. They were huddled in the tight alcove when Nick laughed and pointed at two men kissing in the doorway of a cottage across the street. Christine snapped a photo which she later turned into a sketch. Her father found it months later. Furious about the subject matter, he'd said, "Stop wasting your time on that nonsense. Concentrate on enrolling in modeling classes. Do something that could earn you some real money so we can get out of this dump." But sketching had always been a favorite pastime. As a child she'd sit on the bulkhead outside her home sketching the changing seasons. The summers were rich with color, from the blue-green of Nantucket Sound and brilliant white frothy surf, to the vibrant pinks of the native Rose Mallow and yellows of the Goldenrod. There would be no Goldenrod now; within a month everything would be covered in white. Within a month she'd be surrounded by family again and the Montana winter with its dusky mountains capped in white would go on without her.

****

Nearly two hours later the exit to her childhood home was a short two miles away. Gale Harbor, her youth, her father, her past and her future only two miles down the road. At the city center exit, she turned right and slowly inched down the rain soaked road: past the community church, Summer's Bakery, the post office and Books and Brew. She turned off Main Street onto Breakwater Lane just past the Conoco station and Mark's Fish and Chips where she and her friends spent most Friday nights after the football games at Gale Harbor High School. Breakwater Lane was the icon for the community. The community's stateliest and most expensive homes rose out of manicured lawns, carriage houses adorned bricked driveways, several entrances were blocked by massive iron gates and a few had their own guard houses. The paved lane ended at the sea and intersected with Spit Road. The spit protruded southward from the Cape like an unwanted appendage, anchored by an abandoned lighthouse at the end of the one-mile road where she grew up. Two rocky breakwaters protected the spit from the sea: one from the pounding Atlantic surf on the east side and the other from the gentle slap of Nantucket Sound on the west.

Christine followed the gravel road, dodging muddy potholes, out to the spit where a row of ten tiny sea beaten and weatherworn houses clung to the east side of the rocky breakwater. One belonged to her parents. The row houses were built in the 1920's to provide a home for the families of the Coast Guard station that had long since been shut down. Her father had been one of the first to lay claim to one of the houses when the Coast Guard offered them to retired officers. Since then there'd been several attempts to turn the lighthouse into a bed and breakfast, but they all failed for various reasons.

The setting on the spit was spectacular yet many of the houses were ramshackle. A few had been sold and replaced by houses so large they nearly encompassed the entire lot. Though the street was slowly making a transition, even at night anyone could see the chipped paint, the unkempt yards, broken vehicles in need of repair. Right now the sky was absent of clouds, the moonlight illuminating the street and the frothy surf lapping the shore. Christine dimmed her lights, slowed the car to a crawl and pulled into her parents' driveway, hoping they were asleep. The porch light was on and a light from a lamp in the living room shone through gold curtains that draped the front window. Christine opened her door and took a tentative step onto the slippery driveway. The car door barely made a sound as she nudged it closed. She pulled bags from the trunk and, without thinking, slammed it shut. She held her breath, afraid her mother would come bounding out of the house.

Three months; she'd been gone just three months and it seemed like years. The last time she'd been home was the day before she left for Montana. All of them together: her mother, father, Meredith, Carl and the girls. The conversation had been strained. They all thought she was crazy yet no one said anything. That was the McMurray way; whisper your disapproval to anyone but the perpetrator.

Small black garden lights rimmed the walkway to the front door, some were lit, others flickered, several remained dark. There was always something broken at her house; her father wasn't the handiest of men. A leak from her father's old Dodge formed a leek path of oil that seeped from the closed garage door to the end of the driveway. Her foot slipped and she fell to her knee, dropping one of the bags.

"Shit," she yelled. She waited. No sound. The fall left a black stain on the knee of her jeans. "Shit," she said again. Christine rolled the bags up the concrete stairs onto the porch, pushed open the front door and held her breath. The smell of moth balls and mildew mingling with the distinct aroma of cigarette smoke escaped through the open door. Her father had begun smoking again. She struggled to lift the bags over the door sill and pulled them across the old fir floor. Holding her breath as each wheel clicked a wake-up call, she moved into the dimly lit room. The old lava lamp glubbed its greeting and cast its eerie blue light on the blue walls behind it. It rested on an iron table between two white French provincial chairs covered in plastic. Her father's navy velvet recliner had been moved since the last time she was here and now partially blocked the entrance into her mother's precious dining room. The blue and white Herculon couch took up the space beneath the front window. The flagrant dichotomy of the room was obvious to anyone who visited and often generated subtle, yet disparaging, remarks about its uniquely eclectic mix of furnishings.

Christine and Meredith's bedroom was in the basement, but when visiting she'd stay in the guest room next to her parents'. She tiptoed down the long hallway, a bag in each hand. Halfway down the hall an oversized nightlight beamed upward exposing gold embossed wallpaper and two gold filigree frames that held pictures of female silhouettes. At the end of the hall, her mother's grandfather clock stood silent, stopped years ago at 7:42, no chimes, no minutes ticking away, just frozen in time. As she passed the open door to her parent's room a fluttering motion appeared from under piles of bedding. Her mother waved. "See you in the morning, dear."

The guest room smelled of lavender. Dried stalks lay on top the dresser of the oversized bedroom set her mother had managed to keep from her grandparents' estate. It occupied much of the space and Christine had to maneuver her bags around the bed. The room was her mother's sanctuary, the one place she retreated during the day. Often when Christine came home from school she'd find her mother, eyes closed, humming softly, and rocking gently in the chintz covered rocker. Her mother sat for hours listening to classical tunes emanating from the small antique radio she purchased from an estate sale. Her father had tried to throw it out, but her mother stood up to him, one of the few times she did.

Christine lifted the larger suitcase onto the bed, unzipped it and pulled out a jersey tank top and matching pants. She slipped off her clothes and contemplated taking a shower to wash the dirt from her journey, but decided against it. Waking her father was too risky. She opened the window, buried herself under the covers and listened to the familiar roar of the pounding surf.

TEN

Christine woke to rain and blinds clanging against casing. The aroma of fresh coffee lured her out of bed. Monday. Her mom would be getting ready for her visit to the local nursing home and her father would be at work. Christine dislodged her robe from the corner of the suitcase, attempted to shake out the wrinkles and any lingering Montana critters, put it on and tied it around her. She walked down the hall past her parents' empty bedroom and into the dimly lit kitchen. Cheery orange and yellow flowered wallpaper along the back wall of the kitchen seemed unaffected by the home's dingy occupants and neglected interior. The kitchen had been untouched since her family moved in over thirty years ago; the white porcelain sink had yellowed, metal cabinets were dotted with silver nicks from years of door slamming. The appliances were so outdated that replacement parts were impossible to find.

Christine found her mother hunched over the sink, her thin silhouette visible through the loose cotton nightgown that hung off bony shoulders. Grey had advanced so quickly through her shoulder length dark hair that Christine stifled a gasp, yet when she turned around it was the deep lines around her eyes that made Christine rush to her and wrap her in a quick embrace.

"Morning, Mother."

Her mother pulled back, smoothed her nightgown and ran a hand through her hair. "I must look a sight." Head tilted toward the floor, she shuffled from sink to chair and sank into it. "How are you, dear? You look lovely, but a bit rounder."

It was their standard exchange: a compliment received then abruptly taken away. Christine let the comment slide between them and disappear like a snake down a hole. "I'm doing well, Mother. How are you and Daddy doing? I see you haven't started the kitchen remodel. Is he being difficult?" When Christine received a partial insurance settlement, she'd given them money for a remodel.

Her mother shifted. "It's fine the way it is. You know your father. He heard of a great deal on a stock and had Jim buy into it."

"Damn it, that money was for your kitchen, not one of his hair-brained schemes." Christine sat next to her mother, covering her mother's hands with her own. "It upsets me. I gave that money to you guys so Daddy wouldn't complain about wanting a bigger house. I know you don't want to leave here. I thought it would pacify him."

Her mother gazed past Christine. "Yes, it's really nice here." She sighed then brightened. "The stock is doing very well actually. Your father said we could sell it January and start on the remodel next spring. You see, dear, there is no need to worry about me." She slid her hands free, patted Christine's, rose and walked to the stove. "Now, what can I fix my little girl before I leave? How about pancakes with some nice fresh blueberries? I bought some at the store; I guess they came in from Florida."

Christine shrugged then sighed, "Sure." What was the use? "Do you have time?"

Her mother nodded. "I don't need to be at the nursing home until noon today." She turned to look at the rooster clock on the wall. "It's only nine."

No need to continue the remodel conversation; trying to reason would be futile. Maybe her sister would be an ally. "Say, Mom, how are Meredith and the girls? I haven't talked to her since I left."

"They're doing well. Carl's got a new job; their money worries seem over."

They caught up while her mother pulled eggs and milk from the one door refrigerator, frost spilling from the overworked freezer section. The damn thing must be a hundred years old. Christine's body prickled and frustration got the better of her.

"Think I'll take a quick shower while you cook breakfast."

The shower ran cold at first; pounding her body, pulling the anger from her head, tugging it from her heart and washing it down the drain. By the time the water warmed, the anger and frustration with her mother had cooled and shifted to her father.

He controlled his family with calculated manipulation, sometimes with brawn, but that hadn't happened in twenty years. He'd be difficult to handle; Christine would need a strong will and a clear head when she told him of her plans. She stepped out of the tub onto the shower mat and grabbed a guest bath towel saved for non-existent visitors. A small layer of dust had accumulated on the top where it had been folded over the towel rack. She brushed it off, bits of grey fluff floated through the air; she shook it and rubbed it across her body pulling the dampness onto the rich cotton. The price tag still attached exposed its true origin and price: Filene's Basement, $5.99. Wamsutta had never been so cheap. She avoided the fogged mirror, but looked down at her stomach. She'd gotten used to seeing herself like this yet never got used to the overwhelming sadness that often came without warning. Today, the sadness remained tucked away.

****

"Does Dad really still think that someone would be interested in my story? That they'd do a book or movie about it? Is he nuts?"

Christine swirled a finger around the plate, scooped the last of the syrup and slipped it into her mouth. A few berries lingered. She stabbed them with a fork; a sweet, puckering tartness burst in her mouth. "You know I'm a bit sick of his obsession. No reporter, no movie, no book. And, he can forget his silly ideas about my modeling again. It's never going to happen. I wasn't that good at it in the first place, and I have no interest in putting myself through all that rejection again. Especially now."

Before she'd left Boston for Montana her father had shopped her story to various media outlets thinking it would be a great human interest piece. When only a low level reporter seemed interested, she assumed he'd dropped the idea.

Christine's mother sighed. "Well, dear, it seems like it might be a way for you to heal. You know, heal inside by going back to something familiar. Perhaps just talk to that reporter. If you did, you could do some good by bringing attention to those who choose to imbibe and drive while impaired. You might think about it." She patted Christine's hand then stroked her scarred fingers. "They used to be beautiful." She blinked quickly and looked up; eyes damp. "Well now, enough of that. What are your plans for today?"

Christine jerked her hands away. "Thought I might drive to P'town and relish the few remaining days of fall before it turns cold. I'm not leaving for Boston until next weekend. I have plenty of time to pack the stuff I have here. I could drop you at the nursing home then pick you up."

"I think that's a lovely idea. I hate riding the bus. I'm helping with lunch clean-up, and set-up for afternoon tea, so you don't have to collect me until four. How does that sound?" Christine's mother pushed back from the table, stood and brushed off her nightgown. "I'll bathe, dress and we can go." She paused. "That Miller called again to check on you. He seems like a nice man. You should call him."

She would, but not yet. How could she explain to Miller that the sound of his voice brought back the nightmares? Nightmares so vivid that for the year following the accident she depended on sleeping pills to get her through the night.

In one dream, Miller's hands would appear out of darkness. Images would play in reverse: the fire, the car crumbling, the high-pitched screech of the tires, the car bearing down on them, the yellow light. Then the pain would come back with searing clarity. In the second dream, she would be in the ICU burn unit. White gloved hands would begin peeling away layers of charcoaled skin. Faceless voices interjected their frustration with the unending task. Just as the last bit of burnt skin was pulled away, new brilliant red, raw skin would appear, then it would turn black and the process would start again. The pain, as each patch of skin was torn off, was excruciating. She would wake in terror, her hands and stomach burning. She shuddered. No, she wasn't ready to call Miller.

Nearly an hour later, her mother, hair pulled into a chignon, emerged dressed in a tailored, starched white blouse, black cardigan and mid-calf A-line black skirt. Matronly low-heeled black shoes completed the ensemble.

"Geez, Mom you look like a nun. All you need's a habit."

Her mother frowned. "Well, dear, no one at the nursing home seems to mind how I dress. They're just thankful for the help." She pulled on a black coat and slipped a black purse over her arm. "Shall we?"

The ten-minute ride to the independent care facility became a twenty-minute ordeal. Her mother, obviously miffed, continually sighed while ruffling through her purse. Finally Christine asked her to stop. Her mother snapped the purse shut, clutched it to her chest and stared straight ahead.

Irritated, Christine said, "Oh, god, now you're mad. It's that little whining sound you make. I wish you'd just tell me what you are thinking instead of being so darn passive aggressive."

"I'm sorry, dear. I really don't know what you mean, but it did occur to me as we were driving that possibly you might spend less time worrying about how I look and more time working on yourself." She turned and smiled sweetly. "You really should give that reporter a call."

Frustrated, Christine stopped short of the nursing home, pulled into a tight parking space in the Gale Harbor Market parking lot adjacent to it, shoved it into park and glared at her mother. "I thought we'd left that discussion? No reporter, no story." She slammed her hand on the steering wheel. "Or maybe it's the money it might bring that you care about. You know, I did offer to give you guys more of the settlement and you were the one who said 'No dear, I think we're just fine the way things are.' Or was that another passive ploy so that I wouldn't think you were like him?"

"I don't think that even deserves a response, do you dear?" Her mother gathered her belongings and opened the door. "I'll walk the rest of the way. And you mustn't worry about picking me up, *he* will do it. We shall see you for dinner. Drive safely now."

Guilt sucked joy out of her day. Her mother marched toward the nursing home, nodding and smiling at anyone who passed. Christine rested her head on the steering wheel and cursed. She heard the trunk of the BMW sports coupe in the adjacent parking space pop up; Christine raised her head and glanced in the rear view mirror. A large woman wrapped in a red cape with chubby forearms protruding through massive arm holes lifted bags of groceries into the trunk, gold jewelry bounced on an ample bosom as she bent from cart to car and back. A black knit hat cupped auburn curls tight around flushed cheeks. The woman maneuvered between her car and Christine's, grumbling loudly, "Stupid people don't even know how to park." Eyes bulged and perspiration glistened on her forehead and upper lip, red lipstick spilled beyond the lips natural outline. Once the woman reached the car door, she bent down, and glared at Christine. The shocked look on her nemesis' face told it all. Christine pulled her tongue back into her mouth. The woman opened the door wide so it banged against hers and squeezed into the driver's seat at which point Christine lost all self-control, rolled down the window and screamed, "Hey, there, why don't you go have yourself another cheeseburger. I hear Burger Blitz makes one just your size." Christine filled her cheeks with air and puffed at the woman, immediately felt ashamed and tried to apologize, but the woman backed out before she had the chance.

Remorse prickled the back of her neck, nagging at her to remember the promise made after leaving the hospital: she'd change, no more mean; she'd be more caring, a better person. Not today. She stared as shoppers scurried through the parking lot, pushing carts full of groceries. Groceries they'd take home to their families. Functional families where everyone protected each other because they cared. Normal, not dysfunctional like hers. She wondered if any of them realized how lucky they were.

A young mother dressed in frayed jeans and sneakers clutched a bag of groceries, two small boys held tightly to her pant leg. The woman reached an older blue Mercedes with a side door dent and rested the bag on the roof of the car. As she rummaged in a purse, the smallest boy inched away from her. The mother saw him and yelled at him to get in the car. He ran around the car screeching while she chased him. Other shoppers stared and shook their heads. No one attempted to help. The mother, who looked about Christine's age, was clearly embarrassed. When she caught him she shoved him into the backseat. The groceries were still on the roof as she edged out of the parking spot.

Christine jumped out and ran to the car, banged on the window and motioned upward toward the roof. The woman stopped. The bag had begun to slip when Christine rescued it and handed it back through the open passenger window.

"Thank you."

Close up the woman appeared older. Heavy lines sprang from the outer corners of her eyes and tiny wrinkles rose from a generous upper lip, her brown cropped hair was speckled with grey. She gave Christine a terse smile then brightened, "Christine? Oh, god, it is you! I haven't seen you in ages. I heard about the accident …uh, I'm …" The woman stuttered, stopped, searching to fill the vacuum.

"Lisa?" It couldn't be. They'd been best friends until they drifted apart in high school.

"Yes, yes, it's me." Lisa jumped out of the car and wrapped her arms around Christine. "You look wonderful, you really do." Christine searched Lisa's eyes for the lie, but saw none. "How are you? My goodness, we need to catch up. Hey, you want to grab some coffee? Oh, never mind, you're probably busy and the last thing you want to do is spend time with a crazy childhood friend and her two brats." She scoffed and waved a gloved hand dismissively into the air, her eyes pleading.

A short blast of a horn startled them. The driver of a pickup filled with three teenagers maneuvered around Lisa's car and made an obscene gesture.

Christine's inner voice whispered "don't go." She ignored it. "Sure. Where should we go?"

"Oh, wonderful! This will be great. Promise, I'll make the kids sit quietly so we can catch up."

Fun didn't exactly describe what Christine was feeling about visiting with a friend she hadn't seen in almost fifteen years; a friend she'd not so ceremoniously dumped when she'd been accepted to the cheerleading squad sophomore year; the year she'd instantly became popular.

Lisa had been loyal, Christine had not.

"Follow me and in case we get separated, here's my cell number." Lisa rummaged in her coat pocket and pulled out a tattered white business card along with some cookie crumbs: Lisa Moretti, REALTOR®, Carson and Marks Realty, Hyannis, MA. At the bottom her e-mail and cell number; in the upper right hand corner a smiling, younger and well-coifed Lisa stared at her. The photo must have been taken on a better day.

Christine followed Lisa out of town and onto the highway. They sped past the next exit and Lisa moved in and out of traffic like Jeff Gordon. Christine pressed on the gas pedal; the car sputtered then crawled to the lightning fast speed of fifty-two MPH before leveling off. She moved into the left lane passing two cars and slipped in behind Lisa. Through Lisa's darkened rear window Christine could see arms flailing, first from one side of the backseat, then the other. Lisa's silhouette twisted, arms swinging toward the empty space between the two boys, who immediately pulled their arms inward. What had she gotten herself into?

The next exit was to the center of Eastham; perhaps they were going to Café Bertoletti's. That would be acceptable. No, Lisa passed the city center exit and moved through traffic again. Oh, no, they weren't going to Lisa's house. She picked up her cell to cancel and it rang in her hand.

Her heart lurched. Anders?

"Hi, kitten." It was her father. "What's the matter can't give your old dad a call?" On the surface his tone was playful, underneath it was laced with accusation.

"Hi, Daddy. How's work?"

"Is that all you can say? How about, sorry I haven't called you?"

"Sorry I haven't called you, Daddy."

"That's a glib response. What's going on, baby? Have a fight with your ol' mom?"

How did he know? Of course, she'd call him. They share everything.

"She told you? What'd she do, walk into the nursing home and pick up the phone? You know it's really annoying that you would even take her side. She had no business trying to tell me what to do and not only that …"

"Hold on there, slow down. I don't care whether you two fight it out like cats and dogs." He paused then said, "Though she did have a point. You should really …"

"No, Daddy, I shouldn't really."

"Well, alright then. I can see this conversation will have to wait. I called to give you a knuckle nudge for not calling me this morning. I wanted you to stop by my office so I could show off my best girl."

"Your office? I thought you were consulting?"

"I started a business. I bought some stock with that money you gave us and it doubled, then I sold some and started an agency."

Interesting; he'd sold some and hadn't told her mother. "That money was for a new kitchen, not for you to waste on some stock scheme."

"You need to temper that tone. I'm not some degenerate ranch hand, I'm your father. Show some respect."

Had he ever shown her any? She moved the phone away from her ear, dropped it into her lap and started to disconnect. "Chrissy, are you there? Look, I don't want to fight ..."

She put the phone back to her ear and sighed. "I don't either, but you need to do that for Mom. That kitchen's ancient; she deserves a new one."

"Is she complaining again? She needs to listen better. I told her we'd do it in the spring. By then this business will have taken off and we can redo the whole damn house if she wants to. Now, how about lunch? I can introduce you to Mattie and Jeff, and I can tell you all about my new venture."

Again she toyed with the idea of hanging up. "Daddy? I can't hear you, the connection must be bad."

"Don't be ridiculous; I know you can hear me. C'mon, I miss my little girl."

Hanging up on him would be too easy and it would do no good, he'd just call back. She eased down the slippery slope of flippancy. "Oh, Daddy, you're fine. Call Mom, she'll keep you company."

His familiar barrel laugh cut through her unease; her experiment had worked. "You're just too much, kitten. You have a good day now and I'll see you at dinner."

"Okay, Daddy. Love you."

"Chrissy?"

Maybe she hadn't gotten away with anything after all.

"Yes?"

"We'll talk more about your future tonight."

"But, …" It was no use, he'd hung-up.

She disconnected, then realized Lisa was gone, too—no blue Mercedes in sight, traffic had thinned out and the highway had narrowed to two lanes. She fumbled with Lisa's business card, thumbed the number with the right hand while steering with the left.

"Where'd you go?" Lisa bellowed.

Boyish shrieks shot through the phone line causing Christine to pull the phone from her ear. "Where'd *you* go? I've been driving like crazy to keep up and after we passed the city center exit I lost you."

"Damn it, Jeremy, stop hitting your brother. Sorry. Where are you now?"

"The last mile marker was fifteen."

"Oh, geez, you're miles ahead of me. I turned off right after city center at the second roundabout. I was taking you to a little coffee place I know where there's a kids' play area."

Anxiety fluttered in her stomach and streaked scary scenarios across her afternoon swiping away her tranquil stroll down P'town's main street, replacing it with images of two young boys running rampant through close quarters of a tiny coffee shop.

"Let's make it another day. Is that okay, Lisa? I was going to P'town anyway and it looks like I'm a good seven miles from you." Lisa sighed. The phone connection crackled and as did Christine's resolve but she clenched her teeth, and said, "How about tomorrow? We could meet at the new Starbucks on North Ave.?" Screeching, then an audible wail, presumably from the backseat of Lisa's car, cut through the awkward silence.

"All right, what time? Jeremy, baby, we're going home, honey, stop crying for mommy. Christine, are you there? What time?"

Tomorrow loomed in front of her, a wide chasm waiting to be filled; a yawn of a day with unlimited possibilities. Tuesday was her mother's bridge day, another work day for her father, a basement stacked with boxes from her willfully forgotten past waited to be packed and moved to Montana. But she had time.

"How about ten?"

"Ten at Starbuck's then. See you."

Christine accelerated, rolled down the window and let a rush of frigid air slap at her face. She'd succeeded; the day was in her possession again.

ELEVEN

Clouds had moved in, billowing with the threat of an early snow. A blast of wind rocked the car. It sent leaves from red maple skipping across the parkway and the small scrub-like bushes along the roadside twisted. It scooped sand from the side of the road and sent it curling across the roadway. Excitement tugged; she loved the inclement and unpredictable New England weather.

The outskirts of P'town came up quickly, the terrain flattened except for stalks of brush that poked up through high drifts of sand. The distant rumble of the ocean interrupted Petula Clark's woeful serenade of *You Don't Have to Say You Love Me* which somehow seemed appropriate this morning. During the long ride, Christine's thoughts had drifted to Anders and how much she already missed him. Thoughts of him morphed into memories of Nick and their broken engagement. It saddened her and, instead of turning left into town, she turned right toward the seashore.

The Herring Cove parking lot, a blackened carpet adorned with swirls of sand, stretched out to the sea. Dunes, created when past winter storms had thrown temper tantrums, resembled mounds of caramel colored ice cream. She parked then stepped out into the unsettled weather, unwittingly opening the door to her past.

Toward the horizon the white sky disappeared into a mélange of intense purple, breathtaking against the vast bleakness of the sand and the black of the ocean. Just off shore the waves, capped in white, swelled, curled, then slammed onto the beach, spraying salt water onto her face, seeping into her scars. Its sting reminded her of the last time she'd been here. The day Nick had broken it off. She shut her eyes and heart, and willed the memory away. Still the waves crashed and each release of the sea's power brought forgotten emotions and unwelcome images.

"It's not you, honey, it's me," he'd said. His face bronzed from hours spent in tanning beds in preparation for their summer wedding and Hawaiian honeymoon. The wedding, initially postponed, then rescheduled for a year later, and ultimately canceled forever. Canceled here on this beach last spring with such finality that even now it seemed unbelievable. Not that she still loved Nick. Had she ever? But, she'd felt betrayed, humiliated. "It's not you ..." She knew it was the "you." It was her lost beauty, the thing that had drawn them together in the first place, a mutual attraction that had sustained them until the accident. A façade of love that began to erode the first time he'd seen her in the hospital. Eroding even further the first time she'd reached out to touch him and disintegrated entirely the first time she'd taken off her clothes. It had only taken him two months once she was discharged from the hospital to begin to pull away; it had taken a full year for him to release her permanently.

The wind pushed the sand toward her, wrapping each shoe. It scooped up grains and whipped them through her hair. She stared at the water; mesmerized, remembering. Unconsciously her wrist moved, then her hand. Unknowingly her fingers began sketching the landscape on an imaginary canvas. A forgotten moment years before when life was in sync. The brilliant sun, beating down on two lovers lying on a soft blanket of sand; her head in the crook of his arm, his hand resting lightly on her hip, both spent from an hour of lovemaking. A scene too familiar, too painful.

Christine dropped the hand to her side. "Who cares anyway," she whispered. She kicked the sand off her shoes, buttoned her coat, and knotted the scarf around her head. She walked toward the end of the spit, at first gingerly, afraid her leg would weaken, but by the time she reached the end, she was running, her weak leg feeling stronger with each stride. Seagulls swarmed above, squawking, landing in her path, hopping to one side as she swept by. Her breaths shortened. At the edge of the spit she slowed, finally stopping as a wave tumbled ashore, soaking her shoes. She sucked in the salty air, filled her lungs, then exhaled, extricating Nick from mind and body.

****

The main street of Provincetown looked the same. Storefronts crunched together, many hugging the narrow street, portraying a false intimacy and laissez-faire attitude. Devoid of tourists this time of year, the juxtaposition of the town's quaintness and quirkiness became more glaring and, as always, it intrigued her. She parked and walked, window shopping unless something drew her inside. She paused at a new café that had opened since her last visit; its pink, clapboard exterior butted up against the adult 'toy' store on the right. The aroma of baked bread enticed her and she moved into the small alcove at the entrance of the restaurant. A silhouette deep inside motioned for her to enter. The prospect of anonymity in the new restaurant appealed to her and she went inside. A small fire crackled from the old brick fireplace in the back left corner, heat warmed the honey colored pine floors. Even on this grey day, the white-washed room was bright; light streamed in the large windows along the west side of the building where a few locals stored their bikes and a cobbled walkway led to the beach. Inside, an eclectic mix of antique chairs surrounded each white melamine table. A small woman with long, thick grey hair twisted in dreadlocks stood behind a long counter. Heavily jeweled hands appeared from underneath her oversized paisley caftan and fidgeted with the salt and pepper shakers that dotted the counter.

"Welcome to Moon Café. You're our first customer of the day." She threw her head back in a throaty laugh that seemed too big for her narrow neck and said, "I guess you're our first customer since we closed up in September. We only reopened today after our renovation. I tried to get ready for the weekend, but Theresa couldn't get her act together on Saturday, could you, honey?" An acknowledgement in the form of a grunt moved down a narrow hall from the kitchen and landed in the dining area with a thud between them. "She's just in a bad mood because the stars aren't aligned and she knows this will not be a good day for her. She'll get over it and, please, don't you let it stop you from ordering her pumpkin squash soup. It's to die for."

The woman moved out from the counter, stopped for a breath, then swept her arm across the entire breadth of the room and said, "Sit wherever you like. Some chamomile tea or hot lemon water?"

Christine moved to a table for two next to the window; the woman followed her. Christine glanced at her watch, lunch time. "Do you have any coffee? Strong coffee?"

The woman, who was probably in her mid-to-late fifties, twisted a dreadlock, and said, "Cup of strong coffee. Can do. Anything else?" She flipped her hair back and handed Christine a menu. "Everything," she stooped over and caught Christine's gaze, "I mean everything, is incredible here. Theresa's the cook and she insists on cooking everything with fresh ingredients, no preservatives and nothing artificial. We've been working hard to make sure this place is a destination for those," she wrinkled her nose and rolled her eyes, "with discerning palettes." She straightened, reached for Christine's hand and said, "I'm one of the owners, Moonbeam, but you can call me Moonie, if you like."

"Hi, Moonie. I'm Christine." Christine pulled off her gloves, quickly maneuvered her hand underneath Moonie's, then turned it, palm up, a technique she'd perfected since the accident. People rarely saw the scars, and that way Christine avoided answering a lot of unwanted questions.

"You live around here, Christine?" Moonie pulled a chair from the neighboring table and started to sit when two men entered the restaurant. "Oops, looks like more customers. I'll talk with you later. Remember what I said about the pumpkin squash soup now and, oh, Theresa just made rosemary garlic bread, I'll get you some as soon as I seat them."

Christine slipped out of her coat while perusing the menu. A few items intrigued her: sun-dried tomato ravioli with a white truffle reduction sauce, eggplant baked in fire roasted tomato and garlic sauce, salads, sandwiches, homemade soups. The menu continued onto the next page with desserts and a moderately priced wine list. Christine's mouth puckered and her stomach rumbled. Montana had put a crimp in her previously meatless diet and it felt good to have a lot of wonderful vegetarian choices.

She settled on Boston Lettuce Wedges and Stilton, with a Zinfandel and Shallot dressing. She could almost hear her mother whispering approval: "Good girl; lettuce means lean, dear." Old habits die hard.

Moonie returned after seating the two men at a table near Christine. "Here's your bread. The coffee will just take a minute. Have you decided on what you'd like?" She frowned when Christine gave her order. "No soup? Never mind, you have to at least taste it. I'll bring you a small cup. No charge. Now don't argue." Moonie waltzed away, caftan swaying, jewelry jingling.

"Look, John, I don't want to get into this now. But … the Morrison painting has to go next to the Hayward sculpture. The light in the main room is perfect to show off the depth of …"

"Well, fine then." The man named John, turned away from his counterpart, crossed his legs, right over left and frantically pumped his right one. He picked up leather gloves from the table, crushing them between his hands.

"Now stop; you're getting all worked up." The other man pulled his leather jacket tight, reached across with an apology and when John turned away, the other said, "You are acting like a child." He turned from the table and summoned Moonie, who had gone back to the kitchen and now appeared smiling, a small cup of soup in hand.

She scurried past the men, plopped the soup in front of Christine, offered her ground pepper and turned back to her other patrons. "Yes, Bill what can I do for you boys?"

"You're familiar with April Morrison's work. Don't you think it needs to be next to the Hayward sculpture?"

"Not getting into this again. I told you last time that you'd have to fill that gallery without my input. I don't do well with Libras and I've got two of you sitting right here. If that's not enough you had to go and stick that other awful painting in the window this summer. You do know heterosexuals frequent this town, too?"

"See, see I told you." John swung his legs back under the table, pointing aggressively at Bill with one finger and tugged at the waistband of his jeans with the other hand. "See, you never listen to me. For once I agree with Moonie here. Drape that beautiful red kimono we bought in Japan across the ..."

Christine tuned them out. Might as well try this orange concoction. She tore a piece of rosemary bread and dipped it in the soup. The pumpkin was a soft melody behind the other flavors of garlic, cumin and a hint of butter. Amazing.

"You like it, don't you?" Moonie stood over her, smug.

"I hate to say it, but it is, well, to die for." Christine lowered her voice and said, "What's with those two?"

"Oh," Moonie raised her voice loud enough to be heard in Chatham. "They're just two queens who feel the need to mess up my day. They've been playing with my aura for months, interrupting Theresa and me while we were trying to redo the floors and get the place painted. I tried everything: crystals, chants, meditation, you name it, nothing works." Moonie locked eyes with Christine, but tilted her head toward the couple. "Are they listening?"

Christine looked over; they were staring at her. "You might say that." She lifted her spoon and took a sip of the soup, ignoring them and hoping they'd ignore her.

"Who *are* you?" Bill was still staring at her. A bell sounded from deep in the back of the restaurant.

"Looks like your order's up. I'll go get it." Moonie slipped down the hall.

"Well," Bill said. "Who are you?"

Christine stood and walked over to him. "Hi, I'm Christine McMurray; I live in, well, um, I grew up in Gale Harbor and will be here for a few more days."

Bill asked, "You know art?"

John busied himself with the menu, flipping the pages and ignoring her.

Christine said, "I paint and sketch as a hobby, but I'm not very good. Why?"

"You're a part-time artist, huh?" Bill's eyes roamed up and down, taking in her worn Coach boots, outdated Prada bag and zoned in on her Cartier watch. "Hmm, looks like you have some taste. John here thinks he's an art expert. We own P'town Gallery. I thought maybe if you had any art sense you'd come by and prove how wrong he is. What do you say?"

She loved galleries and in the end her curiosity got the better of her. "Sure, I'll come by. I'd like to see what you're exhibiting anyway. I noticed your gallery on the way down. Very interesting painting in the window, by the way." Okay, she'd said enough. "I'll finish my lunch, give the two of you time to do the same, then I'll come down. Oh, do you know if Books of Merit is open yet? I see most of the shops are closed for the season."

This time John answered, "Yes, they're open, but he closes at two."

Moonie arrived with her salad. "If you'll excuse me then," Christine said and backed up toward her table.

****

"Well, my goodness, if it isn't Christine McMurray. Where have you been?" Harry Merit, the owner of Books of Merit, grabbed her and squeezed. "My goodness, you are thin, girl. Where'd my chubby little eight-year-old helper go?"

"Oh, Harry, she's gone, long gone. Instead, you got me."

"Ha, ha, funny." He released her and stepped back. "You're looking mighty good though. Those scars are healing nicely. Heck, I can barely see the one on your face. How are the ones inside doing?" His blue eyes narrowed beneath his wire glasses, his thin lips pursed. "Hmm, not healing so well there, huh?"

"Getting there, Harry. I'm getting there." She noticed his hair had thinned since last summer, his beard was scruffier, and his osteoporosis seemed more pronounced. When he stood, a small hump was visible underneath his heavy cardigan yet he still towered above her.

"What's this nonsense I hear about you moving to Montana?" He draped his arm around her and led her to the back of the store where a desk covered with papers resided in a small alcove; books were piled on the floor around a worn red couch. Rex, Harry's golden retriever, rose from under the desk, pushed his cold nose into her hand and nuzzled a greeting. Harry pointed to the couch and said, "Have a seat. Would you like a cup of tea?"

"I can't stay long; I've got to get back to pack up a few things." Her stomach fluttered. "I bought some land in Montana with part of the settlement money and it's being excavated and prepped as we speak. The house will be done by spring if the weather cooperates."

"Is this all about that cowboy that sat by your bed for weeks?" He didn't wait for an answer. "You know Nick's around. He pops in here every once in a while when he takes a break from that nightclub of his in Boston. I don't think he's got a gal friend."

"Harry." She looked at him as sternly as she could muster. "He dumped me because I have scars."

Not one to hide behind a curtain of tact, Harry said, "There was a day when you'd have done the same if it had been him."

Had she been that person? Of course she had. "But I'm not that person anymore." She wasn't, she knew she wasn't.

Harry patted her hand. "I can see that."

"To answer your question, no, it isn't because of the cowboy. Which, by the way, he isn't. He's a photographer and a really nice guy. But, we're just friends."

Rex slipped onto the couch between them, flopping in a furrow that had been molded over the years to fit his old body. Harry stroked the dog's head, rubbed his ears and said, "You know your dad's been coming around too. I shouldn't be telling you this, but he's been selling off your old sketches to whoever will buy them. Some are hanging in the chocolate shop down the road and Le Poisson Café has a few. Everyone knows about the accident and we've all heard about that reporter who's interested in doing your story. You've become a bit of a celebrity here. I'm just telling you about the sketches so you won't be surprised if you bump into one."

The ground opened and she tumbled into the black hole of betrayal. Harry's voice reverberated, his image blurred. "You're a sweet old boy, aren't you, buddy?" Who was he talking about?

Her father? She tried to focus, tried to get off the couch. Her leg buckled, she fell back. The dog. Rex. He was talking to the dog. "Sure you are; you're my best friend, aren't you?"

She shut her eyes, blinked, tried again to focus. Harry's head was next to Rex. Was he really rubbing noses with the damn dog? Didn't he see what he had just done to her? But no, her father had done it; oh, god, how could he?

Head down, Harry sighed, scratched his beard and, without looking at her, continued, "I never told you this either, but he gave me that sketch of the two gay men you did when you were in high school. He brought it around years back and told me he couldn't stand it in his house. Said, I should sell it, I think his words were, 'to one of them.' I framed it and kept it over my desk until a couple weeks ago. It's pretty damn good, you know. You should have been doing that instead of the modeling." He glanced at her, his eyes questioning. "Oh, I see I've upset you."

She tried to talk, tried to get the words to form. Tears welled and she turned away from him. Heat flashed through her body with a rush so violent that she lashed out. "Damn it, Harry, what the hell were you thinking?" She leaned back, closed her eyes and forced herself to breathe deeply which did little to diminish her anger. Her hands itched and her neck tightened, and it took all her restraint not to lash out at Harry again.

"I'm mad at him, not you. I'm sorry. Damn, him; damn him; damn him. Why does he do things like that?" But she knew why: the damn money. It's always about the money. She pushed herself forward on the couch, laid her face in her hands, then turned to Harry, her voice raspy, "I need to know what happened to it."

"To what?"

"My sketch."

"John and Bill, new owners of P'town Gallery, bought it. They're nice guys. They've been helping some of the locals with winterizing and renovations and they've given money to the Fine Arts Work Center. Bill saw it here one day and seemed quite taken by it. I sold it to him for three hundred dollars. I called your dad first; he didn't want any part of it. You know how he is about gay people." His eyes narrowed again. "Hope that's okay, dear. I can give you the money; I still have it."

Her leg ached, but she pushed back hard against the couch and grabbed the desk to steady herself. John and Bill, the guys she just met had her sketch.

"Hold on now." Harry jumped up. "Let me help you."

"I need to go." She swayed, used the bookshelves that lined the walls for support.

He cupped her elbow. "Christine, please, please let me help you."

He could help her walk, but couldn't help her heart. No one could.

"Please, Harry, let me go. I need to go on my own."

"Oh, honey ..."

She buttoned her coat, as much to keep the pain in as to keep the weather out. She squeezed his arms and, while he was still saying good-bye, headed in the direction of P'town Gallery.

TWELVE

Christine rushed past Cape Cod Adventures, Made For Coffee, and the Episcopal Church, wanting to run, but felt little strength in her leg or her psyche. In the two short blocks to P'Town Gallery her emotions ran the gamut. She tried to reason away the anger, rationalize his actions, stand up to him, chastise him and at one point beat him to a pulp. Letting go of the pain wasn't an option, it was the only thing that kept her motivated; motivated to tell him once and for all what she thought of him. Then she cried: for his insensitivity, for his greed, and finally for the loss of his love. Or, was it hers for him? By the time she opened the door to the gallery she was conflicted.

"Hello there, may I …? Oh, it's you, our little gal from the café." John rushed up to her. "My dear, you are soaked. Don't you have an umbrella? Tsk, tsk, didn't your mother teach you anything?"

Of course her mother hadn't.

John pulled her coat from her shoulders and shook it. "Now, come on to the back, we'll get you some hot tea."

What the heck was with everyone and tea? Did they really think it was the cure for everything? "No tea, John, but thanks."

Bill appeared from the rear of the gallery. "Well, what do you think of the sculpture next to the painting?"

She'd forgotten all about the original reason she was there. "Can I talk to you about something else first?"

John and Bill sighed at the same time. John's shoulders slumped and he moved away from her, mumbling.

Bill came toward her. "What is it?"

"Uh, Harry said you bought a sketch from him a couple weeks ago. Can I see it?"

"Who's Harry?" John muttered with his back to her.

"Books of Merit," she said. Hands sweaty, body clammy, she maneuvered past a tall, wide marble stand displaying what appeared to be a two foot piece of white quartz in the shape of a whale.

"Oh, that Harry," John said. "Bill, what did we do with that thing anyway?"

"It's in the office above my desk. Why, Miss McMurray? If you are interested in buying it, it's not for sale."

John sighed, a long exaggerated exhalation of air, then paced, straightening each piece of art along the showroom floor. He stopped and turned toward them, "Of course not. Bill thinks it's a sketch of him with his first lover. Can you believe it?"

Bill said, "It is me, John, and just because you don't think it is doesn't…"

"It's the memory, isn't it? You can't let him go. He dumped you for Pete sake; the guy was a prig." John flopped into a leather cushioned armchair, with antler-like arms and legs. "You like him better than me, don't you?"

This time it was Bill who sighed. "No, no. I've told you I don't, now stop pouting and let's help Ms. McMurray with her request." Bill turned to her. "I'm curious, why are you interested in it?"

"I think I may have sketched it when I was in school about fifteen years ago."

"Really? It's quite good," Bill said. "Follow me and you can see for yourself."

"I'll wait here," John whimpered, "I can't stand to see how you look at it."

Christine followed Bill to the back of the gallery, past glass etageres filled with glass figures and jewelry. They passed a display case filled with yarn figures shaped into animals and moved down the short hall past what Christine presumed was John's office: a tiny alcove, with a large window that looked out onto the gallery. She caught a glimpse of crimson walls covered in textile art.

Bill stopped and said, "Here we are." He opened his office door and led her inside. A black art deco desk and matching chair were showcased against soft taupe walls; two overstuffed armchairs in red damask sat in front of the desk. "Turn around, the sketch is behind you on the wall," he said.

And, there it was. Fifteen years came rushing back: the trip to P'town, Donna, Nick, the storm, the photo and the beauty she'd found in it that she couldn't explain. "It is you, isn't it?" She turned to Bill. "There in the eyes; there's no denying it."

He was quiet for a moment then sat behind his desk. "I knew it the minute I saw it. You did a great job; I couldn't take my eyes off it and it has nothing to do with Dirk either. You captured real emotion and love in both our eyes. People don't see that when they see two men showing affection." He picked up a letter opener and flipped it side to side. He leaned forward and stared at her. "Then it's your signature on the sketch? C. Mac, huh? I thought your name was McMurray," he said as his eyes widened. "Oh, I get it—Mac, McMurray. Well, I suppose you want it back now."

No, she didn't. Now it just reminded her of a past she didn't want to remember and a father who'd let her down. "No, you keep it."

Her heart slowed, breathing returned to normal. Bill's earlier compliment calmed her; she'd never had any appreciation for her art. Remembering the intensity she'd felt when she sketched it returned, as well as a renewed excitement for her art. It had been a too long.

Pen and brush had slipped from her grip initially after the accident. The fingers on her left hand, the hand she used to sketch Bill and his lover, were stiff, unyielding. Continuing to try became too discouraging, so she'd stopped. Until one day at the ranch when a filly had given birth; the colt emerged glistening. Tentative and unsteady, unsure that his legs would hold him upright, the colt rose and fell, the filly encouraging the colt until its legs held, steady and strong. It was the first animal birth she'd ever witnessed and somehow the colt's determination to stand had touched her; she'd left the barn tearful. Later that evening Anders came into her room and handed her a pen and sketch pad. He held it out to her and said, "Do something with this." And, she did—she sketched the colt. Her hand, though still a bit stiff, drew the scene perfectly, or that is what Anders said. She'd given it to him as a thank you.

John appeared in the doorway and fiddled with the door knob. "Do you still sketch?"

"Once in a while, and I do watercolor but haven't done it much lately."

John's gaze glided over her like a disapproving parent, "If you *happen* to pick up a paintbrush again—we don't handle sketches—let me know. Watercolors, now that interests me. You are good, even though I hate that one." He raised his arm and, without looking at it, pointed at her sketch. "If you do finish one, bring it by."

Behind her she caught Bill's reaction in the reflection of the glass on the door; he waved frantically, obviously not agreeing with his partner.

"Whaaat? She's good," John said to Bill, then snickered and turned to her. "He hates when I bring in new talent. He's such an old fuddy."

She ignored him. "I have some watercolors at my house in Boston and a few I did in Montana. The landscape there is breathtaking and the light, well, you can imagine."

"No, I can't actually, I've never been there," Bill said. "And, really, I have no desire to go." He rose from his chair, walked toward the door, leaving her no option but to do the same. It was her dismissal; their interest in her apparently gone.

When she walked out of the gallery she discovered the rain had turned to snow. Large flakes matted her hair; dampness seeped into her scalp and ran onto her forehead. By the time she reached her car, it was encased in white. She dusted off the door handle with her coast sleeve and tried to remove the snow from the driver side window with her gloveless hands. Her palms had little feeling, but the icy cold sent shooting pinprick-like pain into her fingers.

A mix of slush and icy rain clung to her boots as she sidestepped gingerly around the car to clean off the rear window.

She fell to one knee; pain shot up her thigh and into the hip. What a mess she was. Ice had formed under the snow; it took several attempts before she could stand. In frustration, she swept the arm of her coat across the windshield. Snow fell into the open sleeve and dropped unobstructed through the flimsy sleeve of the blouse soaking through to her underarm. She cursed herself for not using the scraper in the backseat.

The car started immediately. She eased out of the tight parking space, inching along as her mind filled with the earlier emotions. Though her anger with her father had been temporarily shelved at the gallery, it resurfaced. By the time she reached Hyannis she'd already had several imaginary arguments with him, all of them ending with her father's unrealistic, heartfelt apology. Just as she took the exit to Gale Harbor, the phone rang. Of course, they were calling, she was late.

"Hello."

"In one day you forget all about me?"

Anders. For the second time today the air in her lungs seemed to disappear and her hands immediately grew clammy. "Oh, hi, it's you."

"Oh, 'it's you.' What kind of greeting is that?" His laugh, deep and husky, shot through the phone like electricity.

"Sorry, I thought you were my parents. I'm late for dinner and it's about this time they'd be sending out the cavalry. I've been in P'town all day. How are things in Montana?"

"Good."

"The weather's lousy here, how is it there?"

"Things are fine in my neck of the woods?" He laughed again. "Christine, stop. I don't want to talk about the weather or Montana. I want to know how you are doing."

How was she doing? "I'm good," she lied. "I ran into an old friend today, after I dropped my mom at the nursing home."

"Nick?"

"No, no, not Nick. Lisa something. Can't remember her old name. I went to middle school with her, then we totally lost track of each other in high school. She's married and has two obnoxious little boys, but I promised I'd have coffee with her tomorrow."

"Provincetown today, Lisa tomorrow. When are you going to start packing and get back here?"

"I have plenty of time. I don't go to Boston until the weekend and I don't have very much stuff at my folks."

"How are they? Glad to have you back, I'm sure."

She hesitated. "Anders, can I call you later? I'm almost home and, well, something happened when I was in P'town that I have to talk to my dad about."

"Sure, but why don't you make it Wednesday? I'm meeting Jake's doctor at the hospital tonight then I have to leave pretty early tomorrow morning to pick up Peta. We've decided she should stay at the ranch."

Christine pulled to the side of the road, rested her head on the steering wheel. "I'm being silly, but would you call me tonight after you get back from the hospital? I really need to talk to you."

"Honey, what's wrong? I can tell you're upset."

"Nothing major. I'm just missing everyone." That was the best explanation for now. "I better go. Say hi to Lotte." She started to close her phone. "Oh, wait. Anders?"

"I'm here."

"I forgot to ask about Jake. Is he doing okay?"

"About the same, which is good. I'll know more tonight. But, Christine ..."

"Yes?"

"You need to take care of yourself now so that you can get on with your life here."

"I know; I will. It's just been a really ... well ... confusing day."

"I'll call you when I get back unless it's really late." There was a pause and she thought he'd hung up. This time his voiced cracked, "I care about you."

"I care about you, too." It was their standard sign off; safer than "I love you" and certainly at this point in their relationship, it was truer. At least for her. She closed the phone and drove home with as much trepidation as she had ever felt.

"There you are, dear. We've been worried." Her mother greeted her at the door, kissing both cheeks and squeezing her arms. "Where did you go off to?"

"I went to P'town. I told you when I dropped you off, and Dad knew."

"Boyd, why didn't you tell me you spoke to Christine?"

His voice echoed from the basement. "I told you. My god, you forget everything." His voice grew louder. "Maybe we should have you checked for Alzheimer's."

Her mother frowned. "That's right you did tell me, I forgot." She stepped back and patted Christine's arm. "My, my you look a fright. Go now and get cleaned up for dinner. I made your favorite: pork chops with potato pancakes and applesauce."

"There's my girl." Her father emerged from the basement, removed his glasses, wiped his face with a handkerchief, and walked toward her. "Damn cobwebs are everywhere down there." He pointed at her mother. "You need to get down there and clean it up." He turned to Christine. "No one's been down there since you left. It's full of dust. Let me look at you." He rested his chin on his hand, tilted his head and pretended to scrutinize her. "You're looking pretty good there. No cowgirl rolls, at least that I can see. You must have kept up on the exercise? Aye, kitten?"

"Nice one, Daddy. I'm not even home two minutes and we're already talking about weight. Aren't mothers the ones who are supposed to be obsessive about beauty issues?" She pushed by him, mumbled, "I'm going to change."

"Kitten, I was just …"

She shut the door and, not bothering to turn on the light, sank into the bed. She rolled to her side, drew both knees to her chest and pulled the bedspread over her. Asshole, such an asshole. She wanted to stay curled up, wanted to be in Montana with Anders, wanted to talk to him. She dug in her purse for the phone then stopped. She couldn't, he was too busy. Maybe everyone would be better off without her. Damn it. No more victim. She threw off the bedspread and stormed back into the living room. Her father was sitting in his recliner, paper in hand. He peered over his glasses. "You didn't change."

"That's it? That's all you can say. Not 'I'm sorry, Christine, for betraying your trust. For letting my greed take over my loyalty to you.' Not that. No, not that." Her heart pounded, her fists coiled ready to hit something, anything.

"What in the hell are you talking about?" He threw the paper aside. When she didn't answer, he demanded, "Talk to me, damn it."

She took a breath. "You. I'm talking about your obsessive need for money. You're out-of-control desire to make me into something I'm not. I'm sick of you."

He rose and stood inches from her face. "Who do you think you are talking to?"

"Do you want to know who I'm talking to? Do you really want to, or do you want to keep pretending like you're the best father on earth? Well, do you?" Air burst from her lungs and she couldn't catch her breath. The lights in the room seemed to flash on and off; her resolve weakened. She blinked, took a step back from him. "How could you?" Her voice broke, but she went on, "You gave him my sketch, then you sold, you SOLD my other sketches to anyone who would buy them."

He backed into his chair, caught himself, then sat. "What are you talking about?"

"I saw Harry today. He told me everything. Why, Dad, why? Did you need the money that badly?"

"I didn't sell anything to Harry, I gave him that damn thing. I hated seeing it every time I walked into your room. And you know what? You were gone. You'd left and got that modeling job in Boston. Not a thank you, hardly a good-bye. Just left us with a stack of bills from modeling courses and college, and then you ran off with Nick and Donna. Did we get any money from you after that? Hell no, we hardly heard from you. No, not until your little accident did we see one cent from you to repay us for all we sacrificed."

"Sacrificed? You stopped paying for college so I'd have to model to earn money. Modeling was your f'ing dream, not mine. I was ready to make a career out of my art, but, no, you couldn't support that. Pretending you don't know what I'm talking about doesn't make you less responsible. You didn't support me, remember? Cutting me off; pulling the plug on MY dream, that's your style. 'Sorry, Christine, we don't see a future in art design, you'll have to make it on your own now.' But look at you now. Now my art seems to be paying off for you, doesn't it? And, my 'little accident' seems to be working for you, too, doesn't it?"

"You bet it does." He shot out of the chair again, was in her face, pointing and spitting. "I'll reap whatever I can after you wasted five years at college, to say nothing of the years you squandered running around with your little sketch pad."

"Don't you point your finger at me …" She was screaming now.

"You let me finish. Then what do you do? Run off to Boston with your nose so far up Donna's skirts that you couldn't see opportunity if it hit you in the head. Boston? New York was where you could have made it big. When I think of all those years your mother and I wasted hauling your ass to classes, running around taking you from one beauty pageant to another. The gas, the hotels, the airfare—all for you. Yes, you bet I'm going to pull in as much extra dough as I can from those pathetic sketches. Spoiled little ungrateful brat is what you are."

He looked toward the kitchen where her mother stood, tears running down her cheeks. He turned back to Christine. "And you know the irony of it all? They loved 'em. Every store I went to, loved your sketches. I had store owners fighting over them. Because of your notoriety, Christine? No, because they said you were good; they said you had talent. So yes, I got a few measly dollars for those sketches that were rotting in your room for the last fifteen god damn years." One hand dropped to his side, he pulled off his glasses with the other, pinched the top of his nose and walked away from her.

Somehow they made it through dinner; her mother making small talk, Christine and her father not saying much. Out-of-sorts. That was the best way to describe how Christine felt after the fight with her father. Anger mixed with guilt, brought on by her father's dejected attitude the remainder of the night. Confused, Christine went into the basement to begin packing up the rest of her belongings and wait for Anders to call. He didn't. When she went back upstairs at midnight, the house was dark and both of her parents were asleep. She felt her way down the hall in the darkness, finding some solace in not being able to see where she was going.

****

Light seeped through relaxed lids. Christine squeezed her eyes tighter, hoping to keep the day at bay by ignoring its intrusion into the morning after a fitful night. Her father's anger had echoed through a dream: she was on a beach running away from him, but never getting very far. Incessant twitching and jerking of her body woke her so frequently that each time it happened she felt her throat closing and heart pounding against her ribs.

Exhausted, but determined to make this a better day, she opened her eyes and kicked off the covers. Cold air whooshed in, settled, wrapping around her like a lifeless a body. Though sunlight poured into the room through the flimsy curtains, it had done nothing to warm it. She rolled to the side of the bed, sat up and pushed the curtain aside. The blinding brightness of the sun bouncing off the snow covered ground made her squint. When her eyes adjusted she almost broke into song; everything looked beautiful and pristine. A fleeting moment of giddiness propelled her out of bed. The clock on the nightstand read 8:14 a.m. Reality. She'd have to deal with parents. She listened. Nothing; perhaps he'd left for work. She threw on clothes and grabbed boots from the suitcase.

Christine tiptoed down the hall and quickly surmised her father had gone. Her mother had left a note on the kitchen table:

"Lucille picked me up and she'll bring me home. I'll be at bridge club and a luncheon. Be home around five. Have a nice day, dear."

Saved. She toyed with the idea of calling Anders, but remembered he was on his way to see Peta. Instead she grabbed a coat, opened the door and headed out into the hushed silence.

The street was an unspoiled winter scene straight from every childhood fantasy and holiday song. Snow glistened on branches, tugging them toward the earth; they bowed and swayed when a slight breeze rushed in from the sea. She eased down each icy step, conscious of the ache in her leg, but determined to work through it. The cold air filled her lungs and nipped at her ungloved hands. Except for a few tire tracks, the road was an unblemished blanket of white. Snow crunched underfoot as she walked gingerly toward the end of the road and the lighthouse. A gentle slap of water against the icy shore played a familiar song, one that filled her with joy. This winter scene, this spot, had been one of her favorites as a child. She spent hours sketching the houses, the lighthouse and, her favorite, the sea. Her mother would bundle her in a down snowsuit, hand her a woolen scarf and mittens so hands would stay warm between pen strokes. A thermos of hot chocolate kept her from running back home when she got cold. She hadn't thought of those sketches in years; she wondered if her father had sold them as well.

"Out for a stroll?" Leon Nichols stood on his porch, hands stuffed deep in jean pockets, a cigarette dangled from his mouth. "Lizzie sent me out here to have my smoke. Pretty darn cold if you ask me."

"Hi, Mr. Nichols. How are you doing?" She stopped.

"Oh, been better, not been worse though." He laughed, sucked on his cigarette and blew smoke into the air. "How you doing Christine? Thought you were someplace out west?" He leaned on the porch railing of his blue and white saltbox.

"I'm home for a bit; just long enough to pack up. You take care now." She began to turn away.

"Your dad and I have coffee every Saturday now down at the Legion Hall. He really missed you, you know. He's always saying how proud he is of your recovery. Just thought you'd like to know." He flicked his cigarette into the snow, saluted her and said, "Have a nice day."

She stumbled, optimism disappeared. Her nostalgia replaced by disbelief. Proud of her recovery? She doubted it.

Clouds slipped in from the east and erased the sun, turning the day an ugly grey. The snow no longer held magic; reluctantly she retraced steps toward her parents' house. Once inside she took off her boots and put on slippers. Cold and exhausted, she shuffled aimlessly from kitchen to bedroom and back to the kitchen. The thought of the bed, warm and safe, drove her back down the hall, but as she lay down her cell rang.

"You're still coming today, right?" Lisa's voice boomed.

Christine had forgotten. "Oh, um, ..."

"Good, but I have a favor to ask. My youngest has the sniffles and I need to keep him home, can you come here?"

No, she couldn't. She knew that in an instant. "I'm really sorry, Lisa, but I've changed my plans and I'll be heading to Boston today. Can I have a rain check?" Not waiting for an answer, "I'll be back for Thanksgiving. How about we plan on getting together then?"

"Tony, give that back to your brother." Wailing became the focus of the conversation. "Sorry, 'bout that. Damn it, I said give it to him. Jeremy, stop that crying." Whimpering, then silence. "Look, that's fine. Call me when you get back."

She should have felt guilty, but the relief was overwhelming. It was clear now: enough of her father, enough of the past, it was time to move on.

She dialed her mother's cell phone. "Mom, it's Christine."

"Hello dear. Everything okay?"

"Where are the rest of my sketches? You know, the ones I did as a kid. Or did Dad sell them, too?"

"Now, dear, I don't want to get into an argument."

"Mom, listen please. I just want to know where they are."

"Can it wait until I'm home? I can help you find them."

"No need. I want to do it myself. Any ideas?"

"If they aren't in the basement they might be under the bed in the guest room. I put a lot of old stuff under there. Why don't we look together when I get there?"

It was unavoidable; she may as well get it over with. "I'm leaving today to go to Boston and by the time you get here, I'll probably be gone." No stomach flutters, no shortness of breath; only calm resolve.

She waited for the obvious response, but was surprised when her mother said, "Well, dear, you have a safe trip and we'll see you on Thanksgiving. You're still coming, aren't you?"

"Yes, yes, sure, I'll be here. I'll call you when I get to Boston and we can talk more about it." She had over a month to think of an excuse. The thought of a family holiday gathering was almost unbearable.

"Christine, are you going to call your father or should I tell him you're leaving?"

"I'm not talking to him. You tell him."

"Look, dear, I can't really talk but … yes, Dottie I'll be right there. Chrissy?"

"Go back and play bridge, Mom. I'll deal with Dad later."

"He's not a bad man, you know. He thought you wouldn't mind if he sold them."

"You knew?"

Her mother's voice came back barely audible. "We needed the money. The mortgage was due and …"

"You know, Mom, I don't want to hear anymore. I'll see you." It felt like a fire had been ignited in her chest. So her mother knew. She slammed the phone down.

Christine flew around the house, determined to get out before either of them returned. She rummaged through an entire corner of the unfinished portion of the basement where the previous day she'd found old clothes and keepsakes. Eventually she found the sketches lying flat in an old Filene's gift box in an unlocked cabinet in the driest corner of the basement; the same cabinet where her father kept his coin collection and her mother's

Hummel figurines. She grabbed a rag from the floor and moved it across the top of the box, dust motes rose, floating into the light like old memories pulling away from a dark past. Particles danced through the air, catching the beam of light that poured through the tiny rectangular shaped basement window. She removed the lid and found the sketches still intact, each wrapped in parchment paper. She slipped her hand down the inside of the box, touching the edge of each sketch and counting until she reached the bottom: eighteen, they were all there. Christine lifted the top drawing and gingerly unwrapped it. Heavy, untrained pen strokes sketched a crude picture of the lighthouse at the end of the road. Seagulls dove into a solid green sea, without definition or depth; a product of adolescence, not art. This sketch though had the benefit of watercolors stroked within each object's borders. Most of her sketches were just that, sketches created with black ink outlining the things around her, yet occasionally she would reach for color, depending on her mood.

It was about age five when she first became aware that images and objects could be recreated on paper. Rows of markers, colored pencils, watercolors and acrylics had sat neatly in a box under her bed away from her father's prying eyes and her sister's jealous curiosity. Meredith had always been the practical one with her nose pushed into books, ignoring Christine whenever she could.

The squeal of metal on metal outside the basement window startled her, then footsteps on the porch, a snap of more metal. She grabbed a footstool from next to the washer and peered outside just in time to see the mail truck pull away. Time had gotten away from her; she covered the box, crept upstairs and set it by the front door.

The remainder of the day Christine scoured the house for her possessions so that nothing would be left behind in case she didn't return for Thanksgiving. After lunch, she stripped the bed and changed the sheets, cleaned the kitchen and packed. It was nearly five when she finished loading the car. She took one last look at the house where she grew up, and pulled away. Not another confrontation, no lengthy discussion to resolve things, it was too late now. She'd worry about it at Thanksgiving, unless she decided to stay in Boston. Boston. Another confrontation.

As she approached the roundabout that would take her back to the highway, she dug in her purse for her phone and dialed Anders.

"Say, I'm at the hospital saying good-by to Jake, can I call you right back?"

"Never mind, I'll just talk to you sometime when you're not busy." She navigated the roundabout and moved onto traffic.

"Aw, c'mon, don't get all pouty on me. They're taking Jake up for more tests. If I can't call you back, can you at least hang on a minute?" This time he sounded irritated and her annoyance receded.

"No wait, let me talk to him." She hadn't talked to Jake since his heart attack.

She pressed the phone into her ear listening for the response. The phone muffled and she heard Anders say, "It's Christine, she wants to talk to you."

Then another voice more agitated and unmistakably Lotte's said, "Gimme, the damn phone I'll talk to her."

Then Jake. "Stop bein' bossy, woman. Hand that thing over to me."

Christine felt her spirits lift; Jake always made her feel better. "Hi there, little gal, how's ol' Boston doing?"

"Oh, Jake, it's good to hear your voice. I'm not in Boston yet, but on my way. I had a horrible fight with my dad and I'm just not sure what I'm going to do. I had all this stuff I had to pack up, now I've got to …"

A female voice of authority cut through their conversation, "Mr. Frazier, you're going to have to put down that phone, radiology isn't going to wait for us if we're late."

Shit, she'd gone on about herself and hadn't even asked how he was doing. "Jake, wait, how are you?"

"Got some minor thingy tomorrow. I think they call it a procedure, but it's all good. Gotta go, these nurses are regular drill sergeants. Take care there and we'll be seein' you soon."

A shuffling of the phone then Anders said, "Now I can talk, he's on his way. We have to be back around six in the morning, his 'thingy' is scheduled for nine. Been crazy the last couple days. How are you doing?"

She was worried now. "But he's going to be alright, isn't he?"

"That's what they say. Doctors and hospitals aren't my thing; hate them actually. Anyway, they say it's relatively routine."

Anders sounded worried. She wished she could wrap her arms around him, feel his thick chest against hers, bury her head in his neck, smell the soft musk of his breath on her cheek. Her body throbbed, her voice caught, "He'll be …" she coughed, blinked hard and continued, "good as new before you know it. He's tough."

"Oh, of course he will. We're not worried, are we, Lotte?" All he got for his optimism was a grunt from Lotte. "Say, honey, I know you need to talk and I really want to talk to you, too, but I'm going on the elevator and I'll lose you. Then we'll be driving. Can I call you in about thirty-minutes? I'll be home by then."

Brushed off again; disappointment surrounded her, holding her captive. She shoved it aside and resignation became an easy ally, "Sure. Just call the cell, I'll be driving."

"Where are you going? I thought you were at your folks."

"It's a long story. I'll talk to you in a bit." She hung up on him while he was still talking.

Snow had been coming down steadily since leaving her parents' house; it was collecting on the road, filling in tiny crevices left behind by last summer's resurfacing project. By the time she crossed the Sagamore Bridge, it was dark and the driving treacherous. Christine eased off the accelerator, switched the wipers to high and cursed herself for not leaving sooner. She stabbed at the radio searching for something other than love songs, paused and listened to one that seemed to have an identity problem. It played jazz, then country then Beethoven's Fifth. It became a metaphor for her mood.

It had been over an hour. Anders hadn't call. Several times she picked up the phone and just as many times laid it back on the seat. Why hadn't he called? Why should he, she'd been naughty again. The phone rang; it was him.

She said, "Hello. Selfish, spoiled and sorry girlfriend here."

"Well, hello there, selfish spoiled girlfriend. This is your studly, brilliant, perfect boyfriend at this end. What can I do ya for, ma'am?"

A smile tugged at the corners of her mouth and her heart quickened. She opened her heart and blurted, "Hmm, let me see; I guess you could jump on a plane and get your perfect butt out here."

Before she had time to take it back, he said "I'll be there in the morning, darlin'." And he sang, "I'm leaving on a jet plane …"

Her smile broke and a laugh rumbled from deep inside her. "Stop, oh please, stop. You're cute, but that voice …" Then there was silence. "Anders, are you there? Anders. Hello."

His voice returned, low and gruff, "You don't like my singin' huh? But I'll bet there's something about me you'd like. I know you liked it once upon a time. Remember?"

The blush rose, heating her face. She rolled down the window allowing snow to cool her. The yearning his comment stirred was replaced with a shyness she rarely experienced.

This time it was Anders who laughed. "Got you, didn't I? What's the matter, can't think of anything to say, huh?"

He was right, she couldn't. She giggled—like a school girl for goodness sake. What was becoming of her? She stuttered, "I guess we'll just have to find out how much I like you when I get back then, won't we?"

The promise rested in the void that lay between them, waiting for one of them to take it back. Since he wouldn't and she couldn't, she moved beyond it. "I'm on my way to Boston. I had a fight with my dad."

"Why? What happened?"

Communities flew by as she recounted the highlights of the last two days: the trip to P'town and the fight, but left out Harry Merit's reference to Nick.

"Wow, I'm sorry. You know I'll bet he was trying to …"

She pressed her foot to the floorboard. “Don’t you dare defend him. He’s evil, he’s selfish and he only thinks of himself.” Spit sprayed; embarrassed she looked around the car as if someone had seen her. Breaths came short and shallow.

“Whoa there. I wasn’t defending him. Didn’t you hear me? I said, I’ll bet he was trying to exploit you. You’ve told me enough about him that it only made sense that he was doing it for himself. Are we okay now?”

“Sorry.” What else could she say, she’d overreacted, again. She stared at the road. Her headlights caught the delicate clumps of white as they fell in front of the car. As they floated through the darkness and into the light they appeared as cotton puffs; the same ones released by cottonwood trees she’d seen the summer she and Donna visited Montana. The first time she’d met Anders. The sadness burst through without warning. “Anders, did you hear me? I’m sorry. It’s just that.” The tears fell, blinding her so she had to pull off the road and dropped the phone. The muscles in her stomach ached from the force of each sob.

“Christine, Christine. Are you alright?”

The phone lay in her lap, reverberating each time he yelled. She picked it up. When the sobs didn’t stop, she gulped in air hard and made a feeble attempt at a laugh, grabbed a used napkin from her purse, dried her eyes and blew her nose. Between hiccups she said, “Not sure where that came from. I’m good now. Guess it all built up and, lucky you, you got the brunt of it.”

“Look, you just need to stop being sorry. I understand why you’re upset. Your life’s been turned upside down the last few years and it’s starting to take a toll on you. Things will be better when you get back here. This is the place for you now.”

Relief invaded the bleakness. “Yes, yes, I need to move on.”

“Christine?”

“Yes?”

“I hate to do this to you, but I’ve got to get going here. Can I call you back later?”

She beat down the rejection and said, “I’ll tell you what. Why don’t we talk tomorrow? I need to concentrate on driving and when I get to Boston I've got to contend with Donna. I'm fine now, really. You don't need to worry."

She hung up, pulled back onto the highway and headed to Boston.

THIRTEEN

The gaslight directly in front of the stairs that led to the ivy covered Beacon Hill brownstone flickered a warning: caution, sharp objects ahead, take evasive action, avoid total destruction. Softer light filtered through sheer curtains on the apartment's windows and splayed onto the snowy sidewalk—seducing anyone outside into thinking it was a safe haven. Christine watched as two shadowy figures paced inside the apartment, arms flailing: one male, one female. It meant Donna was home; must be Matthew, too. Fighting again, she was sure.

Christine sat in the car for thirty-minutes summoning courage. Opening, then closing the car door—resolve waning each time she attempted to step outside. For the first time in years she yearned for a cigarette, but she needed to get it over with. She tugged at the door handle and opened it as a dark figure filled the brownstone's portico. Matthew emerged rubbing his eyes as if awakened from a bad dream. He wrapped a scarf around his neck, pulled a knit cap over his hair and walked toward the car. Christine eased the door closed until she heard a click and the interior lights went out. She slumped onto the passenger seat, closed her eyes and took in short, shallow breaths until an engine started, then faded away. She opened the car door again, grabbed her purse and the largest suitcase from the backseat, leaving the other suitcase and the boxes for the morning.

If she was lucky Donna had gone to bed. Christine took tentative steps, peering in the windows. Wishful thinking, Donna was sitting on the couch talking on the phone. Christine fumbled in her purse for keys, unlocked the outside security door, entered and climbed the short four steps to the apartment door.

"You forget something?" Donna yanked the door as Christine put the key in the lock. "Oh, god, you scared the crap out of me; I thought you were Matthew."

Donna stepped back and Christine slipped into the apartment. "What the hell are you doing here? You're not supposed to be here until Saturday."

"It's a long story." Christine leaned in and touched cheeks with Donna, dropped the bag and sunk into the couch. "I'm beat."

"Your room's a mess, I made Matthew sleep in there a couple days ago. I'm pissed at him." Donna glared at her. "If you'd stuck to your timeline, I'd have cleaned it."

Christine's temples pounded. She lifted her legs onto the newspaper covered antique trunk they used as a coffee table and closed her eyes. Before she did she'd noticed half-eaten bowls of chili taking up coveted space on the packed media center while a reality show, one Christine hadn't seen before, hummed in the background.

The voice in her head yipped its way to her mouth. "You could have at least cleaned up the dirty dishes. How long have they been there anyway? A month?"

My god, she sounded like a disapproving wife. "I'm going to bed now." She rose, opened the bedroom door and flipped on the light. The unmistakable odor of alcohol and the overwhelming smell of dirty laundry made her gag. Matthew's clothes littered the floor; she kicked a path to the closet and maneuvered the bag inside before throwing open a window. Exhausted, she shoved Matthew's books off the bed and collapsed.

****

"OMG, can't you just see the look on her face …" The slap of the shade against the window frame and the rush of cold air coupled with the screeching sound of laughter and conversation reached into her dream. Christine woke with a start, sat up and listened. The voices subsided then continued at a distance as the partiers apparently walked away. Her bedroom, which fronted on the street side of the building, overlooked the park; perfect for observing the plethora of 'entertainment' that occurred after dark. If she was into it, that is. In reality the constant buzz of traffic and clickity-click of pedestrians on the cobbled sidewalk was annoying, especially at night. She closed the small window above the bed. The room was freezing and dark; the only light emanated from her digital clock that read 10:23 p.m. She stretched, blinked and sat up. After a few minutes her eyes adjusted to the darkness; Donna had shut the door and turned off the light. The ambiguity confusing at times: Donna, the bitch and good friend all rolled into one. Christine's stomach growled; she hadn't eaten anything all day. She listened—no TV or music. Apprehension and the long car ride had made her shoulder muscles throb and her back tight. She pushed forward on the edge of the bed until chest met knees, felt the release and heard the soft pop; then rolled her neck trying to release the tension that had settled there. Her back had taken a beating in the accident, yet the discomfort she experienced from it hardly seemed important compared to the rest of the injuries. She massaged her thighs and hated that she sometimes felt seventy. Not that it was that old—Lotte had taught her that. Lotte had taught her a lot of things. Should she try to call again? No, let him wait. Right now a shower was a necessity.

Christine opened the bedroom door. "Donna?" No answer.

She slipped into the hall, tiptoed to Donna's room, stood at the closed door and listened. No sound. She went in, discarded clothes carpeted the floor. She waded through and peeked inside Donna's bathroom. Make-up filled the sink, underwear and a wet towel littered the floor. She checked the rest of the apartment. Donna was gone.

Christine went into her own bathroom, turned on the shower and sat on the edge of the tub while it heated up. It felt good to be back in her own bathroom; one that was familiar and stocked with her toiletries. Christine loved the green and black tile. The old ivory pedestal sink with its thick rounded edges was the showpiece. Though rust had begun to seep in around the edges of the faucets, they were sturdy, made of nickel with mother-of-pearl insets. Donna had tried to talk her into letting Matthew's parents update the bathroom when they'd remodeled other parts of the apartment, but Christine liked it as it was. The entire apartment, with its tall ceilings and ornate moldings, had been an elegant statement to the past until the remodel. Scarred fir floors were replaced with wide, dark hardwood planks, the kitchen's original softly worn and slightly chipped marble countertops were replaced with shiny granite and the old white wood cabinets thrown to the curb, contemporary cherry ones hung in their place. The only change Christine embraced was the state-of-the-art stainless steel appliances with more settings and choices than she or Donna would ever use. Still their sleek, unblemished presence in the apartment somehow represented perfection. After the accident, each time she'd turned on a gas burner, taken food out of the refrigerator or loaded the dishwasher, buoyancy had filled and lightened her. In reality, she'd miss the apartment; its proximity to the Harbor, the shops, everything she loved about Boston. She wouldn't miss Donna, her parents or the memories that living here conjured. Moving away from Boston meant her burden would be lightened: people here knew Christine the model. In Montana, they knew the Christine with scars and they accepted her.

The shower washed away the disappointment of the past few days. She let the hot water beat down, driving away the memory of her father's betrayal. Once it ran cold, she stepped out and reached for her old robe. She lifted it, held the soft fabric to her face taking in the aromas while keeping an alert mind. No Matthew, yet there was the familiarity of lavender, laced with citrus and a woodsy scent. So familiar that her hands shook. She tossed the robe aside, resisting the temptation to bury her body in it. It reeked of Versace and Nick. She stood there, naked, scars visible to the entire bathroom: to the mirror over the sink, to the full length mirror on the back of the door and to her reflection that bounced back at her from the shower doors. See, that's why he didn't want you.

"You in there?" Donna pounded on the door. "You finally got up, huh? You were snoring so loud I couldn't stand it so I went down to Johnny's."

Christine wrapped in a towel and opened the door. Donna's tall, lithe frame blocked the doorway, eyes glazed, dressed in a tight black mini-skirt and a white low-cut peasant top with a black bra underneath.

"How's everyone at Sammy's?" Christine asked, and tried to nudge Donna out of the way. In the attempt, Donna lost footing and fell to the floor, upper torso in the bathroom, the rest sprawled in the hall.

"Fuck, you knocked me over," Donna snorted. Pale skin and perfect breasts overflowed, spilling out of the blouse's low neckline. Dark strands of Donna's hair lay in puddles of water left from the shower. Christine wrapped the towel tighter, backed up and sat on the toilet. Donna closed her eyes; black liner and thick false lashes rested on bronzed cheeks and crimson lipstick outlined generous lips.

"Oh, no, you don't. You're not passing out in here. Get the hell up." Christine prodded Donna's head with her toe.

"Stop that. I'll get up." Donna sat up, rubbed her eyes, smearing black onto both cheeks. "Damn boots are killing me. Here, give me hand, will you?" She scooted in a semi-circle so both legs were on Christine's lap. "Give 'em a tug. They'll come off easy."

Christine resisted the temptation to tell her to go to hell, instead, yanked on the heel of the boot so hard the sock came with it. Donna screamed, "Do you have to be so fucking rough?"

Christine shoved her legs to the floor. "Do it yourself then." She stepped over Donna and walked down the narrow hall.

Donna pushed up from the floor and followed close behind. "C'mon don't get all huffy. I missed you. Give me a hug."

Christine's spine tingled as Donna grabbed at her shoulders and tried to turn her around. She pried Donna's fingers away and turned to face her. "Stop. You just need to stop. It's been a really shitty two days and right now I'm starved and I'm freezing … and you're drunk." She elbowed Donna aside, went back into the bedroom and closed the door.

Donna giggled. "Hey! I'm not drunk. I've just had waaaay too much to drink."

What a surprise. Christine put on jeans, a hoodie and some wool socks. Her stomach rumbled a reminder. She yelled, "Did you bring anything back?"

"What?" Donna's voice muffled.

Christine opened the door and shuffled into the kitchen. Donna was standing on a stool rummaging through the cupboard above the microwave.

"I said, did you bring anything back?"

"Yeah, I brought some bad breath." Donna leaned toward Christine and blew.

"Geez, that's gross. What the hell did you eat?" Christine pulled back, waved her hand in front of her nose.

"Sapphire. That's what I ate. Pretty blue Sapphire gin, with a splash of vermouth and lots of olives. Oh, and some onion rings off of Sara's plate." Donna straightened and continued her search in the cabinet where they kept the alcohol. "For food, you'll have to look in the fridge. There's tons of leftovers. Some pizza from last night, I think."

Open containers with undecipherable contents filled the shelves. Nothing looked edible. A large flat grey box took up most of the space above the crisper. Christine took it out and stared at one piece of shriveled pizza that resembled an old shoe with its toe curled upward. Half-eaten crusts littered the box.

"You call this leftover pizza? It's disgusting; I can't eat that."

"Stop complaining or I'll send you back to your folks."

"Just try."

Donna hopped off the stool, hand clutching a bottle of gin, "I'm ready for another one. You?"

"Not for a martini. Got tonic and lime?"

Christine yanked the crisper drawer; it stuck. She wiggled the drawer left to right and pulled again; this time it opened. In the bottom a lonely slightly wrinkled lime rested amongst browned lettuce leaves and rotting tomatoes. "Geez, Donna, you haven't cleaned this thing since I left." She held out one of the tomatoes. "This is revolting."

"Look, do you want a drink or not? I found the tonic, but if you're going to get picky on me, you can make your own."

The lime was soft beneath her hand and when Christine sliced into it, it sunk into itself. Lime juice pooled on the cutting board. She scooped up the mess and dumped it into the garbage. "I guess I'll do without the lime."

"Who needs lime anyway?" Donna shoved a lime-less gin and tonic into Christine's hand; a can of cashews appeared on the counter seconds later. "Grab the cashews, let's go sit and catch up. You can tell me what your crazy parents have done now."

FOURTEEN

Christine spent the next few days packing most of her summer clothes and dealing with Donna's tirades. "Damn it, what am I going to do now?" "Who am I going to get to share the rent?" "You're being selfish?" And on and on.

Never mind that Matthew had told her not to worry about the rent; his parents had given her a 'pass' for the next six months. No, Donna was hell-bent on making Christine's last few months in Boston miserable. So when the call came it was more about getting out of the apartment than a real interest in the caller's proposition.

"Christine?"

"Yes?"

"Strom Peterson, Cape Cod Register. I don't know if you remember me."

Of course she remembered him. He was the reporter who hounded her for months following the accident, hoping to do a story about her.

"Look, Mr. Peterson, I told you, I've told my father, I'm not interested. In fact, I'm moving to Montana. I'm trying to put the accident behind me. Thanks for calling."

She went to disconnect, but heard him yelling.

"Wait, wait. Please, this isn't about a story." He hesitated. "I, uh, got involved in the burn center while I was researching your story and I have a favor to ask."

She hadn't thought about the burn center in months. The images of the scarred and disfigured children had marched through her dreams too often after the first visit. Miller had taken her there, thinking it would erase the self-pity. It did the opposite and threw her into a deeper depression. But she'd promised Miller, so she'd gone back until it was too much, until the rest of her life fell apart; until Nick broke off their engagement.

"What favor?" It was probably a smokescreen. Yet there was nothing to lose. She'd already packed, she was bored and Donna was driving her crazy.

He cleared his throat. "Well, uh, there's a little girl at the burn center who is really despondent. Her parents don't know what to do with her and I told them about you. How you've moved on with your life and how you are still beautiful. I thought maybe, if you had time, you could go and see her."

The lilt at the end of the sentence was a question that hung between them like a proposal from an unwanted suitor. If she said no she'd look insensitive. If she said yes she'd ... well, she couldn't say yes. But in the end, she did.

****

They'd agreed to meet the following afternoon to give him enough time to drive in from Brewster. "Let's get together. I can tell you about Abby and show you photos before you meet her. You'll know what to expect then." Christine knew what to expect and had no desire to revisit the horrific result of parental negligence: adults falling asleep with cigarettes, adults leaving children alone while they went to bars, leaving them to suffer the consequences. No, what Christine hoped was to find a way to gracefully tell him she couldn't possibly help anyone; that she was still just too fragile.

She arrived ten minutes early to Java Bistro, her favorite café just six blocks from the apartment. The brisk walk in the sunny, cool air along tree-lined avenues dotted with some of the oldest houses in Beacon Hill left her exhilarated and feeling much more amenable to Strom's idea. It helped that her leg had kept up, not buckling or aching.

Christine crossed the street dodging potholes and avoiding any ice that remained. She stopped, rested a moment below the huge elm that anchored the corner in front of the café; a westerly wind whined above her. She tilted her face upward, a few remaining leaves floated to the ground. A gust swirled the light dusting of snow off the café's black ornate iron bistro tables that lined the sidewalk along the front of the old brick building. It rustled the ivy that tumbled from planters along the upper windows. She loved this place; loved Boston. It was going to be hard to leave.

The outside tables were deserted yet in warmer weather patrons filled the tiny café and spilled outside, occupying every table. At least twice a week during the summer, she and Donna ordered coffee and homemade cinnamon rolls and sat outside, lingering and visiting with friends and strangers. Small talk would tumble out from the café through the large open windows and spread onto the sidewalk like musical notes— soprano-pitched laughter coalesced with the guttural sound of arguing and mingled with the subdued and sensual whisperings of seduction. More than once they'd eavesdropped on first loves and longtime relationships that had run their course. More than once she had sat with Nick bitterly arguing or passionately making up.

Even with the chill in the air, Christine took her cappuccino and brownie outside, and headed for a table in the sun. She brushed off the seat and settled in to wait for Strom. With the sun beating down she watched people walk by, staring at them to see if they stared at her. Some did; as if she had two heads: the beautiful one in her memory; the grotesque one, her reality. Yet, today she didn't care and preferred to think those who stared were envious.

A horn honked and Christine recognized Strom behind the wheel of a late model black car with dented bumper. He waved and motioned that he was looking for a parking space. She let the sun warm her scars while sipping the cappuccino, enjoying being alive.

"Uh, um, Christine? Uh, I don't want to bother you, but … ." She shielded her eyes with her gloved hand, shifting it slightly to the right, then left until he came into view.

"Uh, Strom, is it?" she said, mimicking him and bit her lip to stop from snickering. The tips of Strom's brown hair looked like they'd been dipped in white paint and stood up in jagged peaks resembling snow capped mountains against a dark sky. He tugged at his ear, fidgeting with a pencil he had tucked there. His thick black glasses clung to the end of his nose, which raged red against his pale skin. It was unreal how he always looked like he had just gotten out of bed. "Slept in, did you?" She giggled and extended her hand.

A rumble rose from his chest and a raspy cough spewed phlegm into his throat. "Sorry, have a bit of a cold." He turned from her, set a newspaper and briefcase on the table while he reached for a handkerchief in his coat pocket. Handkerchief to mouth, spit to handkerchief, handkerchief to pocket. Gross.

She withdrew her hand impulsively and discreetly wiped it on her jeans, then lifted the scarf to shield her mouth and nose. "Go on, get yourself some coffee or hot tea and let's talk." If he noticed her discomfort, he didn't show it. He nodded and went inside.

Months ago she would have left when he coughed; not a word as to why, just left. The fear of infection would have jerked her out of her seat and sent her running into the street. A wisp of wind brushed away any residual fear and caught the corner of Strom's newspaper, shuffling it like a deck of cards; inserts flew across the table and onto the sidewalk. She lunged forward and grabbed them, before they flew into the street. She gathered them, smoothing each section and piled it neatly on the table, perusing the headlines: "School Superintendent Indicted on Fraud Charges;" "Boston Zoo Faces Threat of Closure," and so on.

Nearly two years ago the headlines had been about her. Well not her really. "Local Model and Friend Critically Injured by Senator's Son." The article had given a brief description of the accident. Only snippets of what really happened: going too fast; ran red light; local beauty and top model; young woman from the Cape. No mention of the fact she'd been trapped, cut and burned; only that Donna had been thrown clear, escaping with only minor injuries and the extent of Christine's injuries were "unknown at press time." No mention that the Senator's son had been drinking. Later after they'd agreed to a settlement, a short one paragraph piece suggested they'd settled out of court because of "errors made by all parties involved." No criminal charges were ever filed. So be it; it was history.

The brownie, decadent and dense, stuck to her teeth on the first bite; her tongue swept the chunks of chocolate and she savored its bittersweet richness. Steam from the cappuccino rose against the cold air. Resting one hand on the newspaper, she lifted the cup with the other. Guilt had no place in the simple joy she experienced from a cappuccino and brownie on this day. This day, carved out of yesterday's bleakness, reshaped and presented to her with clarity. Not often enough did she feel this freedom. In a way it felt good to be back in Boston. She closed her eyes, gave her face to the sun again and wished Anders was sitting beside her.

The table shuddered, sending steamed milk across the classifieds. When she looked up Strom was moving his chair, juggling a cup and saucer in one hand and a plate piled with pastries in the other, seemingly oblivious to the fact he'd caused an upset in this perfect day. Tea sloshed onto the saucer and small raspberry filled sugar cookies teetered precariously atop a mammoth cinnamon roll as he attempted to set both down on the uneven tabletop. She rescued the plate and snagged a cookie, then popped it into her mouth. "Hope you don't mind. I couldn't resist."

"No, no, that's fine." Still standing, he ran his hand across his forehead, wiping it clean of the moisture. "Phew, it's hot in there." He jerked his head in the direction of the café causing more tea to spill. "Have as many cookies as you want. There's a cinnamon roll buried down there somewhere." He chuckled. "My wife says I eat too many sweets; she thinks I'll be a diabetic by the time I'm fifty." He looked over at her and smiled. "Least I'll have fun getting there." He sat and tilted the plate toward her. "Here, have another one." She hesitated. He said, "It's fine, really. I can't eat all this myself."

"Don't mind if I do. Thanks."

"Your hands are healing well. I'm glad to see you're recovering. That scar on your face is fading nicely, too. How are you feeling generally?" He raised the cup of tea and took a sip. His eyes loomed large behind thick glasses; perspiration appeared again on his forehead and upper lip. He shed his topcoat and draped it over the back of the chair where slush from the melting snow soaked the hem.

Christine leaned back. Strom's eyes fixated on the cinnamon roll that he held with both hands. Taking tiny nibbles, his nose seemed to move up and down with each bite. Goodness, he actually looked like her childhood pet hamster. That realization and his obvious unease made him seem far less menacing. "I'm feeling pretty good really. A year ago I wouldn't have thought it possible." And, it was true. Right now she felt really good. "I meant to ask you the other day, how did you know I was back?"

He brushed crumbs from his lips. "Actually, I didn't know you were gone. I called your old number and, well, you answered. I've been putting this off for months. I knew you wouldn't want to hear from me."

"You're right." She stared at him and saw no reaction. "Well then?"

Strom drew a large envelope out of his briefcase, slipped his hand inside and pulled out a manila folder. He shuffled through some papers before handing her a single sheet. "Here I had the parents summarize what happened so it would be accurate."

She glanced at the feminine scrawl, pushed it away. He frowned, slid it back to her and said, "Please read it. It wasn't their fault. They're good parents. Please."

It began: *Abby's always been afraid of the dark. She'd get up in the night, crawl into our bed, shivering with fears we could never uncover. We weren't sleeping and neither was she. We decided to buy her a nightlight. We went together and let her pick it out. She loves what she calls, "princesses." She picked out three: Cinderella, Tinkerbell and Snow White—one was for her room, one for the hall and one for our room. We noticed after about a month that the one in her room, Cinderella, began to flicker a lot. We took it back and the store replaced it. When the replacement did the same thing we unplugged it. Abby had stopped coming into our room, and we decided they weren't needed anymore. What we didn't know was that Abby would plug it in next to her bed each night, between the dresser and bed. A place we couldn't see. We found out later that each morning she'd take it out so we wouldn't know. We guess she'd been doing it for about a week when the fire started. We later found out that the nightlights were defective, but had not been recalled. The hall smoke alarm next to her room went off and by the time we got to her room it was filled with flames and smoke. My husband wrapped wet towels around his head and got her out, but not before she was burned over 20% of her body—mainly her face and hands. We've gone through months of skin grafts and she's been so brave. Such a brave little girl, but she won't talk. The doctor said her vocal cords were not damaged—which was a miracle—and yet he can't figure out why. We've tried therapy at no avail. She seemed fine the day the bandages came off, but the next day the only word she said was "ugly." We can't figure out what happened. The nurses told us that no one had given her a mirror, yet we are sure she must have seen herself. Please help us. We've lost our little girl.*

Voices congregated around Christine, reverberating off the sidewalk with echoes of regret, sadness and anger. White noises whirled from windows high above her, landing flat and resting on her mind. Tears formed before she could control them. She brushed her hand across her eyes and tossed the paper to Strom, hoping the distance would give her clarity. "How old is she?"

He coughed and slid his glasses up his nose. Behind them she could see his eyes glistening. "She's five. It's upsetting, isn't it? I'm sorry. I did know it would affect you, but that was kind of the point. I really need your help. You see, this is someone I know. She's my wife's niece." He handed her a picture of a smiling, chubby cheeked, little girl; blond curls created a halo around her, blue eyes, innocent in their transparency. Dressed in a pink checkered sundress, she knelt next to a flower bed holding a daisy.

The distance Christine had hoped for disappeared. Instead of clarity, confusion lashed out along with a flood of indefinable emotions. The photos that followed clouded all reasoning. In the first photo, a white mask covered the lower half of Abby's face, only her lips, eyes and forehead were exposed to the air. Her lips distorted, her eyes bulging, her forehead puckered and red.

The memory of the kids at the burn center slapped into Christine's day. She flushed in shame. She'd tried to help them, moving from bed to bed, reaching out, whispering a kind word, but she'd failed. The sea of masked and blackened faces atop tiny bodies always had made her feel like she was in the middle of a horror film. The kids would stare at her with cold, empty eyes. Fear replaced compassion and it made her want to flee. The day she left and never returned, a severely burned boy had tugged at her jeans. When she looked down, she unknowingly gasped. He ran from her, his parents staring at her coldly—after that she knew she'd never go back.

Strom shoved new pictures in front of her; they were worse. The mask had been removed for a procedure and Abby's face had ballooned, skin puckered around her nose in large clumps that resembled warts. Her lips, clown-like, were large and misshapen.

"They're horrible." She turned them over, sighed. "But what could I possibly do to make her feel any better?" Before he could answer, she continued, "I'm not even sure I can see that place again."

"You won't have to; at least not right away. She's home now; on the Cape. They live near me."

Christine pulled out the picture of Abby before the accident and traced around the outside of her face. "Such a beautiful little girl. Sometimes I wonder what kind of God would put an innocent child through such an ordeal. What do you think, Strom, does the God you know allow such things to happen or are we really on our own?"

Strom shifted and fiddled with his napkin. "Life doesn't always work the way it should. Reporting has given me a whole different take on life. I've seen some really unimaginable things, and to be fair, some truly inspiring ones. There are some stories you never forget—Abby's is one of them."

Christine tried to ignore the rapid thumping inside her chest, put the photo back in the envelope and said, "I'm not quite sure I'm ready for this. Can I call you in a few days?"

FIFTEEN

"Get your lazy ass out of bed." Donna barged into the bedroom, threw Christine's cell phone at her, it landed with a soft thud on the covers somewhere at the foot of the bed. "Darn thing woke me up. You should keep it with you. It's Anders." She left, slamming the door behind her.

The room was dark; Christine struggled to focus on the location of the phone. She sat up, kicked her feet trying to feel where it had landed. She fumbled on top of the blankets until she found it. It was cold against her ear. "Hi." Why the hell had he called so early?

"Hi, yourself. You sound like you were still asleep."

"I was."

He chuckled. "It's damn near ten out there. Looks like we're going to have to re-acclimate you to Montana time when you get back!"

She yawned, stretched and sat up. "My goodness, I had no idea it was that late. We keep blackout shades on the windows, you know, for those late nights. To keep our beauty intact." Now it was her turn to laugh. She slid out of bed, slipped her free arm into the robe and rested the phone on her shoulder while she struggled to put it on. "How's Montana?"

"We're good. Jake's doing really well. Peta's settled. She's bunking in the blue guest room. She wanted your room, but Lotte was having none of it. Told her she should just feel lucky not to be living in a teepee. You know Lotte—no tact."

She heard the smile in his voice. Having him next to her in bed, right now would have been just fine. She missed him more than she wanted to admit.

"Say, there, sleepy head, I thought you were going to call me on Wednesday. It's Friday, you know?"

She'd forgotten. When she returned home after her meeting with Strom, she and Donna went out for pizza and she fell asleep by nine. Then Thursday blew by. Packing and making arrangements to ship her stuff in January was not as easy as she thought it would be. Besides, she reasoned, the last time they'd spoken he was the one who'd been distracted. Who was he to judge her for not calling?

"I figured you were busy with your sister and Janice." It flew out of her mouth before she could stop it.

"Whoa, there Nellie, where'd that come from?" Though the smile remained in his voice, Christine knew he was irritated.

She yawned again and lay down on her side, drawing knees to chest, "Oh, what the heck, may as well say it. I just miss you. And," she hesitated, "I got a little jealous the other day. You were busy and I was, well, I was ... a mess. You didn't seem too interested."

"Ah, babe."

"No, no I'm fine, really, I'm over it. Besides, I have to tell you what happened on Wednesday."

The story about Strom and Abby poured out of her; she gave him little space to comment or any chance to return to her earlier admission.

"I can't believe I actually might do this, but there's something about her. I hope I can help."

"You'll help her just by being there. I know that for a fact." His unwavering confidence in her unnerved her sometimes. Today it boosted her resolve. "When are you going to see her?"

"I told him I'd let him know in a few days. I may visit the burn center first and see if I'm strong enough. I'll let you know once I know," she said. "How is it going with Peta? She wanted my room, huh? Why?"

Donna burst into her room. "You still on the damn phone?" She handed Christine a cup of coffee and flopped on the bed next to her. She pulled the phone away from Christine's ear and said to Anders, "Hi, there, cowboy. You still as cute as I remember?"

Anders laughed. "This must be Donna."

Christine glared at Donna. "No, it's me again. You can ignore her."

Donna threw her arm over her forehead, sighing. "Oh, Anders, oh, Anders, I want you soooo bad."

"Shut-up." Christine glared at her.

"I didn't say anything." Anders sounded annoyed.

The back of her neck prickled. "Not you. Donna's being an idiot. Look, can I call you back after I get rid of her?"

"Of course. If you don't forget, that is. Say hi to 'the idiot.'"

She hung up and tossed the phone to Donna. "Brat."

"Oh, c'mon; don't be so sensitive." Donna bounced off the bed. "Get in the shower. I've got plans for us today. My photo shoot got canceled because the weather's lousy. I want to leave in an hour; we're going shopping."

"Can't go. I've got packing to do."

"Hire someone to pack and move you. You're being ridiculous. You've got tons of money …" She stopped, looked at Christine. "Yeah, yeah, I know, but I didn't get nearly as much as you did." Donna walked toward the bedroom door.

"Shit, Donna, you were hardly hurt. You want the money? I'll trade you—you take the scars. And, oh let's see, how about I give you my leg and I'll take yours. Hobbling down the runway should be a real winner, don't you think?"

Donna tilted her head toward the ceiling, then over her shoulder, she said, "Look, I'm sorry, but you need to toss that self-pity you got going on. You're loaded and you've got that cowboy. Things could be worse, you know."

"You can't be serious!" The anger surged upward until her head felt like an over inflated balloon ready to burst. "I get nothing from you, nothing. No sympathy, no remorse, no sorry. Nothing. You know I'm sick and tired of this attitude of yours. Like the whole accident had nothing to do with you." Christine pointed her finger at Donna and raged, "If you'd been paying attention instead of putting on your damn make-up while you were supposed to be driving, I wouldn't be limping around like a god damn invalid. I wouldn't look like fucking Al Pacino in Scarface and damn it, I would be able to lead a normal life." She pushed down the tears.

Donna's face turned from shock to fear to anger. "Fuck it. I don't want you with me anyway. Stay home and be a fucking martyr." Donna threw the phone at the wall. "For your information, I was worried about you. Both Nick and I were. But, you had to go and be a wimpy little bitch." Her face twisted and she pointed back at Christine. "And I have no responsibility for what happened to you—none." She stormed out of the room.

Donna's denial of culpability in the accident didn't shock Christine. She'd known Donna felt no remorse, no guilt, but the reality of it left her defeated, her energy depleted. She fell back on the bed, pulled the covers over her head and curled into a ball.

****

An hour later Christine got out of bed and walked over to the window, pulled the shade down hard, and let it fly up. The day surged into the room with a whoosh of cold air. Christine was determined to free herself of Donna's earlier rant. Snow flurried through the trees in the park across the street; bundled up Bostonians, heads down, braced against the weather. An elderly woman sat on a bench at the bus stop just outside the park, her arms wrapped around her body, rocking back and forth as if she too needed to protect herself from the pain of a friend's selfishness. The woman glanced up the street, then behind her toward the park. A patrol car crept along the perimeter; the woman stood, tugged at her coat, reached out toward an overloaded shopping cart and inched away from the patrol car.

Christine heard Donna talking on the phone, her voice booming through the closed door. "You still going? Nope, I tried to talk her into it, but she's playing the 'I'm scared and I can't go out' victim." Silence then Donna's voice grew agitated. "Sara, damn it, I don't want to go alone." Then a persuasive and toned-down Donna continued, "Please, I've really got to get out of here; I can't stand to be around her when she's like this." Silence again. "Good, I'll meet you at the entrance to Macy's in an hour."

Christine grabbed the remote off the nightstand and flipped on the TV, letting the volume dominate the room. Donna's banter became a low rumbling adjunct to the constant droning of Kelly Ripa's annoying dialogue with the audience and a faceless cohort.

Christine turned back to the window. The woman had reached the street and pushed her belongings over the curb. She stepped into traffic; cars swerved around her. Periodically she'd glance back toward the park as she hobbled to the other side. The cart bumped into the curb in front of Christine's apartment. The woman struggled to keep it upright, pushed then pulled the cart up over the high edge and continued to walk straight ahead. When she reached the iron fencing fronting the apartment building, she glanced up, eyes wide, mouth agape. She looked surprisingly lucid. Though the struggles of her life were mapped out around her eyes, the rest of her face was flawless. The hair that tumbled out of the scarf wrapped tight around her head was deep brown.

The image of the homeless woman remained with Christine long after the woman gave her a limp salute and turned left. A sketch formed in Christine's mind: the face against the backdrop of a desolate winter park, the isolation, barren trees, dark skies.

While packing books the other day, she'd come across an old set of watercolors. She walked to the closet and rummaged around, shoving shoes, Matt's dirty clothes, old papers and photos out of the way until she found the watercolors and a new sketch pad. She twisted her hair and pinned it on top of her head, threw off nightclothes and slipped into jeans and an old sweatshirt. A heavy overcoat that must have been Matt's hung in the closet; she put it on, pulled an old knit cap on her head, shoved her feet into boots and walked into the hall with her supplies.

Earlier she'd heard the shower in Donna's room start; it was silent now. "I hear you out there. What's going on?" Donna opened the door, head bound in a thick red towel. "You going out? I thought you had too much packing to do? Or is it that you just don't want to be with me?" Not waiting for an answer she slammed the door.

Christine's irritation with Donna returned. Self-focused, narcissistic, materialistic, vain, compulsive—qualities that Christine had never wanted to see in her friend; qualities that she was beginning to see were once her own.

When Christine opened the building's outer entry door, the wind caught a draft from inside and shoved her outside, causing her to drop the easel and paints. She picked them up, straightened and noticed the snow had subsided. The sun broke through the clouds and while warming the street, caused vapors to rise from the asphalt, transforming into a mystical dance of translucent figures. Clouds of mist ascended like ghostly corpses until a gust swirled the images in the direction of the Back Bay and the Charles River.

Christine walked through the lingering haze, crossed the street and set her easel on its tripod, positioning it to face the park near the bench where she'd seen the woman sitting. She placed the heavy card stock on top of the easel and opened the box of paints. Her hand wavered above an array of watercolors before picking up the lone pencil and moving deftly across the blank page initially with slow tentative strokes, then without thought or pause. She sketched the background, outlining the barren trees and moving onto the browned earth, dotted with patches of white. She blocked out the traffic noise and ignored the crush of buildings surrounding the square. The joggers and bikers, the business people who had braved the cold and were enjoying a brief interlude of sunshine to have lunch on the park benches and tables faded into her subconscious. When she finished the background Christine stepped back, leaned against a nearby tree and pondered what to begin next. She reached into her memory and imagination hoping for the woman's image to emerge.

For the following hour, Christine fleshed out the outline of the face, the lips, nose, the slouch of her body, but couldn't reconstruct the emotion in the woman's face. There had been visible sadness in the eyes, but another emotion lay beneath; emotion that was unreachable to Christine.

Sounds became overwhelming and her concentration waned. She longed for the quiet serenity of Montana to help her concentrate, to see what she should have been able to interpret. Then, it came to her: resignation. The woman had accepted her place in this life and Christine saw the beauty in that. Her pencil skimmed across the blank page, trying to capture it, yet she couldn't. Frustrated, she was ready to give up when she heard a familiar voice over her shoulder say, "The beauty of creation comes from within." The voice triggered a rush of emotions, both welcoming and ominous.

"Miller!" Christine whirled around, dropped her pencil and wrapped her arms around his large frame. She pulled back, looked at him and said, "What in the world are you doing here?"

"Well, young lady, if you'd return phone calls, an old man wouldn't have to traipse all over the state trying to track you down. This old man who's fixing to kick your little butt for not letting him know how you're doing." He laughed, held her at arm's length and continued, "My, goodness, you are looking terrific."

"I look horrible. Lost my looks, but I'm working on that."

"Did you forget?"

"What?"

"What Gibran said about beauty? "Beauty is not in the face, beauty is a light in the heart."

She felt a rush of heat rise to her cheeks. "That doesn't answer my question—how'd you find me?"

"Your mom told me. I got tired of waiting so I just showed up yesterday and demanded to know where you were. She said you'd come back here to pack. That you'd been to Montana and you're planning to move there." He elbowed her then winked. "You and that photo nut moving in together?"

At least he didn't call Anders 'that cowboy.' "Nooo." Heat blazed through her body. "But I did buy some land there and I'm having a house built."

"You're what?" He fell back, put his hand over his heart and feigned disbelief before slapping his knee. "I knew it, I just knew it. Soon as I saw the two of you together in that hospital room and saw how he spoiled your ungrateful …" He paused and winked. "Oops, sorry. Let me rephrase … how he kept bringing you flowers every day; stroking your head, holding your hand; talking to you." He winked again. "I knew something was going to come of it."

"You did, huh, Mr. Know-It-All?" She poked at his shoulder. "And what else did you surmise? Look into that crystal ball and tell me: am I going to have ten kids or twenty?" The mention of kids made her think of little Abby; it also reminded her how much she'd missed talking to Miller.

Miller's face had been the first one she saw in the emergency room. For hours, he'd sat quietly by her side until they moved her to ICU. In the hospital he'd quelled her fears, listened to her screams, and in her worst moments allowed her to be selfish and mean-spirited. The day before she was to be discharged, he'd come for one last visit. He had been sitting near her bed, complaining about the traffic, slumped forward, eyes downcast, picking at his jeans. Then, he'd snorted and nudged her hand. "Boy, listen to me, complaining and you're still all bandaged up." His eyes glistened with apology, his dark leathery face furrowed, resembling a Shar Pei.

The air in her lungs had grown sparse. Oh no, he wasn't going to cry was he?

His smile beamed through their unease. "Well," he said and brought his hands together in a loud crack, "you'll be leaving this hospital tomorrow."

"Shoosh, you'll wake up the dying, for god's sake." Feeling in her own hands had begun to return; tiny, almost undetectable, pinpoint-like pain ran through the fingers on her right hand, a new sensation that had replaced the dullness of feeling nothing. She rolled to her side, inching toward the edge of the bed, reached out and touched Miller's face. "Just kidding. You know, I'm happy to have you here." His dark face, haloed against the stark whiteness of the room, remained expressionless. "Oh c'mon, I'm sorry," she said.

He shifted, his ample body protruding over the seat of the chair. She patted an empty space on the edge of the bed. He didn't move, but said, "You got plans when you get home? Thought I'd stop by now and then."

She panicked, sunk back into the bed, pulling the threadbare covers tightly under her chin. Going to her parents' house on the Cape terrified her and she knew Miller wouldn't be welcome. The silence grew uncomfortable. What could she say? When she didn't answer him, he made excuses and left. Until today, she hadn't seen him again.

But he was here now and she was happy to see him. "Say, do you have time for some lunch? I've missed you," she said, and reached out and gave him a quick hug. "You big old black bear."

"Don't start messing with my ethnicity now. I'm a proud black man and you better show some respect." He hugged her back. "You bet I've got time for lunch. Not sure I should trust you making it though. What can I expect? Peanut butter on white bread?"

She put her watercolors away and slipped the drawing into a sleeve with the easel. "You'll have to wait and see. Hope you have a strong stomach."

They walked arm-in-arm back across the street, through the fog of her past.

~ Here I sit between my brother the mountain and my sister the sea. We three are one in loneliness, and the love that binds us together is deep and strong and strange.~ Kahlil Gibran

SIXTEEN

Cape Cod—December 21st

The winter solstice on December twenty-first crept through the Cape without any fanfare. No snow, no wind, no rain, no folklore, not even a traditional solstice celebration of rebirth or return to light. Only Lisa's boys running in and out of the Moretti's cottage that Christine now inhabited. The days were short, the nights long. The early sunsets and grey days created the perfect metaphor for her thoughts and emotions, not only because of the impending Christmas holiday, which would include family gatherings and expected attendance, but darkness hovered because the second anniversary of her accident on January twentieth loomed. A quiet deep-seated panic had already manifested: a quickening of her heart for no reason, a pin prickle rush of anxiety, headaches and, according to those around her, blatant irritability.

The entry door creaked and a lock of blond hair appeared before the five-year-old who was attached to it. "Hi, Aunt Chrissy, what ya doing?"

"I'm not your aunt, Jeremy. Stop calling me that." And, stop coming in here, she wanted to scream. "Where's your brother? Is your mother home yet?"

"He's in the house. Mom got home a long time ago."

"Then go on, now; tell her she's in charge again. I've got stuff to do."

Christine had been there for over two weeks and the boys were still walking in and out of her place without knocking. All she got from Lisa when she complained was, "Oh, isn't it sweet? They really like you." Then, with a pat on their heads, she'd shoo them outside until the next time. Still, Christine told herself, gratitude is what she should be feeling since Lisa offered to let her stay there after Donna kicked her out.

"Do you know where Atlantic View Heights is?" It was not at all what she'd expected Lisa to say when she'd asked for directions that Saturday after Thanksgiving, four days before Donna dropped the bombshell. Lisa had called while Christine was at her parents and insisted on the visit she'd promised.

"Sure, that's where Donna grew up. I used to go there all the time. In fact, the guards were so used to seeing me that as soon as they'd see me drive up, they'd open the gates. It's a beautiful neighborhood. That's where you live?"

"Yes, we do." Lisa said. "We bought the O'Sullivan place when the old guy died and his children didn't want the upkeep. Remember Jimmy and Bridgett? Anyway, I didn't want something this big, but Gino insisted."

Christine didn't remember them; the rich and famous never had too much to do with her. "Well, you're very lucky. When I was growing up, I longed to live there." Some of those old feelings of jealousy and inadequacy resurfaced. "Yes, you're very lucky. Did you know that's where Nick grew up and his family still lives? Do you see ..."

She never got the chance to finish her question, which was probably for the best.

Lisa started yelling, "Jeremy, leave that rabbit alone. Oh, goodness, I've got to go, the boys are chasing the rabbit and I've got to get them packed. See you this afternoon."

After a hectic and sometimes contentious Thanksgiving, Christine was anxious to get out of her parents' house that Saturday. Her sister, brother-in-law and two daughters had left on Friday and she didn't feel like making small talk with her parents. When her father got up early to make coffee, Christine dressed quietly, tiptoed by the kitchen, gave him a quick wave and left to go into town for coffee rather than sit and visit with him. They'd tabled any discussion about their last argument, pretending it hadn't happened.

The walk into town was invigorating; she bought a newspaper and had a leisurely cup of coffee and croissant at Books 'n Brew. By the time she returned, her parents had gone; the note said they heading up to Plymouth to see the Christmas Festival of Lights and wouldn't be home until after dinner.

At three, Christine cruised through the open gate at Atlantic Heights, a tiny hamlet of large homes constructed on a mile-long stretch of sandy beach inside a protected natural cove on the southern side of the Cape fronting on Nantucket Sound. It was made up of a conglomeration of large estates and old grey clapboard houses. The entrance to the neighborhood was no longer manned, perhaps a sign of the times. She drove past the first few homes. Lawns normally lush and green were turning their winter shade of brown. She eased off the accelerator and crept through the narrow streets. Most of the houses hadn't changed. Tradition, strict neighborhood covenants and other local government restrictions discouraged individuality. Varying hues of grey and white wrapped each home in a monotonous coat of sameness. The attraction had always been the seaside location. The longing she used to feel as a child to be a part of the privileged seemed to dissipate with the forward motion of her car. Donna's family home looked a bit tired and worn; paint was peeling off several dormer windows and weeds had sprung up throughout the normally manicured yard and flower beds. Cars filled the driveway of Nick's parents' house; it was set back from the road and nearest to the shore. It had over ten thousand square-feet and included an au pair cottage, pool house and four-car garage. They'd partied a lot in that pool house during high school and college. At one of those parties he'd broken up with her, the first of three times, so he could date one of her girlfriends. That should been a warning.

As she drove by his house, a young couple ran out the front door. Curious, she slowed, peered down the crowded driveway. No one she recognized. She pulled into an adjoining driveway and attempted to turn around, ready to head back to Lisa's. The car's turning radius was nonexistent; she struggled, cranking the wheel first right and inched forward trying not to drive on the grass or desecrate the rose bushes at the edge of the asphalt. Then turned the wheel left and accelerated onto the road, rolling into the rose bush anyway. A sharp rap on the back window jolted her; she glanced in the rear view mirror expecting to see the angry homeowner, instead saw Nick smiling and shaking his finger while holding up a broken rose branch. With one foot lightly tapping the accelerator and a finger on the door lock, without turning around, she waved and pressed harder on the gas, urging the car forward.

"Hey." She heard him yell. "Is that the way to treat an old friend?"

"It is if that old friend is a jerk", she mumbled.

"Hey, c'mon. Hold on."

She glanced in the side mirror; he threw down the branch and walked toward his parents' house, middle finger raised to the heavens.

Only four houses separated Lisa's from Nick's but the short drive zapped her energy. Her heart was still pounding as she drove down Lisa's long birch-lined driveway. The lane took a turn, ambling to the left, ending at a three-car garage and an expansive view of the sea. The house rose out of the yard like a crown, adorned with ornate moldings and turrets. It reminded her of the houses Christine had seen at her great-grandmother's in Wisconsin. It was unlike the traditional homes on the Cape: an obtrusive looking Victorian that glistened in the late afternoon sun. A brick path led to the front door that flew open; Lisa bounced out onto the porch waving at her. Christine got out of the car and walked toward Lisa who hugged her and led her inside.

The home was immaculate. It could have easily been on the cover of any home decor magazine. The interior was the antithesis of the exterior. As Victorian as the home was on the outside, it was modern on the inside. Christine moved from the entry, down a narrow hall that opened into a large room with floor to ceiling windows.

"This is beautiful and, oh my, the view is spectacular."

The ocean could be seen out of every south and east facing window. It was impossible to think two boys, a dog, cat and two adults lived in this part of the house. Everything was in varying shades of white with touches of sea foam green and taupe.

"Thanks. You're lucky to see it on a clean day. The housekeepers just finished up in here, now they're over at the cottage."

"I saw them going in when I drove up. Cute. Does someone live in it?"

"Nope, mainly use it for storage, but we had guests over the weekend so it needed sprucing up. C'mon, sit down, let's catch up."

Christine settled into one of the overstuffed chairs. "This is very different on the inside."

"The darn neighborhood board won't let us do anything about the outside style because of the local laws. In defiance, and because our tastes are different, we've taken down walls inside to make it more open; from too many small rooms to, well," she spread her arms in a wide arc, "to what you see."

They talked for hours. Later, coffee led to martinis, cookies to pizza delivery. Christine hadn't planned on spending the night, but Gino had left with the boys that morning to stay at their grandparents in Springfield for a few days, so Lisa had insisted.

They rose early the next morning and walked down the long stretch of beach. They reminisced and caught up on each other's lives. As they approached the beach in front of Nick's house, Christine became anxious and insisted they turn around, saying her leg was aching. Lisa's glance, sympathetic but tinged with insight, compelled her to insist it was time for her to get back to her parents.

Their goodbyes were strained, Christine feeling exposed and Lisa obviously unsure of what she had done wrong. Yet during that short weekend, they formed a bond that would be the catalyst for the solution to Christine's ensuing problem: arguments with Donna that led to her subsequent homelessness.

After Christine's fight with Donna, the day she'd run into Miller at the park, their friendship became strained, arguments became frequent and more heated until Donna practically threw her out. When Christine realized she had nowhere to stay, she panicked. Her options were limited. Staying with her parents was unthinkable and returning to Montana didn't make sense, the house wasn't finished and Peta and Jake were staying at the ranch. Of course Anders hadn't seen it that way when she told him she'd already made the decision to live at Lisa's cottage.

"Come here. We'll make room."

"I'll be in Montana soon. I need to get these holidays out of the way. Plus, Anders, I've been to see Abby a half dozen times and she's beginning to come around. I can't believe how much helping her has meant to me." When Anders didn't respond, she plowed on, "Look, I can't help it Donna and I had a fight and she took the opportunity to give my room away."

He sighed and finally said, "First of all she had no right to rent it to anyone else. Secondly you have a room here."

"She did have the right, that's what I'm trying to tell you—she's the one on the lease. Plus, I didn't want to be there anymore. And it's too soon for me to come back to Montana. My house isn't finished enough to live in. I'd have to move back to the ranch and it's pretty crowded there now. Right?" His hesitation was all the ammunition she needed. "See, you know it."

"Well, then, I'll expect you in January."

She ignored the ultimatum and changed the subject. "How's Peta getting along?"

"Good. She's wants to meet you. In fact, she saw your sketches and loved them, especially the one of Barney. She wants you to teach her to draw when you get back."

Before she could ask he said, "Don't worry, the sketches are safe. They were leaning up against the window in your room when she went in the first day. After that, I packed them up and put them in your closet."

"She liked the Barney one, huh?" It was one of Christine's favorites. "Is Barney her favorite horse too? Does she ride him?"

"Yes, and she's a natural on a horse. We've been letting her ride. Janice has been letting her work at the café to earn some spending money."

"Got to go. I'll talk to you in a few days. Tell Lotte hi and give Jake my love." By this time Christine had heard enough of Peta and Janice. She'd hung up feeling insecure. It had unnerved her and she decided she didn't like Peta.

That anxiety had lingered and since then she'd had moments of uncertainty about her decision to remain on the Cape and live in Lisa's cottage.

A light knock on the cottage door startled her, "What's going on in here?" Lisa poked her head in. "I hear you're a bit grumpy. I've got lunch up at the house. C'mon, let's talk."

Christine dropped the magazine she was reading and rose from the wicker chair next to the fireplace, stretched and glanced at her watch. "Okay, but I've got to be out of here by two. I'm meeting with Abby again."

"How's that going?" Lisa locked arms with Christine and led her out the door; they walked across the lawn and up the brick path that lead to the house.

"Pretty good, but it's been difficult at times. It's brought back a lot of my own fears. The best part is that Abby's beginning to trust me and she's talking now."

"That's wonderful. I knew you could do it."

"My first visit with her was at Strom's and it was pretty intense. The next time I went to Abby's house; it was awkward at first. I've never been good with kids." She smiled at Lisa. "I guess you surmised that, huh?" Lisa kept her head down and nodded. "But something clicked and I asked her if she had any dolls that we could play with." Christine rolled her eyes. "Kinda lame, huh?"

"No, no, that's exactly the kind of thing to do to get their trust. You did exactly what you should have done."

That made her feel better. Christine stopped and put her hand on Lisa's arm. "It's important to me to have her trust me. I decided to go slow. I never mentioned the fire or her scars, and her face is much better than the pictures Strom showed me. It's been pretty amazing, but sad, so sad." Christine turned and gazed out at the sea; breakers pounded the shore, pulling the sand back into the ocean grain by grain. The sea grass billowed in the wind, the tiny cottage whitewashed against the brilliant sky. "Why does life have to be a struggle? A little girl, for god's sake." She stared at Lisa, whose eyes had filled. "She's the sweetest little thing and, my goodness, so beautiful once."

Lisa's eyes locked onto hers. "You'll help her; I know you will. Now c'mon let's have some lunch."

"I hope so. Strom said her parents have seen subtle changes the last few weeks." They climbed the stairs to the kitchen door. "She still keeps a blanket pushed up against her face, but we're working on that. Toward the end of this last visit—we've had eight—she didn't use the blanket as much and she even laughs at times."

"Good for you." Lisa opened the outer door, stepped inside and screeched, "Jeremy, put that knife down. What in the world were you thinking?" Jeremy sat on the counter, attempting to smear peanut butter across a holey piece of white bread. "Get down from there this instant."

"But, mom," he said, drawing out the "o" and feigning tears. "I was hungry."

Lisa grabbed him around the waist and set him on the floor. "Your lunch is right here, young man. Now sit up at the counter and eat it. Where's your brother?"

Jeremy took a bite. "He was looking for you." Mouth full of peanut butter, Jeremy fluttered his eyes at his mother. "We couldn't find you and we was hungry."

Lisa kissed the top of his head then yelled out the kitchen door, "Tony? Tony, where are you?"

"I'm right here, geez you don't have to yell. And my name's Anthony, not Tony." He stormed through the door, threw his jacket on the floor and marched down the hall toward the stairs that led to the second floor and six bedrooms. At the age of eight Anthony thought of himself as the keeper of the family since Gino traveled frequently. His frustration with the constraints of being a child, and not being taken seriously, was evident every time he spoke. His favorite lament: "I'm eight, you know; I'm not a baby," was what he uttered as he exited the kitchen.

Lisa sighed. "Isn't he sweet?" She opened the cupboards, found two soup bowls and filled them with the chowder simmering on the stove. "I don't know what I'm going to do when he hits puberty." She laughed then motioned for Christine to sit at the kitchen table that was tucked in a windowed alcove that viewed the sea.

Chowder not being a favorite of Christine's, she said, "Not too much for me. I'm not that hungry."

"Oh, but you won't be able to resist this. I have a cook who comes in once a month to prepare about two weeks of meals for us then she freezes them. This is one of her specialties. Here, I've got some real San Francisco sourdough to go with it." She passed an overloaded bread basket to Christine and flopped down next to her. "Oops, forgot to get us something to drink. Iced tea, water, or something else?"

"Water's good." Steam rose from the soup, the aroma of butter and clams laced with a hint of brandy moistened the inside of her mouth. "Wow, this smells wonderful." It tasted even better. "You know," Christine hesitated as if giving up one of her best kept secrets. "I am really hungry; I just hate chowder ... except for this. This is incredible."

"Thanks, but I guess my only contribution was choosing the right chef. Tell me more about Abby."

"It's going to be a slow process to get her to fully trust me." Christine broke off a piece of bread, dipped it in the soup and let it dissolve in her mouth, then continued, "She doesn't really know me all that well and she's been traumatized." She paused, swallowed again. "To say nothing of her disfigurement." She unconsciously raised her hand to her face and ran her finger over her scar. "Though I must say, her face looks better each time I see her. They've had some incredible breakthroughs in burn treatments, even in the last year."

"What do you guys do beside play with dolls? What else is she interested in?"

"I found out that before the accident she loved to dance and was in many recitals, but now she won't have anything to do with it."

"Is her mom one of those pushy moms?"

"No, actually she's pretty centered, as is the dad. They want her to dance again. They want her to get back to her normal life, but she won't. I'm trying to help her focus on other things."

"Like what?"

"Like art. What would you say to my bringing her back here during the day on Christmas Eve? I have all my supplies at the cottage and I'd like to try to get her to express herself. It really helped me recover—when I could finally move my hands."

"Does it have to be Christmas Eve?"

"That's the best day for me and I have a gift for her."

"Okay, but could you make it in the morning? I need your help in the afternoon since your family's coming to Christmas Eve dinner."

"I'll have her out of here by noon; does that work? Oh, no, what time is it?" She leaned out and glanced at the clock on the wall above the table. "Shit, it's late. I gotta run. Thanks for lunch."

SEVENTEEN

The long gravel driveway to Abby's place was littered with wagons, big wheels and tricycles; Christine deftly maneuvered Lisa's Mercedes over potholes, dodging overgrown bushes that jutted out onto the drive. It opened onto a large clearing where the turn-of-the century farmhouse stood on about nine acres. Scorched siding outside one of the upstairs dormers was all that remained of the fire. Abby's family hadn't been as lucky as Christine; they'd been underinsured and the monies they received had mainly gone to Abby's care. Peeling paint and a long porch that sagged at either end further accentuated the Madison's current financial situation.

"We're trying to get a handle on everything," Wendy, Abby's mom, had told her, "but with Abby's constant care, it's been difficult." On her last visit Wendy revealed it was more than extensive medical bills that kept them from catching up. Abby's father, Kurt, had been laid off at his construction job and was barely making a go of it as a handyman; picking up jobs where and when he could. "Max is going off to college next year, and I don't know how we are going to manage." Wendy's eyes reddened. "We always wanted a large family and Kurt has worked hard to make sure we're taken care of, but six kids is a lot. Those five boys practically eat us out of house and home."

Right now three of the boys were circling the house on dirt bikes. A dusty haze swirled around Christine's car and she cursed herself for driving through the carwash on her way. Andy, the youngest boy, grinned and waved as he flew by the car again, spewing gravel. The twins, Tommy and Eddie, followed close behind, neither acknowledging her nor giving any indication they planned to stop anytime soon. They circled her car, drawing closer with each orbit, like predators to their prey. This wasn't the first time the boys had tried, and succeeded, in intimidating her. On the first visit they'd stood on the porch at the top of the stairs, blocking the front door, telling her Abby wasn't home. Eventually Wendy came out and rescued her. Since then, Christine always honked when she got there.

Wendy stepped through the front door and came out onto the porch and the boys disappeared. Christine opened the car door and stepped out onto the uneven dirt drive.

"Sorry about that; they're full of energy today," Wendy said, smiled and raised her arms in a gesture that indicated she had no control over her masculine brood. Her shoulder length hair hadn't been brushed. Blond streaks peppered her light brown locks, her face scrubbed clean of make-up. Even without any she was an attractive woman, but years of smoking had puckered her mouth with wrinkles. A child's arm appeared from behind Wendy, and wrapped around her thigh, another arm appeared from the other side, then Abby slipped out from behind her mother, barefoot and still in her nightgown.

She waved. "Hi, Chrissy." Then disappeared through the door.

Wendy jerked a thumb behind her, gesturing at Abby. "That one's full of it, too."

"Good. I love to see her happy."

Christine gathered her purse and the bags on the front seat, and walked to the front steps. Both hands full, she leaned into Wendy for a quick embrace before entering the house. The room was tidy, but chilly and dark. Drapes were pulled tight across the windows and the only illumination came from the red and green lights that blinked in unison on the massive Christmas tree that seemed to take up the entire room. A few presents were scattered under the tree and a glittering angel secured the top. To the right of the tree and across from the entry, sliding glass doors led to the backyard. To the left an LCD TV hung over a brick fireplace and a grand piano on the other side represented better economic times for Abby and her family. Once Christine's eyes adjusted, she observed Abby's form sprawled on the sofa, hidden under a tan afghan blanket.

Wendy squeezed past Christine in the narrow entry, blocked on one side by a coat rack and the other by an antique desk piled with papers and bills. "Sorry, I know it's cold in here; we've been trying to conserve oil. The last time we filled it, it cost us a fortune." Wendy walked toward the kitchen then stopped just past the sofa. Turning to face it she put hands on hips. "I can't understand where Abby went? Did you see?" She smiled at Christine, put a finger to her mouth and pointed at the couch. They both smiled. "You want some coffee?"

"Sure, but let me help."

Christine hung her coat on the coat rack, dropped the bags and, while following Wendy, made a quick detour toward the couch where she bent over, tickled Abby and whispered, "I know you're in there, but I won't tell."

On her way to the kitchen Christine passed the kids' play area set up in the back corner of the room next to sliding glass doors. Toys were neatly arranged in baskets and the kids' books were stacked alphabetically in a compact yellow and green bookcase. At Christine's suggestion, Wendy had made a space for Abby to do her schoolwork and art. A child's table surrounded by four animal chairs worked as a desk so she could keep up with her schoolmates until she felt strong enough to return. Math papers, markers, and basic stick drawings were scattered on top of the table. One in particular caught Christine's attention. A tiny stick figure with blond curls stood next to a taller stick figure, also with blond curls. The two held hands and a bright yellow sun dripped either rain drops or sunbeams. She couldn't tell. Simple flowers and trees covered the rest of the paper, yet in the lower left corner, an almost indecipherable stick figure with a large head was crudely drawn in black crayon. Heavy strokes of orange and red drawn like blades of grass encircled it.

"Interesting, huh? She drew it with her therapist—just the two blond figures. After the therapist left she drew the dark stick figure at the bottom." Wendy handed Christine a steaming cup.

The cup warmed her hands that had grown colder in the unheated room. She took a sip and allowed the coffee to warm her throat before she answered. "Well, it is better than the drawings I saw when I first met her."

"That's you, you know," Wendy pointed to the larger blond stick figure; then turned toward the couch, "She told me she likes you. Didn't you Abbs?" When Abby didn't respond she continued, "C'mon now; take off the blanket and move over so Christine can sit down."

Abby slithered further into her blanket, moving like an inch worm toward the end of the couch.

Wendy touched Christine's arm. "I've got some laundry to do. If the boys come back in and start to bug you, let me know. I told them this was Abby's time and they were to stay out." She rolled her eyes and said, "We'll see how long that lasts."

Christine set her cup on the side table next to the couch, eased into the tiny spot Abby had left for her, and reached over to turn on the lamp. "Is it okay if I turn on the light?"

"No light." The words rose from beneath the blanket. Abby fidgeted, toes poking through holes in the crocheted afghan, each toe rimmed in remnants of bright pink nail polish smeared onto skin, seeping deep into crevices around each nail.

"Nice toes." The temptation was too great. She reached over and tickled Abby's big toe. It was a giggle this time that tumbled out, escalating to a robust laugh as Christine pushed fingers deep into the blanket and moved from toes to feet.

"Stop, oh, stop, Chrissy."

"Stop what?" Christine's voice squeaked to an innocent pitch before she quit and said, "I'll stop but you have to come out of hiding."

A snort emerged from the blanket along with the breathy five-year-old, long blond hair covering her face, her smile wide. They stared at each other, each waiting for the other to say something. It was like this each time they met; each unsure how to proceed. Their relationship had been hard to define: not mother/daughter, nor patient/therapist, not even child and adult since Christine often felt as child-like as Abby. They were two victims of tragedies that had been beyond of their control.

The silence grew until Christine noticed something different about Abby. "You've lost a tooth!" Abby brushed the hair out of her face, and pulled the blanket back over to cover her head. "No, no, let me see. You look adorable!"

The blanket dropped; Abby emerged with her eyes scrunched shut and a half-smile on her face. "Look silly," she mumbled.

"You're too cute to look silly! What did the tooth fairy bring you?"

"Now you're silly." Abby pushed the blanket toward her feet, crawled over and poked Christine in the stomach. "Are you ticklish?"

Christine wrapped her arm around Abby's waist and pulled her into her lap. "No way. I'm not ticklish. Now what do you mean that I'm silly?"

Abby turned around and drew her finger down Christine's scar. "There's no such thing as the tooth fairy." She wrinkled her nose, pulled away and wiggled onto the floor. "And there's no such thing as Santa Claus, the Easter Bunny, or …", she stood up, tugged at both sides of her pink flannel nightgown, twirled, then stopped, pushed her face closer to Christine's until they were touching noses, " … God."

The forcefulness of Abby's response caught her off guard; anger at a God that Christine herself wasn't sure existed stifled any rebuff, so she took the easy route. "What do you mean there's no Santa? Of course there is. Who do you think climbs down your chimney and brings you presents?"

Abby stared. "But Tommy said Mommy and Daddy do it. He said I was a baby for believing … " Her eyes welled. "He's mean; he said Mommy and Daddy won't tell me there isn't one because … because," she fought back more tears, "of the fire. He said they didn't want to make me sad again."

Suffocating sadness swept over Christine, then anger. Abby stood up and walked toward the tree; she batted at one of the red satin ornaments and yanked on a branch causing the tree to sway.

"Abby, don't …" the words spilled before Christine had time to think.

Abby glared. "Can if I want to." But she stopped and fiddled with the ribbon on one of the wrapped presents. She wiped her sleeve across her nose, then shook the box. "This one's from Dr. Landau at the burn center. He likes me. Do you like me, Chrissy?"

The obvious answer hovered around her like an alien spaceship. The words formed in her mind and before she shut them off she said, "Of course I like you, Abby. Why wouldn't I?"

Christine waited for her own rush of emotion to tell her she was telling the truth. The blank stare that Abby gave her was enough to let her know she'd not been very convincing.

The truth was she'd actually begun to think of Abby as a daughter, which was crazy because Christine had never wanted a child of her own. The idea of an engorged body along with stretch marks, nausea and sagging breasts had given her nightmares the one time she'd missed a period. Nick had been equally horrified, chastising her for being careless. Yet, more and more this year she'd lingered over pictures of babies and once when she and Anders were in Bozeman she'd stopped to admire a baby of a friend of Anders. Later that week they'd run into another friend of his who was pregnant. For the first time, she saw the expectant mother glow everyone talked about. She'd long suspected it was a myth created by a male in order to procreate. When she mentioned it to Anders, he smiled, "Kids are a blessing, or so I've heard." He hesitated, then continued, "Funny, I thought I'd be a father by now." When she pressed him, he clammed up and changed the subject.

Abby tossed the present back under the tree and skipped to the sliding glass doors, resting her forehead on the cold glass. She took a step back, cupped her hands tight around her lips creating a funnel and blew air onto the cold window. Then she traced the outline of a smiley face with her finger, glared at it and said, "What are you smiling about? You got nothing to be happy about." With that she tugged the sleeve of her nightgown over her hand and swept it away. "Wanna go outside?" she asked, staring through the glass. "It's snowing."

"Really?" Christine walked over to her and stroked Abby's hair. "It's beautiful." And it was; tiny delicate flakes floated from a somber sky. A sudden shroud of sadness cocooned her, weighing heavier than normal. In a moment of clarity she knew why. What Abby had done to the smiley face was what Christine had wanted to do many times with her own face.

"You know what?" Christine took a sheet of paper off Abby's table. "Let's draw the snow first, then go out. How 'bout that?"

"No. I just want to go outside." She reached up, pushed Christine's hand off her hair. "Now. I want to go right now." She unlatched the door and using both hands pushed it to one side and ran out onto the patio, sliding on the snow slickened surface.

"Abby, get in here."

Somehow Abby had remained upright and grinned at her from the edge of the patio. Christine held onto to the door frame, leaned forward and tried to reach Abby without going outside. Her knee buckled, her hand slipped and she fell forward onto the wet concrete then rolled.

"Damn it; damn leg." Pain shot through her knee and up into her hip; her hand throbbed where her palm had met the exposed aggregate patio when she tried to break her fall.

Abby giggled. "Chrissy, you fell and you said a bad word." She shook a finger at Christine.

An angry retort bubbled close to the surface. Christine swallowed, sighed, sat back on her thighs, pushed herself up with her good hand and stood. The front of her sweater was soaked from the slushy surface and her jeans were torn at the knee. She stepped toward the smirking five-year-old, setting one foot securely before moving the next. Abby didn't move and when she got close enough Christine grabbed her wrist.

"C'mon kiddo, let's get inside. It's too cold out here, you'll get sick." Abby twisted and tried to wrench free, but Christine held on until Abby relented and came back inside.

Snowflakes dotted Abby's hair that hung in wet ringlets around her ruddy face, reddened from the cold or perhaps just childlike exuberance. "Let's dry you off. Go get a towel; quick now, go."

"I wanna to go back outside. The boys are out there; why can't I?"

"Because, I came all this way to see you and," she paused and winked at Abby, "I brought you something."

"What, what? Lemme see."

"Not until you're dried off. You better get a move on."

Abby ran down the hall toward the laundry room, "Mommy, Mommy Chrissy brought me something. Hurry, hurry get me a towel."

"What in the world …" Wendy's voice faded out then back. "Abby how many times have I told you, you are not to go outside without a coat. Let's get this wet nightgown off."

"But, Mommy, Chrissy said."

"No, I didn't. Whatever she's saying Wendy, I did not let her go outside." It wouldn't be the first time she'd had to answer to one of Abby's fabrications.

"I know. No worries." Wendy's voice echoed before being drowned out again by the thumping of an out-of-balance washer.

Within minutes Abby bounded down the hall dressed in red tights and shirt, and a plaid jumper; her hair tousled and damp around her face, cheeks rosy, eyes wide; she looked more like a Christmas cherub than burn victim. Though her lips were still swollen, the puckered skin on her forehead and around her nose had softened. "Show me, show me. What did you get me?"

"It's over there in that bag next to my purse. Go ahead."

Abby raced over and tore into the bag. "Oh, thank you so much." She turned to face Christine as part of the contents of the bag fell to the floor. Abby stared at it. "What is it?"

"Open it up."

Abby lifted the lid of the deep rose-colored box and ran her hands lightly across twenty-four triangle shaped crayons.

Christine walked over to her and knelt down. "Lift the tray and look underneath."

Underneath the crayons were markers, glitter, a glue stick, small round-tipped scissors, and a tablet of unicorn stickers.

"Do you like it?"

"Oh, Chrissy, it's the best present ever." Abby picked it up, ran over to her table and said, "Let's draw lots of unicorns."

Abby's favorite stories were about Morgan the unicorn and the lessons he learned because he was different from the other horses. Her parents hoped it would help Abby realize that beauty wasn't what made people special.

She plopped down on a chair, twisted around to face Christine and said, "Will you play this with me?"

"Well, I hope so!"

They spent the next hour drawing, cutting, pasting and creating a glitter house where the unicorns lived protected from the sun, which Abby drew as a blazing red ball with orange rays. There were unicorns hanging out of crudely drawn windows, out of a massive door, and peaking out of the roof.

During the height of their creativity and amidst the chaos of the boys running in and out, Abby's dad, Kurt, came home; a strapping man, with brown hair and wide-set blue eyes like Abby. He bent down for a hug, but his only daughter pushed him away with, "Can't you see I'm playing with Chrissy?"

By 4:15 p.m. the sky had taken on the dusky glow of a late afternoon in winter and it was time for Christine to head back to Lisa's. "Abby, sweetie, I've got to go now, but I'll see you on Christmas Eve. That's just five more days. Do you think maybe you could come to my place?" When Abby didn't answer she continued, "I have paints and colored pencils, and I've even got an easel. It might be fun for you. I live on the beach and Lisa has two boys, one your age. And, I'll have Christmas cookies."

"Boys are gross." She stood up and slipped her hand into Christine's. "But I like cookies."

EIGHTEEN

When Christine had gotten back to the house, Lisa, Gino and the boys were outside wrapping Christmas lights around a tall spruce and the lamppost at the entrance to their driveway.

"Sorry, I know I should have asked, but Abby wouldn't come alone and when I mentioned it to Wendy, she misunderstood." Christine took a breath and followed Lisa around the lamppost where the family had gathered to string outdoor Christmas lights. "And, I'm sorry, but I said Christmas Eve and forgot to say in the morning. Wendy thought I was inviting all of them to our Christmas Eve gathering." She tried to catch Lisa's eye. "Are you mad?" When Lisa didn't answer Christine went on, "I couldn't very well tell her no. Besides, all their family is in California and it's been really tough on them this year."

While Christine talked, Lisa continued to concentrate on the entangled maze of Christmas lights in her hand and barely looked at Christine. Finally she said, "Geez, I just wish you'd asked me first. But, I really wish you hadn't invited them. I've already got Gino's relatives coming, then your parents, sister and family, now I have to add eight more." In frustration, she threw down the string of lights and walked toward Gino who had started up the ladder with an armful of lights. Lisa tugged on the hem of his pants and said, "I need to talk to you."

"What's wrong?" The ladder bounced against the tree as he descended; each step sunk the ladder deeper into the damp soil at the base of the tree. The boys ran around the tree sliding in pools of partially melted snow. As they came upon areas where the snow had turned the soft earth into mud they stomped, trying to send it up each other pant legs. When they succeeded, they'd point and fall to the ground laughing hysterically. Both parents seemed oblivious. When Gino reached the bottom rung of the ladder, he collided with Tony. "Anthony, how many times have I told you not to run? Now, stop it. Look at yourself."

"But Jeremy started it." Tony stifled a smile behind a gloved hand.

Unnoticed, Lisa slipped in next to Tony, rested a hand on his shoulder and shouted, "But you're the oldest; you should know better." Tony jumped and this time it was Gino's turn to stifle a smile.

Gino was a short, robust man who, at his own admission, had accumulated fifty pounds of extra weight during his time as a successful chef and restaurateur in New York. He had to sell the restaurant because of an unknown heart condition. The doctor had told him to lose the weight or sell the restaurant because the combination would kill him before he turned forty. Now he traveled around the world speaking and making guest appearances on various cooking shows.

Their life seemed ideal and at times like this, Christine couldn't help thinking that if it hadn't been for the accident it could have been her and Nick. She shoved the thought aside, picked up the discarded string of lights and busied herself unraveling them; trying not to eavesdrop on Lisa and Gino's conversation.

"It's fine." This time it was her turn to jump. Lisa stood next to her. "Gino just told me only his parents are coming, so bring 'em on!" She smiled, "It's the kid part that sent me into a tailspin. This place isn't set up for fifteen kids. Now we're down to a manageable ten."

Though it didn't sound very manageable to Christine, she said, "Oh, then it won't be that bad."

"No, it won't be, especially since you're going to be in charge of those kids if they misbehave. Your sister's too."

A knot ballooned inside her stomach and she felt like she was going to be sick. "I don't know. I don't think I can do that." How could she? She'd never been comfortable with Meredith's girls, her nieces; two precocious little girls who were always dressed in the latest kids' fashions, their hair perfect even when they went to the store. They were demanding and spoiled. And Abby's brothers? How would she ever corral them?

"Looks like you're going to have to." Lisa must have seen the terror in her face. "Oh, not to worry, you'll do fine. You're only back-up, their parents are in charge."

While it sounded good, Christine knew different. Meredith and Carl were essentially unequipped to be disciplinarians. Her sister followed her mother's style of raising children: Discipline with threats you never follow through on, keep your head in the clouds and give children rights and respect they never give back. Consequently seven-year-old Emily and five-year-old Hannah ran the show.

Lisa winked at her. "You'll be fine." She turned to the boys and Gino and said, "Alright, everyone, it's dark and cold, let's get inside. Anyone want cocoa before dinner?" The boys chased each other up the drive. Lisa yelled after them, "You boys take those boots off before you go in the house. You'll track mud all over the entry." She brushed pine needles off her shoulder and stomped her own boots. "I'll have dinner ready in an hour; you wanna come over?"

"Naw, you guys go ahead."

"You sure? I don't think it's that late. Gino what time is it?"

Gino glanced at his watch, "Six."

He finished winding the lights around the base of the tree, bent over and plugged them into the extension cord. He stood back admiring his handiwork.

"Not bad if I do say so myself." He turned and grinned at Lisa. "What do you say, Ma?"

Lisa blew him a kiss. "Looks awesome. Christine, see you about seven?"

"Thanks, but I've got some leftovers I need to eat, then I'm going to call Anders. I haven't talked to him in days."

"Thought he called yesterday?"

"He did. I was getting out of the shower and I didn't call him back."

"Oh, lovebirds have a spat?"

"We're not." Oh what's the use? "Never mind. We're good."

Together they trudged up the path toward the house. Lisa yelled at the boys not to go inside, and Christine was deep in thought. She and Anders were good, weren't they? She didn't even know. Their recent conversations skimmed along the safe and superficial peripheries of Jake's health, Lotte's preoccupation with the ranch, Peta's fascination with horses and Janice's fascination with Peta. Yet it was Janice's unspoken and, in fairness, only suspected fascination with Anders that plagued her in the moments following each phone call. Janice's presence at the ranch seemed like a daily occurrence: Janice came by to take Peta riding; Janice brought over dinner tonight; Lotte said Janice, … and on it went.

The urgency for her to return to Montana should be mounting; instead she felt herself retreating into the world she now occupied. The spaces in each day that were left empty since leaving Montana were slowly being filled by the seduction of the Cape and the effect it always had on her. Abby's needs had kept her busy and, though she still missed her conversations with Lotte, a renewed friendship with Lisa had become an easy replacement for Donna. Excitement for her new home in Montana, which was being built in her absence, had even waned. Though Anders kept her updated on its progress through e-mail, photos and text messages when they weren't on the phone, it had been difficult to get enthusiastic about the project when she wasn't there. Maybe the less she knew the better. It was easier to believe everything was fine with all of it. Head in the sand, head in the clouds, not facing reality: part of her M.O. too, it seemed.

She reached the darkened portico of the cottage and fumbled in her purse for keys. The easy rumble of the surf this morning had intensified. Christine walked to the edge of the porch and leaned out. White froth heaved forward, thrown toward shore by a distant and invisible force. Yet the sky, with its dearth of clouds and a full moon that laid an illuminated path from horizon to shore, made it hard to believe there was a storm brewing out in the Atlantic. The weather service predicted eight- to ten-inches of snow overnight, and blustery winds. A nor'easter.

The anticipation of a storm made her shiver. She loved storms on the Cape. While other people grumbled about the inconveniences of the inclement weather, she'd take it any day over the hot, humidity of their summers, replete with flies and mosquitoes. Summer seemed eons away.

Her keys weighed heavy in her hand, fingers stiff from the cold. The wind picked up, fanned her hair as breakers crashed on darkened sand. More snow would be nice, a needed distraction. As long as she was able to finish shopping by Saturday it would be fine. She'd overnighted a box of presents to Montana on Monday, but still needed to get gifts for her father and nieces. Christmas was Sunday, a few more days to shop. Plenty of time.

The usual whoosh of warm air that welcomed her when she opened the door to the cottage was absent. She forgot she'd turned down the heat to save energy. She flipped the light switch, tossed keys and purse on the chair. Yesterday's newspaper lay on the hearth, unread; she wadded it up, grabbed kindling and a log, stacking everything on the grate in the small fireplace. She struck the match, curled up in the chair in front of the fireplace and covered up with a blanket. The fire moved from paper to kindling to wood and she had a momentary flash of anxiety before the fire sent a rose glow around the room. A fear of fire, any kind, still plagued her. Though she'd gotten much better this past year, a car with smoke billowing from its engine horrified her. It required deep breathing and focused rational thinking to suppress panic. As heat warmed the room she pushed the blanket to the floor and searched for the phone. It would be late afternoon in Montana. Would Anders even be home? She walked to the French doors that led to the beach, dialed, rested her forehead against the cool glass and stared out at the ocean. As a strong gust sent sea grass dancing down the sand, Anders answered.

"Hey, you." His voice gruff, sent her heart into a tailspin.

Her own voice came out raspy. "Were you asleep?"

"It's four-thirty here. No late afternoon naps for me. How's the Cape?"

She could hear him groan like he was stretching, then yawn. "You were asleep; you're yawning," she said.

"Alright, you caught me. I dozed off while talking to Peta. Oh, oh, looks like she left me here alone." Another yawn. "What's up?"

She straightened, turned around faced the room and leaned her back against the doors. "Just wanted to say hi."

"Hi yourself. I miss you. What the hell are you still doing out there?" He didn't wait for her to answer, "Kidding! I was only teasing you." His voice dropped, "Not that I don't want you to come back soon. But, I'll play nice. What's been going on in your world?"

"I saw Abby again." She sighed, walked back to the fireplace and threw another log on. "I don't know, I think I'm getting through to her, but sometimes I feel pretty ill-equipped." She walked around the room, absently moving pillows from chair to sofa, sitting then rising, before walking into the bedroom and collapsing on the bed.

His response was quick and brusque. "Now why would you think that? You know what she's going through. You're patient and, well, pretty damn hot, if you ask me."

"What in the world does that have to do with anything?"

"C'mon now, you need to lighten up a bit. I can tell by your voice that you are on edge, and I doubt this is all about Abby."

Of course he was right. "Okay, you got me. It does and it doesn't. I invited Abby and her family to Lisa's for Christmas Eve without asking. Lisa got mad and now I'm panicky because they'll all be here, along with my sister, her family and my parents. I don't know what I was thinking."

Saying it aloud made it twice as bad. How was she going to cope? She stood, cradled the phone between ear and neck, slipped out of her jeans and sweater. The bed with its blue and white flannel duvet covered comforter drew her in; she crawled between the matching blue flannel sheets, inched her way down and pulled the covers up to her chin.

"Suddenly I'm feeling overwhelmed. Can I come home?" As soon as the words were out of her mouth she regretted it.

"Nope, won't let you do that." He continued, "Look, I've been thinking about this a lot. You obviously feel you need to be there or you'd be here right now. Or …," he hesitated, "you're not ready to come back for whatever reason. So I decided not to press you about it."

It wasn't the response she'd expected. "But just five minutes ago you …"

"I know, I didn't say I had perfected this new found rationale, but I'm working on it. Really, Christine, I want you here, if you want to be here, but not if you're not ready."

"But my house …"

"Your house will be here. If, you come back."

There was something in his tone that made her uncomfortable, like he was pulling away from her; like he was preparing himself for her not to return. Was this a new tactic of his or had she gone too far by not going back to Montana? "What do you mean if? Of course I'm coming back." Saliva filled the back of her throat and she croaked a response, "I really do miss everyone. It's just harder to let go here than I thought."

"I'm not sure I get that, Christine. You've cut ties with Donna, your friendship with Lisa is new, as is Abby's, and you've hardly seen your parents. So, what do you mean?"

She felt like she was a child caught in a lie. "I can't explain it. I don't know. I guess I feel like I have more to learn. Maybe 'learn' is not the right word, but I feel I'm not finished here."

"Is it Nick? Have you seen him again?" This time Anders voice cracked.

"No, haven't seen him since that day in his driveway. No, it has nothing to do with him, but Anders, this is my home. Maybe I'm scared. One minute I feel like I've got it all together, the memory of the accident has faded and I'm ready to conquer the world. Then I catch my image in the mirror and I feel like I'm suffocating; like I'm locked in the car again and all I want to do is run. Run back to Montana, you, Lotte, Jake, my house. But I realize now that's not the way I want to come back. I want to come back because it's the right thing to do for me. I want to do it from a place of strength, not weakness. Even though I was apprehensive at times, somehow the idea of moving seemed easier when I was out there: buy land, build a house, move my stuff and live out there. It doesn't seem that easy right now, and with the holidays looming, and the anniversary of my accident, the only thing that is keeping me from sinking back into that black hole I was in after the accident is the familiarity of this place and my family—as dysfunctional as they are. And Abby; I really think being with her is helping me."

The silence from the other end of the phone was deafening. Unsure, she plowed on, "I know none of this makes any sense, but I'm really trying to, well, 'fix me.'" She pushed down further into the bed, pulling the blankets over her head. And still he said nothing. "Are you there?"

"Uh, sorry, I'm not sure what to say. I get it. I really do. I hope you figure it out and decide to come back, but I can't wait forever, you know. I've been busy the last month so it hasn't been too difficult, but I do miss you and want us to move forward. It's kind of hard to do that with you there and me here."

First a rush of sadness, then tears filled her eyes. She brushed them away, causing her mascara to sting her eyes which in turn made them water more. She cleared her throat, wiped under her eyes with the sheet and tried to sound upbeat. "Soon; I'll be better soon."

"I'm a fairly patient man, Christine, but ...," he stopped, mumbled something unintelligible and came back on the line. "I've got to get going here. We're taking Jake out to dinner to celebrate his doctor's appointment today. Doc says he's doing really well and can slowly begin his normal activities. They told him his quick recovery has been a miracle of sorts. Christine, hold on, will you?" It sounded like he covered the phone with his hand because all she could hear were a few scattered words, Peta and Janice among them. Peta and Janice, again. She wanted to hang – up.

"I'm back. Bottom line is that I really care about you and your well-being and I'd say you were on the right track to recovery. I'm here for you when you're ready." He hesitated. "But don't take too long. Okay? You're the one who has to figure this out, I can't help you. And, Christine," he paused, "I can't be your crutch; I want to be more than that."

"I'm really trying to come to terms with what happened to me." Her composure, fragile at best, was being held precariously in his hands. If he'd gone on much longer she'd have broken down, instead he'd told her she was on the right track. That small acknowledgement gave her the strength to say, "It's not been easy. I really do care about you in ways I never thought I would. That complicates things for me, too. I find I'm working against myself most of the time."

"You'll do it, I have confidence in you, but I've got to go now. Take care there."

She dropped the phone, relieved the conversation was over.

****

She woke the next morning with an overwhelming feeling something was amiss, a sense that something was off kilter. She rolled to her back, flopped an arm across her eyes to keep the morning out. What was it? Abby had made some revelations, Lisa had gotten mad, but neither of those seemed to be the culprit. Her arm grew cold and she pulled it back under the comforter which did little to warm it or keep the cold from penetrating the rest of her nearly naked body. The room was quiet, no telltale sound of air moving; the heat had not come on yet or she had forgotten to set the automatic thermostat again. The brightness that invaded the bedroom told her that either the sun was out or it had in fact snowed last night. It also told her it was late. The gentle rhythm of the distant surf lulled her. She rolled to one side, curled up and tried to fall back to sleep. Yet something tugged at her memory. Dissecting, then discarding each scenario until she remembered she'd said too much, exposed herself, let Anders in too far.

"Oh, geez," she said and covered her face as if someone was observing. But it was done; there was nothing to do about it now.

The heat kicked on without prompting. With the rush of warm air, Christine kicked off the covers and propelled out of bed, landing in front of the dresser and catching her image in the tall mirror above it. Most mornings she ignored mirrors until it was time to put on make-up; today she confronted her body. Same scarred, but flat, angry stomach; breasts the right size for modeling—not too large, but round enough to accentuate the clothes. She stepped back, rose up on her tiptoes and turned. Derrière firm, no cellulite; legs toned and slightly muscular from the running she used to do. Not bad, but time for a reality check. Her face. Her eyes widened. Was the scar going away? The red and ragged edges had begun to fade. Hands? They were the same. But, her face pleased her this morning. Not only did the scar appear to have softened, the hardness around her eyes and mouth had too. She tossed her head, curls fell forward hiding the scar completely.

"I don't look that bad," she said and smiled. Being back at the Cape worked for her right now.

Children's laughter floated into the room from outside. Christine pulled on sweats and a T-shirt, and walked into the kitchen. The window over the sink had fogged, but she could make out snow—lots of snow. The smell of stale smoke lingered from last night's fire, the stench still so familiar that it unnerved her, but oddly though this morning it also made her think of coffee.

While the coffee brewed, Christine made a bowl of oatmeal, added some frozen fruit, sat at the breakfast bar and flipped on the TV. A local newscaster in Boston reported that eight inches of snow had fallen overnight causing minor traffic accidents. Maybe the snow would keep her parents and Meredith from venturing out and she wouldn't have to worry about seeing them on Christmas Eve. But, it was only Wednesday; by Saturday the roads would be back to normal.

"Hey guys, get away from Christine's. She's probably still asleep." Gino's voice boomed through the stillness.

"But, Dad, we want her to come play with us."

Sounded like Jeremy, but Christine was never sure. She slipped off the stool and grabbed the dusty kitchen towel. She walked to the window, swiped the dampness away and pressed her forehead onto the glass.

"Boo." Jeremy jumped up and peered at her, eyes wide, nose smashed against the outside glass. He turned. "Daddy, Daddy, she's awake." Then to her, "Auntie Chrissy, will you make a snow angel with us? Please, please, please." He clasped hands together in mock prayer and dropped to one knee.

She tugged at the lower part of the window, trying to nudge it open, but it was no use. Years and layers of old paint prevented it from opening. She motioned for Jeremy to go to the front door and tucked herself behind it while letting him in. Frigid air rushed in.

"Quick, get in here, it's freezing out there."

"Hey, wait for me." Tony shoved Jeremy aside and stomped past him.

Both boys were covered in snow; it was obvious they'd begun their snow angel creations without her. Their boots, backsides, even eyelashes were adorned with snow. Their noses crimson, their lips slightly purple.

"C'mon." Jeremy tugged at her arm, teeth chattering. "We need you to be the mom snow angel."

Tony brushed past her and flopped on the wicker chair in front of the fireplace. "I'm cold. Got any hot cocoa?"

Jeremy whined, "No, Tony, I want Chrissy to make a snow angel with us. We need a mom snow angel."

Tony kicked the heels of his boots against the pine floor, dropping clumps of snow on the sisal rug.

"Tony, stop that. Your mother will be furious if you wreck that rug."

Her initial enthusiasm waned. Now the idea of getting bundled up in layers of clothes, only to have Tony kick snow on her wasn't very appealing. She knew nothing of the whims and moods of children and, until she met Abby, had little interest.

"Now tell me boys, why's it necessary for me to be your mom snow angel? Why can't your mom do it?"

Jeremy tugged at his knit cap and pulled it off. Static electricity caused clumps of his blond hair to spike then the hat zapped his cheek. He yelled, dropped the hat and rubbed his face. Frustration got the better of him and, collapsing on the floor, he whimpered, "She can't. She's baking some stupid cake to take to Mrs. Smelly."

Christine bit her lip to stop from smiling. Doris Smidley lived next door and reeked of gin and urine. "That's not a nice thing to say about her. She's old, Jeremy. When you get old you might smell, too."

Tony whooped and pounded his hands on the arms of the chair. "Jeremy's going to smell, Jeremy's going to smell." He stopped his chant to catch his breath.

"Okay, Tony, knock it off. No one's going to smell," Christine said as Jeremy wailed; tears rolled down chubby cheeks, his nose dripped and when he tried to wipe it, mucus smeared from nose to cheeks. He was a mess. Oh, no, what had she gotten herself into? Should have kept the door shut. Better yet, should have stayed in bed.

"Jeremy, stop crying. I'll do it; I'll be your mom snow angel. Just go outside and wait while I get dressed."

He leapt up, wrapped his arms around her legs, and stuttered, "You're the best auntie a boy could have."

"She's not your auntie, Dufus." Tony jumped out of the chair, grabbed Jeremy's hat off the floor and ran out the door.

"Mooommm, Tony took my hat " Jeremy ran outside after him.

A moment's reprieve. They'd be pounding on the door again once the hat issue was resolved. Just in case, she locked the door, sank into the cream colored loveseat, draping her legs over the arm, and grabbed the remote.

The 'visit' from the boys had worn her out. The aftermath of accident still held her energy captive, slowly releasing it at its own speed. The doctors hadn't prepared her for that. It wasn't until she complained to them on the last visit before leaving for Montana that they admitted she might never completely get it back. She hated feeling old when she should be at the prime of her life, even Lotte and Jake had more stamina. She dropped the remote to the floor and closed her eyes.

The mountains of Montana became animated figures: crevices became eyes, nose and mouth, and trees became arms and legs. They were in combat with a sea that had risen. The sea's white foamy surface formed a frothy hat, kelp transformed into limbs that slapped and cut into the mountains strength. The mountain pulled free and tugged at her hand, pulling her back while the sea crashed around her and screamed for her to return. The mountain tugged harder and she relented.

A tiny voice whispered, "Wake-up, Aunt Chrissy." Then soft wet kisses covered her cheek.

"Jeremy? Honey, how'd you get in here?" She slipped her hand from his, lifted both arms over her head and stretched. "What time is it?"

"I dunno. I can't tell time yet, Chrissy, I'm only five. When I'm eight like Tony, then I can tell time." He waddled over to the open door, his snowsuit crackling as he walked, and yelled, "Tony, Aunt Chrissy wants to know what time is it?"

The muted response came back. "Leave me alone; I'm busy."

"Shut the door, Jeremy, will you?" The room had grown cold. Christine sat up and pulled the wool throw around her arms. "How'd you get in here anyway?"

He turned, crestfallen. "Tony said I should use the key under the flower pot. He said you'd want me to. Don't you want me to?"

"Yes, yes it's fine, just close the door; it's freezing in here."

He stepped behind the door, stretched both arms out in front of him, grunted and pushed. It stuck. He pushed again and again.

"Can't do it."

She sighed, tossed the throw on the loveseat and rose. She nudged the door with her hip until it closed completely and turned to Jeremy. "It's fine, but next time your brother tells you to use that key, you tell him Aunt Chrissy says she'll tell your mother if he doesn't stop tormenting you."

"What's torrrrmenting mean?"

"It means he'd better stop. Now take off your boots and sit here." She moved a barstool out and patted it.

Jeremy sat on the floor, tossed his gloves aside and tugged at each boot until it came off. He walked over to the stool and looked at her. "Can you help me up? I'm too little."

She grabbed him under his arms and hoisted him onto the stool. "Now stay there. I'll change and be right back." She hesitated, then walked to the cookie jar, removed a gingerbread cookie and handed it to him.

"Ohhhh, my faborite." His eyes scrunched as he pretended to inspect it. "Did you make it?"

"I sure did. With my very own hands." She ruffled his hair and walked to her room.

She slipped out of her sweats and into jeans, a heavy sweater, and pulled on wool socks. She ran a hand through her hair and decided against wasting time with make-up. It was just the kids after all.

****

"Who's that?" Tony pointed in the direction of the driveway where a male figure walked toward them silhouetted against the trees. The sun had just broken through the clouds and its brightness bounced off the snow causing a blinding reflection, making positive identification impossible.

They were in front of the cottage. Christine lay on the ground, flapping her arms and legs up and down to make a "mommy snow angel" for the fifth time—the boys had insisted. Snow had soaked through her jacket and mixed with the perspiration generated from the minimal exertion it required to make the 'perfect snow angel'. She sat up and squinted. The figure was too slight to be Gino;

maybe Tom from across the street. Halfway up the drive, the shape came into focus.

Oh, shit, it was Nick. Her heart thumped; anxiety flushed through her. "Boys, go tell your mom she has a visitor. Hurry, run." The boys ran toward the house shouting for their mother. Christine stood up, backed up the steps onto the front porch of the cottage and tried to open the door. When it wouldn't budge she thrust her hip into it so hard pain shot through her leg and she yelped.

"Christine, is that you?"

She feigned surprise, "Oh, hey, Nick. Didn't know that was you." She touched her hair and twisted a lock, "What are you doing here? Visiting your parents for the holidays?"

"Actually, I wanted to see you. I heard you were staying at Lisa's. I thought we could catch up."

Her heart beat unnaturally; she backed up against the door until she could go no further. "Ah, sure, but I'm kind of busy right now," she said.

He turned, looked down at her handiwork and back at her. He grinned; his unnaturally white teeth seemed to sparkle. "Yes, I can see that." His dark eyes took her in. He wasn't as tall as Anders, yet his presence always made her feel small. Since their break-up she'd come to realize her attraction to him had been mostly physical, and yet even now she felt herself drifting toward him.

She scoffed, "Oh, that. I was just keeping the boys company while Lisa baked." She eased past him and down the porch steps, putting a safe distance between them. "How've you been?"

"You know you could've talked to me after you nearly ran me over at Thanksgiving. I won't bite." He leapt off the top step and onto the snow, nearly landing on her. He leaned into her. "You look good, Christina Marie. Montana must be good for you."

He'd called her Christina Marie since grade school. The first time he used it they'd been in first grade. She'd stomped her feet and told him that her name was Christine and demanded to know how he knew her middle name anyway? He'd laughed and run away, shouting "Christina Marie." At first he used the name to tease her, later admitting it was the only way he knew to get her attention. Antics of young boys never change. He told her after they started dating that the name suited her better. After that he rarely called her anything else.

She felt her face redden. "Yes, Montana's been good." She dropped her eyes. "I'm moving there; in fact I'm having a house built with the settlement money."

"I heard."

It was one of the things she hated about Gale Harbor—everyone knew everyone's business. "I guess that's no surprise. Who'd you hear it from? My parents, yours, or is it being discussed in every restaurant in town?"

He reached over and flipped hair off her shoulder. "Nope, Donna told me. She told me I should try to stop you, that you are making a big mistake." His eyes locked on hers. "Are you?"

She clenched her teeth and said, "Actually, Nick, I don't think that's any of your business. In fact, anything to do with me stopped being your concern when you called off our wedding."

"Maybe I made a mistake."

Now she was pissed. "Maybe? Ya think? Doesn't matter now. I've seen who you are and I've moved on."

"Hi, you two." Lisa walked out of the kitchen door, boys in tow. "Hi Nick, heard you were back on the Cape. How are your parents?"

"Lisa." Nick acknowledged her with a nod.

"Why don't you two come inside where it's warm; I've made some cocoa for the boys. Want some?"

"Not sure Christina Marie would like it if I stayed. I'll jet. Good seeing you." He nodded at both of them and walked back down the drive.

"Damn it why should I feel guilty? He's the one who broke up with me." Christine bit her lip. "I hate it. Why didn't he stay in Boston?"

"How'd he know you were here?" Lisa reached out and touched her arm.

"Donna told him."

"Oh." Lisa dropped her eyes. "That figures."

"What do you mean? I didn't know they stayed in touch." Odd. Donna always said Nick was trouble.

Lisa shifted. "It's nothing; they both live in Boston. It makes sense that they'd talk to each other." She wrapped her arm through Christine's. "Enough of the past. You were always too good for him anyway." Lisa pulled her toward the house, "Let's get inside where it's warm."

NINETEEN

By Friday everything had returned to normal. The roads were clear, planes on time and Nick's visit an unwelcome memory. If the encounter burst into her consciousness, she closed the door. She didn't mention it to Anders the next time they talked and, every time Lisa asked her about it, she brushed her aside. "He's not important to me anymore."

The stores at Hyannis Center were packed with last minute shoppers. In front of Macy's, a massive Fraser fir stood draped in gold ribbon, gold glass ornaments and tiny fairies figures dressed in glittery attire. Christmas music blared. A long line of weary parents and screaming children waited to see Santa. Swarms of people rushed in different directions, bumping into each other without so much as a "sorry." Tempers were short and one man screamed at another because he had accidently knocked against a child.

Christine's anxiety over what gift to get her father made her as short tempered as everyone else. His betrayal still fresh, she'd spent three hours wandering from store to store. Finally at Macy's she bought dresses for her nieces and was about to give up and put cash in a card for him when she walked into the book store and, after finding books for her nieces and Lisa's boys, bought her father a book about self-made millionaires. She gathered her bags and walked toward the exit, while *We Wish You a Merry Christmas* echoed through the mall. Done, except to have everything wrapped by noon tomorrow for the gathering at Lisa's. Only one more day of tranquility before the holiday gaiety would erupt and a façade of family happiness would have to be erected. There was also the issue of Christmas Day at her parents' where she was expected for dinner. Spending Christmas Eve with them would be enough. She planned on feigning food poisoning or a migraine for Christmas Day.

The mall parking lot was chaotic and she was nearly hit twice walking to the car. Christine clicked the opener on Lisa's key ring and loaded the purchases into the trunk. Turned out Lisa's late model blue Mercedes was an extra car and when Christine moved in Lisa gave her the keys and said, "She's all yours. Just brush the crumbs off the seats, fill 'er with gas and she's ready to go."

Christine inched out of the parking spot just as a woman, loaded with packages, rushed behind her. Christine slammed on the brakes, missing the woman by inches. The woman, oblivious to the fact she'd almost lost her life two days before Christmas, hurried to her car. As Christine drove by, the woman turned, stared, and then began frantically waving. It was Lois, Nick's mother. Shit.

Christine reluctantly rolled down the window. "Hi, Lois. How are you?"

Lois rushed over. "Oh, darling, how are you?" She pushed her head in the window and kissed Christine on both cheeks. "I've so meant to call you, sweetie, but my goodness the time has truly flown."

"No worries, Lois, I've been out-of-state."

"Yes, yes I know, Nick told me. He was right, too, darling, you do look wonderful. Come see us, okay?" She backed away chattering.

"Sure, will do." Christine started to close the window when Lois ran back.

"Wait, wait. I'm having a small gathering tonight. Please come. You can't say no. Be there at seven for cocktails, dinner to follow. Ta, ta darling. I'll tell Jane you're coming. She has news to tell you."

She hadn't thought of Nick's younger sister in months. Jane had gotten married last spring right after Nick called off their wedding. Christine hadn't been able to bring herself to attend Jane's. "No worries, girl," Jane said when Christine called. "I know you wish me well and if I were you I wouldn't want to see my brother either. Heck, I don't even want to invite him to the wedding, but, you know, he's family and all."

****

Christine mentioned Lois' invitation to Lisa later that afternoon as they were wrapping presents in the cottage.

"Go. He can't hurt you anymore. You need to get out. Staying in every day isn't healthy."

"I go out to see Abby. Besides it's winter—brrr." She shivered. "Too cold to go out."

"Who are you kidding? You like winter."

"But …"

"Go to the damn party. If you need protection, I'll go with you."

That made her feel like a child. "No, I'll go by myself. I've known them all my life. I'm being silly."

"Since we're talking about you being silly." She stared at Christine. "What's the real reason you're still here and not in Montana? I know you said it's because Donna kicked you out, and because you want to be with family during the holidays, which is a crock because I know how you feel about them. It's not Abby. You've only known her a few weeks. Tell me, Ms. Scaredy Pants, why?"

It was nearly five o'clock, they were on their second Cosmopolitan and the liquor had taken effect. Christine tied a ribbon on the last present, leaned her back against the front of the loveseat and closed her eyes. "It's complicated." When she opened them, Lisa was staring at her.

"That's a copout." Lisa grabbed Christine's glass and said, "Another?"

"Sure. They're in the fridge, already mixed. Just pour, m'dear, just pour." Christine stared into the fire. It was complicated, wasn't it? There was nothing simple about her situation.

Lisa came back into the room, stood over her and handed her the refilled glass. "Hello. You still there?"

"Sorry, I was thinking about how to answer your question."

She took the glass and set it on the trunk that served as a coffee table. "Actually," she glanced at Lisa, "I'm not sure how, or even if, I want to answer."

"Well." Lisa flopped down beside her and held out her glass for a toast. "Let's start with this. Come on, clink me."

Christine did as she was told. "Now what?"

"Let's drink to, say, Anders. You'll drink to him, won't you?" She leaned over and peered at Christine, green eyes boring into Christine's.

"Sure, I'll drink to him." Christine raised her glass, lightly touched Lisa's and blurted, "To Anders, the best guy I've never slept with. Guess I should qualify that one: haven't slept with since the accident."

"Whoa, TMI. But, what the heck, if you want to share, I say share!"

She wasn't sure why, but sitting here with Lisa and discussing Anders seemed right. Lisa wouldn't judge her; wouldn't jump to conclusions and might even give her some sound advice. Something she sorely needed.

She dipped a finger into the pink liquid, swirled it around and took a sip. "I think I might be in love with him." There she said it and now that she heard it, it terrified her. With love came commitment, then exposure both emotionally and physically and it came with Lotte, Jake and now Peta.

"Good for you; now we're getting somewhere. And …?" When Christine didn't respond, Lisa asked, "Loving him is a good thing, right? From everything you've said about him, he's a really good guy."

Anders' image emerged; standing, leaning against the fireplace, hands tucked in jean pockets, legs crossed and smiling. He seemed to be saying, "Now what are you going to say?"

She cleared the image and said, "I've not had good luck with love in the past. Not with my family or friends. I give, at least I think I give, but I don't get it back. If you know what I mean."

Lisa gazed into her drink and said, "Okay, girl, time for the truth. Can you take it?"

She had a pretty good idea of what was to come. Could she take it? She dug her nails into her palms. "Hit me with your best shot."

"First, yes, you're a good person." Lisa shifted and faced Christine. "But … you weren't always. Or you hid it. You may think you gave, but sweetie, for a long time you took more than you gave—from your friends, from your sister and from both your parents."

"But …"

"Now wait, I'm not done. You were selfish, self-absorbed, vain and judgmental." Lisa took a breath. "But, you're not that person now. I can see that."

"You sure that's it? You don't want to add to that list of wonderful qualities?" She knew Lisa was right, but it hurt just the same.

"All right then, I said too much … but you said you could take it." Lisa rested her head on Christine's shoulder and patted her hand. "You didn't deserve to go through what you did, but I think it made you nicer. Maybe it made you think about what is important and what's not?"

Tears flooded Christine's eyes, slowly slipped down her cheeks and plopped into her lap. She tried to speak, but it came out garbled.

Lisa grabbed her shoulders and hugged her. "Oh, no, oh no, I didn't mean to make your cry. I'm so, so sorry."

Christine waved a hand, took a deep breath and tried to talk. "It's okay, really." She wiped each eye. "You're right; I know you are. I've had to take a hard look at myself and …" Tears filled her eyes again, her voice quivered, "I don't want to be that person anymore."

The front door opened, "What's going on in here? You guys can't have this much fun without me." Gino stepped around the love seat and stood above them. His face reddened, "Oops, sorry. Havin' girl talk about us useless guys?"

"Nope," Christine said. "We're talking about how useless I've been." She pushed up from the floor and offered a hand to Lisa, helped her up and kissed her on the cheek. "You're a good friend."

Christine walked to Gino and hugged him, "Thanks for sharing her. And, Gino," she stepped back and looked at him, "thank you for letting me stay here. I know it hasn't been easy, but I appreciate it."

Gino reached for his wife's hand and pulled Lisa close. "Yes, I'm a lucky man." He kissed her then turned to Christine. "As for you staying here, it's been my pleasure."

Lisa's eyes searched Christine's. "I'm really sorry. Are you going to be okay?"

Oddly she felt fine. "I'm a bit lightheaded, but I think that has something to do with those." She pointed to the empty glasses lying on their side and the minute pink stain on the rug next to them. Undeniable evidence drinks had been consumed.

"C'mon, Mom, let's go see your boys. They're tearing the place apart." Gino pulled Lisa toward the door.

She resisted. "You go on; I'll be right there."

"I'll wait." Gino stood in the door. "You go ahead, I won't listen."

Lisa walked back to Christine. "You still going to Nick's?"

"Oh, no, what time is it?" The kitchen clock read 5:48. "You bet I am." She wiped her eyes, "I've got some fences to mend with Jane. She tried to connect with me after Nick and I broke up and I ignored her. The nice Christine is revved up and ready to go."

"You can't drive, though; you've had too much to drink. Gino can drive you."

"Lisa, it's four houses away. I'll walk. You worry too much."

"But it's freezing out there."

She grabbed Lisa by the shoulders, turned her around and pushed her toward Gino. "Take her home." Lisa hesitated. Christine pointed at the door. "Go."

The door had barely closed when Christine dropped into a chair, grabbed a pillow and buried her face in it, trying to clear her head. Thoughts spilled, falling and tumbling, into the haze of vodka, the past and the future. The phone rang in the bedroom, she let it ring. She looked around the room. It would be very easy to just stay here. These four walls had become her protector; the shell that held her after Donna disappointed her. Everything she would ever need was in this cottage, and in the sea. Her renewed friendship with Lisa, mentoring Abby and even little Tony and Jeremy had become like her own family. She lifted her head and leaned it against the plush back cushion, trying to imagine life without Anders, without Montana. The air, the mountains, the sky still lingered in her heart. Maybe that is what Miller meant; maybe Montana was the beauty, the light in the heart. If she was honest, she needed it, and she needed Anders.

She tossed the pillow aside, walked into the bathroom, stripped off clothes and showered. Excitement fused with apprehension— happy about seeing Jane, almost paralyzing fear of seeing Nick. After shaving her legs, Christine stepped out of the shower, wrapped in a towel and stood in front of the mirror. She ran a hand towel briskly over her hair. A mass of shoulder length curls covered her face. After the accident she'd lost interest in her appearance, letting the hair do whatever it wanted, only trimming split ends. She opened the cabinet door under the sink, took out the hair dryer and brush and began drying her hair; drawing each section through the wire brush until all curl disappeared and each strand fell sleek and shiny. The effect was very different; without curl her hair reached a few inches below her shoulders.

What would bangs look like? She lifted a section of hair, raised it up, and swooped it across her forehead—not bad. It was done before she had time to think. Snip—and a thick section of hair dropped into the sink. She evened up the new bangs and tossed her head. The effect was good. Still, it needed something. Christine took a side section and ran the scissors, in a razor like motion, down the side like she'd seen hairdressers do with other clients. Wisps of hair drifted into the sink, the rest fell lightly onto her cheek, partially covering the scar. Then she did the same to the other side and stood back. She felt giddy. It looked good. She looked good.

She slipped on panties and a bra, and walked to the closet. Most of her clothes were in Montana or packed away, ready for shipping. Sweats, jeans, one pair of wool slacks, a couple sweaters and blouses, and one black dress for the holidays were the only garments left. She slipped the dress off the hanger and stepped into it. It fell into place, hugging her body and accentuating each new curve; curves that two years ago would have sent her into a panic with a panacea of crash dieting and purging.

The black strappy shoes, 'borrowed' from a fashion show, were perfect; luckily she and Abby had painted their toenails during a visit. She glanced at the clock on the dresser 6:45 p.m.—still time to put on make-up, lotion on her legs and walk to Nick's.

The deep violet eye shadow made her eyes look sultry; when she added eyeliner and thickened her lashes with mascara the result pleased her. She dabbed concealer on her scar, then finished with foundation and a light dusting of powder. Her heart raced; she did look good. She twirled in front of the full length mirror on the back of the bedroom door. The dress floated high above her thighs, only a bit of scarring visible. It would be all right if she kept the dress down. Her hands … there was nothing to do about them. Instead of hiding them she decorated them with two of her grandmother's antique rings she carried in her purse, and a bracelet Anders had given her. It would feel good to have a bit of him with her.

She grabbed her coat from the hall tree and opened the door. A rush of cold air filled the doorway and along with it a momentary sense of foreboding. She walked into the night air and left the old Christine behind.

TWENTY

Christine stood at the end of the driveway to Nick's house, her earlier confidence diminishing. The two-story blazed with activity, a single candle illuminated each of the twenty plus windows. Snow fell, collecting on the ground and sprinkling her hair with moisture. She pulled the hood of the coat over her head and kicked snow off both shoes, cursing herself for not wearing boots. Her toes felt frozen. She stared at the house, willing it to give her an answer: Go in or go home? The staggeringly beautiful three-acre waterfront estate with a light dusting of snow looked like a Christmas card. The setting always made her feel insignificant. She'd often wondered why Nick and his family were nice to a girl who lived in a modest three-bedroom that used to be government housing.

Voices and music drifted, and drew her in. She submitted, shoving her hands into pockets she put her head down and inched forward, teetering on stiletto heels just as a car entered the drive.

"What's the matter? Afraid you'll get eaten alive in there?" Nick's face scowled at her through the open window.

"Hi. Uh, no, I was ..."

He cut her off, "Relax, I'm only messing with you. Get in. I'll drive you to the door." He reached over to the passenger side of the silver Mercedes coupe and swung the door open.

"Don't be ridiculous, it's right there. I can walk."

"Not in those shoes you can't. Get in."

"Nick, I'm walking." She moved away from the car and started toward the house.

"Suit yourself." He slammed the door, gunned the engine, and raced up the drive.

"Idiot," she said to no one.

She moved back onto the driveway; unsteady and knees wobbly, she was determined not to fall. Her eyes focused on the ground until she reached the other cars. When she looked up Nick was staring at her, a bag of ice in each hand.

"Nice job. Bet you hated it when your legs wobbled."

"They didn't, but thanks for your undying support." Same old Nick. Jerk.

He grabbed an elbow. She pulled away. "Relax," he said, "I'm not going to kiss you or anything."

"Don't flatter yourself, that was the furthest thing from my mind," she lied.

"Look, Christina Marie." He dropped the bags of ice and put his hands on her shoulders. "You don't always have to be so confrontational; I'm not your enemy. We loved each other once, shouldn't that mean something?"

She covered his hands with hers and slid them off her shoulders. "It did to me. Apparently not to you though." He looked hurt, she felt guilty. "Come on, stop pouting."

"That's more like it." He grabbed her hand and opened the front door, yelling, "The beautiful Christina Marie is here; the party can begin."

She stepped inside, tugged at the hood of her coat and let it slip down.

"My, oh my, look at you," Nick said. He stared. "You look marvelous, daaahling, marvelous." He took the coat and hung it in the entry closet, then turned, his eyes sliding over her body. "Seriously, you look incredible. That dress is very sexy, my dear. Who are you trying to impress anyway?"

She didn't dare look at him; instead she rubbed both hands together, and gazed around the elaborate entryway. Nothing had changed; it was massive and gauche. Compared to the entryway at the ranch, which was warm and inviting, it left her cold. She peered into the living room filled with guests.

"Christine!" Jane rushed through the crowd and hugged her. "Good lord, he's right, you do look incredible. I love your hair." Jane reached over and touched it. "What have you done to it?"

Christine, blushed, looked down and started to answer, then burst out, "Look at me? Look at you! Is that a baby bump I see?"

As soon as the words were out, she thought, Oh, please let it be true. Jane always had a problem with weight.

Jane grabbed Christine's hand and rested it on her belly. "Yes, isn't it wonderful? Here, feel him, he's moving right now."

Jane's skin rolled under the pressure, Christine quickly pulled it away. The sensation always made her queasy. When Meredith was pregnant with the girls, she made fun of Christine saying, "What do you think is in there? Some alien?"

"I told you she had a surprise." Lois swooped in, drink in one hand, dragging her husband with the other. "Dick, dear, come say hello to our Christine."

Dick dear responded, "She's not our Christine anymore, Lois."

Christine went in to give him a hug and he intercepted her with a cool handshake. "My goodness, Dick, give her a hug, she was almost family," Lois said.

"Nice to see you again, Christine. You're looking well." Then Dick turned and walked back to the other guests.

"Never mind him. He's grumpy today; some case he's working on has got him all in a dither." Lois tucked Christine's hand under her arm and maneuvered her into the room. "Everyone, for those of you who don't know her, this is Christine McMurray—she was almost our daughter-in-law until our son made a stupid decision." Then she turned to glare at Nick, who had disappeared.

Christine smiled and gave everyone a quick wave. Inside she was screaming. Lois leaned over and whispered, "You mingle, dear, I have to have a word with my staff." She left Christine standing alone in the middle of the crammed room; clusters of people she didn't know, and some who looked familiar, stared at her. When she met their gaze they turned to each other and began talking again. She scanned the room hoping to find Jane, instead inadvertently caught the eye of one of Christine's mother's friends.

"Goodness, Christine, you are looking much better. Your scar is almost completely gone. Now let me see those hands." She took Christine's hands, inspected them and said, "Well you can work on those and I'll bet in no time they'll be fine." She dropped her hands and said, "How is your mother doing? I see her at bridge, but she seemed distressed last time. I think you were in town then and having some difficulties. Everything fixed?" She smiled and took a sip of her drink.

Nick appeared at her side. "I'm sure everything's fine, Dottie. Why don't you let Christine alone, so I can get her a drink." He wrapped his arm around Christine's waist and led her into the kitchen. "What a bitch. I never liked that woman. Don't know what our mothers see in her."

The kitchen was empty except for a few staff cooking at one of the two commercial stoves. The center island was laden with dozens of extra unopened bottles of liquor, wine and mix.

"Geez, do you think you have enough booze?" Christine said.

"You know Mother; she'd die if we ran out. It'd be all over Gale Harbor by tomorrow and by Friday she'd be getting calls from people who assumed we were destitute."

Red glasses in all shapes and sizes were showcased in an open antique cabinet; Nick went to take a wine glass down, stopped and instead asked, "Forgot, you're a martini girl. Still drink them?"

"Sure."

"How about a dirty one?" He winked at her.

She ignored the inference. "Thanks, but I prefer vodka, without olive juice, and a couple of cocktail onions."

"Oh, I see your tastes have changed. Must be the company of those Montana cowboys I hear you keep. Sure you don't wanna beer, little filly?" He slapped his knee then nudged her shoulder.

"Never knew you had such a keen sense of humor." She nudged him back.

He picked up a small silver shaker, measured out vodka and a drop of vermouth, shook it and walked to the freezer. He took a chilled martini glass, set it in front of her, raised the shaker high above the glass and poured, not spilling a drop, then skewered two onions and laid them in the glass.

"I see your bartending skills have improved. The last time you tried that you spilled it all over my dress."

"The last time I tried that I was drunk."

He filled his own glass with scotch and moved to the small corner breakfast booth, beckoning her.

She sat opposite him. "Here's to you," he said and raised his glass. She lightly touched his and took a sip.

Vodka warmed her throat and she relaxed. "I think that's the best martini I've had in a very long time. Been practicing?"

He shrugged and set his glass on the table. "Owning a bar in the Back Bay made me hone my mixology skills."

"How's that going for you? I heard the bar is very popular with the celebrities." After they broke up she heard he purchased an old warehouse and converted it into an upscale bar and dance club.

"It's good. In fact we're expanding." When she didn't ask what he meant, he said, "I'm opening a smaller version in Hyannis. I'm looking at some places a week from Tuesday. Want to come with me?"

She ignored the question. "That's great; I'm glad you found something you enjoy."

"You are, huh?" He waited for an answer; again, she ignored him so he continued. "Yeah, who'd have thought after all those years I struggled through law school and studied to pass the bar that I'd wind up as a bartender."

"But you passed the bar. Aren't you still in practice with your father's firm?"

"I stay current, but I don't practice. He's not very happy about it, but what the fuck. It's not his life."

Nick picked up his glass, stood and stretched. He could have been a model: dark, wavy hair, deep brown eyes, high cheekbones, full lips. Images from the past flooded her mind—Nick naked and erect, standing over her. Her body responded involuntarily; she shifted and swept the memory away.

"I look pretty good, huh?" He smiled at her, "You had that old look on your face. I know you pretty well, you know."

"No, I was, uh, admiring your clothes." They fit him like they were tailor-made, and probably were. The grey trousers sat low on his hips and the camel sweater bulged slightly over his biceps. "But to answer your question, yes, Nick, you look good."

He smiled, obviously pleased. "Well, what did you expect? I always look good." He bent down and picked up her hand. "Shall we?"

He led her into the empty dining room and waved his arm around. "She's gone a bit overboard this time, but with Lois … well, you know."

The staff was putting the final touches on the table. Seven tiny Christmas trees ran down the center. The place settings were the same ones Lois had used for their engagement party: gold chargers, white plates edged in gold, gold silverware and antique crystal glasses rimmed in gold. Christine walked around the long table lightly touching the Irish linen tablecloth that had been Nick's great-grandmother's. She counted twenty-three chairs.

"After she invited you she realized she had an odd number and freaked out. You know how she is." Nick rolled his eyes. "She's seated you next to me. I hope that doesn't freak *you* out." He searched her face. "I'll behave."

"Sure you will." She took another sip of the martini, winked at him and immediately regretted it.

Before he could react, Jane saved her. "There you are. I've been looking all over the darn place. I see my brother has stolen you away."

"Not really, but he was kind enough to get me a drink and whisk me away from Dottie. For that I'm grateful." She tried to keep her tone light, disconnected.

"Then you won't mind if I tear you away from him and we can catch up?" Jane looked at both of them.

Christine said, "That would be nice. I've missed you."

Jane turned to Nick. "All right with you?"

"Be my guest." He lightly brushed Christine's arm. "See you at dinner."

Nick's had touch created an unwanted tingling through her body and she wanted to get as much distance from him as she could. She quickly followed Jane upstairs. They went to the second floor entertainment room; the one on the first floor was occupied by guests watching Sullivan Christmas movies. "Yes, scenes of Christmas past. They all look the same. Lois is drunk, Dad is scowling, Nick is posing and I'm fat!"

"Stop it; you were never fat."

They flopped down on the massive taupe sectional. Jane rubbed her hand over the linen fabric, thoughtful. "Dad's trying to talk Mom into media chairs, but she's having none of it." She leaned back against cushions. "Of course I was fat, especially compared to you and Donna and the rest of that anorexic group. And being Nick Sullivan's younger sister didn't help."

Growing up, Jane had little of the Sullivan good looks. Nick inherited his father's dark wavy hair, Jane's mousy brown hair hung limp, always looking as if it needed a good scrubbing. Now Jane's hair was cut into short layers that fringed a narrower face, blond highlights brightened her hair. Her pale complexion had always burned easily; as she grew redder in the summer sun, Nick's skin bronzed. Nick was lean and muscular. As a child and adolescent, Jane had been a bit chunky, but the nicest one in the family and Christine had missed her.

"You look good, Jane; you look happy."

"I am. Chuck's a great guy and he doesn't care how I look."

Christine touched her hand. "I still feel guilty about missing your wedding. It was too soon after the break up. I wasn't up for it. I know that's selfish, and I was, but it's been a tough two years."

"Is it two years already? I can't believe it, it seems like yesterday that Nick called me—he was hysterical, you know. He was sure you were dead."

Christine cringed; Jane reached out and touched her arm. "Sorry. I can see it still upsets you."

Christine sighed. "Yes, the memory never quite leaves me and when it does, all it takes is someone like Dottie to remind me." She touched her face. Had the concealer worn off?

"You're still beautiful, Christine. You can still turn a head. All the men in the room tonight—even the old ones—took a long look and it wasn't your scars they were looking at. I think Nick is sorry he broke it off, you know. Now more than ever."

"Why do you say that?"

"Nick has changed some. He's not as callous as he used to be. Dad's been really hard on him since he bought the bar. That's affected him." She paused. "He's not dating anyone you know."

"But I am, Jane, and Nick really hurt me. I don't think I can ever forgive him."

"I understand." Jane kicked off her shoes, rubbed her toes and tucked her legs underneath her.

They chatted, catching up on all the gossip, Christine telling her about Lotte and Jake, but mentioning Anders only once. The call to dinner came just as Jane tried to pry more information out of her.

They started downstairs, but midway Christine stopped and said, "Jane, I am sorry I wasn't nice to you in high school. I wasn't the best person and I'm sorry I didn't return your calls after Nick broke it off. It was too hard. I really do miss talking to you."

Jane touched her arm. "We'll have to make sure we keep in touch. Promise?"

"Promise."

When they reached the dining room most of the guests were seated including Nick who jumped up and pulled out a chair. "You two catch up? Should my ears be burning?" He smiled and tweaked her nose.

"No, I think your ears are safe, my nose on the other hand …" She sat, unfolded the napkin and set it on her lap, averting his eyes.

"Here, I made you another martini." Before she could say no he slid it in front of her.

"Not trying to get me drunk, are you?"

"Who, me? Never."

He winked at her and in that moment, she saw the old Nick: the player, the charmer, the womanizer. She'd need to be careful.

But, she wasn't.

After she finished the second martini, a third appeared and once she had the first sip of the Sauvignon Blanc which was served with the baby artichoke and arugula salad, her glass was never empty.

With each course a new wine appeared. A sommelier, hired for the night, told them about the grape, what their nose should tell them about the bouquet and how their palettes should respond with the first sip. After she finished the second glass, each wine smelled, tasted and reacted the same to her untrained and sated palette.

The Chardonnay they served with the potato leek soup and the " … oaky, full-bodied" California Cabernet they poured for the entrée all slid down her throat, barely touching her tongue. While her appetite for food lessened, she managed to finish all the wine, including the 50-year-old port they served with dessert.

Her head ached, conversation became almost impossible. Nick kept taking her hand. She kept pulling it away. Finally, he announced that he was taking her home. When she tried to tell him she was fine, the words jumbled together and made no sense. The other guests smiled politely and nodded.

Jane got her coat, wrapped it around her and said, "It's okay, honey, everyone knows this was hard for you."

"Not so much," she slurred. "It's been a barrel of laughs." Then she giggled.

Christine and Nick stepped out the front door into the pristine air. The snow had stopped, the sky was clear and filled with stars. She stumbled down the porch steps and fell against Nick.

He steadied her and said, "Let's drive; you're in no shape to walk." Then he laughed realizing how funny it sounded.

He looked incredibly cute. "Nope, I'm walking," she said and faltered as she tried to go around him.

"Then you're taking off those shoes and I'm getting you some boots. Stay here."

She gave up, sat on the bottom step and rested her head in both hands, drifting off until she woke with a start when Nick removed one of the shoes.

"Here we go. Not very stylish, but at least you won't fall off them. How'd you get your feet into those things anyway? I thought you hurt them in the accident."

She leaned forward, rested her forehead on his shoulder. "Hurt my leg. It doesn't hold me up sometimes." Then she scowled. "Nice of you to remember."

"No fighting now, let's go."

"But how would you have known? You only visited me what—maybe three times?"

His voice grew angry. "Knock it off, Chrissy, I was there more than that."

They reached the end of the drive before she answered, "Really? Because I don't recall it that way. Did you ever meet Miller? Cuz Miller was there almost every day and Anders, hell, even he was there more than you, and he lives in Montana. He's sweet, you know?"

They turned right toward Lisa's and after a few steps Nick stopped. He tightened his arm around her and tried to turn her face toward him, but she resisted. He said, "I'm sorry."

She pulled away. "Keep walking." But the feeling of his fingertips lightly pressing into her waist chipped away her resolve.

"I couldn't stand to see you in such pain; it killed me." He stopped again, his eyes pleading.

"I said keep walking."A car turned into the road toward them, its headlights flooded their eyes and she squinted. It passed, honking at them.

"Fuck off, you ass hole," Nick yelled.

"Fuck off yourself, dick head," the driver yelled back and sped down the road.

The exchange gave her momentary clarity and all the memories of the break-up rushed back. "How about when I got out of the hospital? For days, you never called. Then what? I hardly saw you the next year. Too busy getting your practice going, you said. It'll be different when we're married is the way you put it. I had to plan the wedding completely on my own while I was still trying to come to grips with what had happened to me. I should have seen it then."

"Seen what?"

"That you were done. Then, two fucking months before the wedding, you call and ask me to go to the beach with you. I thought finally we'd have some time. Instead, it was to call it all off."

They'd reached her front door and he pulled her close, his mouth open, ready to go in for the kiss. Her anger slipped away and she leaned into him. His lips were cold from the night, but familiar. His tongue slid around the inside of her mouth. He pulled back and lightly sucked on her upper lip, a move that in the past always excited her. It had the same effect now. She pressed her body into his. His slid hands down her arms and began unbuttoning her coat. His hands familiar, explored her body, touching her in places that hadn't been touched since the accident.

"Let's go inside," he whispered. "I need you."

She tried to move out of his grasp, her mind in conflict with her body, but his arms tightened, pulling her closer. "Let me go. I can't."

Something wasn't right; Anders face emerged where Nick's should be. Yet, a part of her longed to give in to Nick, to feel desired by the man who had rejected her.

He murmured in her ear, "C'mon Christina Marie, I know you want to." She stiffened and pushed him away. His eyes glazed, questioning. "You can't still be mad about Donna?"

What was he talking about? Donna?

He sighed. "I know. I'm sorry." He released her and leaned back against the porch railing.

She stumbled backwards. He reached out to steady her, grabbing both arms to keep her upright. She stared at him. "Why would I be mad about Donna? She was my friend."

"Never mind, I thought you were pissed." He encircled her waist again, pulling her to him, his lips close to her ear. "We were both crazy worried about you. We were reeling from the accident and how bad you were hurt. It meant nothing; it was just sex. Something to keep our minds off your situation."

"My situation? I damn near died!" Then it registered. "And what do you mean about you and Donna? What was just sex?"

He looked stunned. "Nothing, it was nothing. I thought you knew."

"What the fuck are you talking about?" It hit her full force. "You slept with Donna while I was in the hospital?" She was screaming now. "You fucking asshole." She fumbled in her purse for the key, shoved him away, but before she could get it in the door he was on her. Grabbing, pleading.

"Please. Look, I said it was nothing. Donna's a cunt. She's not your friend."

The keys dropped, tears stung and she choked, "Get away from me."

"Damn it, hold on. It was hard to look at you like that and I needed comfort. It just happened. You understand."

"I understand all right. I understand that you are an egotistical maniac and I'm glad, really glad, you and I are no longer together. Now let go of me." She twisted away from him, opened the door and slammed it shut on his foot. "Get the fuck away from me." When he wouldn't leave she leaned against the door, crushing his foot.

"Then get the damn door off my foot," he said.

When she opened the door slightly so he could remove it, he pushed his body against it preventing her from closing it. He smirked. "You'll always be alone, you know. With scars like that no one will want you." His eyes grew cold and he spewed, "Your dad told me about the chance you're passing up. Your chance to get back into the game. We could have been famous, you and I. A team. Now you'll be nothing but an angry, bitter, has been. You and that cowboy deserve each other."

He bumped his body against the door so she flew backward into the room. He started toward her then stopped. "You're not worth it." He abruptly turned, slammed the door and left.

For the second time tonight she dropped into the chair and crushed the pillow to her face. This time she sobbed uncontrollably, taking in large gulps of air until she felt sick. Her stomach turned and she barely made it to the bathroom; vomiting wine, food, martinis, and a whole lot of bullshit.

****

She woke the next morning, still in the bathroom, curled up on the rug in front of the toilet, head pounding. Someone was beating on the front door and yelling her name.

"What?" she rasped, her voice hoarse from crying, drinking, and heaving all night.

"It's me. Let me in or I'll use the hide-a-key," Lisa said.

"Gimme a minute."

"You've got one minute, then I'm coming in."

Christine got up slowly, she smoothed her dress, washed her face, and went into the living room. She opened the door and Lisa fell inside. "Geez, you could have warned me before you opened it."

Christine bent over and tried to help Lisa up. The room spun. "I've got to sit down; I feel terrible."

"I figured. We heard you yelling at Nick last night. You sounded pretty drunk. What happened?" Lisa followed her, and sat next to her on the love seat. "Well?"

"I'm an idiot, that's what happened. I drank too much, let my ex-fiancé walk me home and discovered my best friend and my fiancé slept together while I was near death. I'm an idiot because I was drawn to him again, thinking he wanted me when all he wanted was to be in a movie with a freak, so he could be famous. I'm an idiot for still being here and not in Montana. There. That enough info for you?"

"Don't take your frustration out on me, sister. I'm on your side." Lisa got up and walked to the kitchen. "Want some tea? Or coffee? How about aspirin, have you taken any?"

Her head pulsated. "Yes, no and no."

"Tea's good, not coffee and you've not had any aspirin. Do you want any?"

She watched Lisa fill two mugs with water and put them in the microwave. "Don't have any. I take ibuprofen. You know what, Lisa, never mind. I deserve this."

"Oh, now we're going to be the martyr, huh? Look, girl, in …," Lisa glanced at her watch, "in less than six hours, I'm going to have a house full and you promised to help. Where's the ibuprofen?"

"It's in the bathroom." Christine stretched out on the loveseat, rolled to her side and drew her knees to her chest. "Oh, no, how am I going to manage that?" She sat up and immediately regretted it. "Lisa, really, my bad leg is aching, and … Lisa? Are you listening to me?"

Lisa walked out of the bedroom, stood in the doorway arms crossed, frowning. "No, you don't. You're not going to play the 'I almost died, and my leg is still hurting' card on me. You're going to get in that shower then you're going to help me."

"He slept with Donna." There, she said it again; she waited for the tears, but none came. "Lisa, did you hear me?"

Lisa walked to the sink and filled a glass with water, came back and handed it to her along with the pills and said, "I know. Well, I didn't really *know* but I suspected. Everyone suspected, Christine."

Everyone suspected? "How? When? Where?"

"Don't know. I do kinda know the when. It was a week or so after we heard about the accident. I was in town and saw Nick and Donna coming out of Bertoletti's. She had her arm in a sling." Lisa stared out the window as if trying to remember. "It's closed now, you know, and I hear Nick might buy it." She stopped. "Geez, the kids are outside without coats."

"And?" Christine waved her hand in front of Lisa's face.

"Okay, okay. Donna and Nick were huggy and she was leaning on him. When they got to his car, he helped her in and they kissed. Not a quick peck and not on the cheek—a long intimate, 'we're sleeping together' kiss. Then they saw me and left. Others saw them together after that, but we all pretended like it didn't mean anything. I ran into him a couple times weeks later, but neither of us mentioned it."

It made sense now. He thought she knew—he figured Lisa had told her.

Lisa touched her hand. "I'm sorry you found out; I'm sorry it was true. I didn't think it was my place to tell you and I didn't know for sure."

"I should have figured something like that happened. Donna was really weird after the accident, but I'd hoped she was feeling guilty. Should have known better. Donna never feels guilty about anything."

"What did you mean about the movie thing?"

"Something he said when he was leaving. He'd talked to my dad. I guess Dad told him about the movie thing that never materialized. Fame was always a big thing to Nick. Never realized how much he and my dad are alike. Now I do." Christine stood up, stretched and rolled her head from side to side. "Hmm, I think I'm better."

"I thought you were upset?"

"I am, at myself. He's not worth it; neither is she. I let him kiss me—and I wanted more. I'm upset about that." She glanced at Lisa.

Lisa shrugged. "He's hot for sure. I can see why. How'd it feel?" She linked her arm through Christine's. "Gimme the juicy details. This old married woman needs some good ol' horny gossip once in a while."

"It felt like I was about to slip into an illicit affair. That's when I stopped. Really; all I could think about was how I wished it was Anders. 'Course then he hit me with the Donna thing and I lost it. Sorry if I woke you guys."

"No worries; as long as you're fine and willing to help me today." She pleaded, "I really need it."

"I'll jump in the shower and be over in thirty-minutes."

"Wear sweats," Lisa yelled as she left, "you'll be getting dirty. The house is a mess."

The water was cold. She didn't wait for it to warm up, penance for being an idiot. She wondered what Nick was thinking right now. She'd told Lisa the truth, but there had been moments last night when she'd wanted him—badly. The water slowly warmed; she let it run into her mouth, over her hair and down her stomach. She lathered soap on her body and let hands linger between her legs; slowly rubbing until she became aroused. She'd felt the subtle throbbing for weeks, but had ignored it; last night had been too much. She thought of Nick, then of Anders; she pinched her nipples and rubbed herself until she felt the explosion, then the release. She'd purged Nick—she felt cleansed.

TWENTY-ONE

"Aunt Chrissy, how'd you get that scar on your face? Mommy said we shouldn't talk about it, but I think it's okay now that you're my auntie. Don't you?" Jeremy squeaked out the question while Christmas music blared in the next room and families made polite conversation.

Christine had escaped to the kitchen with Jeremy, Tony and Abby to make them hot cocoa. Abby wore an adorable red velvet Christmas dress with large satin green bow her mother had found at a consignment store. The boys were dressed in little black suits with red plaid vests. The three looked up at her now—eyes fixated on her face, waiting for an answer to Jeremy's question.

"Little boy, that's a terrible thing to ask someone." They all turned. Christine's mother stood in the doorway, glaring at Jeremy whose lower lip quivered.

Christine knelt down and hugged him. "You pay no attention to her, she's just …" She wanted to say a mean angry woman, but instead said, "She's just trying to protect me, sweetie, but she forgets I don't need protection anymore." She winked at him. "I'm a big girl now." She rose, glowered at her mother.

"But, dear I was only trying. Oh forget it, you never understand me." She pouted and when Christine didn't react, she said, "Well, at least give me something to do."

"Here." Christine handed her a plate of Christmas cookies. "Why don't you pass these around?"

"Certainly, dear." She walked out.

"All right, kids, come here and I'll tell you. What happened was …" She started to explain that what happened to Abby had also happened to her, but in a different way.

Before she could finish Abby's youngest brother ran in, followed by Meredith's daughters. It was too much. She bent down and whispered to the other three, "I'll tell you about it after grumpy Audrey and grumpier Boyd leave. Okay? It'll be our secret." They nodded.

Christine's parents had been driving her crazy all night. Her father continually yelled at the kids to stop running, stop laughing, and stop talking. When he wasn't doing that, he cornered her, trying to talk her out of moving to Montana, coaxing her with all kinds of future modeling possibilities. Each time he brought it up, she cut him off. It became a game. Frustrated, she turned the tables, and confronted him about the sketches.

Focusing her anger on her parents made it easier to forget the encounter with Nick. Lisa said Nick had been calling the house all day asking for Christine's cell number, but Lisa said she told him to get a life.

The microwave dinged. Three cups of hot water were ready for cocoa, but the kids had run into the living room where Gino, dressed as Santa, had begun handing out gifts.

"Get in here, we're opening presents." Meredith appeared in the kitchen and pushed Christine into the other room.

It was quite a scene: nine children sat under the Christmas tree, legs crossed, hands in their laps, whispering to each other. Max, Abby's oldest brother, had said he was too old for "this kind of stuff" so he stayed home, but the others were awestruck. Gino called out names, but before he'd hand over a gift he'd say, "Now wait. Were you good? Because if you weren't I'll have to give this to someone else?" After the first two, the kids didn't even wait for him to ask, just blurted out, "Yes, Santa, I was good."

Meredith turned to her and said, "You know the part they're not saying is, 'Now gimme the present."

The ritual continued until there was only one gift left. Gino grabbed it, turned over the name tag and yelled, "Where's Andy?"

The youngest of Abby's brothers stood up. "Me, me I'm Andy and I've been the bestest boy." Everyone laughed.

Later while the kids were playing with their new gifts and everyone was sipping coffee and making small talk, Meredith touched Christine's hand. "How are you?"

Meredith's concern surprised Christine. True, she'd been upset about the accident, but once it was a certainty that Christine would live, Meredith rarely visited her.

"I'm good. Really good actually," Christine said.

Meredith smiled. "I'm glad."

"Say it looks like the parents and grandparents have this well in hand," Christine said. "Want to see where I'm staying?"

"Sure, I'd like that if I can slip away without the kids and Carl noticing. You go first then I'll follow."

"I'm going to leave through the kitchen—there's a mud room with a door to the back yard. My place is a few yards from the edge of the breakfront … in case they stop you before you catch up with me."

"Oh, I'm going no matter what. I've had enough merriment, and enough of those two." She pointed to their parents. Then she made circles with her finger next to her temple and mouthed one word: "Crazy."

Christine slipped out. By the time she got to the mud room and started down the outside steps, Meredith was close behind. Giggling like two school girls who had pulled a prank on their teacher, the two ran to the cottage. Christine opened the door and Meredith said, "Chrissy, it's beautiful. How can you leave this?"

"Well, let me show you." She pulled out her digital camera and showed Meredith pictures of the ranch and Anders.

"I see now why you want to get back there soon. He's pretty cute. But is he nice to you, Chrissy?" Meredith had never liked Nick.

Christine ran her finger over the picture, "Yes, sis, he's very nice to me. I don't deserve how nice he is to me."

Meredith wrapped her arms around Christine. "Of course you deserve it; you've been through hell."

Tears filled her eyes, but she moved out of Meredith's grasp. "You want to see the rest of the cottage?"

As they walked around the rest of the cottage Meredith said, "This is perfect. I'd love my own little place one of these days.

You know, a place to hide, read, sleep … whatever. Think Lisa will let me come here after you go?"

"Of course she will, but is everything alright with you guys?"

"Things are much better for Carl and me, but Mom and Dad are driving me crazy. They constantly criticize the girls. Dad especially—if they eat too much or if their hair isn't perfect. How did you stand it? He's a real nut case and she's no better. I get sick of hearing 'Now, Meredith, he's your father, you need to show him some respect.' Ridiculous; like he ever showed me any. Respect? He never even knew I was around. It was all about you." She took a breath. "Sorry; I know it wasn't your fault but I got tired of Christine this and Christine that. I hated you most of the time, and I'm sorry for that."

Meredith ignored Christine most of their childhood. The more attention she got, the more Meredith had shunned her. Her sister's sudden unburdening was unsettling. Christine didn't know how to respond, so she said the same thing she'd said to Lisa and Jane, "I'm sorry. I know I was a bitch myself and pretty self-absorbed. It must have been hard for you to have me as your sister." The tears began again and this time she let them fall down her cheeks. "I love you, M. We missed a lot not having each other to lean on. Do you think we can start over?"

Meredith's eyes were red. She took Christine's hand and stroked it. "Yes, please let's start over. Even if I was jealous at times and hated how much attention Dad paid to you, I was terrified we were going to lose you after the accident."

They sat together for a while, sharing happier stories of their childhood until Meredith said, "We'd better get back or Mom and Dad will kill us."

As it turned out, their parents had left and asked Carl to remind Christine that Christmas dinner was at two sharp and not to be late. "And, they were upset that their two daughters weren't here to say good-bye," Carl said.

"Maybe they should have waited for us. I'm sure if we'd left without saying good-bye to them they'd never let us forget it," Meredith said.

"Did Abby and her family leave, too?" Christine peered around the room.

Lisa raised her eyebrows and grinned. "Yes, that was interesting. They had to get the kids to bed and said to tell you thank you for inviting them. I told them they were welcome on your behalf."

Christine squealed, "No, you didn't!"

"Is that an inside joke?" Meredith asked.

Christine explained how she'd invited Abby and family to Lisa's without asking, and Lisa hadn't been too happy about it.

"It turned out fine. They're great little kids. Abby's a doll. Even with all the work she's had to endure on her face, she seems like a happy child," Lisa said.

Meredith put on her coat and said, "I'll see you tomorrow." When Christine didn't answer, she said, "You have to. Please, really. I can't go through that alone. Besides, we've a lot to catch up on."

Lisa leaned over to Meredith and whispered, "Yes, you two do; especially after what happened last night."

Christine glared at Lisa and put her finger to her lips, but Meredith said, "Yes, that's right. I heard you went over to the Sullivan's. How'd that go?"

"Later, Meredith. Right now you'd better get going." Christine gave her a gentle shove toward the door.

Gino's parents left soon after that. With everyone gone, Lisa sank into the sofa, Christine next to her. They stared at the room. Crumpled wrapping paper littered the carpet, dirty plates and cups cluttered the coffee table.

Lisa pointed at Gino. "You get the boys. Christine and I will clean up."

"Come on, boys. Time for a bath and bed," Gino said.

"But, Dad, it's Christmas," Jeremy whined.

"Yes it is, little buddy, but if you don't get to bed Santa won't come." Gino winked at the girls and nudged the boys up the stairs.

"Well, that went really well. You outdid yourself," Christine said.

"It's really nothing. It was easy, for the most part."

"Sure, and I've got a bridge …"

"Really. Okay I cheated. I ordered all the food months ago and Gino picked it up today. But, I did need your help. If you hadn't helped with the kids, nothing would be clean and we'd still be in our pajamas. By the way, you look happy."

It was surprising how good she felt. Earlier in the day Gino had given her a Bloody Mary, telling her that it was his homemade remedy. "You'll be fine," he'd said. "Works every time." And, it had.

She and Lisa cleaned up the living room and when they were finished Christine looped her arm around Lisa's waist and led her into the kitchen where she made Lisa sit.

"What are you doing? I've got this mess to clean up." Lisa started to rise, but Christine gently pushed her down.

"Nope; you're staying right here. I'm cleaning and we can chat at the same time. Gino's taking care of the boys, you just sit and relax."

All the dishes were stacked on the center island. Christine set to work scraping and rinsing before setting them in the dishwasher.

"You win; I'm exhausted. I can't imagine how beat I'd be if I'd cooked, too. I don't know how some of these women do it all."

"Most of the time they don't—they have help. Remember, most of our friends had housekeepers, nannies, and cooks. It's still that way. Don't beat yourself up about it. Everyone had a wonderful time."

"Why'd you and Meredith leave?"

Christine shifted; her leg had begun to ache. "I offered to show her the cottage and we had a sister moment." She twisted around to look at Lisa. "We've never had one of those."

"Oh, come on, you can't be serious. All sisters have at least one of those moments."

Christine sighed. "Not us. She hated me growing up, and later I hated her."

"Naw, I'm sure she didn't hate you."

"She did; she told me tonight. But we're good. We both had some apologizing to do. I think we've forged a new relationship. Too bad I'll be leaving soon." She rubbed her shoulder and rotated her head to try to loosen the tightness. "Oh, and by the way, that little comment about telling her what happened last night—not funny. I don't even want to remember it myself, let alone talk about it."

A groan, then a guttural sound drifted over to the sink. Christine jerked around, afraid some animal had gotten in, and found Lisa slumped over the table, head on her arms, mouth open, snoring loudly.

By 9:30 p.m. Christine finished cleaning the kitchen and went to pick up any leftover dishes from the other two rooms. She bent over to pick up a sweater that one of Meredith's girls had forgotten and saw movement outside. Someone was walking to her place. Nick. She ducked next to the sofa, put her head down and held her breath.

"What the heck are you doing?" Gino asked as he walked down the stairs.

Christine shushed him and whispered, "If he knocks on your door; I'm not here and you don't know where I am, okay?"

Gino said, "Sure, but you can get up now; he can't see you. He's got his back to us."

She crept into the hall bathroom and hid in the dark until Gino came in.

"He's gone. Didn't bother to knock on our door. Good thing. I wouldn't have lied for you."

Nice guy, she thought and scowled at him.

"I'm kidding. But you'll need to face him again one of these days." He raised his eyebrows and shook his head. "Seriously, you did nothing wrong. Maybe got a little drunk, but he's the jerk."

Great, he knows, Lisa told him. "True, but I almost let that jerk in my life again."

"Knowing you these last few months, I doubt that you'd have done that. You're much stronger than the Christine Lisa told me about." He punched her upper arm 'guy style.'

"Ouch, that hurt," she lied.

He tilted his head and mocked her. "Boo hoo, boo hoo, that huuurt."

"By the way, your wifey's out cold in the kitchen. You need help getting her upstairs?"

"With these guns?" He pulled up his sleeve and flexed. "She's all mine."

"Thanks for a nice evening." She gave him a peck on the cheek. "You're a nice guy; Lisa's lucky."

****

The glider on the cottage's rear patio responded easily to the slight backward movement of her torso; Christine pushed harder and it swung past the edge of the patio, thumping as it slammed back. The only illumination came from the moon shimmering on the sea and a bedside lamp she'd left on inside the cottage. Its light tumbled through the cut-outs in the eyelet curtain, casting tiny dots of white on the ground outside. It had been a long day. Truth be told, even with Gino's 'remedy' she still felt slightly nauseous.

With the sea gentle and the air still, she was tempted to strip and run into the ocean to clear her head. She'd delayed going inside, hoping to savor the happiness she'd felt after talking to Meredith, then Gino. A brisk breeze shot off the water; she took a deep breath and tightened her coat. Something hard hit the concrete, making her jump. She looked down; her phone skipped from patio to sand. It must have fallen off her lap. She'd been waiting for the right moment to call Anders, debating whether to tell him about Nick. Another gust of wind sent grains of sand swirling over the phone; she took that as a sign that the time wasn't right. Yet she longed to hear his voice and to tell him about her night, her conversations with Meredith and Gino. Her dilemma: if she told him what Gino said, then she'd have to tell him about Nick. Her confidence lagged. Another gust and the sand cleared away. "Okay, okay, I get it." She bent over and picked up the phone, brushed it off and dialed.

"Merry Christmas." Anders voice, deep and confident, reached into her heart.

It affected her to the point of tears, but she took a deep breath, and said, "And a happy, merry, wonderful Christmas to you."

"Hey, there, Cape Cod, how you doing? I was hoping you'd call. I didn't want to interrupt your dinner party at Lisa's. That was tonight, right?"

She was breathing normally again, her heart had stopped thumping. "Yes, it was tonight. It was wonderful, Anders. Wish you could have been here. Is this a good time to talk?"

"Yep. Sitting on the porch all by my lonesome. Everyone's fed and happy. Lotte and Jake have gone for a short walk. She's been adamant about his exercise routine. Peta's watching some reality show, though I don't know what could possibly be on TV on Christmas Eve. And the guys have scattered. Shoot." He paused, then said, "I miss you."

Her heart did it again. "I miss you, too. How's my house coming along?"

"The weather's been really mild since you left. They've been able to do a lot. I've been over there every day making sure they are sticking to the plans. Outside walls are up, roof is on, and the siding is going on. Most of the interior walls are sheetrocked and they've started putting the river rock on the fireplace. I guess that bonus for an early completion you dangled in front of the contractor worked."

"Really? Wow, I had no idea. Send more photos, pleeeease." Her voice squeaked. "I guess I should start picking out paint colors. Could I do that here and send them to you?"

"Make sure we can get them here. No fancy manufacturers or I'll have to have to go into Billings. Well, what have you been doing? Any sketches or painting? How are your parents?"

She filled him in, but left out anything about the previous night and gave him an abbreviated version of her conversation with Gino. "I'm supposed to go to my parents for Christmas dinner tomorrow. I was going to try to get out of it, but Meredith said she'd kill me if I did. It'll be nice to have a sister to talk to for once in my life."

The wind picked up; a bank of clouds erased the stars. She leaned her head back, watched the clouds race across the sky then closed her eyes. Eventually Anders' voice faded into her subconscious until her phone began beeping. She sat up and pulled the phone from her ear, afraid Nick was calling. Instead her battery was running low.

"Anders?" She cut him off mid-sentence. "I've got to go; the phone's going dead. Will you call me tomorrow night? And, please wish Lotte, Jake ..." she hesitated, "Peta and Janice too, a Merry Christmas."

"Well, honey, I won't be seeing Janice, but I'll tell the rest of them. Take care now and enjoy the time with your parents and sister."

Guilt lingered long after she hung up. She should have told him about Nick. He probably would have understood. But she wasn't so sure. Even she didn't understand.

TWENTY-TWO

January 18th—Cape Cod

Christine stared at the calendar. The second anniversary of the accident was just two days away. The nightmares had returned along with a nagging unease that spilled over into each day. She grabbed the calendar page marked January and ripped it off, wishing she could do the same with the days ahead.

Three weeks of constant anxiety had begun sometime after midnight on December thirty-first, manifesting itself with subtleties that at first she wrote off as 'after the holiday blues,' then later blamed on a lingering guilt over Nick. Luckily, he'd gone away, but not without trying to reconnect by leaving a short note wedged in the door sometime on New Year's Eve. It had fallen to her feet the next morning when she stepped outside. He'd written: "Sorry about the other night. I wasn't myself. I'll be at Bertoletti's on Tuesday at ten. I think we might buy the place. Meet me there, or I could pick you up." And he left his number. She'd torn it into tiny pieces and let the wind take them.

For awhile after that, the puzzling sense of foreboding dissipated. When it surged back a few days later, she convinced herself it had to do with the ten days of brutal winter weather. Snowstorm after snowstorm lined up, pummeling them so badly that for four days they couldn't get out of the driveway. Constant bouts of nausea and headaches made her feel like jumping off a bridge. When those symptoms didn't go away after the snow melted, she feared it was something more serious until Lisa provided clarity with a short statement: "Look at the calendar, silly. The anniversary of the accident is this month." Lucidity should have brought relief. Instead, other fears surfaced; she tried to push them away by ignoring them. When that didn't work, she called the doctor who suggested breathing and visualization exercises. He offered anti-anxiety medication, but she refused.

Dulling all emotion wasn't the answer so when angst incapacitated her, she visualized sitting at her favorite spot on Forest Beach with a soft breeze and the gentle lap of the surf.

Today the fears were overwhelming. She decided to make fantasy a reality. She loaded a sketchbook and pencils in the car, told Lisa she was heading to Forest Beach and would be back later. The weather was supposed to be sunny, with a warm-up into the low forties, a perfect winter beach day and, since it was Wednesday, the beach would be deserted.

Christine traveled on Route 28 and turned onto Forest Beach Road, a residential neighborhood filled with a mix of new and old Cape Cod houses. Narrow lanes led to enclaves of weather worn homes that were designed to look that way; architecture unique to the Cape. A right turn up the hill would take her past homes of high school friends—many with unobstructed views of the Atlantic. To the left along a private road were four or five estates with expansive manicured lawns and back yards that butted against the sea.

At the end of Forest Beach Road, a sand swept parking lot led to a short jetty jutting into the sea; a spot where she sometimes set up her easel. Today it was too breezy on the point, so she set up farther back at the edge of the sand where it gave way to tall sea grass. With her back to the sea, she sketched the driftwood fence that leaned to the left and tilted precariously forward, woven together with rusted wire. Small dunes rose up behind it, cast in a pink glow from the sun that periodically peeked out from its cloud cover. A shore bird landed on one of the fence posts. Christine quickly sketched it on the lower corner of the paper, hoping to include it in a painting later. Her mind relaxed and captured each nuance of the scene. The earlier apprehension floated away as the sound of the surf soothed and eventually reassured her.

Winter on the Cape had its own allure: the nearly monochromatic grey, the dearth of tourists and the reassuring silence. She slipped the finished drawing into her bag and turned to enjoy the ocean. A sailboat, not far from shore, full sail, braved the winter sea, rocking and slamming through the waves. Without hesitation, she pulled out another blank page and sketched it, feeling strong and significant. When finished, she took a blanket out of the car and spread it on the sand. Just as she lay down, her cell phone rang.

"Where are you?" Lisa said.

"I told you, I'm at Forest Beach."

"Well, I need your help."

"Lisa, I've finally relaxed. What's so important?"

"Look, I've got to go. Just get here as soon as you can."

Another calamity no doubt. While Christine had come to love being with Lisa and the boys, and would be forever grateful, she wouldn't miss the drama that seemed to occur every day. Reluctantly, she packed up her blanket and easel and drove back.

When she got to Lisa's there was a car in the driveway she didn't recognize. She trudged toward the front door, feeling apprehensive again. Before reaching the first step, the front door opened and Anders stood there grinning at her. "Well, hello there, Miss Cape Cod, where you been?"

"What … ? Oh, my, what are you doing here?" She scurried up the steps and wrapped her arms around him.

"Now that's the kind of welcome I like." He hugged her tight and they went inside. He paused in the entry and held her at arm's length. "Let me take a look at you. My goodness, you look wonderful." His eyes widened, "What'd you do to your hair?"

"You like?" She twirled, not very nimbly, in front of him. As she came full circle, a slightly built teenage girl with short, cropped dark hair and Anders' eyes stepped out from the kitchen.

"Hi, Christine, I'm Peta." She extended a trembling hand, eyes downcast.

Christine's emotions ran the gamut, from elation at Anders arrival to confusion at Peta's appearance. Anger, frustration, suspicion, and jealousy finally gave way to acceptance.

"Nice to meet you Peta. I've heard a lot about you." She leaned over to hug her and they bumped heads. Both laughed.

Anders laughed too before wrapping his arms around Christine again and whispered, "I missed you."

She turned to face him and, even with Peta watching, kissed him. "I've missed you too. How'd you manage to pull this off?"

He tucked his hand into hers. "Lisa …"

"Oh, Lisa had something to do with this." Christine grabbed his arm and pulled him toward the kitchen, figuring that's where Lisa was holed up. "You come too, Peta." They entered the kitchen, but it was empty. "Lisa where are you?"

Anders said, "She was here a minute ago."

"Coming down." Lisa yelled from the back stairway that was once used by servants. "I'm up here."

Anders stepped back and smirked. "Were you surprised?" He lightly touched her cheek.

"Of course I was. Why …, I mean what, are you doing here anyway? I thought you had an assignment this month."

"I do. I'm assigned to you for the next four days." His voice grew serious. "I couldn't let you go through your second anniversary alone. I knew your anxiety wasn't getting any better. I called Lisa last week and she told me. We conspired to do this. Didn't we, Lisa?"

Lisa skipped down the last step. "We sure did. Bet you had no idea, did you?"

"None." Christine shook a finger at Lisa. "How'd you ever keep this secret?"

Lisa shrugged. "I'll never tell."

Christine turned to Anders and Peta, "She's the worst at keeping secrets, just ask Gino." Her joy turned to confusion, then concern as she began to wonder about sleeping arrangements. "Where are you guys staying?"

"Lisa was kind enough to offer me her guest room. I told her we'd find a hotel, but she insisted."

"Peta can stay with me." Christine said and looked at Peta, "That okay with you?"

"Sure."

Lisa said, "Great. Now that that is decided, how 'bout some lunch? I've made chili and sandwiches."

****

"What was I supposed to do? We're not sleeping together; I couldn't very well invite him to share my bed, could I? Even if I did, with Peta here, it wouldn't have worked." Anders and Peta had gone out to the car to get their bags and Christine had cornered Lisa.

"Hmm, that does make it difficult." She poked Christine in the shoulder. "Glad I don't have to figure it out."

"Thanks, you're a real help." She peeked into the living room to make sure they were still outside. "Well, how'd he sound when you offered him the guest room? Did he say he'd rather stay with me?" Christine awash with conflicting emotions, chewed her fingernails.

"No, he was adamant about the hotel until I told him he had no choice but to stay here. He never mentioned staying at the cottage, and neither did I."

The front door opened and Peta tumbled in with a small suitcase and backpack, Anders not far behind with an oversized duffel bag. "We travel light, huh, Peta."

Peta managed a short, "Uh, huh."

Anders walked into the kitchen. "Now, Lisa, where's that guest bedroom of yours?"

"It's at the back of the kitchen. Used to be maid's quarters; even has its own bathroom. You should be fine. And, oh, it has a private entrance and is a stone's throw from the cottage."

Peta rolled her suitcase into the kitchen and asked, "Where do I go?"

Christine glanced at Anders and said, "Here we go, Peta, I'll show you."

Anders grabbed his bag and followed Lisa. "You girls go on; I'll put my stuff away and meet you back here." Anders turned to Lisa. "Next to the kitchen? Works for me. I love raiding the refrigerator late at night."

Christine led Peta along the path to the cottage. "You wanna share the bed? It's a king and has plenty of room for both of us."

When Peta didn't answer, she quickly added, "Or, you can have the loveseat—it makes into a bed."

Peta shrugged. "Whatever. I can sleep on anything, even the floor." She stumbled on a brick and almost fell.

Christine grabbed her elbow and held her up. "I think we're going to get along just fine—I trip on that same one all the time."

All the nervousness of the last thirty-minutes fell away and she was excited to have both of them with her. The anniversary of her accident didn't loom as large.

She emptied a dresser drawer for Peta, showed her the shower and gave her a towel. "You can shower if you like. I'll meet you back at the house. Do you need anything else?" Peta shook her head and quietly closed the bathroom door.

Anders was sitting on a stool at the breakfast bar eating a tuna sandwich and a bowl of chili when Christine walked in.

"Sorry. Lisa made me eat. She'd already fixed me a bowl of chili and insisted I eat before it got cold. Your sandwiches are in the fridge, and there's more chili on the stove. Lisa's gone to pick up the boys."

Christine walked over to him, rested her chin on his shoulder and wrapped her arms around his neck. She kissed his ear and whispered, "I'm happy you're here."

He turned around and said, "Aren't we in an affectionate mood. You really must have missed me." He pulled her to him. "I hope you don't mind that I brought Peta with me. She's been pretty lonely."

She hesitated then said, "I guess I minded at first, or maybe just surprised, but now I'm glad. It'll be fun to get to know her since I assume she'll be a big part of your life." She grinned at him. "And, since I will, then she should be a big part of mine"

"That's what I like to hear. I was beginning to wonder about you, you know. Out here surrounded by everything you know; your parents, friends, …" he hesitated, turned, and took another bite of his sandwich, "and Nick."

She answered quickly, maybe too quickly. "Nick's in Boston."

Anders gave her a pensive look and gulped his milk. "But have you seen him?"

Guilt prickled at the back of her neck. "I've run into him a couple times. He's nothing to me; for that matter neither is Donna. I've found out that she's not such a good friend." She swallowed. "She did leave me stranded without a place to live."

He stood, picked up his dishes, rinsed and put them in the dishwasher. "You don't have to sell me on Donna; I never really liked her." He frowned. "Aren't you going to eat?"

"I'll eat while you shower." She gave him a playful shove. "You smell like you've been traveling for eight hours … oh, wait, that's right, you have."

He strode toward her, arms outstretched like Frankenstein. "Come here, my little darling, let me give you a big bear hug."

"We're back. You guys still here?" Lisa yelled and walked in the kitchen, the boys on her heels, chasing each other. "Whoa, boys, come here I want you to meet Mr. …?" She put her finger over her mouth. "Ya know, I don't even know your last name."

"It's Larsson. Hi, young men." Anders walked over to the boys and extended a hand to Jeremy. "You must be Jeremy. My name's Anders." Jeremy's eyes widened and he nodded.

Anders strolled into the living room where Tony had gone to sit. "That's makes you the man of the house; Tony, right?"

Tony scowled and folded his arms across his chest. "I'm Anthony and my dad's the man of the house; I'm the boy of the house."

"Okay, then, 'boy of the house.' I'm Anders. Nice to meet you."

Reluctantly Tony unfolded his arms and shook his hand. Jeremy ran up to them and jumped between them. "Are you a real cowboy? Do you ride a horse? Do you have a gun? 'Cause my mom says guns are bad even if you use them to hunt—it's still killing and that's bad."

"All right, Jeremy, let's leave Anders alone now. Both of you go to your rooms and clean them up. You were supposed to do that this morning. Scoot." Lisa shooed them up the stairs and followed. "I'll be right back." She poked her head over the railing, "No fooling around while I'm gone."

"Anders?" Peta's meek voice came from the kitchen.

"In here. Never mind, stay there, we're coming back in."

They walked arm-in-arm into the kitchen where Anders kissed Christine lightly on the cheek and turned to Peta. "This here woman thinks I need a shower. What do you think Miss Peta?"

Peta giggled and pinched her nose. "I think she's right."

Anders moved toward her in monster gait then stopped short and went into the guest room.

"He's lame." But Peta was smiling.

"Are you hungry? Lisa made tuna sandwiches for us and chili," Christine said.

"Sure. Just a sandwich, though. Chili makes me ..." Peta blushed. "Makes my stomach hurt."

"Me, too." Christine took two sandwiches out of the fridge, put them on plates and asked, "How about some chips? We have wonderful potato chips here on Cape Cod."

Peta accepted the plate and sat down. Christine wondered if she would ever get Peta to say more than a few words.

****

"What shall we do?" Christine asked.

Anders rose from the loveseat, walked to the French doors and stared at the ocean. "It is spectacular here; I can see why it's been difficult for you to leave."

They were in the cottage. Lisa, Gino and the boys had gone into Boston for the night to return some Christmas gifts. Peta still said little, mainly giving one word responses when asked a question.

Christine turned to Peta, "What would you like to do? We could go to the beach; it's cold, but beautiful. We could sit on my patio, but it's kind of fun to see the other beaches on the Cape. We could go to P'town. Or, I could take you out to Abby's farm.

What'd ya think?" She could see Peta was uncertain, so she looked at Anders.

"It all sounds good to me, but how about we go to Abby's? I'd love to meet her and it's the shortest drive, right? I don't think Peta and I are up for the long drive to P'town and we have the beach right here."

"Is that okay with you, Peta?" Christine asked.

Peta muttered, "Sure."

Anders said, "Will they mind if we come along?"

"Let me call Wendy to make sure; then we'll head out."

****

Christine drove slowly, pointing out sights and giving them more background on Abby and her parents.

"Are her scars bad?" Peta asked.

"They're getting better. Kind of like mine."

Peta shifted in the backseat and murmured, "Your scar hardly shows, Christine, and your hands look real nice."

Christine glanced at Anders and smiled. "Thanks, Peta. I think they're getting better, too."

She hoped the inner scars were too, but during the last hour the turmoil had returned. She wasn't sure if it was due to Peta being there, the anniversary in two days or guilt because she hadn't told Anders about Nick.

The driveway up to the Madison farmhouse was devoid of the usual obstacles. A snowmobile and snow blower were the only two pieces of equipment still sitting outside.

Christine stopped the car and honked. Wendy came out to greet them as they stepped out of the car.

"You must be Anders. Christine's told me a lot about you. I'm Wendy." She gave Anders a quick hug and looked over at Peta. "And who might this be?"

Anders said, "This is Peta, my sister. She's come with me. We're here to make sure Christine doesn't forget us."

"Perfect timing, too, I'd say." Christine and Wendy had many discussions about anniversary demons. Wendy motioned to them. "Come on in."

Anders reached for Christine's hand, leaned down and put his lips to her ear. "She's heard a lot about me, huh? You've been talking about me, eh?"

She flushed. "Shush, now, behave."

As soon as they stepped inside, Abby flung open the closet door and yelled, "Boo. Bet you thought I was with my dad. The boys had to go with him to fix the fence that Max ran into with the car—he's grounded, but I'm not. I get to stay here with Mom. It's just us girls."

Earlier when Christine called, Wendy told her the boys would be with their father fixing one of the horse fences. They had begun boarding horses to earn some income while he was out of work. It had been so successful that the farm was at capacity.

"Does that mean I have to go outside with the boys?" Anders looked hurt. When Abby grew silent he said, "I'd rather stay here with you girls. I'll bet it's more fun."

Wendy laughed. "Well I'm not too sure about that. Abigail, come out of that closet and say hello to Anders and his sister Peta." While Abby fought her way out of the closet crammed with coats and shoes, Wendy said, "Is it okay if she calls you Anders? We're not too formal around here?"

"Of course." Then Anders dropped to one knee and said, "Hello, Abby, I'm Anders, Christine's friend, and this is my sister, Peta."

Abby raised her hands to her face and fiddled with her lips. "Peta. That's a funny name."

Wendy said, "Abby, you apologize. That's not very nice."

"It's okay, Mrs. Madison, everybody says that. Hello, Abby, nice to meet you."

"Abby, why don't you show everyone the new picture you painted." Wendy turned to Christine. "She's been drawing the horses, and drawing more horses. I can't get her to draw anything else, but then she loves doing it. I figure what's the harm."

Abby grabbed Peta's hand and pulled her to the play area, rummaged through some pieces of paper on the kids' table until she found one. "See. It's kind of bad, but Mom says I'm getting better at it. Do you like horses?"

Peta sat on one of the kids' chairs, knees nearly touching her chin. "Yes, I have a horse called Barney at Anders ranch. He's white. I can draw him." The girls bent over the table and began drawing.

Anders glanced at Christine, then at Wendy. "Would it be okay if I go out and find the boys? I'm in my element out there and a bit out of it here."

"Of course. Go to the end of the drive then about two hundred fifty yards down the tree line. If you can't find them, holler. One of the boys will find you."

"Is that all right with you girls?"

Abby took a noisy breath and crossed her arms. "Yes, you should be with the boys. This is girl time."

He raised his eyebrows at Christine. "Okay with you?"

She nodded.

When Anders was out the door, Wendy said, "Now there's a keeper."

Without turning around Peta asked, "Are you marrying him? 'Cause if you are, I might have to go back to foster care."

Christine stared into the backyard until she found her voice. "You know, Peta, I like your brother a lot. He's a really good guy, but that's all I can say right now. Why would you have to go back to foster care?"

Peta fumbled with the colored pencils. "Folks that get married don't want kids around right away. Least that's what my mother said."

"Is that what happened with your mom? Did she get married?"

Peta shifted away from her and didn't answer.

Wendy touched Christine's arm and lowered her voice. "I made some coffee a bit ago. Do you want some? Peta how about some cookies? Abby?" They both shrugged. "I'll take that as a yes, girls."

Christine pulled up a rocker from the corner and sat between them. "Can I draw, too?"

"You're too good." Abby sniffed.

Peta said, "Yes, she is good. She drew a picture of Barney. My brother let me hang it in my room." Both kept their heads down and continued to draw.

"Peta, why did your mom leave?" Christine knew enough psychology to know that if Peta brought it up, it was weighing on her.

"She left because of some dumb guy, but she'll be back. They always dump her."

"Then when she leaves, you have to go back to foster care? Every time?"

Peta nodded, "After Grammy died and Aunt Lucy went nuts last year, I had nowhere else to go until Anders said I could live with him. But it's okay; the foster people are nice. They got three kids of their own and four of us who don't have any parents."

"You know, Peta, Anders would never send you back—and neither would I. It's important to have people in your life who love you, and I know Anders does."

"Anders does what? What'd I do?" Anders walked through the front door.

"Nothing," Peta said, "we're just talking." She held up her drawing of a grinning white horse with wild big green eyes. "Kinda creepy, huh?"

"Well." Anders scratched his head. "It's interesting."

Wendy emerged from the kitchen. "Didn't find them?" She handed a cup of coffee to Anders and another to Christine.

"I did, but they were on their way back."

The door burst open and the twins ran in, followed by Max yelling, "Mom, they're being brats. Why do I have to be out there anyway? I'm supposed to be working out for football." He stopped, stared at Peta. "Uh, hi."

Peta turned, mumbled, "Hi." Then, she went back to drawing.

Wendy took a sip of her coffee and said, "Max, boys, this is Anders and his sister Peta. They're friends of Christine. This is

Max, my oldest and these are the twins, Tommy and Eddie. Our youngest is Andy—he's probably still out with his dad. We also have a thirteen-year-old who is visiting his grandparents in Weymouth this week. "

"How do you do, sir? Nice to meet you." Max stretched his arm across the twins and reached for Anders hand. "Peta, nice to meet you, too." He walked over and stood behind her.

She stood and turned, her face reddened, but she extended her hand and said softly, "Nice to meet you."

Abby jumped up. "Go away." She shoved Max in the stomach. "She's my friend. Mom, make him go away."

Max ignored his sister and pointed at Peta's drawing. "You like horses?"

Her face brightened and she was breathless when she said, "I adore horses."

"You wanna ride one? Mom, is it okay? She can ride Misty, she's gentle and Mrs. Markenson said we could take her out whenever we want."

Wendy glanced at Peta. "Do you know how?"

"Yes, yes. I love to ride. Ask Anders, I'm really good."

Anders nodded. "She is."

"But I want her to stay here with me." Abby stomped her foot. "Make her stay, Mom."

Peta said, "Abby, I'm gonna go ride, then I'll come back and we can draw. Okay?"

When Abby didn't answer, Peta hesitated, but Wendy told her to go. "Abby will be fine."

Max motioned to Peta. He opened the sliding glass door, waited for Peta to go first and they left together.

"I hate him, I hate him." Abby ran down the hall toward her bedroom.

Wendy yelled after her, "Abigail Madison, you get back here and apologize to your brother, right now."

"Saaaaaarrrrrry." she screamed.

"Abby, he's outside. Get in here so he can hear you," Wendy said.

They heard stomping before Abby appeared, arms folded, lips pursed, tears in her eyes.

"Go," Wendy said.

Abby stormed to the sliding glass door and opened it, screamed her apology again, clumped back to her room. Wendy sighed. "Sorry you had to witness that. I'd hoped you'd leave with a better opinion of this dysfunctional family."

Anders looked undaunted. "No worries. I'd tell you about mine, but we'd be here for days."

"She's having an especially bad day. Christine, I had to tell her you'd be going back to Montana soon and she didn't take it very well. She said she wanted go with you. Can you believe it?" Wendy looked at Anders. "It took weeks for her to even let Christine come over and introduce herself. Now … well, now she wants to leave us. Kids. You can't live with them and you can't live … with 'em."

In the end, Abby emerged from her room, and she and Christine drew while Anders visited with Kurt and Wendy. When Peta returned with Max, flushed and excited, she did as she promised and spent time drawing with Abby before they left.

Peta didn't stop talking about the visit until she fell asleep later that night. Reluctantly, Christine kissed Anders good night on Lisa's doorstep. Had Peta not been with them, tonight Christine would not have slept alone. Tonight would have been the night she and Anders wouldn't have slept at all.

TWENTY-THREE

Morning seeped through the bedroom window like any other January day, but it wasn't—it was the twentieth. The nightmares began as soon as she'd closed her eyes the night before. Around four in the morning she finally dozed off, then woke in terror at 7:15 a.m.—the exact time she'd set the alarm two years ago.

That morning had been filled with optimism about her new modeling assignment and upcoming wedding. Yet later, as she was dressing, foreboding had wrapped itself around her. This morning the same feeling hovered. It was a feeling she feared would haunt her forever. She tried to push it away, tried to recapture the contentment she felt yesterday when she, Anders and Peta spent the day visiting various beaches. As they sat on the sand at Forest Beach, a dazzling sun glinted off the sea and heightened the vivid blue of the sky. Cold enough that their breath condensed into white puffs, they drank hot cocoa and ate roast beef sandwiches.

"Not as good as your picnic lunch on the river, Anders, but I'm learning," Christine had said.

They sat on a wool blanket spread on the cool sand mesmerized by the white foamy surf as it lapped against the white dusting of snow.

"I love the snow here," Peta said. "It's not dirty like at home."

Christine didn't want to disillusion her by admitting that by mid-February the snow that remained along the sides of the road was anything but beautiful. Dusted with soot, dirt and bits of garbage swept up by snow plows as they cleared the streets. No, not so pretty then. But she'd be going home in February. That's how she'd begun to think of Montana—home. Flight reservations were set for February twenty-seventh. Time to ease Abby into the idea—time to start saying her good-byes.

Yesterday had ended at the cottage with store bought pizza and a late evening call from Wendy, inviting Peta over the following day.

But that was yesterday. Today was not a good day. Christine slipped out of bed, trying not to wake Peta who wasn't going to see Abby until later that morning. Christine dressed and went to the kitchen to make coffee. A light tapping on the kitchen window startled her and she unlocked the door for Anders.

"Shush, Peta's still sleeping."

"Hello, my darling. It's a spectacular day out there. The sun's come out, let's go for a walk."

"You're nuts. It's a spectacularly cold, grey day out there."

He scoffed, "You New Englanders are so wimpy. You want cold? Try a winter in Montana." He picked her up, twirled around and said, "Oh, that's right, you will!"

"Put me down, silly boy, or you won't be able to do anything today, let alone walk."

He eased her gently onto the loveseat and plopped down next to her. "Well, little lady, what's on the agenda for today?" Before she could answer, he continued. "Nothing, huh? Well, this ol' boy has a few surprises up his sleeve. You game?"

She wasn't. What she really felt like doing was staying in bed all day with the covers over her head. But she knew Anders wouldn't let her; he'd promised to be with her all day. Would his presence be enough to keep the demons away?

She tilted her head back against the cushion and took in a deep breath. "I don't know what I feel like doing today. I wish I could sleep through and wake up tomorrow. Can you help me with that?"

"Well, m'dear …" he'd started to be flip, but must have changed his mind. "Look, I can't even begin to imagine what you went through or what you're still going through, but let me help if I can. Nothing crazy. Sound good?" He leaned over and lightly touched his lips to hers.

The urgency was suddenly overwhelming. She took his face in her hands and kissed him fervently, running her tongue around his, tugging on his lips with hers. She slipped on top of him and began taking off her shirt.

His voice husky, he said, “Wait, Christine. Not now; not here. Not with Peta sleeping in the other room. Not with you in such a state.”

She slid off him onto the floor, head in her hands, moaning. He bent over and pulled her hands down and said, “I’m sorry, I didn’t mean.”

“I’m fine, really. A little embarrassed maybe.” Her face felt hot, but she looked at him anyway. “I don’t deserve you, you know.”

“You are so, so right.” He lifted her back onto his lap.

She leaned against his chest and said, “I don’t think I can wait a month. I think I’m going to need to have my way with you way before that.”

She looked up at him and rubbed his cheek with the palm of her hand. “Feels weird; can’t feel much, you know.” Then she rubbed it with her knuckles. “When I do have my way with you, you’re gonna have to shave that face of yours. It’s scratchy.”

He reached for her hand and kissed it. “Done. And, my dear, what your hands can’t feel, I’ll make sure other parts of you will.” He winked.

The door to the bedroom opened, Peta peeked out. When she saw them, she covered her eyes with her hands and said, “Eeewww, what are you guys doing?”

Christine jumped up. “Nothing, we weren’t doing anything.”

Peta took her hands down, yawned and said, “What time is it anyway? The darn clock in here says its 7:45 a.m., but it can’t be. I never wake up that early.”

“Well, my child, that’s exactly what time it is.” Anders said.

Peta groaned. “Wake me when it’s over.”

“When what’s over?” Christine said. “No, no we really weren’t doing anything; I mean we’re not going to do …”

Anders and Peta laughed so hard that Peta had tears running down her face and Anders said, “Stop, my stomach is killing me.” He took a deep breath. “She didn’t mean when this …” he pointed to the two of them and mouthed 'sex', "is over. It's something we say to each other that really means nothing." They both began laughing again.

Anders left a bit later to shower and change, and said he'd be back around ten.

****

At exactly 10:00 a.m. Anders knocked on the door of the cottage, dressed and ready to take her out. Christine's stomach did flip flops. She took one last look in the bedroom mirror to check her hair and make-up and yelled at the closed bathroom door, "Peta, Anders is here. Wendy will be here in thirty-minutes. Need anything before I go?"

Peta poked her head out. "Hair dryer?"

"Under the sink."

"Thanks. You look nice."

Christine smiled. Peta was growing on her.

She grabbed her purse, closed the bedroom door behind her, opened the front door and let Anders in.

"Wow, you're looking mighty nice."

"That's what your sister just said."

"Good taste runs in the family," he said and lightly kissed her cheek. "Ready?"

She was apprehensive. "Where are we going?"

"Out and about, and I'm driving."

"But you don't know where to go." She was puzzled, and a little apprehensive.

"But, I do, my dear, but I do."

"At least tell me if I'm dressed appropriately?"

"Turn around." He nodded and smiled. "I'd say you'll do just fine."

She'd rummaged through one of the packed boxes and found a pair of skinny black pants, mid-calf boots, a white blouse and black sweater. Black is always a safe choice, her mother used to say. Safe and traditional. Black is what she had on the day of the crash. She shuddered and thought about changing, but Anders pulled her toward the door. “C’mon let’s get going; time’s a wastin’.”

Christine grabbed a coat and scarf. They both yelled good-bye to Peta and got in the car. Anders behind the wheel, Christine next to him. She suddenly had a flashback: Donna behind the wheel, Christine next to her. The inside of the car closed in on her.

“You alright? You look terrified,” Anders said.

She sucked in air, braced herself, and said, “I’ll be fine; it’ll pass. Please, let’s get out of here.” She glanced at him, “Really, I’m fine.”

His brow furrowed, mouth tight. “Are you sure?”

“Yes. Now go.”

Anders talked nonstop for the next half hour as they headed east, then north on Route 6, which turned onto 6A, then on Province Lands Road and out to the roundabout at the end of the road.

“P’town was the destination?” she said as they rounded the tip and circled the rotary, heading back toward the center of town.

“It’s the first stop. Hope you didn’t mind going all the way to the end of the road. I saw it on the map and was curious.”

She didn’t mind, except for a moment she thought they were going to the motel on the other side of the roundabout. It made her think of Nick. They’d periodically get a room there for a ‘quickie’ when they were in P’town. She slapped the memory away.

Anders drove into town and parked in front of P’town Gallery. Christine hesitated before finally getting out of the car. “Anders, what are we doing here?” She tried to pull him back, but he led her inside.

John rushed up to them, while Bill hung back. “Well, well, you’re back.” John turned to Anders. “You must be the boyfriend, Anders, right?”

“How’d you know that?”

Bill walked up to them with a package. “Here it is. I must tell you it was really hard to part with, but John convinced me it was the right thing to do.” He handed it to Christine. “Hope you enjoy it. Oh, and whenever you're ready, John and I are at your disposal."

"What's going on?" She looked from John, to Bill, to Anders.

John said, "Well, your very handsome boyfriend convinced us to let him buy your painting back. Truthfully it wasn't a hard sell anyway. I've hated the thing … no offense … since Bill bought it. When Anders promised you'd replace it with one of Bill and me, well what could we say? And, he did pay handsomely." John folded his arms across his chest, seemingly quite satisfied with himself.

She looked up at Anders who rocked back on his heels and grinned. She was confused. "How'd you know who to call and where the gallery was?" She couldn't get her head around what was going on.

"I'm a good listener," Anders said. "And the name P'town Gallery isn't all that hard to remember."

"But, when did I? Oh, that's right, I called you after I found out about it." She wasn't sure yet how she felt about it, but kissed Anders' cheek and said, "You're good." And to Bill and John, "Thank you. I'm not sure when I'll get to your drawing, though, I'm leaving for Montana in a few weeks."

Bill piped in, "It's fine, Christine, whenever you can."

John shot back, "Well that's great. No hurry because it's a drawing with me, is that what you're saying?"

Bill sighed. "No, John, what I'm saying is that if she doesn't get it done before she leaves, she can do it when we go to Montana. Anders invited us to the ranch."

All was forgiven. John hugged Bill who said, "But are you sure? It's pretty desolate, I'm not sure it will be good for our skin. I guess we could go."

John cut him off, "Well that just figures …"

While they were arguing, she and Anders snuck out before they were drawn into the disagreement.

"Any more surprises up your sleeve?" Christine asked.

"But, of course, my dear." He led her to the car, opened the trunk and laid the painting inside. "I haven't talked to any of the other store owners who have your stuff, but I thought we could walk around and I'd buy some of the others back for you." He peered at her. "If that's what you want."

"Actually, this is enough. The others don't mean the same. This was the first real sketch I did as an adult. And, silly as it sounds, it means a lot because my dad hated it."

"Curious comment. You want to elaborate?"

"I'm not sure. I'll have to work on that." She settled inside the car. When he got in next to her she asked, "Where to now?"

"You hungry?"

"Starved!"

"Okay, then let's get something to eat."

"There's a little place down there that's pretty good." She pointed up the road.

"Nope, I've already got it arranged. We'll be a bit early, but that's fine."

They entered the highway. Christine leaned her head against the headrest and closed her eyes. When she opened them they were pulling in front of the Gale Harbor Beach Resort. A valet took their keys and helped her out. She stood at the bottom of a long set of stairs, staring at the entrance to one of the Cape's most elite resorts. They both hesitated, gazing up at the sprawling white building that fronted on the Atlantic before walking up to the exclusive resort's entry.

A doorman opened one of the large beveled glass doors and they entered the lobby. Loud voices and laughter coming from a room on the right were in sharp contrast to the lobby's quiet elegance with its sea green carpeting, accent pieces in soft pecan wood and pale green and white upholstered chairs. They walked toward the voices until the concierge stopped them.

"Can I be of service?"

"Yes," Anders said, "we're looking for the restaurant.

"It's behind you to the left of the lobby. This is the bar, sir. It's been reserved for a private gathering."

"Thank you." They turned around and walked into the restaurant. Since it was still winter, very few customers were seated at the tables. A bank of windows that viewed the ocean took up the entire back wall. The sophisticated setting with white tablecloths, French provincial pecan colored chairs and the few elegantly attired diners made Christine feel completely out of her element.

She leaned over and whispered, "This looks pretty expensive; we can go somewhere else, if you like."

He feigned shock. "Are you suggesting I can't afford to buy my gal lunch at a fancy restaurant? I'm not a pauper, you know."

The maitre d' stepped in front of them. "May I be of assistance?"

Anders said, "Yes, we have reservations at one; the name's Larsson. I know we're a little early."

"That'll be fine, sir. Please follow me." He led them to a window table with an unobstructed view.

"Looks like we might have some inclement weather," Anders said to the maitre d'.

The maitre d' wore a mask of boredom. His face barely moved when he spoke. "Yes sir, I believe that's what we've been told. If there's nothing else, I'll take my leave?"

Anders shook his head.

"Well then, Jared will be your waiter; he'll be with you shortly."

****

After an aperitif of sparkling wine from California and first course of crab cakes, Anders ordered a white Bordeaux and they both ordered lobster. For dessert, they split a crème brûlée. The lunch took two hours. They ended the meal with a cappuccino—Anders insisted. The day almost finished, her fear nearly gone, they walked outside to wait for the valet to bring their car. She nuzzled into Anders shoulder and closed her eyes.

"Well, if it isn't little Christina Marie."

Her eyes flew open at the sound of Nick's voice. Panic seized her. Nick stood in front of her, his arm around a blonde, hanging on his every word, both of them glassy eyed. The air reeked of liquor, gagging her. She recoiled, her fear paralyzing.

"What? You got nothing to say to your old fiancé?"

"You're drunk," she rasped.

"Sure am. Me and the little honey here." He turned to the blonde and asked, "Cherry or Sherry?"

She giggled and pushed her breasts into his arm. "It's Charlyn, sweetie."

"So, me and Charlyn here had a little party going on. Finally signed the papers on my new place. Celebrating with Bertoletti and family." He belched. "Mostly martinis. You know all about martinis don't ya, Chrissy. Had a few too many at my Christmas party." He sneered. "Didn't ya?"

Christine tugged at Anders arm, pulling him up toward the front door. "Let's go back inside. They're drunk."

Nick sneered. "Like you were?"

She turned away from Nick, tried to go up the stairs, grabbing Anders jacket. "Please, Anders."

Nick stepped back, hands on hips and said, "Anders, huh? You must be the cowboy. Say, there, cowboy, did our little Chrissy tell you about our kiss, huh? Did she tell you she was so drunk that I had to walk her home? Ah, I can see she didn't."

Christine felt nauseous. She turned to Anders and whispered, "Now. I need to go now."

Anders remained rigid, eyes cold.

"Man, have you noticed when she's had a few too many, she can really lock on? She loves to suck lips. Hell, I had to push her off. Bet she didn't tell you how she wanted some of this."

Nick unleashed his date, and stood straight, chest out, and grabbed his groin. "Naw, I can see by the look on your face, she neglected to tell you any of that. Oh, by the way, I'm Nick, her ex."

Blondie giggled and pulled away. "Come on, Nickie, let's leave." She stumbled to the curb where the valet had just parked their car.

Nick leered, looked them up and down. Then he scoffed and said, "Yeah, let's get out of here. Chrissy's a freak. Waste of time."

Anders lunged at Nick. "You son-of-a-bitch. Get the fuck back here and apologize to Christine."

"Boy, you're some crazy ass mother. Why the hell would I apologize? Look at her. She is a freak. Oh, maybe you're trying to defend her honor. Now that's a joke. I should apologize for what? Being a guy? I wanted some and she was about to give it to me. If you don't believe me, ask her."

Anders glanced at her, then grabbed Nick's arm. "I said apologize."

Nick swung at him. Anders ducked and Nick stumbled forward, then steadied himself, and said, "Get a life. Got nothing to apologize for." He walked toward the car.

Anders went after him. Christine reached for his hand to stop him and yelled, "Wait. He's not worth it."

Anders spun around and glared at her. "I'm not pissed at him, I'm pissed at you. You're right, though, he's not worth it. Too bad you didn't realize that sooner."

Nick turned and waved like a child. "Can't believe you get your rocks off with him. 'Til next time, sweetie." He shoved the blonde in his car, jumped in, and drove off.

The valet arrived with Anders car. Without looking at her, Anders led her to the car, helped her in and slammed the door. He crossed in front of the car, jaw tight, fists clenched.

She couldn't breathe, her stomach churned, her world was crumbling around her.

When Anders got in the car she said, "I can explain. Please let me explain. It wasn't like that."

He stared straight ahead. "I'm sure you can, but I don't think I want to hear it right now."

****

When they got to Lisa's, Anders climbed out of the car and walked toward the kitchen entrance, head down, hands shoved in his pockets.

Christine ran to him and grabbed his arm. "Wait, we need to talk." He pulled away from her. She pleaded, "Please, Anders, let me explain; it was really nothing." She reached up and turned his face to hers—no anger, just a blank stare. "But nothing happened. Nick lied." She tugged at him, pulling him toward the cottage. "Please come with me."

He slid her hand off his arm, walked around to the cottage's back patio and slumped on the bench. "Okay, if nothing happened why didn't you tell me about seeing him? I asked you if you'd seen him. You lied." He leaned forward and stared at the ocean.

She paced; she felt insubstantial again, vulnerable, fragile—like at any moment a gust of wind would blow her away. She felt guilty, though she'd done nothing wrong. She sat next to him, "I … I was stupid."

Then she told him the whole story.

When she finished, he stood. "I wish you'd have told me when I called you on Christmas and again when I asked you three days ago. I knew there was something that you weren't telling me, but I convinced myself I was imagining it." He walked toward the house, stopped then turned back to her. "You say it was nothing, but the fact that you didn't tell me shows that it meant something. It shows that you felt you had done something wrong. It shows that you felt something for him." His shoulders sagged. He started toward Lisa's.

She hurried after him. "But I didn't." He kept walking. She yelled, "Wait, please. Just stop."

He waited; she went to him and grabbed his hand. "It was only a kiss; I was drunk, period. There was nothing more to it."

Anders scowled. "It's not about the kiss, Christine. You lied to me. If you can't be honest with yourself about that, how can I expect you to be honest with me? I've been down this road before, Christine, I won't do it again." He strode away from her.

Her head in a fog, leg throbbing, she hurried after him, hunched over as if gravity was pulling her down. Then she gave up. What was the use? He was leaving the next day, there wasn't enough time to repair the damage. What could she say to make it better? In a way it was true—she did feel something—she'd felt alive for the first time in two years. Nick's rejection of her had been so painful that when he desired her again it awakened something she'd buried. A passion, a longing, but in those few moments she realized that the longing she felt was for Anders. And, with that clarity she understood that she could love herself in spite of her deformities. In that moment her life had been given back to her. How could she explain that to Anders? That being with Nick was the catalyst to lucidity, to things falling into place. Maybe she couldn't, at least not yet. She knew now that nearly giving in to something ephemeral, she had lost something significant.

"I'm sorry, Anders," she whispered to his back.

****

They rode to the airport in silence. It was just the two of them. She'd begged Anders to let her take him alone and let Lisa drive Peta. Finally, he'd given in. Lisa had been harder to convince, "Why would you want to take two cars?" Lisa asked.

"It's complicated. Please, I need to talk to him alone."

Lisa threw her arms in the air. "You dolt, you told him about that night, didn't you?"

"Nick told him. You and I will talk later."

Now, she was again in the passenger seat while Anders drove. Every time she tried to bring it up, he cut her off. They were almost to the airport when she tried again. "Can't we talk about this?"

"I don't know what there is to talk about," he said, keeping his eyes on the road.

"Please, Anders, I care about you so much; I care about us."

He shrugged. "I don't think there is an 'us'." He stared at her then, before turning back to the road. "I've been trying to put myself in your place. Trying to see if I'm being unreasonable, but I can't get the sick feeling in my stomach to go away. I can't seem to shake the fact that you lied to me. At the very least you omitted information when I asked you a direct question. It isn't that he kissed you, or you kissed him, it's that you didn't tell."

"I was afraid. Afraid you'd think that I was drawn to him again; afraid you'd see me as weak."

"I thought you knew me better than that." His eyes, sad, searched her face.

"I do, it's me." She played with her hands, working up courage. "I don't know." She sighed. "Yes, it felt good that he found me attractive. I loved that I felt beautiful again. But my response … the longing was for you, not him." There, she said it.

Without saying anything or looking at her, he pulled the car into the rental lot and got out. He went over the paperwork with the attendant, lifted his bag out of the trunk and helped her out. Both were silent as they walked out to the rental car entrance to wait for Lisa. Anders dropped his bag on the sidewalk and said, "This isn't the ending I'd planned on. I'd hoped I could convince you to come with us today." She started to answer, but he put up his hand. "I don't feel that way now."

Here comes the good-bye, she thought, here comes the pain.

"It's pretty obvious that you still need more time to sort things out, but I'm not sure I can wait around for that to happen."

She wanted to scream, but I don't want more time. I want you. I want to be in Montana. Instead she said, "You're wrong, Anders. I don't need more time, but I couldn't go back with you anyway. There's Abby and…"

"Yes, I know; if it isn't Abby then it's Lisa, or the snow, or the beach. I don't know what to think anymore. Am I going to have to sell that house of yours even before you move in? Will you really come out? Those are some of the questions I've been asking myself for a long time. You know, yesterday wasn't just a date you've dreaded, it was a date I marked on my mental calendar last summer—it was a deadline of sorts. I'm afraid we both missed it."

Lisa pulled up. Anders put his bags in the trunk and joined Christine in the backseat. Lisa twisted around. "All set?"

"As set as I'll ever be," he said.

Their good-bye was disconnected, fragmented. Peta gave her a hug said she couldn't wait for Christine to come to Montana.

"Abby and her family want to come out, too. Max is talking about looking at colleges out there. Wouldn't that be cool?"

Peta was giddy, Lisa perplexed, Anders mad and Christine like a windmill without wind.

****

"Well?" Christine had barely sat down in the car when Lisa quizzed her. "What happened? It can't be all that bad. That guy loves you, in case you can't tell."

"I blew it."

She told Lisa about running into Nick and how Anders reacted.

"What did you expect, silly? He's a man, they're all jealous," Lisa said.

"It's not that. I should have told him. I should have trusted that he would be fine with it." Christine noticed Lisa frowned. "Maybe not fine, but he'd have understood. The sad thing is that I wasn't really attracted to Nick; I was attracted to how he made me feel about myself."

"Doesn't Anders make you feel that way? I can't believe a man like that doesn't."

"He does. I can't explain it. So many times I wanted to let him make love to me again. I don't know, maybe I thought if Nick could do it and not look away, then once I was with Anders … doesn't make any sense, does it?"

"I think I understand, but I've not been through what you have and it's difficult for me to make sense of it. What now? How did the two of you leave it?"

"We resolved nothing. And trying to make up long distance never works. Maybe I'll have to wait until I get out there." She rubbed her hands together and ran a finger along her cheek. "If, I go."

As soon as she was home, she checked the airline's site to see if the plane was on time. When it landed, she waited an hour, called, hung-up before he answered. Three days passed before she tried again. This time she let it ring and when he didn't answer, she left a message. “It’s Christine. I hope we can talk again before I come out. How the house is coming? Will it be ready for me or should I get a hotel?”

Instead of calling her back, he sent her a text that the house would not be completely finished, but it would be livable if she chose to stay in it. Otherwise, he said, Lotte said she could stay at the ranch.

She agonized about what to do and decided to give him some time. She wasn’t leaving for a month. Hopefully that would give him time to calm down.

TWENTY-FOUR

As weeks passed it became more difficult to think of leaving. Christine's relationship with Anders was in jeopardy and she was nervous about returning to Montana, unsure how everyone would treat her when they found out she'd lied to Anders. To fill her days she spent more time with Lisa and Abby, and made arrangements to have some time with Meredith before she left.

"This will be so much fun" Meredith squealed when Christine told her what she planned. "Shopping in Boston, hanging-out with my sis."

"Two nights at the Four Seasons, dinner at a top restaurant, and I'm not telling you which one. We'll take in a show and shop, 'til we drop," Christine said.

"But I can't afford that," Meredith said,

"But I can and we're going to do it.

Once she made those arrangements, Christine decided to make amends with her parents. Since Christmas she'd barely talked to them. Although still angry about her father's betrayal and her mother's apathy, she didn't want to leave without at least trying to make their relationship more amenable. She didn't know when she'd be back in Massachusetts and her parents weren't getting any younger.

Her mother was visibly flustered when she answered the door, but calmed down as soon as she realized Christine wasn't there for some kind of showdown. "Floyd, come here, it's Christine; she's come to say good-bye."

"No, no Mother, I've come to say 'hello' and see if I can't convince you guys to come out and see me this spring."

"I'm not sure about that, honey. Don't get your hopes up. You know how we are about traveling too far."

"There's my little kitten." Her father kissed her on both cheeks. "You're looking pretty good there. Being back on the Cape seems to work for you. Sure we can't convince you to stick around?" He drew her into the room and motioned for her to sit on the couch.

"No, Daddy, I'm going to Montana. My house is nearly finished. I really love it there."

"But what are you going to do?" He studied her face. "Don't tell me you're going to become one of those hippy artists? That's not a respectable profession."

She clenched her teeth, bit her cheek and said, "That was your generation, Daddy. My generation reveres art. Artists are actually respected. But, no I'm not going to be an artist, though I may paint."

"Well, thank goodness, dear," her mother chimed in. "Montana is, well, western. I mean what could you possibly paint but Indians and cattle?"

"Actually, Mother." The idea that had been in the back of her mind for weeks, took shape as the words tumbled out. "I think I'm going to open a camp for disfigured kids. The fresh air in Montana would be perfect for them. I'll have art classes and …" She knew she was going too fast, but the more she talked about it the more excited she became. "I'm going to have some cabins built on my land. Let parents come along." Her heart pounded as the vision took shape. "Families. It will be a great place for families to stay with the kids who are convalescing." Her face felt hot, her palms sweaty. "I'll have a therapist on staff. Oh, my, goodness. Won't it be wonderful?"

As expected, her father wasn't supportive. "How the hell do you propose to do something like that? You don't have any business experience and you've always shown your …" he snorted, " … dislike of children. I think it's a bad idea."

She rubbed her hands together. "That changed when I met Abby. It's okay; I'm not asking for your permission." She looked at both of them. "Either of you. Of course, I'd like you be happy for me."

Her father stood up. "So that's it? You're going to take all your money for some ridiculous camp where kids can draw stick figures? If you're that interested in kids, why don't you open a modeling school? I'm sure those kids out there could use some culture. Or open a modeling school here, for god's sake, where your mother and I can help you. That would make us happy for you."

She gritted her teeth. "Yes, I can see where that might be of interest to you, but it's really not my dream. I do thank you for all the two sacrificed, taking me to all those classes. It really showed me how important it is for kids to have something special of their own—especially kids who don't have any means. Those are the ones that really would benefit."

All of a sudden, both parents seemed nervous. Her mother cleared her throat. Her father's demeanor changed, and he smiled at her. "You know having the means to attain a certain status or a dream is really important at any age. Your mother and I were going to talk to you about this Christmas Eve, but then you girls disappeared." He coughed and swallowed. "Now that you've gotten all of your money from the accident your mother and I were thinking of moving into a bigger house and maybe opening a bed and breakfast. One of your mother's friends recently did that in Truro, and they're making lots of money in the summer. We thought we could hire a chef and specialize in gourmet meals and do some catering. We found this place in Eastham; the owners want a million, but we are pretty sure we could get them down to eight hundred. The money from the stocks isn't going to be enough so what do you think? Time to pay your aging parents back for raising you?"

The burn raged in her chest, but she knew what to say and do. "You know, I love you guys. It sounds like a lot of fun. If you get it going, let me know and I'll send some Montanans your way." She kissed them both, urged them to stay safe and practically ran out.

Christine sat in the car, staring at the house, her childhood home. The worn clapboard siding, the sagging roof line and unkept yard. If they wanted to move to Eastham and open a bed and breakfast, she wished them well. Their expectations of her assistance were no longer a concern to her. She'd already been generous enough and she would need the money for other things. Things, which were much more important.

In the past hour she'd made two decisions: to really let go of her father's dream for her, and to follow her own. Until that moment when she sat in front of them, she thought she had resolved that issue, but her parents' approval was always in the back of her mind. No more. The only approval she now sought was her own. Whether she and Anders had a future together in Montana or not wasn't the question. She hoped they did, but if not, she had one.

She fumbled in her purse for the key, put it in the ignition and started to pull away. The living room curtain parted slightly; her mother peered outside. When she caught sight of Christine, she hesitated, then raised her index finger and opened the front door. She motioned for Christine to roll down the window and said, "We'll be fine dear; don't you worry about us, honey." Her mother's shoulders slumped, she hung her head and closed the door. The final attempt at trying to make her feel guilty didn't work. Christine moved the gearshift to drive, edged away from the curb and headed toward Abby's feeling strong.

The concept for the camp grew as she explained it to Wendy, Abby and Kurt.

"I don't know that we want Abby gone for a long time," Kurt said. "Or even if she's ready to be without us."

Christine drew Abby to her and hugged. "Goodness, no, you'd come too. Stay at the house. The cabins won't be ready for months. I was so excited about my idea that I wanted to share it with you. Well, then, what do you think?"

"I wanna go," Abby said and played with Christine's fingers.

Wendy looked up at Kurt. "I think … we think it's a good idea." He nodded. Wendy knelt in front of Abby and held both her hands. "You liked it when Christine took you to her house to draw, didn't you?"

Abby giggled. "Oh, yes, it was splendid!"

Wendy laughed. "Splendid, was it." She turned to Christine. "It's her new word."

"It's a splendid new word," Christine said. "When you're ready—when she's ready— I'd like all of you to come out. The house has four bedrooms and in the spring I'm going to start building cabins on the back part of the property behind the house. It will be like a Ronald McDonald kind of place; families can come or just send their kids." Her excitement grew as she continued to talk about it. "I haven't thought it all out yet. Obviously." She laughed and hugged Wendy. "But it's going to be splendid!"

****

Her enthusiasm carried her through the next few days. She made several calls to Montana, some to Anders who didn't answer nor call her back. She did connect with Lotte who thought it was " … the best darn idea you've come up with."

She added, "You're really comin' back, huh? After Anders came back like a wounded filly, I was sure we'd be sending your stuff east. Hell, he's been about as useful as warts!"

Christine's heart thumped. "What did he say?"

"Hell, he wouldn't even talk about it. Said you were fine and I was to talk to you if I wanted to know anymore than that. So I'm askin'. What happened?"

She told Lotte everything . When she was done, the phone was silent for a moment before Lotte said, "That boy. He's just being plain dim. I'm gonna knock him up the side of the head. You don't worry 'bout nothing but getting back here. I'll have your room ready."

She decided then. "No, I'm going to stay at my house."

"Good girl; give that boy a taste of his own medicine."

"But I'm not …"

Lotte didn't let her finish. "Not to worry; he'll come round." She cleared her throat. "Now I shouldn't be telling you this, but since he's being bullheaded I'm gonna anyway." She paused, dropped her voice and went on. "'Bout ten years ago when the boy was in California gettin' his photography business goin', he fell hard for one of them high fashion models. 'Bout six months later she up and left him. Went back to an old boyfriend. It was too late for Anders—he was already head over heels. Took him years to get past it. He did a couple years penance with the whiskey bottle and a lot of women before gettin' straightened out. When you came round with Donna that first time, he was still playin' the Casanova role. Wasn't till you got hurt that he let himself care 'bout someone again."

Her heart sank. "Damn it, Lotte, I wish I'd known. Every time I ask him about past girlfriends or why he wasn't married, he'd change the subject. Now it makes sense."

"Listen, don't you go gettin' mad at me … he's the one actin' like a spoiled child. Should've spanked him like I did when he was little."

Christine smiled at the picture that emerged. "Now that would be something I'd like to see." She fiddled with the blinds on the cottage's French doors, gazed at a group of sea gulls racing across the sand and breakers hastening toward the shore. "No worries, Lotte. It'll all work out. Not mad at you, mad at him … and myself."

****

"I think I really screwed up, Meredith." She and Meredith sat on top of their beds on their second night at the Four Seasons. Both had changed into matching nightclothes they'd bought earlier in the day along with new bed linens and accent pillows for Christine's house. Exhausted from shopping they decided to forego dinner and went up to their room. They were sipping on an expensive bottle of French champagne and were too keyed up to sleep.

"I'll bet when you explain it all to him, he'll want to be with you again." Meredith took another sip of champagne and said, "You've changed, Chrissy; even I can see that." She smiled. "You're nice now."

Christine picked up one of the new pillows and tossed it at Meredith. It glanced off her sister's sleek red hair as it sailed toward the window, landing on the sill. "I was always nice."

Meredith rolled her green eyes, scrunched her nose and pursed her lips. "Surrrrrre, you were…

"Okay—maybe not so much. But I wanted to be. At times I envied the ugly girls who didn't care about their looks, who only cared about being smart or nice."

"Like me?"

"You're not ugly."

Meredith peered into her champagne. "But I couldn't be beautiful like you, so I had to be nice. Then dad would love me as much as he loved you."

Tears stung Christine's eyes. She bit her lip to stop them. "I'm sorry."

"That's okay, being nice doesn't get wrinkles."

Christine stuck her tongue out and said, "What makes you think you're so nice anyway?" The pillow came sailing back and caught her in the face while she was taking a sip of champagne, spilling it all over her. She picked up the pillow to throw it back.

Meredith yelled, "Truce!"

Christine got out of the bed, walked to the bathroom, grabbed a towel and dabbed at wet spots on the pajamas, then her eyes. She glanced into the mirror; make-up still intact, the scar nearly invisible. She should feel good, yet tonight, even with all the make-up, the mirror reflected a woman stripped; a woman in agony about the people she'd hurt. A woman who unknowingly chipped away at a father's love for his oldest daughter, leaving her permanently scarred. A woman who'd pushed away the one man she'd truly cared about.

She walked out of the bathroom and flopped on the bed. "I'm sorry about Dad. He's not worth it, you know. He's not really a very nice man."

"I know. I'm surprised you see that."

"It's because of Anders. I've realized what a nice man is like. But, it's too late. He'll never come back to me now."

"Dad?" Meredith swallowed the last of the champagne in her glass and tipped it toward Christine.

"No, dummy, Anders." Christine filled both glasses. She went to the mini-bar and pulled out a variety of small cheeses, crackers and a chocolate bar. "Midnight snack?"

"Sure. Does that mean your knight in shining armor isn't so shiny anymore?" Meredith took another sip, pulled back the bedcovers and climbed in, leaning back against the collection of damask covered pillows.

Christine did the same and snuggled into the bed, placing the plate of cheese and crackers on the nightstand between them. "He's still shiny, it's me that's tarnished. I can't believe I let that idiot pull me in again." She cut a piece of cheese, put it on a cracker and popped it in her mouth.

"Anders?" Meredith yawned and rolled on her side, facing the wall .

"Nick—I'm talking about Nick. Geez, M, can't you follow anything? Have some cheese, maybe your brain needs food."

Meredith rolled over to face Christine and reached for a cracker. "No need to get all grumpy on me. Remember, you've changed; you're nice now."

Christine turned on her side and faced Meredith. "Being nice is hard. Being nice means you care about something, and with caring comes hurt. I care about Anders and now I ache knowing he doesn't care about me anymore."

She stared at Meredith and continued, "My body literally aches from the sadness. I care about you and now I feel sad because I know I hurt you."

Meredith started to say something, but Christine put up her hand. "Please, let me finish. I care about Abby and every time I look at her I want to cry. People stare at her face, then look away. I know what that feels like. I just want to grab her and hug her and make that pain go away. At least she's getting better. When Lisa's boys saw her, they just accepted her. I mean I'd prepared them a bit, but it didn't seem to matter to them that her face was disfigured, that her lips were still swollen, that she has …" Tears brimmed and fell unabated onto her cheeks.

"Oh, honey, please don't cry."

Meredith threw back the covers and got into bed with Christine. She wrapped her arms around Christine's shoulders and stroked her hair. "My poor sis; my little baby sister. You didn't deserve what happened to you. I'm so sorry." Meredith was crying, too.

Between sobs, Christine said, "Oh, it's not just me. I'm crying for Abby, for you, for Mom and Dad, for Anders and yes, a little for me." She took deep breaths and wiped her eyes. "It was a lot easier when I … when I hated everyone. Or when I was younger and thought you were all inferior to Dad and me. I thought I was special and you were all, well, incidental, unimportant. And, M, I was wrong, so very wrong."

PART III
SPRING FORWARD

For of all sad words of tongue or pen, the saddest are these: "It might have been!"~ John Greenleaf Whitter

TWENTY-FIVE

Montana—February 28

Christine felt dwarfed by the massive stone fireplace. It soared above her on the wall opposite a bank of windows that looked out onto the Gallatin Valley and distant Rocky Mountains. It was just as she had imagined.

She sat on the edge of the stone hearth, surrounded by boxes and suitcases, and slowly took it all in. She was in awe of what had been created in the last four months. This was her house, her home—one she'd created on paper, Spencer had refined and Anders had helped build. Well, no, not really built, but oversaw. He kept the crew on track and kept Spencer from changing anything. He'd also hung some of his photos including the one of the moose that had been on her property that first day, and he framed some of her sketches. Perhaps that meant he still cared. Fresh flowers adorned the mantel—Lotte's contribution—and Jake and his crew had begun clearing the land behind the house for the six cabins. They were all too good to her; she felt an overwhelming sense of gratitude.

The rumble of an engine interrupted her thoughts. She walked to the massive window and looked out onto the valley. The top of a truck bobbed up and down as it wove up the driveway. Her heart jumped. Anders? But it wasn't Ander's truck that popped out at the top of the driveway; it was Jake and two men from the ranch, the bed of the pick-up filled with furniture. She walked outside onto the porch and waved.

Jake hopped from the driver's side and saluted her. "Howdy, there. Got a futon, an old couch, a rocker, some lamps, and a table for you 'til you get something of yer own. Got a couple other things, too. Not sure what Lotte packed in there." He walked toward her, slapped his hat against his knee and said, "Brought the boys to help. Lotte told me I was goin' nowhere without help. So here we are. Where d'ya want this stuff?"

The phrase "a sight for sore eyes" popped into her mind. She met him in the drive and, even as dusty as he was, pulled him in and hugged tight.

"Good to see you." She stepped back. "And looking so good, too!"

"And, you," he said, "you little cape crusader."

She scrunched her nose. "Huh?"

"Lotte was tellin' all of us at the ranch 'bout your idea for the young 'uns." When it was apparent that she still didn't understand him, he chuckled. "Cape—you were at Cape Cod. Crusader—you are helping those little ones get better. See? Cape crusader."

"Ah, now I understand. Well, thanks." She linked her arm through his and led him toward the house, "want to see?"

Over his shoulder he yelled, "You boys get busy gettin' that stuff inside. Hurry it up." To her he said, "Haven't been inside yet—Lotte wouldn't let me. Lead the way."

They walked arm-in-arm up the flagstone path, up the steps onto the covered porch.

"I like what ya done to the porch. Nice decking. It's that fake wood, ain't it? They say it'll be 'round long after most of us is gone." He laughed.

The 'fake wood' deck was a soft grey. "Spencer helped me coordinate everyone on the outside. I wouldn't have thought the grey would have looked good next to the logs, but with the grey flagstone path and dark grey roof, it looks splendid," she said, trying out Abby's new word. "I'm glad you like it."

Christine pushed open the heavy pine and glass front door, and they stepped into the great room.

"Ain't this grand," Jake said.

He bent over to take off his boots, but she stopped him. "No need. I've got cleaners coming in this weekend. There's dust everywhere from construction. Anyway, these pine floors look best when they're worn a bit." She stepped into the room and twirled around. "Glorious isn't it?"

"How much room you got here?"

She scratched her head. "Can't remember exactly, but this room's, like, thirty-two by twenty-eight. There's a huge kitchen with a small sitting area for a couch and TV. C'mon, I'll show you." She tugged at his arm and led him straight ahead into the kitchen. "And, there's four bedrooms, three bathrooms and a laundry room. That's all."

Jake whistled. "Sure is a beaut. Bet you could fit twenty people in this kitchen, easy." He ran his hand over the countertops. "Looks like concrete, but it ain't, right?"

"But it is." She'd changed her mind from the original idea of soapstone and had gone with concrete instead. "Pretty, isn't it?"

"Not sure I'd call it pretty, but, heck, it works with those kitchen cupboards—pine, ain't they?"

"You've got a good eye, Jake. Yes, they're pine. I've got pine floors everywhere and pine cabinets. Too much?"

"Nope." He walked to the center island, stood there scratching his head and said, "Where's the stove?" Then turned around, "No fridge? Somebody steal 'em already? They shoulda gone in 'fore that floor."

She giggled. "No, Jake, no one stole them. They had to backorder them; they promised they could install them without scratching the floor. The house really isn't finished. I moved in early. Everything's perfect except the fireplace. It was supposed to go through to the kitchen and it doesn't. I need to talk to Spencer about that. There's painting that needs to be finished—both inside and out. Tiling isn't done in a couple of the bathrooms, windows need to be trimmed," she said, waving her arm around the room, "and a bunch of other little stuff. But I figure I can do some of that while I live here." She took a deep breath and beat her fists against her chest. "I can do it!"

Then she grabbed his hand and led him to the French doors. They stepped out onto the partially finished flagstone patio where mounds of snow melted in the unseasonably warm day.

Jake scrutinized the sky. "Weather's been a bit strange. One day it's snowing to beat the band, the next it's fifty degrees. But don't worry, we'll get it done. Looks like someone's been busy with the flowers, though."

Christine hadn't been in the backyard yet and couldn't believe the dozens of pots of varying sizes filled with hellebores and other plants, many that Christine didn't recognize. She was stunned. "Did you do this?"

"Me? Heck, no—my green thumb is black."

"Who did then?"

Jake scratched his head. "Don't know." Then his eyes widened. "Give ya one guess. Bet Lotte did it. Yesterday mornin' she left. Said she had errands to run and not to expect her before dinner. Gol durn, woman, I coulda helped." He shook his head. "Sure look pretty though, don't they?"

Christine gazed northeast across the backyard toward the willow. Images formed. Under the small grove of aspen rimming the top of the hill immediately to the east, spring was emerging from the earth. A hundred and fifty yards to the northwest, where the cabins would stand, she envisioned summer bursting from the sun. Summer with a gaggle of chirping kids running through the yard, easels set up in each cottage and a larger studio where she would paint and teach.

"It's fantastic, isn't it Jake?" She hugged him again. "I made the right decision. Didn't I?"

"Yup. I'll say."

"Jake, we need you in here," yelled one of the men.

They went back inside where the two men stood in the great room, arms crossed, with the futon on the floor in front of them. It had opened up.

One of the men said, "Damn thing released on us and we can't figure out how to get it back together. Jess here tried. I've tried." He peered at Jake. "You know how?"

Jake snorted, "Pretty damn easy if ya ask me. You," he said and pointed to Jess, "get over here. You, Tom, stand here. Now lift." The two men grunted, flipped one side of the futon over and it went back together. "Now, when you carry the darn thing, make sure to keep it closed."

"Where's it go?" Jess asked.

Jake turned to Christine and raised his eyebrows.

"Uh, how about the office down here? The master bedroom floor isn't finished yet—they ran out of pine—now I'll sleep down here." She led the way down the small hall. It was supposed to be a guest room with its own bath, but when the idea for the camp formed, Christine decided she needed an office.

As soon as they were finished with the furniture, the men went back to the truck and unloaded bundles of linens, a box of kitchen supplies and a small TV.

"Looks like you're set for a couple days anyway. When your furniture get here?" Jake said as he set the last of the cartons in the great room.

"Most of it won't be here for about a month. This is great. Please tell Lotte thank you. I love the old rocker she sent over and the quilts are beautiful."

"She said you should keep 'em. She's got drawers full of 'em. Said the rocker's an antique. Something she got from her ma. Said she wanted you to have it."

Christine followed him outside. "Thanks. You guys really took care of me." She stood on the front porch and took a deep breath, filling her lungs with the breath of Montana, the distant sweet smell of spring intertwined with the intoxicating aroma of hope.

Jake walked toward the truck where the two men waited. He said over his shoulder, "Call us if you need anything. Glad you're back."

He stepped up into the truck and put it in gear; it lunged forward, spitting gravel from the unpaved driveway. The gears ground before Jake gunned it and looped around the tight circle drive. He drove down the hill, then slammed on the brakes and backed-up until he could see her. He stuck his head out the window. "Almost forgot; Lotte wants ya at the ranch tonight for dinner; we're 'quing steaks. You need a ride?"

"What time is it now?"

"'Bout noon."

“No; they’re bringing my van around two—I’ll drive over. What time?”

“Lotte said,” he paused, “let’s see,—she said, ‘ … tell her to get her butt over here now and straighten that boy out.’ Least I think that’s how it went.”

“Tell her I’ll be there around four.”

“Anything else you want to say?”

“Yes, tell Lotte Anders can straighten himself out.”

****

Her new van, which she’d ordered sight unseen from a Bozeman dealership, didn’t arrive until 3:15 p.m. When she’d called at 2:30 asking where it was, the owner told her they delivered “on Montana time.” When she asked what he meant he said, “Whenever we damn well feel like it.” Then he laughed, apologized, and told her it was on its way.

When it finally made its way up the drive, she was sitting on the porch wrapped in a blanket, watching the weather change over the valley. The driver was impatient and only gave a quick overview of the van’s amenities, handed her the owner’s manual then left with another employee.

She’d chosen green because it symbolized growth, life and harmony. She’d researched online and found that “ … one should put green in your life when you want a new state of balance, feel a need for change or growth, freedom to pursue new ideas, and protection from fears and anxieties.” The salesman tried to talk her out of it, explaining that a green van wouldn’t resell, but she didn’t care.

Christine walked around it, marveling at its size. She’d never envisioned owning a van and often made fun of people who did. She climbed into the driver’s seat and took in the new car smell. The leather seat softened under her. She ran her hands over the steering wheel, adjusted the mirror so she could see into the back and envisioned a group of kids watching a DVD on one of two players. It had enough seats for nine—the third row folded down for storage, if needed. A navigation system would lead the way if she got lost on one of Montana's many back roads and OnStar® would alert a central dispatch if she had an accident. Splurging on the van was one of the few luxuries she would allow herself until the camp was up and running.

There were lists of things to do: finish the house; file the necessary paperwork for nonprofit status; solicit volunteers and hire staff. Since she didn't know much about the business end of it, she decided to ask Janice. During one of her strained and infrequent conversations with Anders, he mentioned that Janice had enrolled in classes to be a paralegal.

"She told me to tell you that she started thinking about what you said at the café that day, and I'll quote: 'I decided my dad ran this place for fifteen years without me and he can do it again. I'm not getting any younger."

Christine pressed him for more info and even asked if he'd been spending a lot of time with Janice, but he'd been quite cryptic and changed the subject which irritated her. Her initial feelings of guilt had turned to annoyance these last few weeks. He wouldn't return her calls and, in her assessment, acted like a baby. True, she'd made a mistake by not telling him about Nick, but for goodness sake, he needed to get over it.

****

When Christine pulled into the drive at the ranch, she saw smoke rising from the backyard. The usual constriction of her throat and quickening of her pulse didn't materialize; the only reaction she had to the smoke was a fluttering in her stomach. She turned off the ignition, slid off the seat and winced when her feet touched the ground. She walked around the van to the backyard where the men were gathered around the fire pit. They were wrapped in heavy coats, their gloved hands grasping beers. Each man turned and mumbled a greeting. Mitch tipped his beer to her, said, "Welcome back," and then turned to the others. She scanned the group, but saw neither Anders nor Jake.

"Thanks." Her voice cracked—the crew always intimidated her. She was a prima donna to them. They probably hated her now that she'd hurt Anders. Screw 'em.

As she approached the back door, she heard voices coming from inside. "Don't give a rip. If you keep that up you'll wind up like your father—alone," Jake was saying as she stepped onto the back porch. The kitchen door was open and she could see them clearly through the screen. Neither of them saw her—Anders had his back to her, Jake was rummaging in the refrigerator.

Anders grunted, "Yeah, and you're an expert on women." He stomped out of the kitchen.

Lotte swooped in from the basement, carrying an armful of folded laundry. "What's he talkin' about?"

Jake slammed the refrigerator door and without turning around said, "He's grumblin' 'bout Christine." He turned, leaned against the counter.

Then Lotte saw Christine, set the laundry on the table and pushed open the screen door. "Get in here. What the heck you standin' out there for?" She pulled Christine into a hug.

When Jake saw her, he dropped his head and mumbled to the floor. "Didn't hear you. How long ya been there?"

"Long enough to know Anders was ' … grumblin' 'bout Christine.' But not long enough to know why."

"Why?" Lotte said, glaring at Jake. Then to her, "Because, the boy's being stupid—stupid as arseholes, as my mother used to say," She walked back to the table and began putting the kitchen towels away.

"Who's stupid?" Anders walked into the kitchen eating an apple. He stopped short when he saw her.

Her heart lurched. It was the first time she'd seen him in over a month. He looked tanned and relaxed. His hair had grown and lightened. Strands clumped together and stood up on the top of his head like spikes, making him look like a model. His sleepy eyes, his wrinkled sweatshirt and the untucked shirt underneath made him sexy—incredibly sexy. She'd missed him. She pushed aside the voice that cautioned her and walked toward him. He backed into the wall. She stopped in front of him, stood on tiptoes and kissed his cheek. His face reddened. He sidestepped toward the doorway to the hall. When he couldn't go any farther without exiting the room, he said, "Uh, I got your messages when I got back couple days ago."

"Back?"

He cleared his throat. "I've been in Florida the last two weeks doing a shoot."

"Oh. How was Florida?"

"Hot, humid, buggy, and flat. Not a place that I could live."

"Know what you mean. I never liked it much either. I like it here," she said.

Anders cleared his throat. "Didn't know you were back 'til Jake told me this morning. You been to the house?"

"Yes, it's amazing. Thanks for your help. It wouldn't have gotten done without you and I'm so grateful. Your photos look amazing too…" She was gushing. She needed to stop.

They made small talk until the conversation became strained once Jake and Lotte excused themselves. Finally it felt so stilted that she retreated to the bathroom to hide. She closed the door, leaned against it, thought better of it, took a deep breath and immediately went back out. She found him in the living room staring out the window. He turned toward her when she entered, his eyes sad. Her eyes watered, she dropped her head and blinked, then walked toward him. "Can we talk?"

"Ah, sure." He sat.

"Not in here; let's take a walk."

"Looks pretty cold out there and like rain or snow is heading this way." He pointed toward the mountains where it appeared the sky had turned dark grey under white billowing clouds.

"It'll be awhile before it gets here. It's too …," she peered around the corner into the hall, and glanced up the stairs where she heard Peta on the phone, " … too busy in here." She knew Jake and Lotte were lingering somewhere close.

They walked in silence out the back door and down the path that looped around the collapsed skeleton of the old barn. Anders pointed at the rubble. "We had to tear it down. Wasn't safe anymore. Quite a project. Now we're waiting for some guys who work for Spencer to come pick it up. Guess he's going to use it for one of his projects. Barn wood's become ..."

Before he could continue she blurted, "I need us to be friends." Head down, hands shoved in her pockets, she said, "If we can't be more than that, at the very least, I really want your friendship."

Anders said nothing as they walked past the corrals and out to the open meadow where partially budded aspens ran along the creek. The wind picked up, sending a blast of cold air through the previously warm day. The aspen shifted, dancing to the music of the wind—leaning and passing each other, then leaning the other way as if in search of a partner. It was how she felt about herself and Anders. Shifting, passing and shifting again. As she leaned in, he leaned out.

He continued to be silent so she said, "I know I made a mistake by not telling you about Nick, but I can't change that. I, uh, know that you're frustrated with our lack of, uh, physical contact." This was harder than she thought. The blood rose to her cheeks. Stupid, that was a stupid way to put it. "I'm sorry about that." Thunder rolled in the distance and the occasional flash of light seemed to be moving closer, both an anomaly at this time of year.

"Not the problem, Christine. It never was. It's that wall you put up. It's the way you hold yourself back from me. And, it's that side of you that can be mean spirited." His voice rose, "Then you lie to me. It's not the lack of sex. It's that you won't let me in. Yet you do let in the one person who hurt you the most. Like I said on the Cape, I've been down this road before, don't want to go there again." He rubbed his hand over his face, let his arm drop to his side and looked up at the sky.

It hurt; it hurt more than she would allow herself to feel right now. She turned her back to him, gazed at the house, at the rubble that once was the barn, at the upstairs window of the room where she'd once slept, where she'd rebuffed his advances. She faced him, gulped in the air and said, "But can't we talk once in a while? Have coffee? You know, stuff friends do?"

He looked away, shoulders slumped, after a few seconds he faced her. "Sure," he said. "Let's see how that works."

"Thank you. We were friends in the beginning, remember?"

"It was always more than that for me, Christine." He turned away from her and walked toward the house.

"Wait, please." She reached for his arm to stop him. "I've learned a lot these past few months. I know what I want for myself. If nothing else the encounter with Nick made me see how closed up I've been. I saw that though I thought I'd changed, I still have a long way to go. But I want to change. I want to fully accept who I am now—scars and all." She laughed at the literalness of what she just said. "There have been many people who helped me reach this point, including you. Strangely, even my parents inadvertently made me see what vanity can do and how destructive passing judgment on others can be. I see that I've hurt a lot of people and the only way I can make amends is to change." She paused. "It's weird that I found love and beauty in the most unlikely of places and people."

His eyes bored into hers. "Yes, ironic, isn't it."

Thunder clapped overhead and black clouds rolled in, wrapping themselves around the only speck of blue that remained. He frowned, shielded his eyes and peered at the sky. "C'mon we better get back. Sky's menacing."

She could see lightning flashing over the pasture. A smattering of rain dropped on her face then the rain turned to sleet. "Go, go," he said. "I'll catch up. I need to make sure the gates on the corral are secured."

She hurried toward the house, trying not to stumble on the uneven dirt surface. The onslaught of freezing rain made it difficult to see. She heard a gate slam, the sound of feet slapping behind her. She turned and saw him, head down, running. She looked down and noticed the footprints she'd made on the muddy path were disappearing, swallowed up by the rain. It was as if she'd never been there at all.

When they reached the porch, Lotte was holding the kitchen door open. The wind had changed direction again and was now lashing their backs. Puddles pooled on the porch's wooden surface. Christine slipped. Anders caught her.

"Hurry, get in here." Lotte said.

Anders pulled her upright and grabbed the door from Lotte. "Get inside. You're getting soaked."

Lotte made them wait by the door. "Hold on now; I'll get some towels."

They huddled together on the tiny rug, her shoulder brushing his arm. Christine tried to move away, but there was nowhere to go. She stared at the floor and mumbled, "Did Lotte tell you I'm opening a camp for kids? Burned and disfigured kids."

She looked up at him. He smiled, reached over and pushed a strand of hair behind her ear. "Yes, she did. Sounds like a pretty big undertaking, but admirable. I'm impressed."

Her heart beat faster. "Maybe you could help me? Parents will be coming with the kids. They'll need something to do. Would you be interested in setting up fishing trips and stuff? Maybe teaching a few photography classes and I could also use some photos for my brochures."

"I'm pretty busy the next couple months, but I'll help when I can." He stepped off the rug, shifted his body away from her. "I'm damn cold and wet, how about you?" He tilted his head down, ran a hand briskly over this wet hair.

She'd hope for more from him.

He straightened, glanced at her, rubbed a hand over his face, and said, "As for the friends part, I think I can pull that off."

It wasn't really what she wanted to hear, but she knew she'd be okay and in her heart she knew he'd always be there if she needed him.

"Looks like no barbeque tonight," Lotte said as she handed each of them a towel.

The towel felt good against Christine's skin. She rubbed it briskly over her hair and made a decision. "I think I'll head back home. I've got a lot of unpacking to do."

Home, now the nicest four letter word she knew.

When they were dried off, Lotte took the towel then pointed at Christine. "Sit. You gotta eat, girl. No reason why we can't fix them steaks under the broiler or fry 'em up." When Christine didn't respond, Lotte glared at both of them and said, "Didn't get it worked out, I see."

Christine flushed. "It's not like that. I really have a lot to do and I picked up some food at the store. I'll be fine."

"Where ya keeping that stuff? You ain't got no fridge, girl."

"Cooler. I picked one up yesterday. Look, I'll be fine." She backed out the door.

"Suit yourself." Lotte shrugged and followed Christine outside.

"Looks like the storm passed," Christine said, then paused on the porch, reaching for Lotte's hand, "Thanks for everything you did. The flowers are beautiful; the furniture's just what I needed."

Lotte's eyes narrowed. "By the looks of what I saw in there …" she said and tipped her head toward the house, "you didn't patch things up with our boy, eh?"

Christine shook her head.

Lotte said, "He's stubborn, that one—like his dad. Arle closed his heart when Anders ma up and left. Don't think he ever opened it up again. Too 'fraid of gettin' hurt again, I 'spose. Maybe Anders gonna' be like that, too." She searched Christine's face. "Then again, maybe give him some time. Maybe he's smarter."

"I've hurt him, Lotte. Over the last two years I've clung to him, then pushed him away, pulled him closer and pushed him away again. I know how lucky I am to have him in my life, but it's too late. Guess it's the classic scenario of you don't know what you've got until its gone or, in my case, on his way out."

"Damn it girl, don't wait. Catch him and get him back here."

She squeezed Lotte's arm and headed toward the car. As she drove away, she noticed the sun had broken through the clouds. Steam heaved and rose from the ground like the glistening flesh of a horse after a race.

TWENTY-SIX

By the time she turned off the main road onto the long driveway up to her house, daylight had faded and the night sky soared high above her. Stars emerged on the horizon, rhinestones on a sea of black velvet, the earth rotating toward the dark, embracing the night sun. No lights guided her across the bridge over the creek and up the steep narrow drive toward home. No panic ignited a fire inside her. It was as if she'd been heading up this path her entire life, its familiarity confounding, yet, oddly comforting. As she reached the top, light activated by the motion detector spilled onto the drive and glowed, a beacon beckoning her to safe harbor. When she opened the front door a familiar aroma floated around her. A scent so intoxicating that for a moment she believed Anders was in the house until she remembered both Jake and Anders wore the same woodsy cologne. But it wasn't Jake she wanted to remember. If she closed her eyes, breathed deeply and let her mind fill with Anders, she could almost believe he was there.

She flipped on the can lights, walked to the office, tossed her coat and keys onto the futon, and then walked back into the great room, its emptiness overwhelming. Darkness crept in and thoughts of what she had lost crushed earlier optimism.

Then Lotte's words, "Catch him and bring him back," gave her hope. Not only hope that he would come back to her one day, but it gave her confidence to tackle what was ahead of her. While she knew the road would be long and fraught with bouts of indecision and uncertainty, confidence fed her determination to move on without her parents, without Nick or Donna, and without Anders. In a way, she felt he'd let her down. He'd given up on her and that made her more determined to succeed.

She slid the rocker in front of the fireplace, plugged in the floor lamp and turned it on before shutting off the overhead lights. Jake had left a few self-starting fire logs, but no grate so she propped a log upright against the back of the brick firebox, opened the flue and struck a match. Fire licked its way up the paper covered log until it was fully engulfed. She searched through the box of linens and found a quilt, wrapped it around her and sat in the rocker. Amazing how beautiful, yet how deadly, fire could be. Odd that it could immediately make her feel comforted.

****

Curled up in the rocker and still wrapped in the quilt she woke the next morning to the wind whistling outside. She untwisted her legs and rubbed her calves to get the circulation back, stretched, leaned forward, touching fingertips to toes and rotated her head to get the kinks out. Rain cascaded down the skylights in the ceiling. Behind her it slapped at the windows. Dampness seeped into the day. But a day that would be replenished with positive action: the house, the camp and with Anders as a friend—nothing more.

Christine draped the quilt around her shoulders and wove through the maze of boxes to the windows overlooking the valley. Wind swirled around the front yard. The edges of a large blue tarp piled with construction debris flapped furiously. Scraps of insulation and small pieces of wood littered the ground. A small piece of ductwork tumbled toward the edge of the yard and disappeared down the hill. More construction rubble had probably collected at the bottom; she'd have to erect a fence for safety.

Across from her land, on the other side of the road, the foothills that lined the highway all the way into Yellowstone were barely discernible as the rain thickened and turned to snow. The clouds wrapped around the hills as if protecting them from an unknown or unwanted force of nature much like an adult would protect a child from negativity and brutality. Much as she would with the children who came into camp. Her camp. Panic seized the air in her lungs. Would she succeed? Where to start?

She turned back into the empty room, realizing the blank canvas she'd been given. Not only with this room, with this house, but with her life as well. She'd start now by filling the 'canvas' with layers of growth, with good deeds and with love.

The snow continued throughout the day while Christine stored her clothes in the master bedroom's massive walk-in closet. Its rich mahogany eco-friendly wood interior, carpeted floor, custom drawers and shelves was so inviting that she decided to haul the futon mattress upstairs and sleep on the floor in the closet. It was a decision that had been much easier to make than execute. She slid the mattress off the frame in the office, struggled with it until she had it upright, folded the ends of the mattress together, and dragged it down the short hallway to the bottom of the stairs. Just as she reached the staircase, she tripped and fell, released the mattress, it opened up and she landed on it with her feet in the air.

"That's an interesting pose. You learn that in modeling class?"

Fear clutched at her throat, she scrambled to her feet, ready to lunge at the intruder. "Oh, my god, Janice, you scared the crap out of me."

"Sorry. The door was unlocked. I kept ringing the bell and I was getting soaked out there. The snow's that sloppy wet kind, it's saturating the porch."

"Doorbell isn't hooked up yet." Christine's heart was still pounding. "What are you doing here anyway?"

Janice frowned and took a step back. "Well, I guess I could go." Her voice wobbled as did her feet that appeared locked in three inch platform boots; her skinny jeans were soaked at the thigh and her jacket dripped moisture on the wood floors.

"No, no, stay. Just give me the darn jacket—you're dripping water all over the place." While Janice struggled with coat sleeves, the soles of her boots slipped on the wood floor. Christine groaned, "Wait, just wait. Take off the boots first."

"Damn it, there's no place to sit." Janice's eyes searched the room.

Christine pointed. "Over there. On the rocker by the fireplace. Sit. I'll help."

They pulled off the boots and Christine laid them in front of the fireplace. "Stay here and get warm. I'll light another log." She handed Janice the quilt and lit a fire log.

"That's not going to give you much heat." Janice grumbled. "Why's it so cold in here?"

"Good question—truthfully, I hadn't noticed." Christine wandered around the room looking for a thermostat. "They said the heat's hooked up." When she found it, it was set on sixty-two. She turned it to seventy and sat on the floor across from Janice. "Nice to see you. Sorry I was grumpy. You scared me."

"Again, sorry about that."

"What can I do for you?" Christine asked.

"I'm here to help."

"As you can see, there's nothing to do. Don't have much furniture and I'm nearly unpacked."

"I meant I'd help with the camp … or whatever it is. First, you know, you'll need to get a business license. Anders said you want it to be a not-for-profit. I know what papers to file and how to structure it. You'll also need to start doing some fundraising, unless you plan to fund it by yourself?"

"In the beginning, but in a couple years I'll need some backers to keep it going."

"Okay, then, after the camp has been running for a few months we should put together a business plan to present to prospective contributors."

"But how can you help me?"

Janice smiled. "I can see you're not quite sure what to make of this. I've been taking classes to be a paralegal. Thanks by the way. If you hadn't made me feel so guilty about being such a loser, I'd still be shaking my fanny back at the café and listening to my dad remind me it's all I'm good for."

"I didn't say you were a loser. If you remember …"

"Cool your jets, sister, I was kidding. But really, thanks. I'd like to help; besides it's something I have to do for my class anyway. Well what do you say?"

"Sure," Christine said. "Where do we start?"

"Oh, shit. I forgot my briefcase in the truck. Hold on." Janice threw off her blanket and ran toward the door without putting on her boots.

"Wait. You don't have any shoes on." Janice kept going. "Wait, I'll get you some ..." It was too late, she was out the door and back from the truck by the time Christine returned with a pair of slippers.

"Uggs, huh? Nice. Bet it's nice to have a lot of money." Janice said, short of breath, her words tumbling out in disjointed raspy syllables.

"I'd rather have ..." Christine stopped, she was going to say my looks—but, would she?

"Sorry." Janice tried to brush her words away. "Tact isn't one of my best assets. Dad says my tits are." She scoffed, "But then what does he know?"

They spent the next hour filling out paperwork. Janice seemed competent and by the time they were done, Christine felt confident.

"What are you going to call this camp? I'll need to know that before I can send it in."

"Can I change it once it's sent in? I mean if I think of something better?"

"Not sure. I'll check. What should I put down now?"

"Oh, just put down Christine's Camp."

Janice raised her eyebrows and pursed her lips. "Well, that's original."

"I'll come up with something and give you a call."

Janice rose and grabbed her boots from the hearth. "Awe, they're warm. Thanks." She carried them to the front door and pulled them on, hopping on one foot while pushing the other inside. With a hand on the doorknob, she said, "I'll help with the camp if you want. I love little kids. And Peta will help, too. She told me to tell you. Heck, she begged me to tell you!" Janice paused, "I'll bet Anders will, too. If you ask him." She seemed embarrassed but continued, "I hear you two are sort of broken up? That true? Don't mean to pry, but he's been pretty testy lately. I asked Lotte what was up and she told me. Sorry to hear that, I think you're good for him."

"Uh, it's fine." What else could she say?

Janice didn't seem to know what to say either so she opened the door. "Shit, is this crappy weather ever going to stop?" She stepped outside. "Oh, by the way you've got a shit load of garbage at the foot of your hill. You might have the guys get rid of some of that. Garbage gets picked up on Wednesdays. You've got lots of time. See ya. I'll be in touch." She covered her head with the briefcase and ran to her truck.

Janice had barely gotten down the drive, when the house phone rang.

"Ms. McMurray this is Sam down at Apple Appliance. We got your stove, dishwasher and fridge in. When do you want us to install 'em?"

She scheduled them for the following day, called Jake to find out who was in charge of finishing the tiling and window trim, called the painters and scheduled them for the following week. It took an hour arguing with them about why the painting wasn't finished and she finally explained that they were the ones who dropped the ball. She made an appointment with the designer at Rocky Mountain Furnishings for Saturday and called Spencer.

"Hello, Christine. You're back?" His tone clipped, uninterested and annoyed.

"Why, yes, Spencer I am. How have you been?" she said, her tone light, as if they were best friends.

Not acknowledging her question, he said, "What can I do for you?"

"Well ...," she stopped and waited just enough time for him to get agitated.

"Now anything that is wrong at the house isn't my fault. I told Anders not to let you move in. It's not finished—which isn't my fault either." His voice grew tense. "I wasn't the general on this, in fact, if you'll remember I turned it over to Ken."

"Nothing's wrong Spencer. I only called to thank you for your wonderful plan. It turned out better than I thought." She smiled, knowing that it wasn't the response he expected.

"Yes, yes, you're welcome." He sniveled, "I'm glad you like it." He cleared his throat and said, "I guess you should take part of that compliment since you gave me a rough sketch on that disgusting napkin. That said, I'm happy you are happy. Now if you'll excuse me I have another call."

"Actually, Spencer, I did have a couple things I need to ask you. The plans called for the fireplace to be open to the kitchen and it's not."

"It's not what?"

"It's not open to the kitchen."

Silence, then he said, "Ask your contractor."

"I did. The plans you gave him do not show the fireplace on both sides whereas the one you sent me before I left, did show it. How'd that happen?"

She could hear him tapping his fingers. Finally he mumbled, "Don't know. I'll look it over and call you back." He hung up before she had a chance to address any other issue.

He called her later that afternoon with a feeble apology, but no restitution. After haggling with him, she suggested they solve the issue by having him fine tune the cabin design for the camp at no charge. "Just one plan and we'll use the same one for all the cabins," she told him. He promised to have it to her by the end of the week.

If you love somebody, let them go, for if they return, they were always yours. And if they don't, they never were. ~ Kahlil Gibran

TWENTY-SEVEN

Montana—April

Christine decided to take a break. Her leg ached. She limped over to the patio, reclined on a teak chaise, and watched Jake and the crew finish the siding on the last cabin as the first raindrops fell.

Since early morning, she, Lotte and Peta had pounded nails, carried bundles of siding and kept the men hydrated. They'd all helped. Anders was the only one conspicuously absent. "Off on assignment," Lotte told her. Even Jake had been cryptic when she asked, "Haven't seen him much. Not sure. Now what did you want us …" and he'd be off on a tangent about the cabins. They needed to get the last one watertight before more rain started again. Since her return, snow then rain had been constant. The continuous storms, which were backed up to the west coast, wore on her. The low clouds took her hostage, wrapping her in a blanket of grey, waiting for the right moment to send her back to the Cape. And, some days she was a willing captive. The cabin process had been painfully slow because of the weather. Behind it, meteorologists promised a high would push in with warmer temperatures and sun. But they couldn't wait. Abby and family would arrive in a week—for a trial run of sorts before opening the camp in June. The entire family was coming—even Max, who'd been calling Peta daily.

In the past few months things had improved for Abby and her family: Kurt had a job and Max had been accepted to Boston College with a football scholarship. Peta had been disappointed he wasn't going to college in Montana, but Lotte said Anders was relieved. "She's too young to get involved," Anders had said.

Wendy told her Abby was getting better all the time. "She misses you a lot, so this will be good for her. It's really nice of you to buy our tickets. I hope we can repay you one of these days."

They would be there for a week during spring break. While Christine was excited to see them, the prospect left her feeling panicked and vulnerable again. The weather hadn't helped.

"Cold?" Christine jumped. She hadn't seen Lotte standing there holding a blanket. The raindrops had abated and it looked like the sun might poke through the cloud cover. Great, just in time for sunset when they couldn't do any more work.

"Thanks." Christine reached for the blanket and flipped it over her legs, tucking it under her. "Sit, Lotte." She pointed to the end of the chaise. "I'll share the blanket."

Lotte shook her head, "Gotta get back to the ranch and start dinner. You rest, you done too much already. You still coming over?"

Christine leaned her head back. "If I can keep my eyes open."

They were all tired … and irritable: Peta grumbled about not being able to try the new paints and easel they'd bought for each cabin, Lotte complained about her back and the men were always hungry. Yet they'd worked cohesively and tirelessly for the last few weeks. Every morning trucks from the ranch lumbered up the drive, bouncing as the tires splashed through the water filled potholes. Every day Christine stood at the window as the sun broke the horizon. A mug of coffee cupped in her hand, she'd watch as the trucks reached the top of the hill and Lotte, Peta, Jake and the crew tumbled out bleary-eyed. Every night before she fell asleep a question settled, lingering until the next morning: would Anders be with them?

"Looks like we're done for today." Jake walked over, with the men following him. "At least we don't have to worry now about critters making themselves at home inside the cabins. We got the doors and windows in, too. Sheetrock's comin' tomorrow. Where they gonna store it 'till Monday?"

"I thought you were coming back tomorrow." Two days wasted. If they didn't get it done, she'd have to put Abby and her family up in the house and there weren't enough beds yet.

"Guys are beat, Christine." He lifted his hat and scratched his head. "You forget, they've got stuff to do at the ranch. And it's

Friday. Crew's got work to do in town." He winked. "If you know what I mean."

She stifled her disappointment. "Sure, no worries, but the sooner, the better."

Jake turned to Lotte. "You ready? Where'd Peta get off to? That girl's always disappearin'. Anders needs to rein her in or they'll send her back to her ma. 'Course no one knows where her ma is."

"Leave her be, she's gettin' along just fine," Lotte said. "Anders got temporary custody." She turned to Christine, "He went to court. Told the judge everything. Ain't ever seen him so pissed. Was pretty proud of our boy." Lotte turned toward the house and yelled for Peta. "Get out here, little one, time to go."

"Let her stay here with me tonight," Christine said, and caught a dubious look from Lotte. She added, "If she wants to."

"Hell, I'm pretty sure she wants to, it's Anders I'm worried about. It's a thirty-minute inquisition when we want to take her anywhere."

Christine smiled. That sounded like Anders. "Tell you what; have him call me if he has any questions." Let's see what he does with that, she thought.

"Ain't gonna work, you know." Lotte smirked.

"Whatever do you mean? I have no idea what you're talking about." Christine lifted the blanket over her face.

"Sure, ya don't and I got me a twenty-year-old lover back at the ranch," Lotte said, yanking the blanket away and pointing at her. "Look at that face, Jake. She's a lyin' to beat the band." A blush rolled up Christine's neck and onto her cheeks where it blazed the truth. "Not so cute now, are you? That ivory skin a yours tells the story, don't it?" Lotte and Jake laughed.

"Who tells what story?" Peta stood in the doorway, a pint of ice cream in one hand, spoon in the other.

"Nothing to do with you there, little miss nosey." Lotte looked up. "Say, what ya got there?" She moved toward Peta and grabbed for the ice cream. Peta spun away from her and ran back inside. Lotte pursued, shrieking like a teenager, "You can't eat all that;

it'll ruin that petite little figure a yours. C'mon, gimme some." They disappeared into the kitchen.

Within minutes Peta ran back outside with Lotte tickling her. When Peta tried to push her away, Lotte yanked the ice cream out of her hands.

Christine stood, hobbled over and maneuvered herself between them. "Stop you two. I've got plenty of ice cream in there. No need to fight over it."

"Well, why didn't ya say so?" Lotte handed the ice cream back to Peta. "Here, ya go. I'll get m'own."

Once they finished off the ice cream, Lotte and Jake left and Peta stayed. Christine made dinner: scrambled eggs and toast. They were sitting at the breakfast counter, perched on two new barstools.

"You're not much of a cook, are you?" Peta said as she shoveled eggs onto the toast and took a bite. "Got any ketchup? Can't have eggs without it."

"I never learned to cook.. My mom never took the time to teach me." Christine slid off the stool, grabbed a bottle of ketchup out of the fridge and set it in front of Peta.

With elbows on the counter, Peta leaned over the plate and took another bite. "My mom's nuts, but she's a rockin' cook."

She leaned back stared at Christine, then rested her head on her hands, strands of black hair catching bits of ketchup on the ends. "Oh, shit," she said, as she licked ketchup off the ends, peering at Christine through thick black lashes. "Sorry. Anders says I've got a potty mouth."

Peta's dark hair had grown out. Cut in choppy layers, it reached her shoulders, thick bangs covered her forehead, just touching eyebrows. Coupled with bronzed skin and a trim body that had filled out appropriately, she had model potential, though Christine wouldn't tell her. Anders thought Peta was beautiful and Christine guessed he was right. Peta seemed happier, too, not as withdrawn. In a rush of unexplained emotion, Christine patted Peta's hand, realizing she'd taken the gesture from Lotte. It felt good; natural.

"What's she like?"

"Who?"

"Your mother."

Peta turned away and asked, "Got anything to drink?"

"Sure. Bottled water, ice tea, milk or soda?

"Water."

Christine walked to the pantry, grabbed two bottles, and handed one to Peta. "Sorry I asked; I know talking about your mom must be difficult."

Peta shrugged. "It's cool. She wasn't much of a mom anyway. I lived with my grandma and aunt most of the time."

"Did you ever live on the reservation?"

"Nope. Mom liked white men." Peta stood, picked up the plate and set it in the sink, then turned toward Christine and leaned against the counter. "When my aunt got sick I went to that foster family I told you about 'til mom told me about Anders."

Christine slid the last of the eggs into her mouth, swallowed, then said, "What about your dad?" As soon as it was said, she regretted it. Anders had told her Peta didn't know her father. Too late to take it back. She hoped the question would be ignored.

Peta glanced at Christine, eyes dull. Her hands fiddled with hair, twisting it into tight spirals. She sighed, let it loose and looked over her shoulder, out the kitchen window, staring intently as if trying to remember. The rain had turned to a soft drizzle, low clouds clung to the fir trees in the back yard, droplets spotted the crocus that had pushed through the earth. Peta walked over to the built-in desk next to the pantry, grabbed her purse and pulled out her phone, "Don't know who my dad is." She played with the keypad and mumbled, "Neither does my mom."

"I'm sorry, Peta." Compassion had never been easy for Christine; empathy always eluded her until this year when she experienced it so much that she often wished it had stayed buried. At that moment, she embraced it. "You know sometimes knowing your dad isn't all it's cracked up to be."

Peta nodded, yet remained looking at her phone. Christine slid off the bar stool and put an arm around her. Peta tensed and backed away. The obvious rejection Peta felt made Christine reach out and touch her hand. "Really, I know who my dad is and sometimes, I wish I didn't."

Peta faced her. "That's nice, but at least your mom is still around. She didn't run off and she's not doin' every guy that looks at her." Peta's brown eyes were hard, yet her mouth yielding, slack with sadness. She tossed the phone back in the purse and said, "I don't want to talk about this anymore."

"Sure, I get it. We don't have to. I know parents can be a pain."

A high-pitched tone from inside Peta's purse startled both of them. She pulled out her phone again and glanced at it. Her shoulders hunched, her back to Christine, she made tapping sounds with the keypad, presumably texting someone. Moments later she giggled. The giggle tore away at the awkward moment. Christine ventured, "A friend?"

"Kinda." She grabbed her purse and moved toward the door. "I gotta text him back."

"Him, huh?"

"It's Max." Peta rushed upstairs.

The room seemed empty after Peta left, hollowed out by echoes of dysfunctional families and absentee parents. While Christine was relieved that her parents were thousands of miles away, it didn't take away the reality that they hadn't been the best parents. She missed the head in the sand feeling that years of deniability had provided her. Reality sucked. But that was in the past. She knew eventually she'd find a way to have a better relationship with them.

After putting dishes away and cleaning up from dinner, Christine flopped on the couch and mindlessly flipped through channels on her new LCD which hung on one wall in the small sitting room open to the kitchen. The TV, surround sound, a blu-ray player and game console rounded out her sources of entertainment most nights.

"Next up at seven, we'll see if Meg can track down Jonas in our season finale of "Who's Your Daddy Now." A commercial cut into the announcer's monolog with some mundane ad selling a prescription drug that had a litany of precautionary warnings. Christine set the remote down and got up. This was one of Peta's favorite shows.

"Peta?" Christine hollered up the stairs, "You wanna watch the finale of *Who's Your Daddy*?" She glanced at her watch. "It's on in twenty-two minutes." The irony of the title wasn't wasted on her and she wondered if Peta thought the same. When she didn't answer, Christine climbed up to the middle of the staircase and tried again.

The door at the top of the stairs opened, Peta's voice reverberated down. "Yeah, I hear ya. I'll be down in a few."

"You alright?"

"Why wouldn't I be?"

"Just checking." The door closed.

Christine grabbed a wool blanket from the couch, made herself a cocoon and settled in to watch, unsure if Peta would really join her. Cookies. Cookies would lure Peta out of her room. The smell alone would do it. Peanut butter was Peta's favorite, chocolate chip hers. Thank goodness for frozen cookie dough. Keeping the blanket wrapped around her, she waddled to the new stainless steel refrigerator that gleamed in the softness of dimmed can lighting. It was packed with food from Stock and Save, a new warehouse food outlet. She'd spent hours perusing the massive store shelves which reached almost to the ceiling, filling the enormous steel cart with food. It had been the first shopping trip for her new home. She tugged at the chrome handle of the freezer. A whoosh of cold air blasted her face. She tightened the blanket, grabbed two boxes of frozen dough and set them on the counter.

"Oh, cookies, yum!" Peta stood in the doorway, hair pulled into a ponytail. She'd changed into baggy flannel pants and a tank. Her face scrubbed of make-up, her skin glistened. "Sorry about before. I hate talking about family stuff, especially since I don't have one."

"You could do a lot worse than Anders. He is family, you know." Christine moved slowly, methodically setting small round clumps of dough on a cookie sheet. The preheat buzzer dinged on the oven and Christine slid the cookie sheet inside.

"I know; he's cool. Guess I'm luckier than Abby."

Christine peered at her. Peta's eyes were glassy. Had something happened? Fear gripped her. "Oh, my, what's wrong? Is Abby okay?" A setback, could Abby have had a setback?

"Oh, no, I'm sorry. No, no she's fine. It's just." Peta shifted. "It's a bummer living with her face like that. I don't' know how she can be that cheerful. Max said she's jazzed about coming here though. I'd be, like, get me outta here."

"It's not …" Christine's scar throbbed, her stomach began to itch and her leg ached all at the same time. She pushed the pain away—psychosomatic pain—she knew that much psychology. "It's not that bad, really." Saliva had formed in her throat. She cleared it. "Once you get used to it … and if you have lots of support, you soon realize you're lucky to be alive and that there are more important things in the world than being beautiful."

Peta was crestfallen. "I'm sorry, my bad … I forgot about your …" An uncomfortable silence rose between them.

"Shit, shit." Christine looked at Peta. "Oops, sorry, no swearing, right?" She'd forgotten to set the timer and rushed over to open the oven. Safe. No browned edges, no burnt cookies, no bumps, no blisters, no scrapes—no bruised feelings. No one got hurt. Cookies broke through the barrier.

"OMG, can you believe she won? She was a total tool. I totally wanted the big girl to win. She was nice."

They were huddled together on the couch under one blanket.

Christine said, "My goodness, it's freezing in here. What's up with this weather?" They both turned their heads toward the window where the rain had turned to hail. "More cookies?"

"Naw, I'm going upstairs and text Max." She stood and stretched. "Christine?"

"Yes?"

Peta lowered her eyes. "What happened?"

"Where?"

"What happened to you?" She slumped back on the couch, eyes downcast. "You don't have to tell me if you don't want; I asked Anders but he said you should tell me."

No constricting throat, no queasy stomach, no sweaty palms; she felt fine with the question. "He didn't tell you anything?"

"He said you had an accident, that's all."

Christine told her the story beginning with the accident through the long hospital stay. Peta was quiet at first, then mumbled, "That's hardcore. Is he in jail?"

"Don't know where he is; don't care."

"What about your friend? Are you mad at her? I mean, if she'd been paying attention instead of looking in the mirror, maybe it wouldn't have happened."

"Anger is destructive. It's dark. There's no light with anger. You know, it's like I said before, you realize there are many things, and people, that are more important."

"Like my brother?"

Christine tried, but she couldn't suppress the smile. "Yes, like Anders."

"He's still in love with you, you know. I heard him telling Janice."

Her heart jumped. "Really?"

"Yeah, I heard them arguing. Janice called him an idiot. Said he should never let a little thing like jealousy stop him from seeing you. I couldn't hear everything, but then I heard him tell her that he does still love you. Then she swore at him and told him to come see you. He said he would, that he's been trying to figure it out. He's a bit of a tool, too, you know."

TWENTY-EIGHT

Peta left Christine's and returned to the ranch the next morning. Christine tried not to think about what she had told her about Anders' conversation with Janice; afraid of getting her hopes up, afraid of being disappointed. To keep her mind off of it, she called Janice and asked for help with marketing materials for the camp.

They spent the weekend creating brochures and mailing some to hospitals and burn centers in adjoining states. Later in the week they'd distribute them to facilities in the local area.

Monday, the crew began sheetrocking and by Tuesday night both cabins were taped, primed and painted. Wednesday, Christine, Jake and some of the men moved furniture in, stocked the kitchens and made up the beds. When they were finished, and as they were walking back to the house, Jake pointed to the eastern edge of the yard. "You need a fence over there."

Another project. When would it end? Christine said, "I know. I've been meaning to talk to you about it."

"Walk with me and I'll show you."

The men continued on to the house; she and Jake walked to the ridge. He kicked some rocks over the side. "See. One of those kids is gonna take a nasty spill." He peered down the hill. "That's long way to the bottom." He glanced at her. "Want me to get the guys on it?"

"Sure. That would be great. How soon can they do it?"

"Soon as I tell 'em." He chuckled, stretched. "How 'bout next week? That soon enough?"

"Sounds like a plan." Christine rested her head on his shoulder. "Thanks, for helping me, Jake. I know sometimes I can be difficult."

"Ah, go on now. Yer doin' fine. " He grunted and patted her head, straightened and leaned out over the edge. "Now, will ya look at that," he said and pointed down.

Christine scanned the landscape below her until she saw them: two moose standing in the creek; one round, the other with new antlers just beginning to show. The bull perused its surroundings while the female drank. In the stillness of the late afternoon, with the sun setting casting a rose haze across the eastern sky, an unfamiliar sound rose. A low growling, like a foghorn.

"What's that?" Christine asked Jake.

"Sounds like the male. Too early for mating season and it looks like he's already done the job, if ya catch my drift." Jake nudged her. "Cud be he's just warnin' us to stay clear. Hell, I ain't goin' down there. You?"

"Nope, not me." She wondered if the male was the same one she and Anders had seen that first day. A day that now seemed like a lifetime ago. She sighed, allowing regret to creep in. "They are magnificent, aren't they Jake?"

"Sure are, but I gotta get a movin'. Lotte'll be lookin' for me."

Christine forgot about the moose until later that evening when she caught a glimpse of their silhouette under the willow about a hundred yards off the kitchen patio. She'd been inside pacing, obsessing about the camp. Was she doing the right thing? Would it be successful? Her anxiety was growing when outside the kitchen windows she noticed movement to the right of the cabins. The bull's head suddenly appeared from the grassy area under the tree; its tiny antlers silhouetted against the moonlit sky.

Over the next few days, the moose seemed to settle into their new environment. If a vehicle drove up, they'd move swiftly toward the woods behind the cabins; when it was quiet they'd return. Their presence was reassuring and they'd be a nice welcoming committee for Abby and family who were due to arrive Sunday.

While there were still things to finish before they arrived, Christine was feeling upbeat and hopeful. Hopeful that all would go well; hopeful Anders would stop by to help as he'd promised. But whenever she pressed Peta for information about him, Peta clammed up.

If Christine asked about him, Peta would smile and say, "He's tight." Whatever that meant. Mad? Tight jeans? Or like Janice told her, tight meant cool? No matter what it meant, each day Christine hoped he'd show up. Each day she was disappointed.

****

Christine woke Sunday morning with a knot in her stomach; anticipation and trepidation had rumbled all night. She pulled on jeans, grabbed an unwashed blouse off the floor and walked downstairs. She grabbed a jacket, slipped on flip flops and walked outside to inspect the cabins.

By ten, satisfied everything was in order, she was in the kitchen sipping coffee, staring at the backyard. She smiled; her mind filled with a mental checklist of what she accomplished. She couldn't believe she'd actually done it. Only a few minor things needed to be done. Peta promised to help and was due at ten-thirty, Abby and her family by noon. Christine would be ready.

"I've got two cabins for you guys," she'd told Wendy. "Each has two small bedrooms, a bathroom, and comfortable sitting area with couch, chair, and TV. The kitchenette has a coffee maker, hot plate and tiny refrigerator. Don't worry about cooking, though. I hired a chef for the camp and he's agreed to cook for you guys as a trial run." The kitchens were equipped with enough amenities for future guests to do a few things on their own, yet not enough to make insurance costs rise.

Each cabin had a small alcove with an easel and art supplies if kids wanted to paint or sketch on their own. In addition, a larger studio was being built where she'd be giving classes. Eventually they'd add a cafeteria.

The sound of an engine startled her. Under the willow the female moose rose and walked away. A car must be coming. Christine refilled her cup and walked into the great room where she could see the top of Anders truck bounce along the drive. Her heart fluttered and her throat constricted. All saliva disappeared. She hadn't seen him in over a month, the last time at the ranch when they'd agreed to be friends. What would she say? What would he?

The truck jerked to an inauspicious stop at the head of the driveway in front of the new garage and shop. She lingered, hiding in the space between the window and front door. He was alone. She tilted her head until she could just see the drive, hoping to see another car or truck, but none appeared. Why would he come alone? To see her? She leaned back against the door frame waiting for him to knock. When he didn't, she peaked around the corner again. He was gone.

"Looking for someone?"

She whirled around, spilling coffee on her white shirt. "Damn." She looked down then up.

He was standing in the kitchen doorway scrutinizing her. His hair damp, cheeks ruddy, not tanned like last time. She needed to sit. "Where'd you come from?" She walked to the rocker and pointed to the sofa. "C'mon, sit. I won't bite."

He flushed, and shoved his hands in the jean pockets. "I came in through the kitchen off the patio. The door was unlocked. I, uh, thought Lotte and Jake were here, but when I didn't see their truck I thought maybe one of 'em was out back."

Guess he hadn't meant to see her alone. No "I love you" plan. Maybe Peta had it all wrong. Heat raced through her body. "No one's here," she croaked, "but Peta's due anytime now." Confused, she asked, "Weren't Jake and Lotte at the ranch? How was Peta getting here?" It made no sense, unless it was a conspiracy to leave Anders and her alone.

"Supposedly Jake was dropping Lotte off here, then he was going to Jenkins Feed to pick up the gas grill you ordered. Guess it came in this morning. They must have decided to go together. Mitch's bringing Peta; he should be here any minute. I was out at Big Sky yesterday and last night doing photos for the new hotel's marketing brochure. It was easier for me to come straight here. Now, there you got the whole story." He didn't sit, but walked back into the kitchen. "Got any coffee left?"

"Yes. Help yourself."

"Say, did you know there's a moose at the edge of the woods?"

"I know; there's a male hiding somewhere. There are two of them; they're here all the time. They rest under the willow." Her palms were clammy, her throat still dry. She took a sip, saw the coffee stain and cursed. No make-up, hair unruly and there he was all perfect.

"Think one of them is the one we saw last fall?" he asked from the kitchen.

"I wondered. Guess it could be. Are you going to come in here?"

A loud rumbling broke the silence followed by doors slamming. Lotte and Jake walked in the front door as Mitch drove up the drive with Peta.

Lotte nodded at her and said, "Got the barbie. Mitch'll take it round to the patio. What else we gotta do? Can't be stayin' too long; got lots to do at the ranch." Then she stomped through the great room into the kitchen. "What the hell you doin' here? Thought you changed your mind and weren't comin'."

Jake trailed behind her. "Yeah, thought you was stayin' in Big Sky."

Christine lagged behind Jake, walking slowly toward the kitchen. As she approached it she heard Anders say, "Changed my mind. That okay with the two of you?"

Jake's voice dropped, "Well, ya said you didn't want to see her, so I thought …"

Lotte snapped, "Jake, will you just shut the hell up."

Anders whirled around and saw Christine. "That wasn't it, Christine, really."

Despair, rejection, anguish collided. Hope turned into hopelessness. The anticipation she felt when he first entered the room vanished. Air exploded from her lungs, she gasped and doubled over. Tears filled her eyes. She ran without thinking, through the kitchen, through French doors, outside past Mitch who stood there stunned. Ran blindly across the patio, away from the house, toward the willow, voices screeching behind her.

Anders yelled, "Wait. Please let me explain."

Then Lotte: "For the love of Mike, Jake, now see what ya done. Men can't ..."

Christine ran harder, fighting for air, fighting for the strength that had brought her this far. Away from the cabins, past the Aspen along the ridge. Branches slapped at her face and blackberry bushes caught on her jeans. She stumbled on the uneven ground, but kept going. When she reached the willow, she stopped, bent over and tried to catch her breath. Her leg ached. Her heart ached. She wiped the tears and berated herself. What had she been thinking? She saw it clearly now. He hadn't forgiven her, hadn't really wanted to be friends. She'd let herself care too much. She leaned back against the trunk of the willow.

She hadn't seen the moose yet she must have run by it. Now it rose up in front of her, just feet from her face and at least two feet over her head. The male moose heaved and stomped the ground, then took a step toward her. Christine jumped back and stumbled sideways, lost her footing and fell, tumbling down the embankment. Her head grazed a boulder. Pain shot through her. Her hand grasped for a branch— anything to break her fall. She landed hard between two large rocks, her feet dangling to the empty space below.

Her head throbbed, blood trickled into her eyes. She looked down to the creek. It was too far to jump; it would kill her. Fear paralyzed her. Her head pounded, she felt dizzy, nauseous. She tried to get her footing, but there was nothing to secure her; nothing to hold onto while she tried to push herself up. She felt herself begin to slip through the space between the boulders. "Not now, no please, God," she whispered. "Not when I've come this far. I can't die now."

She heard Peta scream and call, "Help, Anders, help! Christine fell!"

She lifted her head, gazed up toward the top of the hill and saw Anders at the edge of the cliff.

"No; oh god no. Christine, oh god. Hold on! I can't lose you now."

Rocks began tumbling around her. She looked up again. Anders was sliding down the hill above her, kicking up dirt, loosening rocks and plants. He stopped just above her, reached for her; his arms wrapped under her shoulders and he pulled. "Hold on, honey. I've got you." His voice drifted, darkness engulfed her and she passed out.

RECOVERY

Out of suffering have emerged the strongest souls; the most massive characters are seared with scars.~ Kahlil Gibran

A Light in the Heart Camp—June

Christine lay naked under the blanket, Anders asleep beside her—her head on his chest, his arm tucked under her. She pushed up on an elbow and glanced around the room. The fire from the night before still smoldered, adding a pink aura to the early morning light that streamed in through her bedroom windows. Quietly untangling herself from him, she reached for Anders' shirt on the chair next to the bed, stood up and slipped it on. She buried her nose into the cotton fabric; the scents of pine and leather filled her with the same desires she'd felt last night.

Voices drifted up from the back yard; she tiptoed to the window. They were gathered there around the cabins, planting flowers, pulling weeds, making ready for the children: the damaged, the scarred, the blessed. In two days they would open the camp to five children and their families. Laughter, then Lotte said, "Shush, for pity's sake, you'll wake them."

They were the ones who saved her: Peta, Lotte, Janice and Jake—her friends, her family. And, in their midst she saw the images of Abby, Miller, Lisa and Meredith. They'd all looked beyond the scars to the beauty that slept inside her. Miller was right: beauty was not in the face; beauty was a light in the heart. And this day her heart glowed.

In the past two years, she'd learned so much, and in the process found herself. The beauty she sought now was not in her face, nor her hands—it was in her heart, in the hearts of family and friends, in Anders and the children she would help. It was clear now: the decision to open the camp had been made the day she talked to Strom about Abby. From that day, providence had led her here. She whispered, "A Light in the Heart Camp—that's what I'll call it."

Christine tiptoed back to the bed and watched Anders sleep. He had shown her so much—that the love of a place, the love of someone else and ultimately the love of oneself could bring you home. Home to Montana where beauty was in the mountains, in the depths of the valleys, the dullness of the hills at sunset, the quiet rumble of a river as it meandered through this rich earth, in the soft squeal of the baby moose that now lived under the willow. Montana, too, had become a light in her heart, Anders the light in her soul.

She slipped off the shirt and crawled in beside him. His face serene, his breaths shallow. When he breathes out I breathe in, she thought and ran her fingers along his arm. She raised her own hand upward, where the light caught the redness and made it pure. Beautiful hands, she thought—long, graceful and no longer beckoning to the heavens.

Anders stirred. He stretched, yawned and pulled her hand toward him, kissing each finger. "My darling, you have exquisite hands." He rolled to his side and gazed at her, the tenderness in his eyes terrifying and exciting, "Someday soon, my dear, you will marry me."

"Well," she said and kissed his cheek, "we'll just have to see about that." She smiled at him. "But, just so you know, I'm not totally opposed to the idea." She moved a hand across her stomach. Not feeling the scars anymore, she imagined a new life growing there one day.

ACKNOWLEDGEMENTS

To Chris: You are never far from my heart. I wish this story could have been your destiny.

To my dear husband Mike, who, when I wanted to quit my 'day' job to pursue my dream of writing, told me to do it that we'd manage. Your support has meant everything .

Thank you to my children, Colleen, Michael and Justin, and their spouses, Jose, Kate and Amy, who never wavered in their belief that I could finish this story, and enthusiastically encouraged me every step of the way.

To my writing 'pals' and dear friends, Jan and Mary: Your friendship, constant encouragement and consistent interest in the progression of my novel allowed me the freedom to write, make mistakes and finally FINISH.

To the Wednesday night writers' group: Thanks for listening, encouraging and critiquing so expertly.

To Jackie Mitchard: Thank you for allowing me to reside in your lovely Cape Cod home and do nothing but write for nine glorious days. Your generosity is boundless.

To Diane, Dianne and Katie: Thanks for being my friends and forever supportive.

To Montana and Cape Cod: Your beauty is the light in my heart.